The
Coil

L.A. Gilbert

Dreamspinner Press

Published by
Dreamspinner Press
5032 Capital Circle SW
Ste 2, PMB# 279
Tallahassee, FL 32305-7886
USA
http://www.dreamspinnerpress.com/

Cover Art by Anne Cain
annecain.art@gmail.com

ISBN: 978-1-62380-020-8

Printed in the United States of America
First Edition
October 2012

eBook edition available
eBook ISBN: 978-1-62380-021-5

Dedicated to any parents reading this book who accept and love their children unconditionally.

Prologue

THREE years could be a long time, or not long enough, depending on what you were waiting for. For Mattie, it had been a torturously slow period, though now that the waiting was over, he found himself more than a little anxious at the prospect of seeing Simon again.

Simon, who was his silent pen pal, his biggest supporter, and the love of his fucking life. Simon, the guy who had helped him get where he was today and had waited patiently ever since, was in this very building. The notion of him being nervous at finally seeing him again was understandable, he supposed, but the idea of him actually being *afraid* of seeing him felt ridiculous.

Surely the cover of Simon's new book was indication enough that the writer's feelings were unaltered. Looking down at the book he held in his hands, he felt his throat grow thick as he studied the picture. It was a photograph taken of a small child with a man crouching beside him, the pair of them studying something on the ground and the image silhouetted in a way that made it obvious that it had been taken by an unskilled hand.

He remembered that day—the old saying ringing so true—like it was yesterday. It was taken during their trip to the zoo, just the three of them. In fact, he still carried around with him a small gift given to him that day by Simon. A small smile played on his lips; he wondered if Jamie still had his giant panda.

He knew that the picture had to be some sort of red flag meant for him, he just didn't know whether it was a good thing or a bad thing. That Simon had ventured to New York in part to see him was a given. Surely the stack of postcards marked from San Diego back at his apartment proved as much, those postcards being his only link to Simon at all. Like clockwork, a new one would arrive every two weeks, not a single word written on it but serving as a silent "I'm still in this." His were much the same. What was throwing him off was Simon's sudden, unexpected visit to New York.

They were approaching the end of their agreed separation, but they hadn't actually discussed how to go about ending it, or who would be the one to speak first. They'd maintained radio silence as per their rushed agreement to make the separation easier. If the postcards stopped coming during their break, then it was time to move on. It was as easy as that. But they hadn't stopped. In fact, the last one he'd received had been only five days ago—only this one had broken the rules. This one had the words "The Corner Bookstore, 1313 Madison Avenue" written in Simon's elegant handwriting, but with no mention of a date.

So naturally he'd Googled the hell out of Simon's name for any upcoming book-related visits to New York, and discovered that the acclaimed writer was due to visit the independent bookstore for a book signing. Now, heart in his throat, he waited at the back of a long queue which he assumed led to Simon.

He was undecided, but there was still good a chance that he might throw up or pass out or both.

"Excuse me, but are you...?"

"Oh. I'm sorry, ah...." Mattie blinked, startled out of his daydreams. "Why don't you go ahead?" He gestured with his book, an "after you" gesture. The woman offered him a friendly, if not slightly unnerved smile, and gladly took his place in the queue, putting him once again to the back of the line with a clear escape route to the storefront, which was becoming more and more appealing by the second.

If he hadn't been so busy fighting off a panic attack, he'd take a moment to be proud. Utterly and blindingly *proud* of the only man he had ever loved so completely. He knew what this book meant to Simon, and what Simon hoped it would mean to his son, Jamie. To actually hold it in his hands now, after being the very person to convince Simon to break away from his comfort zone to write it, just about blew his mind. And if the lengthy queue and happy chatter amongst the people in line was anything to go by, then it had thus far been well received.

However, every time the queue shifted forward, he found himself taking one step back and offering his place to the individual behind him. He needed more time to think. Five days had not been enough notice to get his head together for a moment he had been gearing up for for three years.

That Simon was here and had notified him (in a roundabout way) that he would be, should be reassurance enough. But three years was a long time. Three years was long enough for feelings to fade or cool. It was long enough to banish them to the space in your memory entitled "fond," or "whimsical," or even, "what the hell was I thinking?" It was enough time to move on, though Lord knows he couldn't. He supposed his biggest fear was that Simon had finally decided that enough was enough and it was time to let go, but was too much of a gentleman to just let their correspondence cease, ironically, without a word. A breakup in person would provide closure, he supposed.

His thoughts strayed to Jamie, as they had done over the past few years almost as much as they did to Simon. He'd be eight years old now, and he wondered where he was—if he was here in New York with Simon too, or back in San Diego, waiting for his father to return with perhaps an old familiar face in tow. On the one hand, he would love to see Jamie again. He was the sweetest goddamn kid he'd ever met, and Jamie had honored him by letting him be a part of the very small, very trusted few he would allow into his life. The kid was a gift. That was the word that came to mind when he thought of him. He was innocent, loving, and so enamored of the things in life that regular folk were blind to. People like him were so few, and simply made the world a better place.

On the other hand, he doubted Simon would bring Jamie with him. Jamie, for the brief time he'd known him at least, had not liked new places, was *frightened* of them, in fact. He'd hazard a guess that if Jamie was not with Simon, then this visit to New York would be a short one. Simon would not want to be away from Jamie for too long— any longer than necessary, he'd warrant. But that would beg the question: just who was looking after him now? Simon was desperately protective of his son, and would never leave him with just anyone.

The line shifted forward, and once more he took a step back. Three years was a long time, but it wasn't long enough to stop loving the man at the front of this queue.

Chapter
One

Three years previously...

"DAD?"

Simon abandoned the toast he'd been buttering, licked his thumb, and headed into the lounge at his son's beckoning. Jamie kneeled next to the sofa, peering into his Ninja Turtle backpack with a frown. Holding in a sigh, Simon sat on the edge of the sofa behind Jamie and looked over the child's shoulder to draw the bag closer for inspection.

"Did I miss something?"

Jamie looked back at him, his expression earnest in its anxiety. "Where are my grapes?" He tugged at the bag and opened the inside net pocket that usually held a small tub of grapes that he'd eat during recess.

Simon could have slapped himself upside the head. How could he forget the grapes? "It's okay," he reassured. "They're still in the fridge."

"They're supposed to be in here."

"I know, baby."

"I have them at recess. I sit with Miss Protrakis on the bench and I have grapes."

"Daddy was silly and just forgot to put them in. We'll do it now, okay?"

"'Kay," Jamie said quietly, looking in the bag to check nothing else was missing. "Purple grapes?" he quickly added before Simon had even stood up straight.

"Purple." Simon nodded, gently smoothing down the cowlick he secretly adored above Jamie's left ear.

"No seeds?"

Simon held back another sigh. One little thing like forgetting his grapes, and his son would feel unsettled for the rest of the day. From now on he'd write a list and stick it on the fridge, then do a check through his backpack before Jamie woke up. No child should have to worry over grapes.

"Absolutely no seeds. Come and bring your bag in the kitchen and you can pick your grapes. Then it's time for breakfast."

Simon looked over his shoulder to see Jamie dragging his Turtle backpack along behind him. He glanced up at his dad and gave him that small, sweet smile that always, *always* melted his goddamn heart. He smiled back.

"Okay, up?" Simon asked. He always asked, even if he was Daddy. There was no sudden lifting or gabbing.

Jamie held his arms up in answer, and Simon lifted him up onto the counter worktop, near the fridge. "Here you go," he said as cheerily as could, and handed Jamie the small tub with a red lid. He pulled the grapes out of the fridge and untwisted the knot in the bag. The grapes were, of course, purchased in a clear and flimsy plastic container, but Jamie didn't like how they tasted when left in the container—so, the bag. "Go ahead, pick."

Jamie looked in the bag. A tiny line forming between his brows in due concentration for such a serious and onerous a task, he reached into the bag and very carefully selected his grapes. When done, he placed the red lid on the tub and held it up for inspection. "Twelve grapes," he said happily. Despite everything, he was a happy boy, which was something Simon was desperately grateful for.

Simon nodded. Always twelve grapes. "Down?" He lifted his son under the armpits, and couldn't help but cuddle him close for a second before setting him down on his feet. "Go sit."

Jamie sat himself at the table, waiting patiently and tracing the pattern on the tablecloth with his finger while Simon poured his Lucky Charms into his spaceman cereal bowl. After taking a minute to pick out the rainbows—Jamie didn't like the rainbows—Simon sat the bowl in front of him. "Eat up," he ordered, and pulled out a small plastic cup from a cupboard and poured his son some good old-fashioned OJ.

"No bits?" Jamie asked around a mouthful of Lucky Charms.

"No bits. Smooth orange juice." Simon went back to his now cold toast and sat opposite his son as he scanned the newspaper.

"Fireman saves six from inferno." Jamie spoke slowly.

Simon lowered the paper, blinking in surprise. "What's that now?" he asked patiently.

Jamie's cheeks bulged comically, one hand curled around the spoon lodged between his lips and his pinkie pointing to the back of the paper Simon was reading. Simon turned the paper around, and, sure enough, there was a spread about a local off-duty fireman saving six people from a burning building. He glanced back at his son, pride swelling in his chest. At four years old, he could read and write at the level expected of a child twice his age.

"You're Daddy's clever boy, aren't you?"

Jamie beamed, his small feet in his favorite sneakers that lit up when he ran banging happily against the side of his chair as he nodded. "I'm a clever boy," he chimed happily.

Simon saw it a second before it happened. Jamie's hand, still holding the spoon, came down hard on the table, knocking over his orange juice. The juice quickly bled into the tablecloth and spread outward. Simon used his paper to stop the flow and leaped up to grab a small hand towel.

"Whoopsie daisy," he said airily, not knowing where he'd first heard the expression, but knowing that it usually made Jamie smile. He glanced at Jamie and was dismayed to see big brown eyes filling with tears and his small chin quivering ominously.

"I spilled."

His voice, so small and upset, got Simon every time. Ignoring the lump forming in his throat, he quickly plastered on a bright smile. "Hey," he said softly. "Come here." With his hands already out, showing Jamie that he was going to pick him up, he gently pulled Jamie from his chair and hugged him close, swaying slightly. "It doesn't matter, not at all."

"I knocked over the juice." Jamie hiccupped, winding his arms tightly around his dad's neck.

Simon rubbed his back soothingly, shushing him gently. He hated that his child suffered like this, that knocking over a cup of juice could disrupt his calm and upset him so much. But this was the way it had always been and would be for a long time. It was a part of Jamie's condition. It was a mild case, and there were a lot of other children with the disease that fared far worse, but the effects were difficult to deal with nonetheless.

At four years old, Jamie had in fact only begun to speak a year ago. He'd been diagnosed when Simon had been so concerned by Jamie's seeming disengagement with the rest of the world that he'd taken him to a doctor. It was explained to him that his son's condition was a brain disorder—a problem in his neural development. The night Jamie was diagnosed, Simon hadn't slept. He'd sat at his computer until the sun came up, researching, desperately trying to understand why. Why his boy? Hours of surfing and torturing himself led him to the same answers. There was no reason for it; it just... *happened* sometimes.

He was not Jamie's biological father. Technically, he was his uncle. Legally, he was his guardian. He was devastated when his sister passed away during childbirth. Devastated and angry. Who died of childbirth nowadays, anyway? Apparently it still happened, or it at least still occurred when women like his sister insisted on a home birth with zero drugs and then promptly bled to death. He knew he was being bitter, and that plenty of women who decided to give birth in such a way had healthy babies and lived to see them grow up, but not Carol-Ann. Not his sister. And though he'd been assured it wasn't the case, he couldn't help but feel that if she'd been in a hospital, Jamie might not be the way he was.

He'd felt bewildered too, and despite any residual resentment he may feel, he was in no small way honored that she had named him the next of kin for her baby—the biological father remaining a question mark and their mother not even considered—but the responsibility had hit him full-on. He'd been close to his sister, and grieved for her still, but he'd felt ill-equipped to provide for Jamie *before* he'd realized what that would fully entail. After he'd been diagnosed, he'd felt like an absolute fraud, as if child services would be knocking at his door any moment to take Jamie away from him.

They didn't, of course, and Jamie was legally his son for always. This was something he'd attempted to explain to Jamie a short time ago, and he'd been surprised by the lack of emotion that such a gentle but potentially rocking revelation had gained from the young child. He'd soon come to realize that Jamie had understood, but that he just didn't care. This was, of course, all a part of his condition, which was nothing more than a pervasive developmental disorder.

There were so many symptoms and different ways Jamie's impairment could affect a child. Generally, the condition showed itself in two ways. The child's IQ was either below normal or above normal. Jamie's was above normal, particularly when it came to numbers. But where he excelled at such a young age academically, he lacked dreadfully in social situations.

Jamie did not have any friends. Not really. There were two other boys and one girl, all with the same ailment of different degrees, whom Jamie's teacher, Miss Protrakis, had told him Jamie would occasionally, only *occasionally,* speak to. Otherwise, he spoke to his teacher and his dad. Absolutely no one but Daddy was allowed to pick him up, and the number of people Jamie would look in the eye could be counted on two fingers. That was one of Jamie's biggest challenges, and something that was very difficult for Simon to swallow.

His other symptoms were evident in his inability to initiate a conversation. He would really only speak when spoken to and was otherwise perfectly content to play with his building blocks, utterly oblivious to his surroundings. Except Jamie's building blocks took on the form of towering skyscrapers in repetitive blue and green blocks. (He didn't like the reds or yellows, they were far too bright.) And living on the outskirts of downtown San Diego, he'd often pointed out the large buildings and high-rises to his son when they'd go on one of their walks or to the park. He could swear it was the downtown landscape his brilliant son replicated, though that was most likely the proud father in him speaking.

And he was proud. *Damn* proud.

Jamie could repeat every line from *The Hobbit*, and would only have Tolkien read to him at bedtime or he simply would not sleep. His motor skills were slow, hence the plastic bowls and cups. He couldn't quite grasp another person's perspective, thus his lack of a reaction upon hearing that Simon was not his biological father. And everything, *everything* was literal.

It was draining. It was so absolutely draining that sometimes he would miss how his life had been before his son was born. But he loved Jamie. He loved him so much that quite often when he held him close, as he was now, all he could do was just breathe him in. He was sure that, if asked, he wouldn't be quite able to put into words the love he felt for this beautiful little kid, and that was saying something, given his profession.

He rubbed Jamie's back soothingly, swaying gently. He swallowed hard, hearing Jamie's voice, interrupted by an intermittent sniff, recite a long list of prime numbers. It was his default for when he was upset. He always went back to the numbers.

"Nineteen, twenty-three, twenty-nine…."

"Shush, now. It's all right. Everything's all right."

"Thirty-seven, forty-one…."

"Do you know where orange juice comes from?"

"From oranges?"

Simon barked out a quiet laugh and pulled his head back slightly so he could catch Jamie's gaze. "Good guess, but where do oranges come from?"

"Trees. Trees make oxygen."

"Yes, they do. They also grow oranges." Jamie was quiet, calmer now, watching his dad. "Do you know how many trees there are in the world?"

"No."

"There's *millions*. Millions and millions of trees. And there are millions and millions of oranges."

"Millions and millions," Jamie repeated quietly, no longer crying, no longer reciting his numbers.

"So one cup of juice won't make a difference, all right?" he said quietly. Jamie didn't react, didn't answer. He rested his cheek against his dad's shoulder, blinking slowly as if he were sleepy. And if anything, he appeared mesmerized by his father's voice, almost soothed by it.

"Daddy's gonna give ya a big kiss," Simon said in a silly voice, earning himself a small smile.

Jamie lifted his head from Simon's shoulder, and giggled when the kiss to his cheek turned into a soft raspberry. Simon was never more grateful than at those moments that Jamie was a high-functioning case for his condition, and that such small, innocent acts of affection were acceptable to him when coming from his father.

"All better?" Simon asked, and with a final smoothing to that adorable cowlick, he set him down. Jamie nodded, pulling his cape close around him.

That cape. Some kids had a blanky; others sucked their thumb. His kid wore a cape. Every day. And it was currently, Simon noticed, stained with spilled orange juice. He grabbed a dishcloth and, without thinking, reached to wipe the damp mess down Jamie's front, right near the neckline. The reaction was instant.

"No! *Don't!*"

Simon flinched when Jamie squealed, his little hands immediately covering his own ears. Simon tried his best not to show his frustration and anger at himself for being so thoughtless. It always had to be slow movements with Jamie. He dropped the cloth and immediately began to shush Jamie.

"Jamie! Jamie, Daddy's sorry. Daddy's sorry, baby."

To his utter relief, Jamie stopped his agitated cries, only breathing a little heavily and blinking at his dad. In worst-case scenarios, where Jamie would feel that little stretch beyond agitated, he knew his son would not accept any form of touch, even from his own father, and would be rolling on the floor in an instinctive attempt to calm himself. Only a doctor or parent would know that it was actually an attempt to relax his sympathetic nervous system by applying pressure to large areas of his body (a hug without being hugged). To anyone else it was awkward and difficult to witness. Being a parent, it was at those times that he could only sit back and watch unhappily until Jamie calmed.

"Daddy's being very silly today, isn't he? Silly Daddy, huh?" His voice wavered ever so slightly in upset, and he *slowly* reached to tenderly stroke Jamie's baby soft cheek. "Silly Daddy," he said softly, soothingly. "There's juice on your cape. We don't want that now, do we? I'm going to wipe it off so it's nice and clean, all right?"

Jamie nodded and watched patiently as Simon knelt close and wiped slowly at the stain. Simon pursed his lips in frustration, knowing that he'd have to wash it when Jamie was asleep, seeing as it was the only time Jamie would take it off, and even then he had to have his dad's bathrobe draped over his bed in its place.

"Okay, all done. I want you to finish your cereal and brush your teeth. Then we'll head off to school, okay?"

"Can I play with Gizmo?"

Simon smiled. Jamie loved his hamster. "If there's time. I want you to finish your cereal first, though."

Jamie sat back at the table, going back to his Lucky Charms, his sneakers once again banging happily against the chair's legs as if nothing had happened.

Simon ran his hands over his face and left the kitchen for a second. Out in the hall, he leaned his brow against the wall and fought against the tears he could feel stinging his eyes.

Grapes and juice. And it was only 8:00 a.m. He took a deep breath, pulled his and Jamie's coats from their hooks, and walked back into the kitchen. Jamie glanced at him, and there was that smile. That small, sweet smile.

God, he loved his son.

IT WAS so difficult to leave Jamie when he was unhappy. That morning's events had been enough to unsettle him, enough to make him cling to his dad's hand and hide his face against the side of Simon's thigh. Simon stood there, feeling helpless, with one hand cradling the back of Jamie's small head, the other limply holding his backpack.

"Don't you want to say 'hi' to Miss Protrakis?" Simon tried, and received nothing but a shake of Jamie's head in response. Sarah, the teacher in question, gave him an understanding smile and knelt next to Jamie.

"Hi, Jamie, it's time for school. Smart boys and girls go to school, don't they?"

"Yes," came Jamie's whispered response.

"You're a smart boy, aren't you?"

Simon's smile was strained when Sarah glanced up at him quickly. God love this woman for being so patient and kind with kids like Jamie.

"Well, how about you give me your hand, we can wave bye to your dad, and then you can show all the other boys and girls how smart you are today in math class, huh?"

Simon bit back a sigh when Jamie shook his head and refused to look up at his teacher. Sarah stood again, frowning.

"Did something happen this morning to unsettle him?" she asked quietly, and Simon was grateful for the lack of judgment in her words. This woman understood his day-to-day struggles. Nonetheless, Simon fought the wave of guilt he felt, swallowing, and nodded yes as he gently stroked Jamie's hair. "I forgot to pack his grapes, and we had a little upset when we spilled some juice." He looked down, trying to get his son's attention. "Didn't we, kiddo? But it's okay. It's all cleaned up, and we're ready for school now, aren't we?"

"There's millions of oranges," Jamie replied quietly.

Simon smiled sadly, looking back at the teacher. "I tried to clean his cape, and I startled him." He swallowed when Sarah nodded in understanding, her expression showing nothing but sympathy and support. "I was stupid and wasn't thinking—"

"Hey," she said quietly and touched his arm briefly. "We all slip up. Don't beat yourself up. You're a good father."

To an outsider, her touch may have looked flirtatious, but Sarah knew he was gay and was perhaps one of his closest friends. It was an unexpected friendship, one that, if it was not for Jamie, might not have otherwise formed at all, but nevertheless was genuine and important to him.

He glanced down at his son, who was hugging that damn cape around him, clinging to his leg. "I've disrupted his day. He was okay after the juice, but then… perhaps I shouldn't leave him today?"

"Simon," Sarah began as if gentling a startled animal. It took him a second to realize that he was that animal; he was a second away from taking his son home to where he'd feel safe. "I know how protective you are of him, but we've talked about this. You know how important it is to get him to interact with others while he's still so young. We have to keep him engaged. It's difficult, yes, but believe me, we've got to push him past his comfort zones, slowly but surely. Ultimately, it'll make him more independent, self-sufficient. He'll make more friends, eventually become curious about more than just numbers, and—"

Simon nodded. He understood; it was just so fucking *hard*. "You're right, you're right. Jamie?" He tried to carefully pull away from him to catch his son's gaze, but Jamie stared at the ground. Simon glanced at Sarah and then pulled Jamie off of his leg, holding him gently by the shoulders and going down on his haunches to look him in the eye. "You're going to be my brave boy today, all right? Daddy wants you to go learn lots of new things. I want you to go with Miss Protrakis."

Big brown eyes that were sad and not a little bit betrayed looked up at him, and Simon fought against the urge to snap him up in his arms. "Can you do that for me?"

Simon felt his resolve begin to crumble as that little chin started to tremble again, but then Jamie was nodding.

"Okay, Dad."

Pride, like a goddamn tidal wave, washed clean through him. Until then Jamie had always relied on his father to take him away from situations that unnerved him or made him unhappy. But here he was, doing as he was told first time around, even though it upset him. Simon smiled, glancing past Jamie to where Sarah stood, giving him an approving nod.

"That's my boy. That's my big, brave boy. You take Miss Protrakis's hand, and I'll be back before you know it. If things get bad, then you tell your teacher, and she'll call me, okay?"

"Okay," Jamie echoed.

"Come give me a big hug."

Jamie tiptoed and wrapped his arms around his dad's neck, and Simon clenched his jaw tight. He completed the hug, gently cupping the back of Jamie's head. "I love you, Jamie."

No response came, and really, he knew better than to expect one, but it always hurt a little when he had to ask. "Do you love Daddy?"

Jamie nodded furiously, and Simon laughed softly. He gently pulled him back, aware that the bell signaling the start of registration had rung some minutes ago, the other children now in class and the playground empty. He kissed Jamie's cheek, and then slowly picked up the Ninja Turtle backpack and threaded Jamie's arms through the handles.

"You're being a good boy, Jamie. Can I have your hand?" Sarah asked, holding out her own. Jamie nodded and slipped his hand into hers. "Wave to your dad." She waved to show him.

Simon smiled and waved back, watching as Sarah led him up to the double doors that were the school's entrance. Simon glanced up at the large sign above them.

"Golden Acres School," and below, in smaller writing, *"San Diego's leading school for Asperger's Syndrome and Autism."*

He let out a deep breath.

MATTIE was running late. He rushed off of the bus and down the street to the diner he worked at, cursing himself for falling back asleep after turning off his alarm. Being late twice in the span of one week was a surefire way to go about getting your ass canned. And damn, he needed this job. Not that it was particularly interesting or anything, or even remotely gratifying, but it did have its advantages.

It was easy. Any fool could work the sandwich bar at a diner, even one such as himself who couldn't read or write all that well. The people were nice. In fact, that's where he'd met Tyler, a full-time employee who worked the cash register and took orders. He knew Mattie was gay, and didn't care. He knew what Mattie did sometimes to supplement his bills, and didn't care. He was funny and a general screw up, just like Mattie, and was probably the closest thing to a friend he had.

And then there was, of course, the clientele. In particular, the absolutely gorgeous, adorably quiet, and somewhat nerdy single dad that got him all worked up and hot under the collar every time he came into the diner.

He didn't talk much, seemed sometimes like he might be carrying the world on his shoulders, and he always sat in the same booth, hunched over his laptop and typing away for hours. Mattie couldn't pinpoint why he was so head over heels for him, but he was. Oh *boy* did he carry a torch for this guy.

Tyler liked to tease him, tell him he had a crush on a geek, but he'd just shove the guy in the shoulder and tell him to shut up. Ty was only kidding, finding him and the gay thing in general to be weird, but with an indifferent attitude that made him kind of awesome.

No, he didn't know exactly what drew him in, but he couldn't help but blush a little every time the guy ordered himself a sandwich. In fact, when the guy glanced up at Mattie to say thanks before taking his lunch to the cash register to pay, it was probably one of the best parts of his day. He was slim, maybe a fraction taller than Mattie, and always wore a baggy sweatshirt or turtleneck. His hair was short and graying at the temples, and his glasses made him look somewhat distinguished and clever—*not* geeky. At a guess, Mattie would place him at around thirty-two, a whole six years older than himself, and then there was the whole single dad thing, which just made him want to melt.

He didn't know what the guy's deal was. There was no wedding ring, and he'd never seen a woman with him. It was always just him, or him and the cutest little kid you'd ever hope to see. But gay or straight, single or involved, he without a doubt revved Mattie's engine.

He got the feeling that the kid was… special? He didn't know the PC term for it. The kid was clearly not dumb. He'd seen him sitting across from his dad, always wearing that cute cape, running his fingers along the menu and slowly reading the lunch special (which was more than he could do, for damn sure). But the kid was… he didn't know. It was more than shyness that stopped the little guy from even looking at anyone other than his dad. It was something in him that was born that way. Just watching this guy smile at his kid, watching him gently stroke his hair or hold his hand and take him to the bathroom, hit all of Mattie's mush buttons, and he was man enough to admit he had such buttons.

So, yeah, the place had its advantages. It was just a shame that the pay was for shit. Renting a tiny apartment and sharing a bathroom with ten other people was quite costly, believe it or not. And then there was the cost of his canvases and paint supplies, but he got around that. Mattie shook his head and pushed the door to the diner open, the familiar bell ringing above his head.

"Hey, the boss around?" he asked Tyler as he ducked behind the sandwich bar and shoved his jacket under the counter.

"Nah, you lucked out."

"Sorry to leave you hanging." There was only Tyler and himself in the diner. Though undoubtedly the waitress, Daphne, was out back having a quick smoke, and Jules, the overweight, introverted chef who he occasionally helped out, was probably reading the paper in the kitchen.

"It's not like they're lining up around the corner, Matt, so no worries. Just don't let Don catch you coming in late again."

Tyler was counting the cash register, the black apron with the simple "Don's Diner" logo hanging loose from his neck. Having finished counting, he closed the register and then pulled the strings of the apron around his body to tie at the front. He nodded toward the door. "Flip the sign, would you?"

"Sure." Mattie looped an identical apron around his neck and flipped the sign to say "open." "I'll come in early tomorrow and help you set up, promise."

"Cool." Ty slapped him on the shoulder as he walked by with a couple of refilled napkin dispensers, and set them on the tables. "Hey." Ty looked up, leaning against one of the tables. "There's this band, 'Residue', playing at the Noisy Cricket tonight. You want to come check it out with me?"

Mattie shrugged. "Na, I can't. Thanks, though."

"Sure? I know you don't like that bar but they're supposed to be good, kind of a cross between Rage Against The Machine and the Chili Peppers."

No, he didn't like that bar, though he'd never enlightened Ty as to why. He breathed out heavily through his nose as he started to slice open the baguettes and butter them. He pictured the rope inside of him, or what he thought of as the coil. He always thought of the coil when his thoughts strayed into not-so-great memories. It was at the Noisy Cricket that he'd picked up his first... what? Customer? Client? He shook his head minutely. He didn't want to give them a label, didn't want to make it in any way official. All the same, he didn't go there, to that bar, anymore.

"I can't, got… stuff to do."

"Oh."

Mattie looked up and saw the brief look of comprehension on his friend's face. There was no judgment, but perhaps a hint of pity, which in a way was worse, but Ty would never be unkind to him. Mattie bit the inside of his cheek as Ty walked over to lean against the sandwich bar, glancing at the diner entrance to check that no customers were about to walk in. His voice was quiet, understanding.

"You need to borrow some cash, Mattie?"

The coil inside him pulled tighter, the thick rope with its frayed ends creaking and burning around what he supposed was him in the middle. His jaw clenched, but he glanced at Ty when his hand touched his shoulder.

"It's okay. Tips have been good this week. What do you need?"

He forced a smile. This was Ty after all, and it wouldn't do to snap at the one good friend he had.

He made minimum wage shifting boxes, cleaning the bathrooms, and making sandwiches, and obviously, the cash didn't stretch too far. It *always* came back to money. It wasn't as if he didn't have any higher aspirations. He'd love to be doing something else, something better paid, but seeing as he couldn't fucking read or write like a normal twenty-six-year-old, he was staying put for the foreseeable future. But he was working on changing his circumstances, attending night classes for illiterate adults at the central library at 820 E Street, only a bus ride away. But those classes were not free, and neither were his paint supplies. And he had to paint; sometimes it was the only thing that would let the rope go slack. All of these things, the vital and his one indulgence, cost more than what minimum wage provided. So, he made money another way while juggling the low self-esteem and self-hatred that came along with it.

He'd had a rough upbringing—he hadn't been beaten or abandoned, but he'd grown up invisible to a drunken father, dropped out of school at an early age, and ended up sleeping on different couches until he was eighteen. He'd simply slipped, unnoticed, through the cracks of all child service and educational authorities. His father was gone now, and he was trying to make his life better, but if he had to occasionally hook to do it, to get by? Fuck anyone that wanted to look down on him for it.

"I'd only have to pay you back, Ty," he said quietly, slicing open another baguette. He cut Ty a quick glance, and it was obvious he was struggling to come up with another solution. "Hey," he said quietly, glancing around the room to ascertain they were still alone for the moment. "Thanks, but it's okay. You know it doesn't mean anything to me."

It was a lie; it made him feel dirty and unlovable. And judging by the look Ty was giving him, he wasn't a very persuasive liar. He sighed and put the knife down. "Actually, tonight this guy I...." *This guy I'm blowing for money.* "This guy I'm seeing has a spare ticket to the Voice 1156 Gallery show tomorrow night." He shrugged. "I gotta go see him to pick up my ticket, so I can't hang, sorry."

Ty contemplated him for a second, then smiled, convinced. "You love that art stuff, don't you? You still sending shit off?"

Mattie laughed. "Yeah, I'm still sending parts of my portfolio off, though printing and shipping is killing me. It'd be easier if the Art Institute of New York wasn't in fucking New York, but what are you gonna do, huh?" He shrugged, kidding.

"Well, why not somewhere else? Somewhere local? That's gotta be cheaper, right?"

Mattie sighed. How to explain? He shook his head. "It sounds stupid," he began quietly, "but I've always wanted to go to New York." He shrugged, glancing up at Ty. "Everyone has goals and aspirations, right?"

Ty nodded.

"Well, I've got just the one. New York." Licking his bottom lip quickly. "I remember this one New Year's Eve, I was sleeping on someone's couch, and they were having this party." He shook his head briefly. "I think I was seventeen, and life had pretty much gone to shit round about that point. I didn't want to be at the party, so I snuck down into their basement to hide out." He grinned and shrugged. "Happy people pissed me off, for some reason."

Ty smiled, nodded. "Yeah, I know the feeling."

"Anyhoozles," he sighed. "They had this old TV set, and I decided to watch the ball drop and…." He bit his lip. "You know what?"

"What?" Ty asked quietly.

"It looked so great there. So… *big*. Like it wouldn't matter if you're a screwup there."

"You're not a—"

"Ty." He shook his head. "It looked like a place to start a life, to *make* one. Just… so big, with so many opportunities to start again."

Ty was quiet. "Jesus, just about everything you tell me depresses me. Asshole."

Mattie laughed. "Sorry. You know, it's a *great* school. I've looked it up online." He shook his head. "One of the best, they cater to so many different medias, and I could learn so much. It's just getting in that's proving to be a son of a bitch."

"*Pft*, you'll get in, full ride, just you wait and see." Ty pulled the dishcloth from where it was tucked into the back of his belt and flicked it at him as he pushed off the counter with his hip.

"Have to get my GED first, and to do that, I have to learn to fucking read." He shook his head, a tinge of "why the hell am I bothering" sneaking in.

"Hey," Ty said firmly. "You'll do it."

"Ty, I have to write an entrance essay, I have to provide high school transcripts. I'm a twenty-six-year-old who makes fucking *sandwiches*." He flushed faintly. "All the other students would be coming out of high school. I'll be old compared to them."

"Oh, fuck off." Ty leaned close. "Goddamn senior citizens can go back to school if they want, so that ain't a reason, and if you truly believe you don't have a chance, then what are you doing sending work samples off?"

He had him there. A part of him still hoped that something would happen to pull him out of the pit his life had become. So he continued to paint; he continued to check all possible avenues open to him. At first, he'd sought after financial aid, because there was no way in hell he could pay for tuition. A sincere and humbling conversation with a very kind and understanding admissions representative over the phone had dashed most of his hopes, but they *had* discussed the few options open to him.

He could take out a loan to cover half, and then work part time. The loan itself wouldn't have to be paid off until he was earning a higher salary. There had been a confusing conversation about credits and written references, but there was no getting in there without a high school diploma or GED test scores. There were just so many hurdles.

"Look." Ty leaned close. "You're going to your night classes, yeah? The one for adults?"

"Yeah." He nodded, wiping absently at the counter as he looked anywhere but at his friend. He hated it when he got all sullen, and appreciated a swift—although metaphorical—kick in the ass sometimes.

"Right. And don't say you can't read, because you're getting there." Ty shrugged, almost apologetic. "I've seen you reading the menus, and that's awesome."

Mattie looked up quickly and pressed his lips together in a tight line. He didn't think anyone'd been looking. The idea of someone seeing him hunched over a menu, trying to break down the words and sound them out in his head was mortifying. He swallowed and dug his hands into his pockets.

"So you keep going to your classes. Then you study for your GED. I can help you with that. *Then* you apply."

Mattie smiled. "You rock as a friend, you know that?"

"Ah, shut up."

"No. You're awesome. You keep me from pulling out the violins and going all maudlin and shit." He smiled almost shyly, just the corner of his mouth lifting as he affectionately pushed at Ty's shoulder. "Thanks, man."

"Yeah, yeah, no problem. Just remember me when you're a rich and famous artist, all right?"

The bell above the door sounded, and a familiar, gorgeous face appeared, heading to his usual booth.

"Oh look, lover boy is here," Ty teased quietly as he picked up the coffeepot.

"Shut up."

"It's one thing to choose balls over breasts, but you don't even have good taste in guys."

"You've got no idea what you're talking about," Mattie practically whispered back, and grinned as he stole a quick look at the customer in question.

"Hey, I may not be gay, but I can appreciate a good-looking guy when I see one. You, for instance, are hot."

Mattie laughed despite himself. "You switching teams on me?"

"Hell no. Just means I wish I looked like you. You could be a fucking model."

"Shut up, asshole."

"Seriously, all the attention you get from women—"

"I swear that's the only reason Don hired me—to pull in horny cougars," he interrupted.

"—and nothing. It's like Superman not using his powers."

"Oh, I use my powers, just not on women."

Ty rolled his eyes. "The guy's a *geek*."

"No, he's not. He's all sophisticated looking. You know, good-looking in a down-to-earth way."

"You getting your period, or something?"

"Fuck you." Mattie barked a quiet laugh.

"Are you telling me that if, I don't know, that blonde dude from *90210*—the one that plays a gay guy—or someone like that walked in, you'd pick this guy?"

Mattie shook his head. "That guy knows he's hot. This guy?" Mattie nodded discreetly toward their patron. "He's totally unaware of how cute he is, which is a whole other level of hotness in my opinion."

"I'd pick the *90210* guy, personally." He rolled his eyes at Mattie's questioning raised eyebrow. "That's just common sense," he explained. "I don't have a gay bone in my body. If I did, I would have worked the magic on you by now."

"*Pft*, you wish."

"You'd choose four-eyes over there instead of me?"

"In a heartbeat."

"You need your head examined."

"You know who he does remind me of?"

"A science teacher?"

"Shut up. You ever watch *Frasier*?"

"Duh. That's some classic TV right there."

"You know Frasier's brother, Niles?"

"*What*?" Ty laughed.

"I'm not talking about the germ phobia or the snobby attitude, but just how intelligent he is, how sweet and earnest—"

"Actually, you may have a point there. I got no problem admitting that I teared up when Niles and Daphne finally got together. Man, they don't write sitcoms like that anymore."

"Well, there you go."

"So you're telling me you'd pick Niles over… say, I don't know, Shepherd from *Grey's Anatomy*?"

"Yup."

"You'd go for cute over hot?"

Mattie sighed. "How can I explain this in a way you'd understand...?" He drummed his fingers on the counter. "Ah! Okay, it's like picking Jennifer Anniston over Angelina Jolie."

Ty narrowed his eyes in thought, but slowly began to nod, a grin tugging at his lips. "So you mean you've got the super-hot vixen versus the gorgeous, sweet girl next door?"

Mattie smirked. "The irony being the vixen is overexposed and loses that something that makes your dick that extra bit hard, while—"

Ty was nodding. "While the girl next door you want to not only introduce to your parents, but then take home and bang the hell out of in private." Ty laughed and held his hand out for a fist bump. "Dude, we are so on the same wavelength. I get you now."

Mattie bumped his fist, grinning. "Finally."

Ty nodded, wiped his hands down his apron, and waited a heartbeat before: "He's still a geek, though."

Mattie shook his head. "You're clueless." He glanced back over at the booth where the guy was turning on his laptop. "He's gorgeous, end of story."

Ty shook his head, muttering something about being a lost cause as he strode away, coffeepot in hand. Mattie sliced open another baguette and settled in for what was one of the best parts of his day—watching Mr. Handsome click away at his keyboard.

Chapter
Two

SIMON huffed as he flicked through the stack of postcards he'd picked up from a newsstand on the way to the diner. Generally, when his writing wasn't flowing as smoothly as he'd like, he'd look for sources of brief inspiration. Anything from a song, a passage of a poem, or even an old photograph could usually inspire something.

Not today. He wrapped the red rubber band back around the stack of postcards depicting various landscapes, and dropped them back into his satchel. He was finding it more difficult than ever to get the gears turning with his latest manuscript, and with deadlines set not all that far off in the future, he was starting to worry.

He reached into his bag for his laptop, frowned, and then pulled out a crumpled juice box. He snorted softly. When was his boy going to learn that daddy's bag wasn't a place for his trash? He looked up when hearing someone—the waiter—clear his throat, and smiled his thanks at the young man who filled his mug. The guy smiled back, and Simon frowned slightly. That hadn't been a smile so much as a knowing smirk. Why did he always feel as if he were the butt of some joke when he came here? He shrugged absently. It didn't matter. It was close to the school, it was usually quiet, and they allowed their clientele to hang around as long as they kept ordering. He usually got there at around nine thirty, got himself a coffee, and wrote for a few hours until lunch. He'd buy a sandwich, write for two more hours, and then pick Jamie up from school. He smiled. Sometimes he'd bring Jamie back here; he liked the kid's menu.

He couldn't quite pinpoint what type of diner this was. You could sit and hang out here, order coffee and sandwiches, but you could also order a cooked meal and use their Wi-Fi. It wasn't exactly a five-star restaurant, but it had a cool fifties theme with black and white framed photos of Frank Sinatra, Chuck Berry, Jerry Lee Lewis, and Elvis hanging on the walls. The employees were friendly and laid-back, and they played dated music, just quiet enough to be pleasant and ignorable. Most importantly, he liked to write there. It had a glass front, and he could look out and people-watch during moments of writer's block, not to mention that Jamie loved the mac 'n' cheese.

And if he were to be honest, the lecherous old man in him liked to catch a glimpse of the young guy who cleaned up and made the sandwiches. Because, good God, he was utterly, *utterly* charming. He was a similar height to his own, had the prettiest blue eyes, dimples that peeked out when the guy smiled, and mousy brown hair with short back and sides and bangs that begged to be tenderly brushed away from his brow. His body was trim and in shape, he had the smooth curve of muscle, his T-shirts clung nicely to his slim biceps and hinted at a beautiful abdomen, which somehow made him appear all the younger. He couldn't be more than twenty-two, twenty-three, probably a good ten years younger than himself. There was an irresistible hint of vulnerable bad boy to him, sexy and tough, maybe a little sweet.

Gah, I'm a pervy old man.

But really, he was the kind of typically gorgeous Adonis you'd see in an Armani ad. Simon ventured a quick glance, and wouldn't you just know it, as if the guy could feel his stare, he looked up from the bar and offered Simon a half smile—a shy hello, almost. Simon glanced away, feeling heat bloom in his cheeks at being caught looking.

It'd been a while since he'd looked, more than a year, in fact. He wasn't so sure if there was actually any point in attempting to catch another man's eye. First off, he was no longer the catch he sort-of-almost-was before Jamie. He'd had a modest number of lovers, the intellectual writer apparel appealing to a certain few, but any care taken with his appearance, his clothes, just felt insignificant now. Who had time to glance in the mirror when he had a son who needed his constant care? It wasn't as if he could just leave Jamie with a sitter and go out dating. Sarah was the one exception and genuinely cared for Jamie. She was happy to watch him on the odd occasion Simon had to be away from him, but even that felt like an imposition. The woman had her own life to get on with, after all.

He knew he needed to invite more people into Jamie's life. He needed to get his son to interact with others in a way that other parents didn't have to worry about. The integral interaction and the social rules that came along with growing up came naturally to other children. Not his child. All social rules had to be pounded into Jamie, *taught* to him. *Please* and *thank you. May I. Excuse me. Hello, my name is Jamie.* None of this would ever be forthcoming from Jamie; he had to be pushed. And it was all well and good teaching him these words and the reasons for them, but without putting them into practice, how was Jamie to understand the importance of them?

He could stand to be a little less protective, perhaps. He needed to get it out of his head that anyone new would hurt or disappoint his son. But how to explain to that person their significance to Jamie, if his son were to ever allow them into his life? For Jamie to learn to trust another person, only for them to leave when the going got tough, would be devastating to his son and any routine of his that involved this fictional person. It'd happened before.

He'd been in love with Tim Arnold: a flirtatious and generous man, four years younger than himself, a wannabe actor with a love for life that had inspired Simon. They'd been together for five years, and he had actually thought that, *yes, this is the person I could spend the rest of my life with.* But then his sister… Jamie….

He had to give Tim a little credit. He hadn't signed up for being a parent—a parent of a high-functioning autistic child, no less—but neither had he. The only difference was that Tim hadn't been obligated to stick around. Only loyalty had kept Tim with him for so long, but even that had not been enough.

The Coil

Their lives had been turned upside down. They'd gone from concerts, traveling, and mornings spent leisurely fucking, to changing diapers and midnight feeds. And then later, rigorous doctor appointments had occupied their time, extremely upsetting temper tantrums from a child that was faced with a world with colors that were too bright, noises too loud, and hands that wanted to touch when being held was terrifying. He and Jamie were settled now, they had their routine, but at the time when Tim was still on the scene, they'd still been trying to find their way, fumbling as they went, and the tantrums that had been fucking traumatic for all parties involved took their toll.

Tim couldn't cope. *"I never wanted this, I don't want this, I'm so sorry,"* he'd said, and then left. Two years together, blissfully happy, and then three years together as a small, struggling family. To be fair, he'd half wished he'd been the one to say that, the one with the luxury of walking away. Jamie had been three, diagnosis new and still earth-shattering. Every moment revolved around what he'd considered at that time to be their child. Somewhere along the way, they'd just stopped looking at each other, and life with him and Jamie had become a chore for Tim: painfully exhausting and totally encompassing.

He remembered sitting on the bed watching Tim pack. They both cried. He'd surrendered his last ounce of dignity, taking Tim's hand, pressing it to his brow as silent sobs wracked his frame, and he'd begged. He'd begged Tim to not go, to not leave him alone, that he couldn't cope without him. And there'd been this horrible moment where Tim had flinched and pulled his hand away, as if he couldn't bear his touch. Simon knew now that his touch had been a shackle to a resigned life that was suffocating Tim, but he hadn't known that then, and it had hurt him like hell at the time.

All Tim could do was say that he was sorry, his mind utterly made up and desperate for escape. The worst of it was that Jamie had *noticed*. He'd only just begun to speak, but Tim had been one of his caregivers. He'd been a strict part of his routine that, thanks to his ex, had gone completely up in smoke. It hadn't mattered that he was heartbroken, that Daddy needed a second to catch his breath or a few moments to grieve the life he'd envisioned for himself, because there was absolutely no understanding empathy for Jamie. Not when he was three, and not when he'd be a grown adult.

They'd somehow, *somehow* managed. It had been a tough year for both of them, but they had their routine down and Jamie was making progress. He was verbal. He'd started to learn how to dress himself and to tell his dad when he needed to go to the bathroom so he didn't mess himself. The care and attention, though draining, made for a relatively calm life for his child.

How was he supposed to introduce someone new into that mix? If Jamie learned to like another adult, to trust him as he did his own father, and then they left? It would be so much worse a second time around.

So he supposed it was kind of safe to look at the handsome young man at the sandwich bar, maybe even fantasize a little. Because there was no way anything could ever happen, and that wasn't the pessimist in him speaking, it was the realist. Guys like that? They had the world at their feet, people lining up around the corner for their attention.

He sneaked another look, and almost laughed as the other guy caught his gaze again. He caught sight of a dimple, and the cute guy raised his hand slightly in a small wave not meant for anyone else to see. Apparently he was polite too. Simon smiled uncertainly, dipping his head slightly in response, and turned back to his laptop.

Just do some work, Simon.

"HERE, go give him a refill. And that's not a euphemism for anything."

Ty set the coffeepot in front of the sandwich counter and gave Mattie his best shit-eating grin. Mattie laughed and shook his head.

"I'm busy. Can't you tell?"

"Wiping an already clean counter?"

"Um. Yes. Get lost."

"You're making disgusting goo-goo eyes at him. And I'm a guy. I should never have to say that to another dude. Look at what you're doing to me, man. I'll be knitting next."

"No one's asking you to interfere."

"No, they're not. But luckily for you, I'm an awesome friend. Go top off his coffee."

"No."

"You waved at him earlier. God, I can't believe I'm having such a girly conversation."

"He was looking at me." Mattie shrugged, embarrassed. "Seemed the polite thing to do."

"He was looking because he thinks you're hot. I'm losing masculine points by the second here."

"Scratch your balls or something."

He discreetly scratched his balls. "That's better." Ty drummed his fingers against the counter. "Titties."

"Excuse me?"

"Big-ass titties."

"Um, okay. You're weird."

"Just trying to compensate for the following...." He took a deep breath. "Ah, Jesus. Okay, look. You really like this guy. *Really*. I can tell. You moon over him every day. He's always looking over his shoulder at you and clearly wants to make a playdate with the lower half of your body. *Dude.* Just go *talk* to him."

"And say what?"

"Uh, how about: *'Hi, I'm Mattie. Date me. Now.'*"

"Very smooth."

"You're hot. You don't have to be smooth."

"Ah, shut up, I am not. Hetero boy."

"Yes, you are, you ungrateful shit. You have biceps and everything. I bet your stomach has those bumpy things...." He clicked his fingers, looking for the word.

"Abs? A six pack?" Mattie laughed.

"Yeah! You got muscle where there should be a nice soft layer of skin. Freak."

Mattie shook his head and laughed quietly. He wiped his hands on his apron before discreetly lifting it and the corner of his T-shirt beneath a few inches. "You mean these things?"

"You are such a douche. Do you even say anything to him when he buys food?"

"Not really."

"*Why?*" Ty lowered his voice, looking around him as a customer walked past toward the restroom.

"*Because!*"

"Lame."

"Because when he speaks my IQ drops a hundred fucking points!" he hissed.

Mattie sighed as his friend's shoulders dropped, and flushed when Ty raised a single eyebrow at him that practically screamed "pathetic." He shook his head, leaning on his elbows across the counter, and kept his voice quiet. "You have to step it up with a guy like that. You have to know shit, be able to talk about books and philosophy and God knows what."

"I think that's called stereotyping."

"You're the one who said he was a geek."

"Doesn't mean he's not into sports, cars, action flicks, and dirty bad sex like the rest of us."

Mattie frowned and pushed away from the counter. He untied his apron and drew it off over his head. "I ain't got nothing to offer a guy like that, so let's just drop it, yeah?" He shoved the apron under the counter. "It's quiet, so I'm going for a quick break. Get back to work already." He gave Ty a halfhearted smile to take any sting out of his words, and headed out back for some fresh air.

Ty rolled his eyes and watched as Mattie headed toward the door marked "Employees Only." *Why do gays gotta make it so complicated?* Narrowing his eyes at Mattie's retreating back, he picked up the coffeepot and headed over to the big ol' scary nerd's booth.

"HI THERE, refill?"

Simon was jolted out of his work by the friendly question, and he offered the waiter a polite smile and nodded. "Thank you."

"No problem." Ty poured the coffee and stole a quick glance at the open laptop, expecting to see anything from porn to kitten videos on YouTube. Disappointed, he spied an open word document. "So, you a writer, or...?"

Surprised at the initiation of conversation, Simon looked away from the laptop and fought the compulsion to turn the screen away from view. "Uh, yeah, actually."

"And 'Don's Diner' is a source of inspiration for you?"

Simon smiled. "No, not really. But you give free refills and have Wi-Fi. And my kid likes it here too."

"Oh yeah, cute little guy in a cape? He's a favorite around here."

Simon felt his polite smile turn into something more genuine. "He is?"

"Oh yeah. Daphne—our waitress? Thinks he's adorable. And Mattie—the guy who stares at you sometimes because he thinks you're all hot and stuff? Well he thinks your kid is the cutest thing alive, swear to God."

Sputtering hot coffee, Simon quickly dabbed his chin with the cuff of his sleeve. "Excuse me?"

Instead of answering, the waiter grinned and took a glance around them before slinking into the booth, sitting opposite him. He leaned forward, his head low and voice quiet. "You are gay, right? I mean, you keep looking at him too."

Simon swallowed, feeling his cheeks flush alarmingly. "Uh, well...."

"Or have I got this totally wrong?" A look of horror flashed across the waiter's face. "Oh man, you won't tell the boss I've been hassling you, will you? Geez, I'm sorry. Look, I can get you a free bagel—"

"No, no, it's fine. I mean, uh...." He laughed uncomfortably. "I mean, I *am* gay, but...."

The waiter sat back, a totally relieved and somewhat satisfied smile spreading across his lips. "Oh, well... *great*! So you'll ask my boy Mattie out, right?"

"I don't think—" Simon paused and then leaned forward, curiosity for the moment winning over his usual realistic self. "Just to be clear, we're talking about the guy at the sandwich bar?"

"Yup."

"The one with the baby blues and dimples. The twenty-year-old?"

"Twenty-six, and yeah, that's the one."

"The ridiculously gorgeous guy with the perfect stubble and shy smile? That guy?"

"I just said—"

"And he's interested in *me*?" Simon couldn't help it; he laughed.

"Yeah, I don't get it either. No offense or anything."

Snorting in amusement, he shook his head and reached for his coffee. "I don't know what kind of joke the two of you are playing—"

"No, dude. Seriously, I'm not yanking your chain here. He thinks you're the shit. He doesn't know I'm talking to you, though, and he's too intimidated to do it himself, so don't let on I said anything."

Simon couldn't think of a single thing to say; the idea of it was so preposterous. He just huffed out a disbelieving, halfhearted laugh and looked at his Blackberry when it began to vibrate on the table next to his laptop. He picked the phone up, frowned, and set it back down without answering. The waiter gave him an odd look and then glanced to the back of the room.

"Look, just think about it, all right? Mattie's a great guy. He's artistic and laid back, a real cool guy. He's funny too. Sometimes even on purpose. And for some reason, he thinks you're the best thing since sliced bread, or something." The waiter picked up his coffeepot and walked away.

Somewhat stunned, Simon looked back at his computer screen, feeling utterly dumbfounded. Well, well, well. Gorgeous fantasy guy not so unattainable after all. A small smile spread across his face. It was impossible not to be flattered. Of course, he wouldn't be doing anything about it. The fact that his secret crush seemed to return his feelings didn't change anything. He couldn't have a relationship. Not with all the complications Jamie attracted, and not after what happened last time. Still, he was flabbergasted that the option was there. He frowned. Was the option there?

The waiter had seemed genuine, but perhaps something casual was what would be more appropriate—the *expected*, of a relationship with such a knockout younger man. There was nothing wrong with casual. Casual he could do. The small flashing red light on his phone caught his attention, and pressing the center key to light the screen up, he could see he had a voice mail.

A small groan escaped him. He wouldn't have answered that call even if it hadn't been in the middle of one of the oddest conversations he'd ever had. He didn't take calls from his mother anymore. Still, a small part of him that missed having a family outside of Jamie was curious as to what it was the witch wanted now. Biting his lip, he let out a quick breath and dialed his voice mail.

"Simon, it's your mother. I'm glad to see you haven't changed your number, though I—I... um... can you call me back? Please? I'd like to speak to you. I think all this nasty business between us is entirely unfair. I know what I did was terrible, but I'm his grandmother, and I was just doing what I thought was—"

Simon hung up and deleted the message. Three years, and she still couldn't say the two words that would begin the mending of fences between them. But then, as mule-headed as she was, he would probably be waiting a long time, and even then, he might not be able to forgive her.

He shook his head, his mood drastically heading downhill after his momentary high. That she had disapproved of his "lifestyle," or of who he was, was one thing. But to bring lawyers into the mix and attempt to take his son from him, on the basis that it was *wrong* to bring a child up in a same-sex partnership, just brought to the surface all the bad blood and tension accumulated between them after so many years.

It'd made him as sad as it had angry. There had been a time when they'd been close. He'd never known his father, so it had been just the three of them when growing up: Carol-Ann, Mother, and himself. They'd loved each other up to the sky and back, but then he'd come out to them, and while Carol-Ann had supported him and told him that she only loved him more for finally knowing who he really was, his mother was a different story altogether.

She was a conservative woman, and what started out as confusion on her behalf somehow morphed into a feeling of betrayal and anger. As much as he attempted to explain that he was not trying to hurt her, that he was the same person he had always been, the same person she had loved before she had known, it had all fallen on deaf ears. She just would not listen, and therefore could not understand that it had actually been she who had betrayed him by turning her back on him.

Having Jamie, he could not imagine, could not *conceive* of ever thinking him morally backward. Nothing, absolutely nothing, could make him not love his son. Especially something as insignificant as whom he was attracted to. Just as he could not change Jamie's autism, his mother could not change his sexuality. Whether it came down to nature or God, people are what they are, and it's never wrong. Nature is not wrong. Nature is the one certainty, the one truth that is visible to people, and he hung on to that.

And yet he missed her. But Jamie came first, and he would not risk her upsetting him. The main reason she had not been successful in dragging him to court was the simple fact it was very evident that he was number one in Jamie's life. Jamie needed him; his entire routine revolved around and relied upon his father. If he were to be out of the picture, the consequences for Jamie would be devastating.

No. It would be just him and Jamie, and no one would ever come between them, or ever give any form of authority any reason to even question to whom Jamie should be entrusted. He wondered again, like he had many times before, if Tim had resented him back then for just assuming that he would have his back and want to be a second father to Jamie. He shook his head minutely. There was no point in thinking about it, not when it didn't even matter anymore.

The vibration of his phone against the table top drew his attention, and he steeled himself to answer if it was his mother. They would have to speak sooner or later, and unless she had a genuine apology ready, it would be an extremely short conversation. A glance at the screen showed that it was not his mother, and he quickly answered. "Hello? This is Simon Castle speaking. Is everything all right? Is Jamie—my son—"

"Simon? It's Sarah."

Simon let out a breath. His heart always jumped into his throat when the number for Golden Acres flashed up on his cell. "Sarah, is everything all right?"

"He's okay, Simon. He's not hurt or anything, but I do think you may need to pick Jamie up early."

He was already closing his laptop down and fishing out his wallet to lay a few bills on the table. "What happened?" He heard her sigh, and stood straight when she explained. "Are you sure?"

"Yes, I saw it happen. I've called the other parents in and explained the situation."

"Oh God."

"Relax, their son is autistic too, Simon. They understand."

"I'm on my way now."

He quickly zipped his laptop into its carry case and slung the bag across his body. He grabbed his jacket and weaved his way quickly past the other patrons and out the diner doors, not even sparing a glance or noticing the concerned gaze of the handsome young man at the sandwich counter.

The elderly woman he'd come to know as Margaret, and who sat at the school's reception desk, had been happy to take him to Jamie's classroom. She was also kind enough to reassure him briefly, explaining why he'd been called in by his son's teacher. Apparently she'd seen her fair share of frantic and overprotective parents in the time she'd worked at Golden Acres.

"Sarah?" she said as she popped her head inside the classroom.

A young man came to the door, shushing his class and telling them to listen to one of the other support teachers as he pulled the door to. He offered Simon a smile and his hand to shake.

"Hello, Mr. Castle. Jamie's with Sarah in one of the quiet rooms. I'll take you to him now. Thank you, Margaret."

"Is the other boy all right?" He'd never been in this position before, but then Jamie had never struck another child before either.

"Tommy's okay. He went home a few minutes ago with his mother. He's not even upset anymore."

"Do you think you could give me Mrs....?"

"Mrs. Sadler."

"Can you give me Mrs. Sadler's telephone number? So I can call and apologize?"

"Unfortunately, I can't, it's against school policy. But—with your expressed permission—I can forward your details on to her and ask her to contact you instead?"

"That'd be wonderful, thank you. Sarah has my number."

"I'll get that from her as soon as you leave. She's just through here."

"Thank you... uh?"

"You can call me Adam." The support teacher smiled and offered his hand again.

Simon shook it, said his thanks, and headed through the door held open for him. With just one glance, he knew he would be in for a tough evening. Jamie sat on one of those small orange plastic child seats, and Sarah sat opposite him, her neck stretched forward as she dipped her head as if attempting to catch his son's gaze. She glanced up when she noticed his presence, and offered him a sad smile. Looking back at Jamie, she reached for his hand.

"Your dad's here—"

"I don't like that!" Jamie snatched his hand away from the teacher, pulling his cape tightly around him.

"Jamie, Miss Protrakis is being nice." Simon knelt beside his son's chair, knowing better than to just pick him up as he'd like to. He barely held in his sigh when he heard Jamie mumble his prime numbers. He looked at Sarah.

"It was break time, and he was playing with the blocks. Tommy wanted to play with him, but he wouldn't let him, so Tommy knocked over his tower," she explained. "Jamie smacked him."

Simon frowned and looked back at his unhappy son. "Jamie, that was very bad. Do you understand me? We never, *ever* hit."

"Tommy's fine, Simon. His mother picked him up a few minutes ago. She mentioned ice cream, and he forgot what he was upset about."

"I'm glad." He looked back at his son, attempting to gain his attention. "But you should never have hit Tommy in the first place, Jamie."

"He knocked them all over," he replied sullenly.

"That's not a reason to hit, Jamie. We never hit."

Jamie didn't answer, but his breaths came quickly, and Simon soon realized that his son was beginning to cry. He wanted desperately to comfort him, but this was a rule he truly needed to push home for Jamie. He could not have him hitting other children.

"Did you say sorry to Tommy?"

This time Jamie did look at his dad, and shook his head no. His mouth pulled down at the corners, and he looked absolutely miserable.

"Do you think we should?"

Jamie paused, thinking it through, and then nodded. "Sorry," he said quietly.

"It's isn't me you need to apologize to, is it?"

"You told me to be good, and I was bad," he said in a small voice.

Unable to stop himself, he reached his hands out for Jamie, and his son—thank God—willingly went to him and allowed Simon to pick him up. He gently shushed him and rubbed soothing circles into his back. "We all make mistakes, and it's all right, because that's how we learn, isn't it?"

Jamie nodded against his shoulder, and Simon caught a brief, approving smile from Sarah. "What are you going to do next time you see Tommy?" There was a loaded pause before Jamie answered.

"Let him play with the blocks?"

Simon smiled. "And?"

"And say sorry for smacking him."

"That's my good boy. Perhaps we can even go to the store on the way home and pick up some gummy bears. Don't you think it'd be nice to give Tommy some gummy bears tomorrow?"

Jamie nodded, and when Simon went to set him down, Jamie wouldn't allow it, refusing to let go. He was more than happy to comply, taking Jamie's backpack when Sarah handed it to him and shifting Jamie onto his hip.

"Thank you for calling."

"Of course."

"The other support teacher, Adam? He said that he'd get my number from you to pass onto Mr. and Mrs. Sadler. I'd like to apologize and reassure them that Jamie won't do anything like that again."

"I'll make sure to do that. I think they'll appreciate it. Though, honestly, Simon, she seemed to understand. All the parents here are in the same boat."

"I'd still like to call."

She nodded and then once again attempted to catch Jamie's gaze. "Tomorrow will be a much better day, Jamie." She spoke as they headed toward an exit. To his relief, Jamie lifted his head and looked at Sarah.

"I'll say sorry to Tommy."

"Good boy. And then later I'll be over to watch a movie with you while your dad is out."

Simon had almost completely forgotten. His editor, Andrew Camp—a man who was a complete and utter ass but was nonetheless very good at his job—had given him a ticket to some sort of art exhibition for tomorrow evening. Andrew had edited his previous two books, and despite a certain lack of affection on his behalf for the crude man, they had a solid professional relationship, and he couldn't imagine working with anyone else at this point. He had a suspicion that this was Andrew's way of trying to stir his writing muses, but hell, an evening out just sounded plain nice. Usually his instinct was to turn down any sort of social event. The only person he was happy to leave Jamie with was Sarah, and he didn't want to abuse their friendship and ask her to sit too often. But it had been so long since he'd gone out for an evening, whether it was by himself or with someone else. He was simply eager for a night off.

Tomorrow night, he'd be by himself, but his editor would be there with a few other authors, which would be interesting. He couldn't say that he knew much about art, but there would be free champagne and adult conversation. He'd been looking forward to it for some time.

"You're still okay to sit?" he asked, turning to face Sarah, who paused by the exit.

"Of course." She smiled. "Tomorrow we're going to watch *The Two Towers*, right?"

Jamie nodded, and Simon was glad to see his son wasn't looking quite so upset.

"There's a battle at Helm's Deep in the second one, with lots of orcs," Jamie piped up.

"There certainly is. Shall I bring some popcorn?"

"He doesn't like the kernels." Simon smiled, swaying Jamie gently. "But feel free to raid the cupboards for anything." He touched her arm briefly. "Thank you, Sarah. I really appreciate you sitting."

She waved him off. "Think nothing of it. Now I have to get back to my class. I'll see you tomorrow around seven."

He nodded and told Jamie to wave good-bye. He was happy when Jamie did, and decided that they'd go for a walk through the park before heading home.

SITTING on the bench with Jamie beside him, he found himself content to watch as his son threw pieces of bread for the ducks. They'd had another talk about why it was bad to hit people, and Jamie had promised him that the next time he felt angry, he would tell a teacher. They'd gone to the store to pick up a few vitals, including bread to feed the ducks and gummy bears to feed Tommy, which had made Jamie giggle. Now they sat together, his hand gently stroking Jamie's head. Jamie's feet swung happily as he chattered quietly to the ducks.

"That one's called Boromir," Jamie announced, pointing to what could be any one of five ducks.

"All right then," he laughed.

"And that one's Frodo."

"Is there a Samwise Gamgee?"

"That one!"

"I see. Do you like ducks?"

"Yes." Jamie nodded.

Simon worried his lip for a moment, debating something. "How about one weekend soon, we go to the zoo?" He laughed when Jamie's head snapped up to look right at him. It wasn't often Jamie would show such excitement.

"Will it have ducks?" he asked excitedly.

"Yes, there'll be ducks. And there'll be all other kinds of animals too."

Jamie hesitated. "Will there be orcs?"

"No, baby," he laughed.

"Good." Jamie nodded.

"There's just one condition. If we go, you're going to have to hold my hand the entire day. And it might get a little busy and noisy, but if that starts to make you unhappy, you just ask me to pick you up, okay? Can you do that for me?"

Jamie nodded eagerly, and Simon felt a little less guilty about leaving him tomorrow evening. He smoothed down that little cowlick and laughed when a piece of bread meant for the ducks made its way to Jamie's mouth instead. "Feeling hungry?"

"Yep," Jamie chirped.

He'd pushed him—albeit very gently—on the swings, and helped him on the monkey bars, and then they'd fed the ducks again. It had been a long day for Jamie, and they should think about heading back soon.

"Shall we head home?"

"Can we go to the place with the funny music?"

Simon frowned while he stood to gather the few bags they had. "You mean the diner?" Instantly his conversation with a rather nosy waiter and the image of baby blues and very kissable dimples returned.

"Yes." Jamie nodded as he struggled to put on his backpack.

Simon placed the two carrier bags on the bench to help Jamie thread his arms through. He untwisted the strap on Jamie's shoulder, picked up the two bags in one hand, and offered Jamie the other. "Okay then, the diner it is."

HE COULDN'T help but look to see if the cute guy—Mattie, apparently—was still there. Unfortunately, he seemed to have finished for the day. In his place stood a rather portly and sour-looking man with a dark complexion. Simon ignored his disappointment and walked over to the sandwich bar, where the less-than-friendly man stood, already glaring at them.

On the way there, Jamie had already said he wanted a sandwich instead of the usual mac 'n cheese. While this surprised Simon, it also pleased him that he was getting some different foods into Jamie's diet. The child was notoriously picky when it came to what he'd eat.

"Okay-dokey, up?"

Simon set the bags down and picked Jamie up to rest against his hip while they looked into the refrigerated glass case where the different sandwich fillers sat. "What do you fancy?" he asked, bouncing Jamie on his hip a little, and thought absently that he'd miss it dreadfully when Jamie would be too big for him to hold. Jamie leaned forward, pressing a hand on the glass.

"No touch the glass!"

The gentleman's gruff and accented command startled both Simon and Jamie. Simon looked at the guy, more than a little annoyed that he'd spoken so sharply to his son, and Jamie turned his face away, against his father's shoulder.

"Pick sandwich."

Simon could only blink at the completely ridiculous man. Whether this stranger did not possess an "indoor" voice, or was just naturally rude, he had no idea. He opened his mouth to tell him to keep it down—he could already hear Jamie begin to hum unhappily—but the dour-looking guy continued, picking up a sesame seed bun and slicing it in half.

"The boy like pickle? I make pickle sandwich for him."

Simon sputtered and rubbed Jamie's back soothingly. He was about to tell the guy to shove his pickle sandwich when movement at the "Employees Only" door caught his eye. He watched as the person he'd for a long time harbored a crush on strode over, dropped his backpack, and clapped a hand on the rude man's shoulder.

"How's it going, Jules?"

"I make pickle sandwich for the boy."

Mattie looked up and offered him an apologetic smile. Simon shifted Jamie on his hip nervously.

"Why don't you let me do this one before I head off? I'm sure someone needs their coffee topped up."

That's when Simon noticed the casual attire. He wore jeans with a rip in the knee that fit like a glove, a plain heather gray T-shirt that hugged his sides and upper arms perfectly, and a black string necklace tight around his throat with two beads in the middle. He must have been on his way out, and though he looked casual enough, he was downright drop-your-pants-on-command gorgeous.

"Sorry about Jules. I'm heading off early tonight so he's covering for me. We don't usually let him out of the kitchen."

Simon laughed and found himself smiling brightly. "Oh, that's...." He waved it off. "It's fine, honestly. Where's he from, anyway?"

"Really? We have no idea, but he makes a great omelet, so...." Mattie shrugged and gave Simon a crooked smile as he leaned both hands on the counter.

"Well, um, thanks. Don't think Jamie liked that fella too much. Did ya?" He pulled his head back to speak to his son. Jamie had stopped humming, something he tended to do before his prime numbers came out to play, but he wouldn't look at either of them.

"Sorry, he's kind of shy," Simon explained.

"Aw, that's okay, Jamie," Mattie said brightly, completely friendly, and then continued in a hushed, conspiring voice. "Sometimes Jules is kind of rude, but he's just a big teddy bear, really."

Simon knew no reply would be coming from his son and was about to apologize further, but Mattie interrupted him, taking the beginnings of a pickle sandwich and swiping it into a bin under the counter.

"I know what this little guy wants," he said as he pulled on some hygiene gloves and untwisted a bag to pull out two slices of white bread. "You want a peanut butter and jelly sandwich."

Simon looked in the glass case. "I don't see that in there."

"That's because we only keep it for our very favorite customers." Mattie winked and pulled the jars out of a small fridge behind him. "And don't worry; it's the smooth kind of peanut butter. I've seen the little guy eat in here enough times to know he doesn't like lumps in his food."

Simon blinked in surprise. He looked down and was pleased to see that Jamie—although he wouldn't speak or look Mattie in the eye— was watching his every move as he made his sandwich.

"And I'm guessing that you like it without crusts?" he asked as he carefully sliced off the crusts and then cut the sandwich into two perfect triangles and placed them on a plate.

"What do you say, Jamie?" Simon asked, flabbergasted.

"Thank you," came the quiet response.

"No problem, kiddo. Oh, no—" Mattie waved him off as Simon began to dig in his back pocket for his wallet. "It's on me."

"A-are you sure?" Simon stuttered in surprise.

"Yeah, don't worry about it."

He watched as Mattie tugged off the gloves and pulled his backpack up onto one shoulder, walking to the part of the counter that swiveled up for staff to walk through, and felt his cheeks heat slightly when Mattie took the plate and nodded toward the booths.

"Looks like you've got your hands full. Let me take this over for you."

Simon smiled his thanks, picked up their bags, and carried them, and Jamie, over to his usual booth, where Mr. Too-Good-To-Be-True set the plate down in front of his son.

"Thanks, that's real nice of you. Shame you're heading off, otherwise I'd ask you to take a seat and join us."

A somewhat surprised and pleased smile spread across Mattie's face, and he dug his hands deep into his pockets. Simon was utterly charmed.

"That'd be real nice, but, uh, I gotta take off. Maybe another time?"

"Yeah, sure. I'm Simon, by the way." He held his hand out and Mattie took it, shaking it once but holding on a second longer than was necessary.

"I'm Mattie, Mattie Green."

"It's really nice to meet you, Mattie."

"Yeah." Mattie practically beamed. "Yeah, you too. I'll um… I'll see you around, then." Mattie ducked his head but kept his distance from Jamie. "Bye, Jamie, enjoy the chow."

To Simon's utter surprise, though Jamie didn't look away from his plate, he said good-bye around a mouthful of peanut butter and jelly. He smiled at Mattie, thinking how unaware he must be of how very special an individual he was to even garner a response from his boy, and then watched him walk out of the diner with another quick wave over one shoulder.

"Nice man."

Simon's head snapped back to Jamie. "What was that?" he asked, pleased with his son's uninvited comment, but no response came, and he leaned back against the booth as he watched his son wolf down his specially made sandwich.

MATTIE damn near floated as he approached the apartment block, his brief conversation with who he now knew to be Simon and Jamie replaying in his head. Ty would be so damn smug when he told him about it tomorrow.

Stopping outside the building and looking at the familiar buzzer, he stored away the pleasant memory, shrugged into what he hoped was an impassive persona, and buzzed. A voice crackled over the speaker.

"Who is it?"

"It's Justin," Mattie replied. He never gave a john his real name.

No response came, but he was buzzed in. He took the stairs slowly, just wishing the evening was over with, and knocked on the door. The door opened, and one of his regulars stood there, moving aside to let him in without a greeting. The apartment was nice. Nicer than his place, anyway, but that wasn't saying much. The kitchen had black polished counters and every kind of appliance imaginable. The bathroom had a large bath with jets and a shower stall. The living room boasted the largest flat screen TV he'd ever seen, and a leather couch and chairs. He'd only ever seen all this in passing, however, and walked straight on into the one room he *was* familiar with. The bedroom.

He sat on the edge of the king-sized bed, dumping his backpack and leaning back on his hands as he waited. He could hear the guy tinkering about in the kitchen with something and sighed with boredom.

Come on, already.

He just wanted to blow the guy, get his ticket, and get out. He looked at the door when a shadow fell across the bed, and raised an eyebrow in question. The guy was six four, six five, maybe. He was heavyset, with dark hair that was receding, and had pockmarks on his cheeks. Not his type at all, but he certainly paid well. Fifty dollars for a hand job and sixty dollars for a blowjob. What he didn't like was his smarmy attitude, like he was used to being in charge. He thought he'd heard him on the phone once talking about a publisher or something, and figured he must be some sort of journalist. He'd snuck a glance at his mail once on the kitchen table, and at least knew his real name.

Andrew Camp already had his pants undone and was stroking his unimpressive erection as he walked over to where Mattie sat on the bed.

"Got something for you." He smirked.

Lucky me.

"Open those lips for daddy. I want you to hold still while I fuck that pretty face."

"Rubber," was Mattie's only reply.

Mattie watched dispassionately as Andrew rolled on the rubber, and spread his knees for the larger man to stand between them, his cock now in direct line with his mouth. He closed his eyes, but was ordered to open them and watch as Andrew held the base of his cock and then, none too gently, tapped it against Jamie's face.

"Dirty cocksucker."

Mattie's fingers gripped the bedspread tight, willing his mind to wander away as he felt the fat head of the short, stubby penis rub over his lips, the scent of latex assaulting him.

"Open up. Come on, take it."

Mattie opened his mouth and forced himself to look as if he was enjoying the feel of the asshole's cock roughly thrusting in and brushing the back of his throat, or at the very least, he attempted to appear as if he didn't hate it. He much preferred it when they'd just lie down with their head back and eyes closed to let him get on with it, but not this guy.

"Oh fuck, *yesss,*" he hissed, gripping the back of Mattie's head and slamming in forcefully two, three more times before spurting his load into the rubber.

Mattie pulled away as quickly as he was able, taking a deep breath and inching away when Andrew made to stroke his hand through his now messed up hair. Andrew took the hint. Oddly enough, once he'd blown his load, he was less of an asshole and almost polite.

"Money's on the kitchen counter. Help yourself to a drink before you leave if you like."

Mattie watched as Andrew stripped off and headed to the bathroom.

"W-wait, um...."

Andrew turned, raised an eyebrow. "What?" He smirked. "Finally gonna let me fuck you?"

Mattie shook his head. "You know I don't do that."

The taller man continued to strip off and rolled his eyes. "Yeah, I know. For a prostitute, you're not the most adventurous in the bedroom."

He squeezed his eyes shut a second. "The ticket? You said if I came over last thing I could have a ticket to the art exhibition tomorrow? I left work early so I could—"

"Yeah, yeah. It's on the table next to the cash. I wasn't going to rip you off, kid."

Mattie stood and picked up his backpack, muttering his thanks. He kept walking as Andrew called after him.

"If you see me talking to someone there tomorrow, probably best to act like you don't know me unless I approach you."

Mattie rolled his eyes, counted the cash, and stashed the ticket in his back pocket. "Like I'd acknowledge you for free," he muttered as he let himself out of the apartment.

It was done. He'd be able to buy himself two new canvases, and he'd scored a ticket to an exhibition. He headed down the stairs, taking two at a time.

He could feel it, the coil inside of him. It pulled tight, chafing and burning. He knew he could justify it to himself all he wanted, but the transaction was dirty, made him feel as if he weren't quite a part of the human race like everyone else.

He'd go home, do at least half an hour of his reading assignment, tune the radio into the jazz station he liked, and then paint for a few hours. Maybe then the coil would loosen its grip.

Chapter
Three

IT'D been a while since Simon had actually given any thought to his appearance. Usually he'd just throw on what he had clean and pressed, run a hand through his hair, and he was done. Tonight, however, he was hoping would involve some adult conversation, and so he'd paid a little extra care to his appearance. He wore a simple outfit, nothing ostentatious. Just his good shoes, some khaki pants, a crisp button-down and tie, and a sports jacket. He'd even gone as far as to get his hair trimmed, and had picked up his new glasses.

Not bad, Simon. Looking dapper.

He rolled his eyes. *Who says "dapper" anymore?*

Hearing a giggle coming from the kitchen, he gave himself a final glance in the mirror and followed the laughter into the room. Sarah stood leaning against the counter, smiling at Jamie as she stirred a bowl of pudding and listened to him chatter about something to do with class that day.

He took a moment to reflect that, in another life, this would have been one of those Hallmark moments you hear about so often or see on those greeting cards. In another life he would walk over to Sarah and dip his finger in the pudding. She would swat at him and call him mischievous, but then turn her cheek to him for a kiss. Another life where he was straight and Jamie wasn't autistic and everything was just easy.

Jamie looked over his shoulder. Smiled at him.

This life was just fine.

"Are you off?" said Sarah.

Simon patted his pockets, checking that he had his wallet and keys and ticket. He nodded and looked around the kitchen. Had he forgotten something? Surely there was something else that needed doing before he left for the evening.

"Everything's fine," Sarah mollified him.

He looked over Jamie's shoulder and saw him coloring with a worn-down crayon. He'd pick some more up from the store soon, he decided. He proudly noted that the coloring was all within the lines—a perfect picture of a sailboat. That would be one for the fridge, or perhaps another for his briefcase. "What's all the giggling about?"

"Jamie?" Sarah urged.

She never stopped working, he noticed. She was always subtly encouraging Jamie to offer the information himself. Simon looked down at Jamie and barely held in a chuckle at seeing the tip of the boy's tongue peek out of the corner of his mouth as he finished his boat. Jamie looked up and brushed the hair off his forehead with the back of his hand. Damn, it was getting too long again; he'd need to trim his hair again soon. He didn't like to cut Jamie's hair himself—he was no good at it, obviously—but the one time he *had* attempted to take Jamie to the barber had been terrifying for his son *and* the poor hairdresser. He brushed the hair off Jamie's brow, waiting for an answer.

"I gave Tommy the gummy bears. He had the red and yellow ones, and I had the green and blue ones." Barefoot and in his pajamas, he swung his feet happily. "He said we're friends now."

Sarah had let him know that all was well with the boys, but apparently she'd been waiting for Jamie to share this little nugget of information. A delighted smile split Simon's face. "That's great."

"They sat together at recess," Sarah said significantly.

"I asked him if he wanted one of my grapes, but he doesn't like grapes. He likes gummy bears, and so do I."

They may have their setbacks, but when the achievements came along, like Jamie making a friend, it was as eventful for Simon as if Jamie had just scored his first home run or passed his driving test.

"I'm very proud of you, Jamie." Oh damn, his voice was going to crack.

"Shouldn't you get going?" Sarah licked the pudding from her thumb. "We've got a movie to watch, don't we?"

"Yes!" Jamie nodded.

"Okay then, come give me a hug." Simon crouched, holding his arms out. He gathered Jamie to him, holding him gently and taking in the just-bathed scent of his son's skin. "Be a good boy for Miss Protrakis. I'll be home soon."

"Why don't you go fetch the DVD for me, Jamie?"

Jamie rushed out of the kitchen, cape flapping behind him.

"Thank you again, Sarah. I really do appreciate you sitting for me."

"It's fine, Simon, really."

"All the same, I owe you a bunch of flowers, or lunch or something."

"I like tulips."

"Excellent." He winked. "And that's wonderful, about Tommy." He couldn't help but smile proudly. "You know, I was terrified that he'd come home every day from school crying. I even considered homeschooling him, but I still hoped so *much* that he'd make some friends at Golden Acres." He nodded. "I know I made the right decision now."

Sarah patted his arm and walked with him to the front door. "Yes, you did." He offered her a smile, and thought again that it was a shame that such a sweet woman was unattached, and that he was not so inclined. He frowned, however, when he noticed her worrying her lip. "Everything all right?"

Her eyes darted up at him, caught. She laughed quietly, suddenly sheepish. He opened the door but paused on the threshold.

"I wanted to suggest something, but it might be overstepping my bounds."

"Sarah, there's no such thing." He laughed affectionately. "I trust you implicitly. Out with it."

"No, there is. I'm Jamie's teacher and your friend, but I'm not his parent. That's your role, and I don't want you to think for a second that I—"

"You're waffling, you silly woman."

She inched closer and lowered her voice. "I was just going to suggest something."

"All right...," he drew out. He should really get going.

"It's Jamie's birthday soon."

"Yep, not long now. I was going to take him to the zoo. He seemed quite excited about it."

Sarah's face lit up. "Oh, that's lovely, Simon, he'll really enjoy that. You know, one of the other kids brought a kitten in—well, his parents brought it in. It was show and tell..."

Show and tell. Yes, he remembered that. Jamie had taken his hardback, vintage, and fully illustrated copy of *The Hobbit*.

"...and Jamie loved it. Kept asking if he could hold it and pet it. Have you ever noticed how some autistic children have an affinity for animals? I think it's because their natures are so sim—"

"Sarah, you said you were going to suggest something?" He laughed.

"Right! Sorry. Well...." She shrugged. "I was going to suggest that perhaps a small birthday party would be nice." She smiled. "He could invite a few children from school—and their parents, obviously. I could be there to give you a hand if you like. I know how it can snowball if even one in a small group of children—particularly autistic children—becomes unhappy. But you know, a little cake, coloring, some harmless games, maybe a treasure hunt, that sort of thing. It'd be a wonderful way for him to interact with other children outside of the classroom."

Simon began to smile. He had to admit, he loved the idea of Jamie being the center of attention, but in a controlled environment so that he could enjoy it, rather than feel overwhelmed. He leaned against the doorjamb and waited for her to stop babbling.

"And I only mention it because of how well he and Tommy got on today. I mean, Simon, he looked so happy to be just sitting with another child." She touched her hand to her chest. "But of course, it's just an idea. He would absolutely adore the zoo. I'm sure of it."

"I think he'd like both." He smiled. "A party, just a small one. Jamie could make the invitations. He'd like that, and perhaps you could pass them on to the parents?"

"Of course I will." She all but clapped. "Would you like me to be there to lend a hand?"

"Sarah, I seriously doubt that Jamie would be as happy as he is if it wasn't for your help. You can talk yourself into the ground trying to define your role in his life, but whether you like it or not, you're family to us. You're important. So yes, please be there."

She blinked up at him, and he laughed softly as her face began to crumple, and she reached her arms up to give him a hug. She pulled back after a moment and patted his arm. "You should still take him to the zoo."

"Oh, I will, definitely, but another day."

"Well...." She discreetly wiped her cheek. "You should get going; you don't want to be—"

They were both silenced when Jamie impatiently called from the living room, ready to begin his adventure into Middle Earth.

"Yeah, I should be going. I won't be back late, or at least not late enough to turn into a pumpkin."

She smiled and crossed her fingers. "Fingers crossed that you meet Prince Charming."

Simon snorted. "You'll have to cross more than your fingers. I have my phone if you need me."

"We won't." She gave him a gentle push. "Have a good time."

"OH, HEY." Mattie flagged down one of the waiter guys walking by with a tray of wine or champagne or whatever. "Can I get one of those?" He offered the waiter a smile and took a glass, but felt his smile fall as the waiter none too discreetly looked him up and down with obvious condescension.

"Dick," Mattie muttered, digging one hand deeply into his pocket as he watched the asshole walk away. He was wearing a tie and sports jacket, wasn't he? Wasn't like he hadn't made an effort to look smart. Okay, so he'd borrowed them off of Tyler, but his shirt was tucked into his jeans, and he'd thought that maybe he could pass for smart casual, at least.

He strolled over to one of the paintings, away from the small groups of people talking about stuff he had no interest in and couldn't follow anyway. Shit, half of them weren't even looking at the work on the walls. They seemed to be there for the sake of it, all dressed up and looking down at him.

Fuck 'em.

He took a sip of his bubbly, decided he liked it, and took a few gulps and then discreetly wiped the corner of his mouth with the heel of his hand. He wished he had a friend here with him, someone who he could discuss what they were looking at without that uncomfortable feeling of not belonging. Just one friendly face would be nice, someone to share the evening with. He took a sip from his glass, glanced around the room, and nearly choked when spotting a certain someone across the way looking equally out of place.

Having not been able to get his brief but actual—not imaginary, he reassured himself—meeting with Simon out of his mind, he felt suddenly caught off guard with finding himself once again and unexpectedly within his vicinity. He had to smile at how awkward Simon looked. He had the look of someone who was eager to mingle, but had been out of practice for far too long. He was looking *fine*, too. Tugging at his shirt collar nervously and sipping at his wine, tilting his head marginally to one side with a frown as he studied one of the pieces on display. He was absolutely gorgeous, but utterly oblivious to it. And wasn't *that* just sexy as hell.

Go talk to him. Go talk to him. You know stuff about art; go impress the pants off of him.

He'd just about talked himself into going over to Simon, had a clever opening planned even, when Andrew Camp stepped up behind Simon. He watched unhappily as Andrew laid a slimy but familiar hand on Simon's shoulder.

Mattie swallowed as he watched Simon turn and offer Andrew a tight smile, and any clever words instantly fled him. He suddenly felt ill. Andrew Camp and Simon knew each other. His client and the uber adorable guy he fantasized about on a daily basis knew each other. The thought of Simon knowing, of him finding out and then looking at him the way others did, like Andrew did? Mattie shook his head and downed the rest of his drink. That simply *could* not happen. He quickly made his way through the crowd, away from Simon and Andrew and toward a thankfully deserted looking veranda. When the coast was clear, he'd make a quick exit. He could talk to Simon at the diner.

HE TILTED his head to one side, trying to hazard a guess at what the painting in front of him was supposed to depict. He knew next to nothing about art, but he'd hoped he might strike up a conversation with someone who did. A warm hand on his shoulder startled him slightly and made the wine in his glass slosh a bit, and he turned to see his editor standing beside him.

"Simon, decided to join the rest of the world after all, I see?"

"Yes, I suppose so." He tugged at his shirt collar, unused to wearing a tie.

"Well, it's about time you got yourself out and about. Next thing you know, you'll be blowing one of the waiters in the cloakroom." He laughed.

Jesus, always so crass.

"And you never know, a little romance may even inspire you to finish that book of yours."

Simon offered an uncomfortable smile, rubbing the back of his neck. "I don't—that is, I'm not really looking for... uh, I mean I'm not in a *position* to look for—"

"All right, all right, don't hurt yourself." Andrew snorted, clapping him roughly on the shoulder again. He bit his lip briefly, glanced at the writer, and then laughed softly. He drew Simon close by the shoulder. "You know, all jokes aside, a good roll in the hay doesn't have to involve dinner and dancing."

Simon's eyes widened slightly in alarm before he could stop himself. He'd thought they'd put this behind them, that he'd made it clear he had no romantic interest in his editor. Was that why Andrew had insisted he come, to have one more shot at the prude?

"You can take the look of horror off your face. I didn't mean me."

"Oh." He was flooded with relief, and quick on the heels of that was mortification. "I mean, it's not that you're not, ah...."

"Relax. We're like night and day, I get it. No, my awkward and strangely ineloquent writer friend, I was referring to something else. Some*one* else, actually."

"I don't understand."

"I know a twentysomething-year-old Adonis I could introduce you to."

Simon actually laughed. "Yes, because that's my usual type, Andrew. Have them lining up around the corner for me."

"I'm serious. He's here, actually, at the gallery." He shrugged. "He's into this sort of thing, apparently, and not to just rub shoulders with the right people like the rest of us, believe it or not."

"Wait, are you actually trying to pimp out your date? You want to introduce me to him with the intention of breaking my dry spell, my very *long* and painful dry spell?" Simon asked in utter confusion. This was without a doubt the oddest conversation he'd ever had with his editor.

"Oh, good God, he's not my date." Andrew laughed. "But don't get me wrong, he's a nice enough guy, and very easy on the eyes, but I'm not dating him. No, I couldn't get a guy like that the good old-fashioned way."

"Then what on earth makes you think that I could?"

"Do you have any cash on you?"

"Of course, why, do you need to borrow—" Simon automatically reached into his back pocket, but Andrew stilled his arm.

"If you have fifty dollars on you, then he's not out of your league."

Simon frowned, and then his eyes widened comically as understanding dawned on him. "Wait, he's, he's a...."

"Yes. And a very good one, if you don't mind boring." Andrew leaned close to continue their already quiet conversation in a near whisper. "Oral only, I'm afraid. And always with a raincoat. I know that should be reassuring, but he's not even into the occasional cream pie, if you follow me. Tried that once with him and he very nearly burst into tears, if you can believe it." He shivered. "Made me feel like a complete bastard."

Simon had to fight to not let his lip curl in disgust. Andrew actually thought he was so desperate as to pay for it? Just the thought of sharing that kind of intimacy, and then *paying*? It made him shiver. Apparently his feelings were written all over his face, because that hand on his shoulder was squeezing.

"Hey, don't look like that. Kid's hard up for cash and trying to make his way. Not everyone is as comfortable as us, you know."

His look of apparent disgust hadn't been so much for the guy Andrew had been describing, but more for his editor and the idea that someone would choose to do that. Shame tugged at his conscience, however; perhaps choice didn't come into it. All the same, he couldn't be further from aroused now if his mother was pirouetting naked in front of him.

Andrew sighed. "All right, perhaps it isn't for you. But at least keep an eye out for him and know that the option is there. You don't exactly have the easiest time of it, Simon." He shrugged. "And this could just be a way of taking the edge off for an hour without having to worry about rearranging your schedule or introducing someone new into your dreadfully complicated life."

Simon nodded, ignoring what he felt had been a hint of sarcasm aimed at his home life. He knew Andrew didn't understand the pressure or the privilege that came with raising Jamie. Nobody did, except perhaps Sarah, but there was not a chance in hell he'd be making any such transactions. It was too awkward. Too depressing. He hadn't even met the guy and already felt pity for him. What sort of life was that?

"His name's Justin. He's about five eight or so, mousy brown hair, has a real slim, fit body. Oh, and he's wearing an awful blue tie."

Simon looked down at his own blue tie. The description didn't exactly narrow the field down, but it didn't matter. He suddenly felt rather tired and decided that perhaps he'd cut the evening short, chalk it up to a disastrous attempt to integrate himself back into society, and make a run for it as soon as Andrew disappeared off to schmooze.

So much for a little adult conversation.

HE WAS relieved to find the veranda empty and that the weather was holding up. It'd looked like rain earlier, but instead of damp, it was a pleasantly cool and crisp evening. He found himself itching for a cigarette, something he had managed to wean himself off of six months ago, due to the rising cost of the little cancer sticks and the complaints of one of his regulars, who tipped well but hated the smell of smoke. Mattie glanced back through the double doors, considered sneaking back in there for another glass of bubbly, but decided against it and shoved his hands deep into his pockets. He hunched his shoulders against a cold breeze, straddled one of the benches, and looked out over the garden.

He wasn't sure if the gallery had been adapted from an old apartment complex, but it seemed likely when looking through the shaded trees. It was dark, but he could tell that this would have been a communal garden of some kind. Given the purpose of the building now, the garden must have been tended to by a landscaper or something. It was pretty. He could just about make out a swing seat under a small canopy across the way, and decided it was almost romantic.

He smiled to himself, imagining bringing a date—an actual non-transactional date—to a place like this. Man, did he even know *how* to date anymore? At twenty-six years old, he'd never really had an actual boyfriend. Sure, he'd dated a little, but that had pretty much stopped when he took to hooking to pay the bills his minimal salary didn't cover, like his adult reading and writing classes, for example. There was no way to make prostitution acceptable to someone who, quite rightly, expected his fidelity and exclusivity. The guy would have to be Prince Charming to even *try* and understand why he'd fallen into this life. To look past the sordid, preconceived notion of what prostitution was, and to see it for it for what it was: desperate, dangerous, and isolating.

Mattie doubted such a guy existed, but consoled himself with the promise he'd made to himself some time ago: when he had his GED, he would look for a better job and drop the hooking altogether. Then he could let himself look at other men romantically. He'd never, *ever* mention how it was he'd gotten by, and he'd meet some nice guy who wanted to do regular stuff. Like going to the movies and arguing over the Sunday morning crossword. Like spending the day in bed making love. He just had to hang on a little longer, and then he could have a normal life, just like everyone else. Maybe he'd even move, so no one would know him. Or he could just stay out in New York, if he ever got that far.

His thoughts were interrupted by the sound of the glass door swishing open, and he glanced over to see someone quickly closing it again behind them. He couldn't tell in the dim light that it was Simon until he'd turned around, looking relieved to have left the milling, chattering crowd behind him. Mattie's instincts were to quickly stand and hide.

It was stupid, but if he could have dived into one of the shrubberies without drawing attention to himself, he would have. He looked around quickly and made toward the tree line as casually as possible, but Simon's voice caused him to pause. He sighed and turned around, plastering on a smile that insinuated he was as surprised as Simon to see him again, and that he had not been running away at *all*.

"Mattie?" Simon said hesitantly, giving him what seemed a muted version of a smile that wanted to split across his handsome face. He couldn't help but feel a little flattered.

"Hey." He smiled politely. "It's Simon, right?" A voice inside his head laughed. In what life could he forget this man's name?

"Yeah, fancy running into each other outside the diner, huh?"

Mattie watched as Simon awkwardly walked toward him, shy smile in place, hand nervously tapping the side of his glass as if unsure if he were welcome.

Fuck my life. He is so adorable I could die.

"Small world." He shrugged. There was no sneaking away unseen now, might as well enjoy himself. "I got a spare ticket from a friend, so…." He trailed off, his hand twitching up nervously to check his tie was straight.

"Oh. So you're um… you here with someone?" Simon dug a hand into one of his pockets and tapped the side of his glass with a finger again as he casually looked away.

"No." He was quick to clarify. "Here alone, just an art buff, you know?"

"Great." Simon smiled, winced, and instantly backpedaled. "I mean the art thing, not that you're… I mean, I'm sure if you wanted company you could e-easily… uh…."

Mattie had to press his lips together to smother a delighted smile as Simon trailed off uncomfortably, rubbing the back of his neck. It was actually nice to realize that perhaps this man wasn't as straight as he'd originally thought, that maybe this crush was not so one-sided after all. He was about to say something to help Simon muddle out of the awkward moment, but the sound of the glass door swishing open gave them both pause. Someone unknown to him hunched their shoulders, there was a brief glow of an ember, and then they were leaning against the wall, clearly settling in for a smoke.

"Man, is the old monkey on my back screeching away right now," Mattie joked.

"You can light up if you want. It won't bother me."

"That's okay. I quit a while back."

Simon nodded. "Good for you."

Mattie smiled, and an awkward moment passed as they both stalled out but clearly wanted to keep company for a while longer.

"The uh… the garden's nice, huh? I think it may have been an apartment complex or something."

"Yeah, yeah. Nicer out here than in there, anyway." Simon smiled, feeling equally as awkward, and taking a sip of his drink.

"You're not into the show?"

"It's not that. I mean, I do appreciate art. I just don't know much about it, you know?"

Mattie grinned, finding himself pleased with Simon's comment but unsure why. "You don't have to understand what it is you're looking at to know it's beautiful."

Simon let out a breath of laughter. "Are you a romantic, Mattie?" he teased.

"I know art. I love art." He bit his lip. "It saves my life every day." At Simon's raised eyebrow, Mattie cleared his throat and shook his head, offering a self-deprecating roll of the eyes. "Sorry, that was a bit heavy for polite conversation."

"No. No, it's…." Simon shrugged, offering a gentle smile. "It's clearly important to you. That's nice." He looked back toward the glass doors on the veranda. "No one in there seems to actually be here for the artwork."

Mattie snorted. "Yeah, tell me about it, bunch of snobs."

Simon laughed. "Not your sort of crowd, huh?"

"Not really. Even the waiters here look at me like I'm something they stepped in. I'm here to see the work, but I thought perhaps... I don't know, maybe there'd be likeminded folk about, but...." He shrugged. "I don't really fit in here."

Simon's smile faded, sensing the genuine discomfort in his posture. He touched Mattie's arm briefly with the back of his hand that was holding his glass. "That makes two of us, then."

"Not your crowd either?" Mattie asked almost hopefully.

"Well, technically they are. The majority in there are publishers, editors, and other writers, but—"

Mattie's eyes widened. "Oh, man. I'm sorry, I never meant to insinuate or insult—"

Simon laughed, touched his arm again. "Relax. They *aren't* my kind of crowd." He shrugged, looked away a moment. "They used to be. Hey, a couple of years ago, I would have been in there schmoozing with best of them. But, uh, I was really just looking forward to a little conversation, you know? Just... appreciating some beautiful paintings, talking about regular stuff, that kind of thing."

They were quiet for a moment, and Mattie looked back to the doors, hearing laughter and more people congregating on the patio-like porch. "Hey, you want to, uh...." He scratched the side of his cheek. "You want to walk a little? There's this swing thing over there...." He trailed off with a shrug.

Simon smiled. "Lead the way."

They walked toward the canopied swing seat, and Simon chuckled softly as Mattie held it still enough for Simon to sit, before joining him. It was a cool evening. The buzz of chatter and laughter was quieter now, quiet and distant enough for them to hear the cicadas, the rustle of the leaves above them, the faint squeak of the swing seat. It was a pleasant silence, and Mattie imagined moving his hand across the short space between them, taking Simon's.

"So you're a writer," he asked instead.

"Yes," Simon sighed. "Though the words aren't coming as easily to me as they used to, I have to confess."

"No?"

"I have two novels published. I'm just struggling with the third."

"Why's that?"

"I'm a father now."

Mattie looked at him, nodded, but was unsure of how to respond.

Simon glanced at Mattie, hazarding whether to share such personal details with the young man. Hell, Mattie seemed to be the sharing type. "It's… my son takes up a lot of my time. And even when he's in preschool, I'm thinking about him—worrying about him."

Mattie glanced at his lap, bit his lip, and then met Simon's gaze. It was such a sensitive question. "Jamie. He's uh… forgive me for not knowing the PC term, but um… there's something different about him, something special, isn't there?"

Simon took a deep breath and let it out as he looked around the garden. How Mattie would take his response would decide whether they would continue to share this private swing, or if it was time to say goodnight. "Jamie's autistic."

Mattie didn't bat an eyelid, just nodded. "I feel like the appropriate thing to say would be that I'm sorry to hear that, but…." He frowned. "Your kid…." He shrugged. "He's a happy little guy. He seems bright too."

Simon smiled. "He is. He's always got a smile for me. And he's a high-functioning autistic." He shook his head. "We're so lucky in that respect. I mean, don't get me wrong, I would have loved him no matter what, but other autistic kids… worst case scenario? They never learn to speak and would be completely dependent on a caregiver for their entire lives. Jamie, he's ah…." He shook his head, and missed the gentle smile that spread across Mattie's face in response to the look of pride that showed on his own. "Jamie's incredible. He only began to speak a year ago, and he's very quiet by nature, but he can read and write. He's very gentle—most of the time." Simon frowned slightly, thinking back to the incident with Tommy. "Regardless of everything else in my life, he is the very best thing that ever happened to me."

"That's so great," Mattie said softly, the respect he felt gleaming in his eyes. "Is he with his mom right now?" He still had no clue as to the situation with this guy, but just had that feeling that they had one *particular* thing in common.

Simon had to smile. It was big question, with a very revealing answer. But, hell, he already knew he had nothing to worry about. The nosy waiter at the diner had seen to that. "There is no mother. I'm...." He took a deep breath. "I'm actually Jamie's uncle. My sister passed away during childbirth." He shook his head minutely. "You just don't expect that kind of thing to happen anymore, not in this day and age, anyway."

"I guess not, no."

Simon took a deep breath and let it out quickly. "Anyway, I adopted him as my son. And...." He wet his bottom lip briefly. "And I'm gay. There isn't a woman in the picture, unless you count Jamie's teacher, who happens to be a close friend and who's sitting for him right now."

While Mattie was pleased by this clarification, he knew to show this would have been inappropriate. "Were you close to your sister?"

"Oh, man," Simon sighed, his shoulders slumping. "Yes. Yes, I was."

Mattie dipped his head to catch Simon's gaze and touched his knee briefly to get his attention. "I'm very sorry."

Simon held his gaze and was touched by the sincerity he saw there. He nodded. The hand left his knee, and he took a breath, offering Mattie a smile. "So. You and art, huh?"

Mattie smiled, rubbing his hands on his knees. "I dabble." He shrugged in mock modesty, making Simon laugh. "Yeah, I paint. In fact I pretty much divide my time between the diner and painting."

"Are you any good?"

Mattie laughed, shrugged. "Maybe. Could be better. I, uh, I actually want to enroll in art school."

"Yeah?" Simon smiled. "Which one?"

Mattie bit his lip, his hands curled over the edge of the seat as he took in the open, friendly, and interested man sitting beside him. *Why not?* He didn't answer, and decided on a rather brave question of his own. "Simon? Would you… uh…." He broke off, laughing nervously, and rubbed the back of his neck. "Would you like to—maybe when, you know, when you're free—can—can I take you out? Sometime, maybe?"

The beginning of a smile curled at the edge of Simon's mouth, but before he could answer, like some kind of inevitable soap opera, he was interrupted.

"Simon?" They both looked up to see someone out on the veranda, searching the garden, spotting them, and then making their way over. Mattie's stomach turned over, realizing who it was.

"I've been looking for you. I want you to come meet—oh." Andrew stopped short, a slow smile, almost a smirk, appearing. "I'm sorry to interrupt."

Mattie hastily stood, his voice breathless and wavering when he spoke. "Actually, I have to be going."

"Oh, please, no, don't let me interfere." He held his hands out to stop him from leaving, and Mattie backed up. "Simon, I wanted you to meet with someone, but it can wait for another time." He glanced between the two of them. "I'm glad you took my advice."

Simon frowned. "I don't follow."

"Here." He dug in his back pocket and threw his keys at Simon. "Call your sitter and tell her you'll be late getting back. You can use my place."

"What the hell are you talking about?" Simon frowned. He'd been having a nice conversation and was pissed to have it interrupted.

"Don't worry." Andrew nodded over to Mattie. "Justin knows the way."

"Oh God." Mattie closed his eyes, digging his hands deep into his pockets, unable to look at Simon.

"Just—" Simon's eyes widened. "Justin?" He looked at Mattie, stood, and saw how Mattie—or Justin—cringed away. "I don't understand."

"Glad to see you've climbed off your high horse, Mr. Self-righteous." Andrew smirked.

"Wait, you're Justin?" Simon asked firmly, feeling like a fool.

Mattie felt his face grow warm, and was alarmed when his eyes began to sting. "I um… No. No, my name's Mattie."

Andrew frowned, but said nothing, looking between the two. "Does it matter?"

"Yes!" Simon raised his voice before quickly looking away and clearing his throat. "Of course you're a prostitute. Of course." He laughed with little humor. "As if you'd ever… ugh." He broke off, shaking his head.

Mattie flinched at hearing the word "prostitute" come out of Simon's mouth, but the look of disgust on his face was more than he could deal with. "I have to go," he whispered, pushing past the both of them, back toward the veranda, through the crowd, and started out at a jog when meeting the sidewalk outside the gallery. He didn't slow until he was two blocks away. He ran his fingers through his hair, pulling tight.

"Fuck. *Fuck.*" His voice hitched. He dug his hands deep into his pockets once more as he made his way back to his apartment. It was a long walk, but flagging down a cab, having to use his voice to give his address, to talk to anyone at that moment would be impossible. He was a prostitute. He was a fucking prostitute and the coil was choking him.

SIMON had shrugged off Andrew's concerns, thrusting his keys back into his hand, and gone on after Mattie. He couldn't decide if he was more shocked at the revelation, angry with Mattie, or angry with himself. All he had wanted was to have a nice evening out. That nice evening had quickly developed into a lovely evening in the company of the handsome young guy from the diner. He'd been enjoying their conversation, had felt his heart leap in a way it hadn't since Tim when Mattie had tried asking him out. But then reality—horrible, disappointing reality—had come rushing in.

Simon couldn't see Mattie anywhere, and with slumped shoulders and a resigned sigh, he flagged down a cab and headed home. He leaned his head against the window, staring out at the sidewalk rushing by as he tried to figure out what it was that had passed between Mattie and himself. Having never engaged in such activities, he couldn't gauge whether Mattie had genuinely tried to make a date with him, or was setting up some sort of transaction.

The part of him considering only his interaction with Mattie, before Andrew's interference, claimed that a good looking, funny, interesting guy had sincerely been interested in him. The part of him that had been too damaged by his last relationship to be optimistic told him to let it go, to go home and write and put his son to bed and forget the entire ridiculous encounter. To learn, and to know better the next time a handsome young man showed interest in him. The kind of meetings and romances he so often read about were popular for a reason, and that was because they did not exist in real life.

Paying the driver, he headed on in and met Sarah in the living room. She looked up from her book.

"Hey." She looked over at the clock on the mantel. "You're home early, aren't you?"

He shucked his jacket off. "It wasn't really all that great. Just a lot of schmoozing and a lot of phony people." He shrugged. "At least there were free drinks."

"Shame." She folded the page of her book and stood, stretching. "Here's hoping Prince Charming will be at the next shindig."

"Jamie asleep?"

"He's as snug as a bug."

"Any trouble?"

"No, we had a grand time. We watched the movie, and he convinced me to watch the DVD extras, but his eyes started to droop five minutes in, so…." She smiled, shrugging.

"Well, thank you for sitting, and as always, you're a star." He pulled his wallet from his back pocket and handed over a couple of bills.

"Thank you, Si." She folded the money and headed into the hall. She slipped on her pumps and pulled her jacket from the coat rack. "Let me know when you need me to sit again."

Simon shook his head and hugged her briefly. "I do feel like I take advantage of you."

"Simon," she groaned quietly. "We went through this. I adore Jamie. And...." She trailed off, zipping herself up. "Well, times are rough, you know?" She patted the side of her handbag where she'd put her purse and money. "Teaching doesn't pay much, and being single with a car that's on its way to the scrap heap and all... every penny helps. All right?"

"You know that if you ever have problems with money you can come to me, right?" He rubbed her arm. "I meant it when I said you're family."

She smiled at him. "I'll be just fine, but thank you for the peace of mind. I'll see you tomorrow."

He kissed her cheek, and waited at the door until she had driven away in her car, that did in fact have an exhaust that sounded like a tank, and then closed the door.

He toed off his shoes and pulled his tie loose and then over his head. He looked into Jamie's room briefly before going on into his own to change into his sweats. Changed and more or less ready for bed, he headed back into Jamie's room.

Jamie lay curled up on his side, fast asleep and with his thumb in his mouth. Simon smiled tenderly, extracted the thumb, and sat on the side of the bed gently so as to not wake him. He leaned against the headboard and sighed happily as Jamie turned in his sleep and instinctually curled up against his dad. With Jamie's head resting against the side of his stomach, he stroked that little cowlick and wrapped his arm around him. Jamie's cape was askew between them, but he'd put it right before he went to bed.

He sighed and leaned his head back against the wall. There was no hiding from it. He felt terrible. He felt terrible that he had to rely upon Sarah so often because he trusted so few people with his son. He felt terrible because, deep down, he knew his third novel wasn't working. He felt terrible that he hadn't had a relaxed, normal evening. And he felt terrible because he could not shift the look of mortification and shame on Mattie's face from his mind.

That look alone was enough to tell him that what Andrew had said was true, that it was something Mattie was not proud of, and that it must surely be out of necessity. What had Sarah said? Times are rough. Hadn't Andrew said something similar? Simon knew he was fortunate. Privileged, even. His first two novels had done exceedingly well and were still on the shelves. He didn't need to worry about the cost of replacing an exhaust, or money for Jamie to go to school. He owned his home. He was comfortable and had the means to take care of himself and his son.

Perhaps he needed to pull his head out of his ass. He did something he loved for a living. He spent half the day writing, and the other half with a son he loved more than life itself. He knew next to nothing about Mattie's life, or the man himself, other than he had been kind to his boy, had attempted to ask him out in an alarmingly bashful but endearing way, and that he made sandwiches and wanted to go to art school. That was it.

He didn't know the circumstances, and couldn't rest knowing that he had made this perfectly nice guy feel miserable. Perhaps it was all in his mind and Mattie had already shrugged it off, but tomorrow he would have to speak to him, and if need be, apologize. It would go no further than that. Mattie was too young, anyway, and he certainly had enough complications in his life already.

Chapter
Four

THIS was ridiculous. He'd been loitering across the street from the diner for an hour almost, afraid to go in. Or perhaps not afraid per se, but attempting to put off what would be a very awkward and uncomfortable conversation in Mattie's place of work. Simon didn't want to make him feel any worse, he truly didn't, but a selfish part of him knew that he liked the diner. He could write there, and it was close to Jamie's school. His hopes were to, at the very least, reassure Mattie that he wouldn't pass on what he knew already and that he thought no less of him. (Even if part of him sincerely recoiled at the thought of Mattie being treated harshly or unkindly, despite their limited introduction to one another.)

After Sarah's reassuring him about her sitting for Jamie, he felt less guilty in asking her to sit for him again so soon. She would keep him with her while she packed up for the day, and would then take him home for his supper. (He had long ago trusted her with a spare key to his home.) He'd made sure to repeat this break from Jamie's usual routine a number of times, so as not to cause him upset when home time came around and he wasn't there to pick him up. He had a feeling that Sarah knew that this "last minute meeting with his editor" was a cover for something else, but oddly enough, he had sensed her approval, and he now had the afternoon free. Whether it was to hopefully buy Mattie a coffee after his shift to apologize, or to find himself another place to write and give himself time to lift his morose mood, he was, as always, infinitely grateful to her.

But first, he needed to go in there, offer him a friendly, approachable smile, and wait until he perhaps took a break to ask for a private word. As it was, he was sitting at the bus stop across the street with his laptop case in his lap, looking over at the glass front of the diner, attempting to grow a pair.

Was he being selfish? To approach him at his workplace may be flat-out unkind, but in a way it felt as if it were his workplace too. He knew the thought was unfair, because he could technically write anywhere, but only other writers knew that when you found the right spot—that comfortable, tucked away spot where you could allow your mind to let go of its surroundings and engross itself in the story—it was an important thing and not to be taken for granted.

And I want to see him, still.

Simon groaned as another bus came to a deflating stop with a *"whoosh"* beside the curb, its doors opening and the driver looking his way. Simon gave an apologetic shake of his head, and the driver pulled what he assumed was a lever, closed the doors, and pulled away.

Simon watched the bus pull away, and then glanced back to the diner to see Mattie leaving. He stood abruptly, nearly dropping his laptop case in the process, and stayed there stupidly, his heart in his throat, watching as Mattie zipped his jacket and hunched his shoulders with his hands in his pockets, as if a strong wind was pushing against him.

He was nearly out of view when Simon finally came out of his stupor, hastily hooked his satchel with laptop inside over his head, and quickly glanced both ways before crossing the street at a jog.

"Mattie!" he called, somewhat breathlessly. (He blamed his inactive career for his less than Olympian health.)

Mattie looked back over his shoulder and visibly flinched. He stood rooted to the spot, as if caught, and looked around, contemplating a quick getaway. He looked back at Simon, his shoulders slumping in resignation. Simon came to a stop, still clutching his bag to his side, where it had been clapping against his hip, huffing and fighting the instinct to bend at the waist with his hands on his knees to catch his breath.

"Mattie," he said needlessly, wanting to take away the look of caution and utter discomfort from his unhappy face. "You're leaving work early today?"

"You're not going *in* to the diner today?" Mattie replied, ever so quietly, a look of hurt ill-concealed.

"I've been sitting across the street like a coward, trying to think of something to say. And I didn't want to make it difficult for you to work."

Mattie nodded, looking to the ground with a sniff. Meeting Mattie's gaze once again, the writer was relieved to see that the sniff hadn't been caused by tears. He stood closer, one shoulder lifting unconsciously in apology. "Mattie," he said quietly, "I barely know you, but I know I've upset you, and I'm sorry."

Those gorgeous hazel eyes that looked so sad regarded him, and Simon felt such a compulsion to protect, to take away the upset he saw there. "Can I please buy you a coffee? Can we talk?"

Mattie's brows drew up sadly, and he looked away to the side before quickly shaking his head. "You said sorry, Simon, that's enough. You don't gotta spend time with me or avoid the diner. It's fine."

He's a sweet guy. There can't be a bad bone in his body, despite how he may make his money. "Then will you let me buy you a coffee just because I want to?"

Mattie's gaze was wary, not leaving his even when someone shouldered past, knocking into him. "I don't want pity, Simon, or your disapproval. Even if I deserve both."

"Just coffee, coffee and talking. I liked talking to you last night," he pointed out.

That got him a hesitant smile, and Simon felt himself smiling back. "That a yes? Café Latte on me?"

Mattie bit his lip, hesitant, but then nodded. "Yeah, I guess so."

"Great."

THEY'D found a secluded booth in the back of a Starbucks, and Mattie unfolded and folded his hands restlessly on top of the table, watching as Simon walked over slowly with a tray. He'd wanted to sink into the ground when he heard Simon call his name on the street, but was glad that it appeared Simon was kind enough to approach him after the incident at the gallery.

He'd told his boss he was sick and left work early. As time'd ticked by with no appearance from Simon, he'd steadily begun to hate himself more by the minute. But this, *this* was promising. Perhaps it wouldn't have to be awkward at work, and he could go back to just looking.

"Here we go." Simon set the tray down and placed a small saucer in front of Mattie. "I got you a lemon square."

He smiled sadly. Despite the encounter at the gallery, Simon seemed to be a stand-up guy. "Thanks, you didn't have to."

"And a Cinnamon Dolce Latte." He placed the mug next to the saucer. "It looked so good I got myself one too."

He broke a corner off the lemon square and watched Simon take a sip of his drink, mumbling something about it being good before an uncomfortable silence settled over them. Mattie ran his hand over his hair and sighed.

"This is so awkward."

"It is a little, yes," Simon agreed.

"I'm guessing that... I mean, you're either a really decent fella or you're not all... you know, disgusted by me."

Simon shook his head. "No, no, I'm sorry, I must apologize for my uh... my rather *harsh* reaction last night."

Mattie snorted. "That wasn't harsh, believe me. Don't get me wrong. It was humiliating and kind of crushing, but it wasn't harsh." He took a sip of his drink. It was cinnamon-y.

Simon's voice was strangled. "I don't want to make you feel that way. *Christ*," he sighed. "I don't even know you. I've got no right passing judgment on you."

"That's true," he said quietly, "but... I don't know. I wish I could have kept that from you. It was nice getting to know you."

"It's not like we can't ever talk again."

Mattie watched him, swallowed. "You forget that I asked you out? All right, not very *smoothly*, but...." He trailed off with a shrug.

"No, I remember." He cleared his throat uncomfortably. "I guess I, ah, I guess I don't really know what you... what—"

Mattie's eyes widened, and he turned his head away with a grimace. "You thought I was trying to make a deal?"

Simon said nothing in response, and Mattie let out a small, sad laugh. "I think you're handsome, okay?" He kept his eyes on the drink. "I think you're good-looking and a nice guy. I didn't want your money. I wanted to date you."

"Oh. Oh, that's...." Simon looked down at his drink, frowning.

Mattie winced and pushed the plate away, starting to stand. "Chalk it up to a simple mistake, but I'm heading off now. You're a nice guy, but I don't need to put myself through this." He paused when Simon grasped his wrist.

"Please don't. Please?"

Mattie sighed and slowly sat back down. He held no animosity toward him. Hell, Simon was being a gentleman right now, but he didn't want any more apologies. He wanted to pretend that the entire exchange last night never happened; he wanted to go home and paint.

"I'm so—"

"*Don't*," Mattie bit out and closed his eyes to calm himself. "You don't gotta do that. Don't apologize, and please don't feel bad for me.

Just—just treat me normal-like, okay? I know you're not going to want to date me, but you can look at me like a normal person, can't you? I'm no different. No different at all. I just have financial problems. I'm a little stuck, and I have to dig myself out sometimes, but I'm not what you're picturing. I don't do drugs, I don't... I don't hang out in any gangs, I just... I struggle, that's all."

"Well," Simon said quietly, "that's one thing I certainly can understand."

"Struggling?"

"Yes, but not in the same way, I think. I have financial security, but, well... the rest of my life is very complicated. I'm bound to it, to my son. I love him to death. I would never give him up, but that freedom I used to have is gone. My life revolves around his routine. Whereas you... you're young, you could do anything, but money— well, it can cripple a person, can't it?"

"That it can." Mattie leaned closer over the table. "I want you to understand that I don't... I don't *enjoy* it. It means nothing." He shook his head. "This is hard to talk about. I don't even know you, but I feel like I've dared to try and do something normal, like ask you out, and now I almost... *owe* you the details."

Simon shook his head. "You owe me nothing. But if you want to talk to me about it...." He sat back, wiped his hand over his mouth and chin. "Well, we're here, talking. You're not working, and I've got the time." He smiled. "And for some reason, it is inexplicably easy to talk to you."

Mattie leaned back, and they eyed each other. It felt neither unfriendly nor cautious, merely curious. "Do you want to know?"

"Know why you do it? I think so, though you've kind of alluded to that already. But we can just as easily sit here and talk about the weather if you want. It doesn't have to be about that."

Mattie watched him, took a deep breath, and leaned forward to rest his elbows on the table. "There's never a good reason to get into it—hooking. I just need the extra money."

"Your job?"

"Minimum wage. I make sandwiches, for crying out loud."

"Family, friends?"

Mattie shook his head. "Family is a no-go. Friends...." He tilted his head and wet his lips. "There's a few, and sometimes I can accept a little help when I can't stand the alternative, but I don't want to be a burden. Friends—good ones—are important, and I want to keep them, not sponge off of them."

"Why the diner? Why not an office or somewhere that pays a little better?"

"I... ugh, I'm not really qualified."

"You're inexperienced? Everyone has to start somewhere."

"No." Mattie controlled the urge to whimper and looked away. "God, as if you don't have a low enough opinion of me already."

"Mattie...," Simon encouraged softly.

"I kind of...." He shook his head. "Okay, here's the thing. My mom took off early, my dad took to the bottle, and my teachers never really noticed that I never quite learned how to read." He sat back, trying to gauge Simon's expression, which appeared, ironically, to be unreadable. "I just fell on through the cracks, dropped out of school, and here I am."

"That seems so unfair."

"That's how the cookie crumbles, I guess."

"So... manual labor is pretty much...?"

"All I'm qualified for? Yes. Although...." He shrugged, self-conscious. "I'm, uh, I'm putting myself through this adult reading and writing course at the central library, over at 820 E Street?"

Simon had been leaning forward, his chin resting in his hand, but at that revelation his brows rose and his arm splayed down across the table with a thunk. "Mattie, that is entirely admirable."

Mattie bit his lip, raised his eyebrow. "How do you think I pay for that course?"

Simon's expression froze, and he leaned back against the booth with a quiet "Oh."

"Still think I'm admirable, mister writer?"

Simon frowned. "Yes, as a matter of fact, I do admire a person who's trying turn their life around for the better."

"Well… as long as you know it's not a career choice—hooking, that is."

Simon contemplated his next words, as if anxious they might cause upset. "Andrew, he… he said some things."

Mattie immediately pulled himself up straight, something in his eyes shuttering closed. "And what was that?"

"I'm sorry. We don't have to talk about it."

"I want to know what he said."

"He said… he said you'd only do… certain things?"

Mattie cleared his throat, glancing away and clenching his jaw. "And you want to know this why, exactly?"

Simon blanched. "I didn't—no, forget it, I should never of—"

"Oral only. I *cannot* let someone fuck me, and I can't fuck any of them. That sort of thing has to stay intimate, you know? Just the thought turns my stomach. Don't kiss 'em either. I figure I have to keep those things away from johns if I ever want them to feel good in a real relationship. And yes, I am always, *always* careful."

Simon nodded, looking down at his mug and turning it slowly. Mattie's brows drew together sadly, and he fought the urge to reach forward and touch the writer's hand.

"Simon, it's… how do I explain?" He huffed in frustration. "It's casual. I can get by on casual. It's important that it be just… *un*important. I can't let that sort of thing mean anything to me. I mean, of course I crave something more… you know, *real*. But I have to keep it easy. I have to keep it casual. Do you—*can* you understand that?"

SIMON was surprised by the outpouring of emotion and the sharing of such infinitely personal feelings, the pity he'd felt for Mattie slowly being replaced by grudging respect. He still didn't like it. He didn't like that anyone would have to resort to that way of life to get by. It seemed infuriatingly unfair. But he couldn't in all truth say that he never wanted to speak to Mattie again. There was a great deal of strength in the man sitting opposite him. It was merely smothered in some sort of guilt or self-hatred. It didn't seem right.

"I think I understand. In fact, yes, the casual thing? Yeah, I get that."

Mattie smiled. "Yeah?"

Simon smiled, rolled his eyes, and leaned forward with his hands clasped together on the table. "I find myself in a similar predicament. *Not—*"

Mattie let out a gentle laugh. "I know you don't hook. Mister good-looking, sophisticated writer guy."

Simon felt his cheeks flush slightly, but he shook his head and continued. "Seeing as we're sharing and all… I, uh, I had a relationship. The permanent kind with a guy I was head over heels for, but then Carol-Ann—that's my sister—she passed, and I was suddenly a father. He couldn't take it. He stayed long enough to become important to Jamie and then cracked under the pressure." He pressed his lips together in a thin line. "That's the kind of thing that makes 'casual' seem like a lifesaver, doesn't it? For us it's different reasons, but…."

"You understand," Mattie said quietly, his voice sounding almost relieved. "You actually get it."

Simon lifted one shoulder slowly, an "I don't know" gesture. "I will never risk my son being upset like that again, so if I do ever decide to date again…." He trailed off with a sigh. "Any future relationship for me would have to be totally on my terms, which sounds wholly unrealistic and unfair. What's the male equivalent of spinsterhood?"

Mattie laughed softly and shrugged.

"Well, that's what I've got coming, I think." Simon laughed.

"I don't think that's true."

"That's kind of you to say. Naive, but kind."

"No way, man. I hope it's okay for me to say this, but the guy that let you go? The guy that let your *kid* go? Out of his mind. Out of his ever-loving *mind* to let something like that slip through his fingers."

Simon smiled. Fuck it. It was good to talk to Mattie. Whether it was just friendship or kinship manifested from understanding of their individual struggles, he liked him. He was a *good* guy, and it felt good being in his company. He noticed Mattie checking his watch and felt disappointed that he probably had somewhere else to be. On the heels of that thought was a question of where it was he had to be.

"I suppose you have to pick up Jamie soon, huh?"

Simon blinked in surprise, pleased that Mattie didn't appear to making an excuse to leave and touched that his thoughts and concerns had been for his schedule and son. "Actually, I have someone taking care of him this afternoon."

"Oh? You... you want to go for a stroll or something, then? Seeing as our drinks have gone cold, and all."

Simon let out an amused huff, looking down at his Cinnamon Dolce Latte that was practically untouched and had gone stone-cold some time ago. "That sounds good."

"I'VE never seen him upset. He's always seemed perfectly content at the diner." Mattie sidestepped an empty McDonald's bag that had been left on the park pathway. They were walking aimlessly, just following the concrete path through the trees, passing the now-deserted swing sets and monkey bars as the sun went down.

"That's because he's used to the diner. It's unfamiliar situations that upset him."

"That must be tough."

Simon nodded. "It can be. When he started preschool, I actually took him there a half dozen times before his first day, just for a half hour at a time, so he could get used to the people there, the sounds, the activity."

"Sounds?"

"Sounds, colors." He nodded. "Anything too loud or bright can make him anxious. It *hurts* him, panics him."

"How'd his first day go?"

Simon smiled. "I struck gold with Golden Acres—no pun intended. I enrolled him early on, and he took to his teacher right away, even after the first visit. Her name's Sarah. She's with him right now, actually. He even lets her hold his hand sometimes."

"But no one else?"

"No. Though…." He rubbed the back of his neck. "I don't know if that's my fault. I'm… I'm reluctant to let anyone near him, really. I don't want him upset. It breaks my heart when he's upset. But maybe that does more damage than good."

"That's understandable, though. He's your boy."

"It's not an excuse, though." He laughed quietly. "Thank God for Sarah. She is amazing when it comes to kids with special needs. I mean *amazing*. She has the patience and compassion of a saint."

Mattie smiled. "She sounds like a cool chick."

Simon laughed. "She's a gift from heaven. She's constantly pushing the both of us. She knows exactly what Jamie needs when I don't, and she knows exactly how to calm me down when I start to fret."

"Shame you don't swing that way. I mean, yay for the male sex, but not so much for her."

"You're very free with the compliments." Simon flushed.

"Only when deserved." They shared a quick look; both glanced away. Mattie cleared his throat. "So… is it okay that I'm asking you about this stuff? It's pretty personal."

Simon lifted one shoulder. "It's nice to be asked. It's usually an awkward topic of conversation. People tend to get quiet and sympathetic when you tell them your kid is autistic, like you've just told them they're dying of cancer, or something."

"Oh, *come* on."

"It's true, and it makes me want to smack 'em silly."

"You know the guys at the diner. They'd never—well, aside from Jules, who just doesn't know how to interact with *anybody* normally—but everyone else, they're not like that at all." He shrugged. "I think they know there's something different about Jamie…." He glanced at Simon to check that he hadn't caused any offence. "But he's still just a cute little kid to them."

Simon nodded. "Why do you think I like that place so much?"

Mattie snorted. "I was hoping it had something to do with the dude making the sandwiches."

Simon cracked a grin. "I'll admit that was a bonus." He shot Mattie a sidelong glance. "Did you know that your friend, the waiter, came over to me and blew your cover?"

Mattie stopped still, his mouth comically hanging open before he rolled his eyes and groaned. "That asshole."

"He seems like a nice enough guy, gave me confidence enough to go talk to you at the gallery, anyway."

"Hmm, maybe I won't murder him, then."

"Ain't you a sweetheart."

Mattie laughed. "I do believe your funny bone is alive and well, Mister Castle."

They walked a while in an oddly comfortable silence, just ambling, really. Eventually Mattie broke the silence. "Can I ask you something else?"

"Sure."

"Just remember that I'm not the brightest bulb in the box here, but… what *is* autism? You've said what some of the results of it are, but… I mean, is it a brain thing?"

"Don't feel dumb. It's a glossed-over subject and doesn't affect most people's lives, but what it comes down to is, yes." He nodded. "It's a brain disorder, a problem in his neural development. And really all that means is that, in Jamie's case, he has a significant impairment in social situations. Other than that he's a healthy, normal—albeit above average, very bright—kid. He's just another child, but he has to work a lot harder at the things that come naturally to other children. That's it in a nutshell."

Mattie nodded. "No less, just different."

Simon nearly stopped in his tracks. Mattie didn't seem to notice, but Simon had to swallow and clear his throat to make sure his voice didn't come out as a squeak. That had been the absolute *perfect* thing to say. Even Tim had never quite grasped in three years what Mattie seemed to understand or realize in a walk through the park.

"That's it exactly," he said quietly.

"So… when he gets upset, does it happen often?"

Simon offered him a sad smile. "You sure you want to know all this stuff?"

Mattie's eyes widened slightly. "I'm sorry if I'm being nosy…."

Simon nudged him back into a walk with an elbow. "Not at all." He smiled. "Just tell me when to shut up."

"Not likely. It's not often you get to connect with someone new like this, you know? It's cool."

Again, Simon found himself baffled at Mattie's insight, and thought distantly that he'd make a decent writer in another life. He nodded. "That's true enough."

"So tell me about it."

Simon ran his hand through his hair, but for once is wasn't an agitated gesture. "Well, it's inevitable that he's going to have to go through stages that frighten him." He shook his head sadly. "I have to keep pushing him into these situations for him to adapt to them, otherwise he'll never be independent. But when I do, it can be quite upsetting."

"For both of you, I imagine."

Simon nodded. "*Oh,* yeah." He glanced at Mattie when he felt a touch to his arm, and followed him over to a bench. He sat normally, but Mattie opted to sit on the back of the bench, with his feet beside Simon and his hands deep in his pockets. Simon leaned forward on his knees, his hands clasped tight.

"I can usually catch it quick. He'll begin to hum, and then he starts with his numbers."

"His numbers?"

"He recites prime numbers when he gets agitated. I think it's his mind's way of distracting him or taking him out of the situation."

"That's… wow."

"But if I don't catch it, if I can't calm him down in time… he starts to cry." He was unaware that his voice had cracked until a warm hand squeezed his shoulder. "He'll cover his ears, he'll pull his cape tight around him… when it's really bad, he'll roll on the ground or spin as quick as he can—and it's *not* him having a tantrum. That's what people assume. That's what they think when they look at me as if I'm the worst parent in the world, but it's not a tantrum."

"What is it?"

"He…." He gritted his teeth. "He can't bear to be touched, not when he gets into that state. Do you have any idea what it's like to see your kid go through that, and not be able to hug them?"

Mattie didn't answer, but he rubbed Simon's shoulder. Simon glanced at him in thanks.

"When he rolls or spins… it's because he needs pressure to his nervous system, the same pressure any other child would receive from a hug. That constant, deep pressure to large areas of his body decreases his pulse rate, his metabolic rate, and muscle tone. It relaxes his sympathetic nervous system and calms him down. When it starts, I just have to sit back and let it happen."

It sounded like something right out of a textbook to Mattie. "God, that's gotta hurt to watch."

"It does, but you have to keep calm. It only makes things worse for him if it looks like his dad is upset too."

Mattie didn't respond, but slunk down on the bench to sit beside him. He cleared his throat and looked at Simon. A small, private smile touched his lips, and Simon felt himself smiling back.

"Confession time." Mattie spoke quietly. "I am insanely attracted to you."

Simon couldn't help it. Despite every hint and every word they'd spoken that had indicated as much, hearing Mattie say that made him snort with laughter and look away with a flush. He looked back to see Mattie grinning at him.

"You don't have to say anything, and I know it's not going anywhere, but... my *God*, you're cute."

"Would you stop that?" Simon laughed quietly, feeling nervous. "If you're not careful, you'll make me blush."

"You're already blushing."

"I'm thirty-three. I don't blush anymore."

"Oh yeah, you do. And it's doing all sorts of things to me."

Simon smiled; it was nice to flirt again. "You sure it's not the single-dad thing?"

"Let me guess, you got all those moms at Jamie's preschool sighing and fawning over you."

"It's not *that* bad."

"Don't lie, and yeah, seeing a guy so devoted to a little kid does send the old heart a-fluttering, but that's not it."

He was hesitant to fish, but.... "Then what is it?"

Mattie shrugged. "It's just you. Quiet, intellectual, unassuming, human, struggling-like-the-rest-of-us, and cute as hell you."

Simon blinked in surprise, and, oh hell, he really was blushing now. "Goddamn," he said quietly.

"What?"

"In another life, one far less complicated, I'd be swept off my feet right about now."

Mattie looked down at his lap, a sad smile touching his lips. "Shame. Maybe we'll run into one another and have a go at it next time around."

"Maybe," Simon said quietly, then shook his head. "We got all serious again."

"Yes, we did. We keep doing that."

Simon forced a bright smile. "So tell me about you. Something happy, I want to see you light up. Tell me about your art."

"'My art', that always sounds so pretentious to me."

"Shut up and talk," Simon laughed.

"Okay, well, I paint."

"Oil? Watercolor?"

He smiled. "Depends on my mood or what supplies I have."

"Well elaborate, mister ar*tist*," he teased.

"I like to work on canvas, and I usually use oils, but recently I tend to lean more toward water-soluble oil paint, rather than traditional oils." He rubbed his thumb and first two fingers together. "It's a different texture and has something called emulsifier in it which allows the paint to be thinned by water." He shrugged, his hands going back in his pockets. "Gives a different, almost… wistful effect, and it stretches the paint—makes it last."

"Everything you just said—all sounds very impressive." Simon grinned.

Mattie laughed. "I don't know much, but art is one thing that seems to stick with me."

"So is it just painting for you?"

"Well." He rubbed his chin. "I've never been one for installations, but I do love to sketch, and I've always wanted to get my hands on some clay."

"Why don't you?"

Mattie shook his head. "Messy and expensive. I can barely afford canvas."

"Aren't there some classes or something in the city you can go to for that?"

"I already pay for my reading and writing classes." He shook his head, looking away. "At the moment that feels more important."

"So you can get a better job?" Simon asked softly.

"Not so much that…." He bit his lip. "I'm aiming to take my GED soon. There's this… this art school in New York, and I want to go there. I want to do better for myself."

"Mattie," Simon said softly and without a hint of condescension. "That is *great*."

"Thing is, you can't get in without a GED, and there's an entrance essay too." He sighed.

"I think you've got it in you."

"You do, huh?" He smiled.

"I don't know you well, but it's like you said, it's not often you make this kind of introduction or connection with someone new. So I say yeah, you've got it in you."

Mattie pressed his lips together to keep the smile from splitting across his face. "Thanks," he uttered quietly instead.

Simon looked away, suddenly desperate to get onto a lighter topic. "So," he said brightly. "What's your poison? Composition, conceptual, abstract, symbolism, portraits, landscapes?"

Mattie laughed. "I have to pick just one?"

Simon was about to say something teasing when his stomach interrupted him with a gurgle. Mattie laughed and raised an eyebrow.

"Is papa bear hungry by any chance?"

Simon grinned sheepishly. "It would appear so, and I am *not* a bear."

"This is true." Mattie stood up from the bench. "I guess you'd better head off, unless… I mean, if you don't have to get back yet, we could…." He trailed off, one brow raised in question.

Simon stood, hooking his bag back over his head. He hesitated. "Um… that'd be nice, but—"

Mattie waved his hand in a dismissive, casual gesture, his cheeks pinking slightly at being turned down. "No worries. You get back to your little tyke."

Charmed was the word to describe how Simon felt at that moment. What would a little dinner hurt, a little more flirting? Mattie got it; he *got* it, when it came to the complicated stuff, the need for casual. "Let me just call home, make sure everything's okay and Sarah can sit a little longer."

Mattie's face brightened. "Great!"

Simon grinned at him and then pulled out his cell. He waited three rings before Sarah picked up. "Sarah, love, it's me. How is everything?" He paused, listening. "Yeah? Good, good, listen, is there any chance you might be able to—" Another pause. "Are you sure?" He glanced at Mattie, who was trying to give him some semblance of privacy by looking away. "Um… I don't know, an hour or two? Can—" Another pause, and this time Simon was smiling. "There's some leftover spaghetti and meatballs in the fridge. There should be enough for both of you. It was a big hit with him the other night." He glanced at Mattie, moved the phone away, and mouthed "sorry."

"It's fine," Mattie whispered with a wink.

"Can you put him on a sec?" There was another brief silence, and then the most loving smile Mattie had ever seen spread across Simon's lips. "Hi, baby boy. You having fun with Miss Protrakis?" There was another pause and another smile. "Are you being a good boy?" Simon laughed and nodded. "Daddy's going to be little bit longer." He adjusted his bag strap with his free hand. "No, I'll be home in time for tucking-in and stories."

MATTIE bit his lip against a smile, something inside of him just absolutely *melting*.

"Okay, baby. I'll be home soon, love you. Put Miss Protrakis back on."

Mattie waited for Simon to finish up his telephone call and knew without a shadow of a doubt that he was utterly and completely smitten. He didn't think there was a chance they could become anything more than friends, but then, not a few hours ago, even friendship had seemed impossible. And here they were, going to grab some supper after having shared intimate details that no stranger should be privy to.

"Okay." Simon smiled, sliding his cell into his pocket. "Where do you want to head?"

"Actually, my place isn't too far away from here. You could see some of my paintings, and I make a great...." He trailed off, seeing the look of sudden apprehension on Simon's face. "Or we can totally go down to this little Italian place, cheap as hell and quite clearly not as scary." He chuckled. "Relax. I know it isn't in the cards. I wasn't propositioning you."

Simon winced and offered an apologetic smile. "Sorry, sorry. It's not that... it—it's just been a while since I've been out there, you know? I don't know when someone's just being friendly or... not."

"It's fine. So... Italian?"

He mulled it over. "You know what? No. No, show me your paintings. And you can feed me."

"I make awesome ham and cheese omelets."

"Hell, you should have said. Lead the way."

"SO, WHAT do you think?" Mattie called from his miniature kitchen, flipping Simon's omelet.

"Well, I'm no critic," Simon called back from the living room that contained no more than a two-seat couch, a coffee table covered in sketch pads, an easel by the window, some stacked-up canvases, and surprisingly, a small rudimentary pen with an open and rather large cage. He'd done a double take when seeing the small rabbit curled up asleep on a cushy-looking pad. "But I'd say you are a very talented artist."

Mattie grinned and slid the omelet onto a plate as Simon entered the kitchen. "Come get some grub." He poured more omelet mixture into the small pan and placed Simon's plate on the circular kitchen table for two. "Go ahead and eat up."

Simon sat, then quickly reached into his pocket for his cell when he felt it vibrate. Worried that it would be a call from home, he was quick to check the screen, but groaned, seeing his mother's number. He sent the call to voice mail and tucked the cell back in his pocket.

"Not feeling sociable?"

He shrugged, picking up a fork. "Unknown number."

"Ah, well then."

"This looks great, by the way, thanks."

"No problem. I can make more than sandwiches, you know."

"Well, that's for damn sure," Simon said around a mouthful.

Mattie smiled, seeming pleased, and flipped his own omelet and let it brown for a few seconds, then slid it onto a plate and joined Simon.

"Glad you like it." He took a mouthful of his own and then frowned. "I think the thermostat is on the blink again. It's warm as hell in here."

"You *were* just standing over a stove," Simon pointed out with a wave of his fork.

"Na, this place always has something on the verge of breaking. I guess I should be grateful to have indoor plumbing. Though even that is communal and down the hall."

"Really?" Simon asked before he could stop himself, surprised that apartment complexes so outdated still existed.

Mattie just smiled, ducking his head. "I bet your place is real nice, huh?"

Simon thought of his spacious living room with its leather three-piece suite and flat screen TV, his kitchen with dark marble counters and stainless steel appliances, his office, Jamie's playroom, and his two bathrooms. And he thought that, yes, his place was damn nice, but strangely enough, he felt reluctantly envious of Mattie. He was a young single guy in a single guy's apartment. Albeit it was kind of bare, and Mattie didn't seem to... *belong* in it, but to Simon, it seemed to represent some sort of freedom or lost youth.

"I like my house. It's not too far from here. Baker Street."

"I think I've been by there before, nice neighborhood. Don't they all have different colored doors?"

Simon smiled. "Yeah, ours is the blue one."

"Better than this place, right?"

"It's not bad, but I bet if...." He trailed off, distracted when Mattie put his fork down and pulled his thin sweater over his head, balled it up, and carelessly chucked it into the living area, leaving him in nothing but a wife beater that showcased his gorgeous, slender torso. He looked slim, but still had good-sized biceps, strong-looking shoulders and forearms, a chest that—

"Simon?" Mattie asked, smirking.

Simon felt his face heat up and snapped his gaze away from the Adonis before him and back to his plate. He shook his head minutely. "I—I was just saying that...." What had he been saying? "That... um, oh yes! If you were to put some of your work up, maybe, it'd... um...."

"You were totally checking me out."

"Oh... *pft*, I was just... I was, um... Yes. Yes, I was totally checking you out. My apologies." Damn it, there was nothing left on his plate to look at.

"Don't apologize, man. You just made my day. I was starting to think you thought I looked like a gremlin or something."

"Oh, please, you're gorgeous and you know it. How could you think that?" Simon laughed and then felt something inside of him soften at how genuinely surprised and pleased Mattie appeared. That, combined with the almost bashful glance away, just about did him in. This guy had to deal with so much ugliness in his life that he had no realistic perception of what it was he actually looked like. "Come on," Simon urged teasingly, his voice soft. "You have a mirror, don't you?"

He shrugged one shoulder. "I have a shiny toaster." He made it sound like a question.

Simon smiled, looked down at his empty plate, and gently pushed it away a bit. He shook his head, almost sadly.

"Let me get that." Mattie took both of their plates to the sink and stayed there, his back turned. "Simon?"

"Yes?"

Mattie turned, wiping his hands dry on a towel and biting his lip. He seemed to force himself to relax his shoulders in what appeared a casual manner. "Come here a sec?"

Feeling unease spike through him, he wiped his hands on his thighs as he stood and walked over to stand next to Mattie. "Everything all right?"

"You like me, right?"

"Yes, yes of course." He smiled.

Mattie's smile lit up the room, and with a quick glance to Simon's mouth, he took a step forward and tilted his head to the side, brushing their lips together. He raised his hand to cradle Simon's neck, but Simon stopped him, gently easing away.

"Ahm. Mattie… *no,*" he said with a soft shake of his head, feeling like a shit at the brief look of confusion, followed by a flash of hurt and then mortification.

"Shit." Mattie squeezed his eyes shut a second. "*Shit,* I'm sorry." He backed up, shoulders hunched and reaching for that dishtowel to twist in his hands. "You don't... I'm not...." He shook his head, offering a smile that was blatantly masking his discomfiture. "Any chance you can pretend I didn't just do that?"

Simon was at a loss. Mattie looked humiliated, and *he* had put that look there. "Oh geez, Mattie," he said softly, "it's not like... I mean, you're gorgeous, sweet, and funny, but...." He felt helpless as to how to save the very uncomfortable situation.

Mattie watched him as if waiting for something else to come out of his mouth, some nice, face-saving words, but when nothing did, Mattie looked away. He tossed the dishtowel on the counter and tucked his hands into his back pockets. "But," he continued for Simon, his voice rough, "I'm a prostitute, so...." His gaze travelled no higher than Simon's neck, unable to meet his eyes.

"That's not—" He licked his lips quickly. "That is *not* why."

"Yes it is, Simon." He finally met his gaze and offered him a sad smile. "Hey," he said, all soft-like. "It's okay. I don't think you're a jerk or anything. It's perfectly reasonable."

"You just caught me off guard. I wasn't ready."

"I overstepped. You've practically hinted a thousand times you're not interested." He lowered his head to hide his heavy frown. "And why would you be?" He laughed, kind of sadly. "I got no business thinking someone so classy and great would ever—" His voice caught, and he cleared his throat. "Man, would you listen to me?" He forced a laugh. "Could I be acting any more clingy or weird right now?"

Simon stood closer and shook his head. "I don't think that."

"I'm sorry. I hope... I hope we can still kinda be friends?" He met his eyes. "I really am sorry. You're just so... you're so *nice*."

He said the word with a sort of sigh that made something inside of Simon hurt. He frowned sadly, and before he could think twice about it, he stepped up to Mattie, his hand hooking around the back of his neck, and pulled him into a firm kiss.

MATTIE sucked in a quick breath, his eyes closing at the last second as his head was held firmly and he was kissed, just as he'd always wanted to be. There was hunger, arousal, and a hint of desperation that sent his heart racing. But there was also something undeniably tender about it. He pressed back, trying to take the lead for a second, but then Simon was pulling away, resting his forehead against Mattie's, breathing deeply.

Mattie froze, afraid of scaring him away. "Simon? You're kind of giving me mixed signals here."

Simon let out a small, breathless laugh and opened his eyes. "Sorry, I… I don't want you to think it's just you. You're so not alone in this. It's just really, *really*…."

"Complicated?"

"Oh yeah."

"Because of what I do?" There was no sadness in his voice. He looked cautious, if anything, as if afraid of saying the wrong thing.

Simon pulled back a little but then gently touched Mattie's elbows. "I won't lie. That does come into it. But… I'm also older than you, and—"

"*What*? You don't get to use that as an excuse!"

Simon smiled. "I'm seven years older than you."

"Seven *shmeven*."

"The fact that you just said 'seven shmeven' only proves my point." He chuckled affectionately.

"You look me in the eye and tell me that, after everything we've talked about tonight, you don't think I'm mature enough for you."

Mattie thought he had him there.

"It's not only that. I can't…." Simon ground his teeth, sounding frustrated. "I can't offer you anything. My life isn't exactly my own, not anymore."

Mattie raised his hands and touched Simon's face, stroking down to his shoulders. "You think I don't understand that?"

"I don't think you know what it fully entails, no."

"We don't have to jump into anything. It's not like we're gonna go from one kiss to meeting your folks."

Simon sighed. "Do you remember what we were saying about—about being casual?"

"Simon, I understand that Jamie comes first with you and always will. And I am well aware that we only *really* met a few days ago. I'm not expecting you to get down on one knee here."

"And what about you?"

"What do you mean?"

"What you said, about… about it has to be casual for you too?" he urged gently.

Mattie nodded, running both hands through his hair and then entwining his fingers behind his neck. When he was with a john, he kept it casual. He took himself away in his mind and turned it into something that meant nothing so it wouldn't mean something shameful. He let his hands fall to his sides, his stare serious.

"I don't let it affect me, Simon. It just is what it is." He shrugged helplessly. "That's all I can think to say. I really do understand if that's not okay with you." Hell, how else could he explain prostitution?

Simon looked relieved by Mattie's response. He started to nod. "Okay, okay."

Mattie bit his lip against a smile, his hands hesitantly reaching out to Simon's shoulders. "Yeah?" he whispered. He dared hope Simon understood that what he had to do sometimes meant nothing, and that they could still have something good. That they could take it slow, and develop into something amazing, something lasting. "You're saying yes?"

"Just… slow and easy?"

Mattie beamed but quickly smothered it and nodded. "Absolutely. Slow and easy. All the time in the world. No rushing."

"As long as we're on the same page."

"How long until you have to head off?"

"Uh...." Simon frowned, glanced at his watch. "Around forty minutes?"

"Will you...." He searched Simon's eyes, aware that they'd literally *just* said the words "slow and easy." "You wanna go to bed with me?" he murmured, crowding closer.

Simon gripped Mattie's waist, the wife beater bunching in his hands. His answer was nothing more than a shuddering breath. "Yes."

Mattie licked his lower lip. "Then we're on the same page. Come with me," he said in a low voice, taking Simon's hand and beginning to pull him toward the bedroom. He looked back when he felt a slight resistance.

"Slow and easy?" he reiterated.

Something in Mattie's eyes softened. "I won't hurt you."

"No, I...." He squeezed Mattie's hand. "I mean, truthfully, it's casual for you?"

In a way, Mattie was pleased that Simon wanted to know flat out that the hooking meant nothing to him. He found it encouraging. He squeezed Simon's hand back. "I promise you, it's water off a duck's back for me."

MATTIE'S casual approach toward relationships was allowing Simon to dare hope that Mattie understood it could never be anything but friendly, *casual* sex. And it had been so *long*. Satisfied that there would be no hurt feelings or misunderstanding—that there would be no reading into things that could never take root—he gave a nervous smile. "Then lead away."

A few moments later, Simon was trying hard, *hard*, not to laugh. It was flattering, really. He'd got as far as placing his glasses on the bedside dresser, and then Mattie was *on* him. He found himself on his back, his sweater on the floor beside the bed along with his shoes and socks—Mattie had been so kind as to rid him of these items in, oh...

three seconds flat—and was lying there in his jeans and a T-shirt. Mattie, however, had yet to take off anything and seemed quite distracted with running his hands absolutely everywhere, kissing him like he had the holy grail of lips, and generally making him feel ten years younger.

"Mattie, *Mattie*," he finally chuckled.

"Hmm?" he murmured between quick kisses against Simon's neck.

"Up here," he laughed.

Mattie looked up at the amused but flustered look on Simon's face and closed his eyes with a wince. He squinted one eye open, smiling apologetically. "Shit." He laughed softly. "How many times did we say slow and easy? And here I am—"

"Making me feel like the sexiest thing alive." Simon grinned, his hand snaking behind Mattie's neck to bring him down for a soft kiss. "I know we're on a time limit here, but, uh… you've gotta take it down a notch."

Mattie let out a breathless laugh, resting his brow against Simon's chest for a moment, and then leaned up for a soft kiss. "I'm sorry, it's just…." He bit his lip. "You know when you've wanted something for so long, then *bam*, you've got it and you just don't even know where to start?"

Simon took a deep breath, his brows rising in surprise. "Wow," he said, letting out that deep breath. "Anybody'd think you were kind of into me."

Mattie gave him a downright rakish grin. "That's *exactly* where I want to be." He dipped his head for a deep, passionate, toe-*curling* kiss. "And FYI, you *are* the sexiest thing alive."

"Um… all right, usually I'd call bullshit on that, but you've got this crazy 'I'm gonna freak if you don't shut up and let me get on with this' look in your eyes, so… as you were."

Mattie laughed and dived down for another kiss. He grunted, however, when Simon suddenly pushed him back. "Do you actually want to see me cry? Do you want to see a grown man *cry*?" Mattie groaned, making Simon chuckle.

"No, but I do want to see you naked. If you'd be so kind as to oblige."

Mattie raised a cocky eyebrow. "All right." He slinked off the bed and had the wife beater off in one swift moment. He snapped open his jeans and pulled them down along with his boxer briefs, toeing off his socks and stepping out of the puddle of clothing.

If Simon's mind hadn't been busy reverting back to that of a horny-as-hell teenager, he would have been impressed with the speed at which Mattie'd disrobed. As it was, he was too busy staring blankly at a body that would turn *God* gay.

"That enough of an eyeful?" Mattie smirked.

"Are you fucking *kidding* me?" Simon barked with laughter. "Look at you, come on! Who gets to look like that? *Seriously*!" He made a show of squinting as he counted. "One, two, three, four, five—yep. Six pack. A damn *six* pack. You know the last time I saw one of those was on my computer screen. I didn't think they existed anymore."

"Anyone would think you were kind of into me, Simon," he mimicked as he climbed back onto the bed.

"I'm not even kidding here. You know there's such a thing as too gorgeous, right? *You* are too gorgeous." He shook his head. "That's just too much pressure. My clothes are staying *on*."

"Don't. *Even*," Mattie warned.

"Nope. Screw that. I'll lower my pants a little, but other than that—" Simon was cut off with a yelp when Mattie gripped him behind his knees and yanked him down the bed.

"I've got about twenty minutes left to blow your mind," he said in a distinctly huskier voice. "So I am going to undress you, and then I am going to *have* you, all right? Just nod your head 'yes'."

Simon nodded.

THEY were twenty minutes spent well. Twenty minutes of flesh grinding in a slow, sweaty tandem. Twenty minutes of having Mattie's hot breath against his neck, his beautifully toned shoulders moving above him and his grip on them sliding, leaving unintentional red marks. Twenty minutes of that smooth, chiseled chest rubbing against his own somewhat average one. Twenty minutes of his fingers gripping Mattie's wringing wet hair in tight fists as he steadied himself on one hand at Simon's side, the other gripping the headboard as their movements became quicker, *harder*, their flesh slapping together.

It was twenty minutes of utter heaven.

They lay side by side, panting as they fought to catch their breaths with the sheets pushed aside so their slick skin could cool.

"Have—have you ever seen someone debone a fish before?" Simon asked breathlessly.

Mattie turned to look at him with an amused expression. "This your idea of pillow talk?"

Simon laughed, feeling utterly slinky. "Have you?" he asked again.

"Uh… think so. Some dude on a cooking show once, why?"

Simon found himself mesmerized by the rise and fall of that beautifully smooth chest beaded with sweat. He licked his lips. "I'm pretty sure that's what you've just done to my spine."

Mattie grinned, looking rather smug. He rolled onto his side, and Simon felt a momentary spike of unease travel through him when he saw a look in those hazel eyes that was decidedly tender.

"You were pretty incredible yourself," he said softly. He leaned forward and kissed Simon slowly. "And as much as I really, *really* don't want to let you out of this bed, I believe you promised someone bedtime stories."

Simon felt a wave of relief flow through him. It was time to go, and it was Mattie that had gently suggested it. He was even a little touched that Mattie'd recalled the promise he'd made Jamie on the phone. He groaned and sat up. "I guess it's back to the real world for now. I'm going to be walking like a cowboy for a week."

"For *now*, and I like cowboys." Mattie grinned, climbing out of the bed and snagging Simon's clothing. "There are tissues on the dresser. Do you want me to call a cab for you while you get dressed?"

Simon slipped on his glasses and was strapping on his watch. "Yes, please. I didn't drive today. I usually try and walk everywhere as a rule, but not tonight. It's nearly eight o'clock, and a certain someone will be in his PJ's, waiting to read the next chapter of *The Hobbit*, which he already knows by heart, I might add," he said fondly.

"That's both cute *and* impressive." Mattie smiled as he slinked on his underwear and searched for his cell.

Simon dressed while Mattie strolled into the kitchen, ordering a cab and filling a glass of water from the faucet for Simon. Simon walked out of the bedroom, feeling rumpled and ravished, and if Mattie's proud grin was anything to go by, that's exactly what he looked like. He wouldn't have minded a quick shower, but the idea of walking down the hall to the floor's shared bathroom while smelling of sex didn't appeal.

"Thanks." He accepted the water, gulping it down, and then impulsively drew Mattie close for a kiss. "Thank you," he repeated, his voice lower and heavy with meaning.

Any post-orgasm awkwardness he would expect to feel quickly melted away with a soft sigh when Mattie slinked his arms up and around Simon's neck, pressing their bodies together to kiss him. It was a kiss he felt right down to his bones and in every nook and cranny of his body. His hands instinctually held Mattie close, and despite the fact that Mattie had topped him that evening, the way he held him now made him feel like a *man*. He allowed one hand to stray lower and splay over Mattie's perfect backside, and could feel Mattie grin a little when he gave it a squeeze. The sound of a car's horn—a cab's horn—caused them to pull apart a fraction.

"You'll be at the diner tomorrow to work, right? Like usual?"

Simon gave him one last quick kiss and nodded. "Just like every day." He reluctantly pulled away and slung his bag across his body. "Maybe you could take your lunch break with me, or something?"

Mattie pressed his lips together to hide what he thought would be too pleased a smile, and nodded. "Sure, I'd like that." He walked Simon to his front door and untwisted the strap of his bag, which had tangled across his chest. "And we can work out when we can maybe next get together." He looked Simon in the eye, and his hand patted where he'd untwisted the strap. "Whenever is good for you and Jamie."

All but blown away by the day in general, let alone that generous and understanding statement, Simon leaned in for a final soft kiss. "I'll see you tomorrow," he murmured, and headed out of the door.

"HEY, I'm home," he called, dropping his keys and bag on a table in the entryway and heading on into the living room. "Hey," he repeated, quieter. He smiled, spotting Jamie fast asleep on the sofa. "Everything go okay?"

"Absolutely fine." Sarah stood, bookmarking her page.

"I'm so glad he's getting used to being around someone else other than me occasionally, even if he does see you during the day."

"It's baby steps, but it's ultimately good for him." Sarah nodded. "He wanted to wait for you to get into his pajamas, though. That's your job and your job only, apparently." She laughed. "And I would have put him to bed, but I didn't want to risk waking him while I was holding him. I don't think he's ready for that."

"Not yet, no." He checked his watch; it was eight fifteen. "He's not usually asleep this soon. What did you get up to?"

"We had a great time. We made some towers, and you have a drawing of Gimli waiting for you in your office."

"That's the dwarf, right?"

"I think so, yes."

Simon smiled. He'd go have a look when he'd tucked Jamie in; then he'd pin it up on the fridge. But first…. "You wouldn't mind hanging on for two more minutes while I grab a quick shower, would you?"

"Of course." She patted his arm and then paused, her delicate eyebrows rising in surprise. "Um…." She all but giggled. "Have a good evening?"

He flushed damn near scarlet and backed away, smiling sheepishly. Someone had taken stock of his rumpled hair and possibly caught a whiff of something that was not aftershave. "I uh… oh, damn it," he laughed sheepishly.

She held her hands palms up. "None of my business, though it's about time Prince Charming made an appearance."

"I'll be back in two ticks."

"Make it three," she chuckled and sat back down.

Five minutes later and looking and smelling more appropriate for polite company, he pulled his wallet out of his bag and pulled out fifty dollars. Sarah looked up as he handed over the bills. Usually she would fold them and put them into her purse, as she was now, and then peck him on the cheek and be on her way. However, this time she paused, taking note of how much he'd handed over, and looked up at him, surprised.

"Simon, don't be ridiculous," she laughed.

"You've been here for hours, and you cooked him supper."

"I heated up leftover *meatballs*."

"Yes, but then you caught me coming in looking all… um…."

She squinted her eyes, looking him up and down. "Lighter, you look lighter."

"That's one way to put it." He grinned when she slapped his arm.

"Here." She handed back ten.

"Don't be silly."

"It's too much. Take it." She pushed it back into his hand. "Now walk me to the door like a gentleman."

He followed her into the hallway, worrying his lip as he tried to think of a way to broach a potentially embarrassing subject. "Sarah, you mentioned that you'd be happy to sit a little more regularly?" He knew he was busted when she snorted and gave him a sly smile.

"Yes?" she drawled, pulling on her jacket.

He couldn't help but smile in embarrassment. "I was wondering if we could maybe make it… I don't know, two, three nights a week?" He was surprised when her shoulders slumped and a look of relief swept over her face.

"That would be fantastic."

"Really?"

The look of relief was quickly replaced by a look of utter aggravation. "I took my car to the shop to get the exhaust replaced. Turns out there were a heap of other stupid mechanical things wrong with it. I paid two hundred in the end, only to be told it should hold out for about another month and to just scrap it as soon as possible. Can you believe that?"

It was at times like this that he felt guilty about having a Mercedes sitting in his garage, infrequently used. "Well, if you're having car troubles, I could always drive him over to your place and pick him up three or four hours later? It'd save you gas money too." And that way he could drive to and from Mattie's apartment.

"That would be great, and that'd introduce him to a new environment at the same time."

"How about I come over one evening this week with him, let him get used to it while I'm there?"

She wrapped her scarf around her neck. "Make sure you bring his blocks and crayons and such. But yes, I think we have a deal." She looked at him seriously a moment. "I know you think I'm doing you a favor here, Simon, but honestly it goes both ways. The money would really help me out right now, so two or three nights a week would be absolutely fine. Think about which nights and let me know."

He smiled, relieved. "I will. I'll still pick him up from school, spend a couple of hours with him, and get him fed. Then I'll bring him over probably between five and six." He waved his hand in a casual manner. "We'll iron the details out later."

"Sounds like a plan." She tiptoed and pecked his cheek, and he opened the door. "I'll see you tomorrow."

"Drive safe."

He watched her pull away and then headed on into the living room to scoop up his baby boy. He didn't have to worry about checking if Jamie was happy to be picked up when half asleep. Usually, in this state, his instinct was to curl up into his dad's arms. He shouldered open his bedroom door, and Jamie mumbled quietly but otherwise didn't stir as he laid him out on his bed.

"Hey, little man." He smiled when Jamie blinked sleepily at him. "Let's get you into your pajamas."

"'Kay."

Simon held back a snort of amusement as his half-asleep son allowed him to remove his cape and pull his Spider-Man T-shirt up over his head. He wiggled him into his cowboy and Indians onesie, making him giggle. He noticed the PJ's were getting a little short in the leg, and made a mental note to pick up some child pajamas on his next shopping trip. He smiled sadly, realizing he would have to buy the size four to five years old, rather than three to four.

All tucked in, he asked if he still wanted to read *The Hobbit*. Jamie nodded even as his eyelids began to droop, and explained sleepily that Bilbo was just about to load the dwarves into the barrels. Simon smoothed down that little cowlick and picked up where they'd last left off.

Half a page later, Jamie was fast asleep.

Chapter
Five

"HEY." Mattie slid into the booth opposite Simon with a bowl of soup for himself and a tuna baguette for him. "Are you at a stopping point?" He lifted his chin as if he could see over the top of the laptop, hesitant to interrupt.

"Just give me one minute." Simon clacked away at the keys for a few more moments before leaning back in his seat, rolling his eyes, and then closing his laptop, pushing it to one side.

"Not going well?" Mattie asked, blowing on his spoon to cool his tomato soup.

"No. No it's not." Simon frowned. He looked up at Mattie, wanting more than anything to just moan at someone about the damn manuscript.

"What's wrong?"

"I'm stuck."

"You mean writer's block?"

He harrumphed unhappily. "Not really. I know where I want it to go; I'm just not... *feeling* it anymore."

"Well, talk it out with me. Tell me about the story, and maybe you can feel out where it's falling flat for you."

Simon sighed, knowing that Mattie was just trying to be nice, but he supposed it couldn't hurt to try. "It's a thriller."

"Like your other ones?"

"You know my other books?" He grinned when Mattie lifted one shoulder, as if it were no big thing.

"A part of completing the reading and writing course was to choose a book from the library, write a short essay or critique, and then read it to the rest of the class." He went back to stirring his soup. "I chose *The Cracked Bell*, by Simon Castle."

Simon smiled in surprise, feeling flattered. "You read one of my books." It wasn't a question, and he grinned when Mattie's response was to mumble something affirmative while occupying himself with his lunch. "I wouldn't mind hearing what you thought of it."

"It was good." Mattie dodged.

"*Pft*, I want to hear this essay."

"Um. No," he laughed.

"Why, did you totally trash me?" he teased.

"No! Of course not, you're brilliant." Mattie looked shocked.

"I was only teasing you, and I'm far from brilliant, but that's very kind of you, you lovely, lovely man. Now come on, cheer me up here. What did you say?"

Mattie sighed. "I wasn't the most articulate or anything, but I just said, in a nutshell, that I found it very suspenseful—which is a bitch to spell, by the way—and that despite the fact that I found myself utterly engrossed, the ending still managed to take me by surprise." Mattie glanced at him and offered him a crooked smile. "That was pretty much my review, and then I just told them about the book's storyline, and to go read it for themselves."

"Thanks. Did you really like it?"

"Yeah, I did."

"Why'd you pick that one instead of my other book, just out of interest?"

"Uh. It was shorter," he offered with a laugh. "I only had a week to read it, and I'm still kind of slow."

"Well." Simon toyed with a napkin. "Thanks for reading it. Are you glad you're done with the course now?"

"Sort of. I have to keep on reading. That's what they tell you. And I guess I can save a little bit of money now that they're done, but I'm not really getting my time back. I'm studying like crazy to sit for my GED."

"I'd be happy to help you any time."

He instantly regretted the offer. Although he really wouldn't mind helping Mattie study, and wanted nothing more than for Mattie to do well, they had, over the past few weeks, carved out a routine of sorts. A few nights a week, when Sarah could sit for Jamie and when Mattie didn't have his reading and writing class or… other commitments that he tried to not think about, they would be at Mattie's apartment. And on the days he saw Mattie, his day would follow the lines of: take Jamie to school, go to the diner and write for a few hours, eat lunch with Mattie, go pick up Jamie and take him home for supper (he'd stopped taking Jamie to the diner for now, both unwilling and ashamed to admit why), drive to Sarah's to drop off Jamie, and then over to Mattie's for a max of two, two and a half hours. It was going exactly how they had discussed it would. It was easy, casual… it was *nice*. His only problem was that it was *too* nice.

The sex was starting to feel suspiciously like lovemaking. It was becoming more comfortable to spend time in bed talking and lying close, getting to genuinely know one another. Mattie's touches were becoming more familiar, and he found himself enjoying, even welcoming the touch of Mattie's hands at his back when being led into his apartment. He enjoyed the kiss goodnight, as if he were being seen off to work by his doting partner. He found himself jealous on the very rare occasions when Mattie had prior engagements, which allowed his imagination to torture him with images of Mattie with other men.

He was not supposed to be feeling this way, and he certainly was not supposed to be offering Mattie help with his studying. Fortunately, he was saved from having to retract the offer when Mattie declined with a nonchalant shake of his head. He made a mental note to perhaps lay off on his time spent with Mattie, as much he enjoyed and looked forward it. They really needed to get back to the mind-set of friends with benefits.

"Thanks, but Ty already has this little study plan thing worked out. He's turned into the GED Nazi."

"He seems like a good guy."

"My best friend, yeah." He pushed his empty bowl to one side, glancing at his watch. "I still have fifteen minutes left of my break." He nodded at the laptop. "Tell me why you're having problems with your book, seeing as you already know what it is you want to write."

Simon worried his lip, hesitant to respond. Mattie's quiet laugh made him glance up.

"Why have you gone all shy?" Mattie asked softly.

Simon huffed, sitting up straighter. "I'm not. I just, um...." He pressed his lips together and then allowed himself to slouch back down, feeling himself flush as he spoke. "I don't want you to think I'm some sort of... *nerd*, I guess."

Mattie spluttered. "Oh, hardly. Come on, you're no more a nerd than I am a super model."

"That's a bad example."

Mattie rolled his eyes. "Come on. Talk to me about being 'stuck'."

Simon sighed. "Well, I guess I just... I'm not feeling it anymore. Usually I have this passion about the story, and discounting the days where the words just don't want to come, I can usually sit down and get on with it." He shook his head. "I think it's taken too long. It's gone stale."

"Why do you think that is? What's different with this one, compared to the other two?"

Simon knew the answer to that; he just didn't want to say it. He tore off the corner of his baguette and chewed, buying some time, but apparently Mattie already knew him better than he originally thought.

"Oh, I see. When did you start this one?" he asked.

Simon winced. "I started it just over five years ago. It got put completely on hold when Carol-Ann died. Then being a new dad... and Jamie...." He hated to use Jamie as an excuse, even if it was the truth.

"That's quite a gap to start a novel and then try and pick it up again."

"You don't understand. After the first book was published, I was offered a contract for my next two books, but they expect it to be within a certain time frame. They got their second hit out of me, but the third...." He removed his glasses to clean them on the edge of his sweater. "They've already granted an extension due to personal circumstances, but they're getting impatient. You've met my editor, Andrew—" As soon as he said it he winced and noticed how Mattie glanced away quickly.

"Yeah, I know him," was the quiet response.

"He's constantly on my ass now, trying to suggest different things to get me motivated or inspired. What he doesn't get is that... well, I'm not the same person I was when I started the novel."

There. He'd finally admitted it out loud.

"Well no, your life's been turned upside down in the last few years. You're bound to feel different about a few things."

"Try explaining that to my editor. He doesn't show any outward disapproval of my home life. It's more like he thinks I should just suck it up and get on with it. He doesn't understand how much of my time is devoted to Jamie. And not only time, but thinking space: I'm always thinking ahead when it comes to him."

"I think I get that. Like you said," Mattie added softly, "Jamie has to tackle the things in life that come naturally to other children. He's not less for it, but he needs more understanding and time. Simple stuff like, I don't know, a trip to the movies. You'd have to plan that ahead; am I right?"

"You're dead on," Simon murmured, once again shoving away those fluttery feelings that were beginning to stir. "I could probably write this book, but my heart wouldn't be in it. That's why I'm having a problem committing to it. I can't imagine having something published that doesn't *mean* something to me. I'm trying to get that feeling back."

"I think that just means that you have standards."

"Even when I wrote the first two, they were both thrillers, but they were important to me. Each character was real and had an entire history of their own. Now… now this book just feels frivolous to me."

"Can't you just… you know, write something else?"

"And throw away a novel that I've—albeit intermittently—spent years working on?"

"Let me ask you this. You said you could probably write it despite feeling this way, correct?"

"Yes."

"If you plowed through, finished it in that state of mind and had it published, would you be proud of it?"

That stumped him. It was a damn insightful question, and Simon was afraid he knew the answer without having to think about it. "Probably not."

"Well, the way I see it, then, is that you have a simple choice to make. And I in no way mean to underplay the importance of this, or anything," he was quick to point out.

"No, it's okay. Go on."

"I think it comes down to whether you're comfortable with putting something out there that you don't feel completely happy with. People who enjoyed your last two books are going to read it. Don't you think they'd feel disappointed if it read as half-assed? And all for the sake of not wanting to have wasted the past few years on a failed novel."

Simon slumped back in his seat with a sigh. "You make a damn good point."

"Let me ask you this: is there anything else that you feel you *would* like to write about right now?"

He worried his lip. "Actually, I've been playing around with an idea, just brainstorming in my head, really. I haven't put pen to paper yet, but it's way out of my comfort zone."

"Which is…?"

He sighed. "Well, with writing thrillers. Ever since I was a teenager, I've loved horror. I always wanted to be Stephen King or Richard Matheson."

"I have to admit that, up until recently, I've never really had an affinity for horror."

"Oh you should give these guys a go. They're legendary. Ever seen *Shawshank Redemption, The Green Mile,* or *I Am Legend*?"

"The last one, wasn't that the one with Will Smith trying to cure a virus that turned people into zombies? That was awesome."

"The book is a little different, but you should give it a read. You know if you decide to pick up reading as just a hobby, I'm the guy to come to for a recommendation. You should see my library at home." And there he went again. Saying something that was outside the parameters of what it was they had agreed they were. He didn't have to backpedal, however, because Mattie was determined to turn the conversation back to his work. And rather than feeling merely relieved, he felt reluctantly pleased at discussing the problem that had been preying on his mind for some time. It felt good to have someone take an interest.

"Maybe, but back to what we were talking about. You were saying something about comfort zones…."

He nodded. "I've only ever written in the horror genre. I just fell into it. It always came naturally to me, and I've always enjoyed it."

"But not anymore?"

"Not right now, I think, but I wouldn't say I was done with it."

"But this idea you said you'd been thinking about, what is it? Romance? Comedy?"

"No. I—" He bit his lip. "It'd be painful to write about, which is why I've only ever thought about it and not spoken about it. I've never taken the idea seriously before, but… I—I was thinking of writing about a single parent raising an autistic child. *Fictional*, of course. Not autobiographical."

A soft smile slowly spread across Mattie's face. "Now, I imagine *that* is something you could put your entire heart into."

"There's a lot of pressure with a book like that, Mattie."

"But you *know* that life, and you're a talented writer."

"I may know that life, but there's still the matter of making people understand it and doing the struggle justice *without* it sounding like some sort of burden. Jamie might read that book someday, and I couldn't bear for him to think that I was either cashing in and playing on the reader's sympathy, or that I felt entitled to some sort of recognition for raising an autistic child. *God*, if he ever—"

"Simon." Mattie reached across the table and touched his hand. "At every instance when talking about Jamie, you've made it totally clear that you would be lost without that kid. He is your entire world, and if he ever read the book—if you ever write it—I think there's a good chance that he may begin to understand just how loved and how special he is."

"And if he didn't see it that way? He may be high-functioning, but he struggles with empathy just like any other autistic individual."

"Then you explain it to him, but I don't think you should count your chickens before they're hatched. You tell me all the time about how you push him, that you drum these social rules into him every day. With a father like you, there is no saying how Jamie will turn out. You have no idea."

"It's still… it's frightening, Mattie." He had never once admitted to being afraid of anything to anybody. When he was a teenager, he had protected himself when it came to his sexuality, never showing weakness even when he was made to feel immoral. As a young adult, he had faced his first editorial meeting head on, despite feeling like an amateur. When Jamie had come into his life, it had been a case of staying strong for the baby and honoring his sister's memory when he had never felt so alone in all his life.

He'd never admitted to a soul that he was frightened. And here Mattie was, not looking at him like he'd hung the moon, but with a respect and understanding that resonated with him. There was a lending of strength and an offer of support that spoke of more than their casual arrangement.

"You really think I could do it? It would mean asking for another extension."

A beaming smile split across Mattie's face. "We may not have known each other all that long, and I've only read one of your books, but I can say with complete confidence that you *could* do such a story justice, simply because I know how dedicated you are to your son. You've made it clear how others sometimes look at Jamie, but hearing the things you say, the good and bad, and having seen how you are with him the few times he's been here, I don't think I'd ever be able to think of an autistic individual, child or adult, as anything less than equal to me. It would be a commendable message to try and get across, and you never know, it could be like… therapeutic for you or something."

Simon was gritting his teeth. "Something you said there is actually probably what terrifies me the most."

"What do you mean?"

"It's one thing when they're children—people with special needs, that is—but when they grow into adults, society seems to lose what little patience it had for them as children." He sipped at the orange juice he'd been nursing for the past hour. "Have you ever seen it? How uncomfortable and sometimes disgusted people become when around an adult who can't help but jerk or slur their words? The polite ones hide it, but it's there. I sometimes think about when Jamie'll be in his twenties, or older, when I'm no longer around. I wonder if he'll be alone, and if people will look at him in that horribly distant way, as—as if he were *dangerous*."

"Then all the more reason for you to tell your story and try and change that perception. I'm serious, Simon. You are so passionate about this subject. You've actually spoken to me more about this story, which at the moment is just an *idea*, than you have the book you've been working on for more than five years. That should tell you something."

It did tell him something. It told him that Mattie was right. It told him that a very awkward and potentially unpleasant conversation with his editor and publisher was long overdue. It told him that Mattie was possibly one of the most intuitive, compassionate people he had ever met, and that he was fast beginning to think of him as his closest friend—a friend he had feelings for that surpassed sexual.

He thought it was perhaps about time for him to stop hiding behind his failed novel and be brave enough to start anew in a genre in which he had no experience or credibility—yet. He also knew he had to shake these feelings for Mattie, because it would only lead to a broken heart for him, and he could *not* go through that twice in one lifetime.

"My break's over. I've got to get back to work." Mattie huffed and stood with his empty bowl in hand, and took Simon by surprise by casting a quick glance around before stealing a quick peck on Simon's cheek.

Simon couldn't help but smile; there really was something naively sweet about this guy. "I got a sitter tonight. Will I see you later?" He wasn't expecting a break from their little routine, but some small, insecure part of him always needed to double check. He felt something inside him shrivel when an uncomfortable and apologetic look passed through those gorgeous hazel eyes. He knew that look.

"Ah, I'd love to, but I can't tonight. What about tomorrow? And hey, I'll even cook for you."

He could feel something bitter curling in his gut. Some subconscious part of his mind knew it wasn't true, but he couldn't help but feel like an afterthought. "Studying with Ty?" He knew it was a low shot. His voice alone conveyed disapproval, even though his words were innocent enough. He knew good and well Mattie wouldn't be studying.

His jab took a direct hit, and he felt ashamed when Mattie looked down at the bowl he carried, then back up with small, forced smile. Those eyes of his had dimmed considerably, and Simon suddenly felt like a total bastard.

"Yeah. I'll see you tomorrow," Mattie murmured and then headed on back through the "Employees Only" marked door.

"Simon Castle," he murmured to himself. "You're an asshole."

Mattie hadn't deserved that. He knew the effect his words—or the insinuation behind them—would have on Mattie, and he didn't deserve that. What the hell was wrong with him? They had agreed from the start: *casual*. Mattie had never hidden what it was he sometimes had to do to pay the bills, not after the night at the gallery, anyhow. He had no right to throw it in his face, even if he *was* jealous.

He'd thought time and time again of just offering Mattie some cash to help him along, or just leaving it in his apartment so that he wouldn't have to hook. But that smacked too much of a payoff for their time together, and that was *not* the relationship they had. Such a well-intentioned solution would only destroy their friendship and hurt Mattie and was, therefore, not an option.

There were no options. This was the way things would have to be between them, and he would just have to get over his feelings toward Mattie's moonlighting and his feelings toward Mattie, period. He was too young, too gorgeous, and had too many issues to become a permanent fixture in Simon's life. Because, when he was being completely honest with himself, what it boiled down to was that his life was also Jamie's life, and Mattie just did not fit into that equation.

He was having fun. The sex was fantastic (even if they had wordlessly ruled out anything oral for now) and zapped some of the tension out of him. He genuinely enjoyed his time with Mattie, but perhaps he should put a stop to what it was they had going on before he became any further involved. If he was already taking cheap shots and getting jealous, then that told him he had allowed things to develop too far already. It was just a matter of finding the words, of finding the *will* to break things off.

The very thought filled him with unhappiness, and rather than think it through further or discuss it with Mattie like an adult, his instincts were to pack up his things as quickly as possible and leave the diner before Mattie returned. He couldn't work right now, not after what they'd discussed about his writing. And he certainly couldn't watch Mattie, all handsome and sweet, smiling at him every now and then from the sandwich bar while he contemplated a way of breaking off their arrangement. It was too much, and he fled like a coward, completely missing the suspicious glance Ty shot him as he looped his bag over his head and headed out the door.

MATTIE stood outside, staring at the intercom a good ten minutes before actually buzzing. After composing himself in the cloakroom of the diner—his conversation with Simon having rattled him—he convinced himself he was imagining things and returned back to the restaurant floor, only to stop dead in his tracks when seeing Simon's booth empty. He thought for a moment that perhaps he was in the customer restroom, but then all of his things were gone, save for his barely touched tuna baguette.

He tried texting Simon to ask if everything was all right, but only grew further disheartened as the hours ticked by and no response was forthcoming. He had a feeling he knew what was going on, and he was kicking himself for being unprepared and so hurt by it. They'd had their moments where he'd been unable to meet with Simon in the evenings, and this had been mostly due to Ty being over to help him study, but occasionally, it had been something else completely.

He was broke. He'd found himself flat out of painting supplies a week ago, but now he was even a few dollars shy of his rent, and he'd already borrowed from Ty twice that month, so there was no choice. He'd avoided hooking as much as possible because, where before he had been able to distance himself when with a john, he now found it difficult to zone out. Now that he had something that felt natural and real to him, something romantic that regular people had, the idea of giving head for money made him feel fucking sick.

As far as he knew, Simon was under the impression it was still a frequent occurrence. He'd actually been naive enough to think Simon understood the situation and accepted it. Not today. For the first time in the past several weeks during the pleasant haze he'd been in, he'd felt ashamed. And Simon had been the one to make him feel that way.

Whether it had been intentional or not, for the first time in a long while he'd felt like his old self. He'd felt dirty.

He tried to tell himself that it was encouraging, that this meant Simon wanted more from him. Perhaps he'd even ask him to quit the hooking. That was really what it came down to, wasn't it? He was waiting for that request. And as difficult as that would make his life financially, he would do it for Simon if it meant something more permanent for the both of them. If it meant actually going somewhere other than his apartment, or being able to call him his boyfriend, meeting his friends, seeing Simon's home, and meeting Jamie officially… then he'd do it. Lord knows he hadn't brought the little guy to the diner since they'd first got together, and he tried his best not to think about why that might be.

Hearing the door buzz and click open distracted him from his thoughts. He pushed the door open and made his way upstairs to Andrew's door, and it was already open a crack for him. This was the one specific place he did not want to be, but Andrew was the most generous when it came to money, and he was hoping he could pay his rent with this one trick with Andrew, rather than with two johns. He pushed the door open.

"In the bedroom," Andrew called.

He walked on through to the bedroom, seeing Andrew in a towel, his hair wet, sitting at a dresser while distractedly going through what looked like a bound stack of papers.

"Make yourself comfortable," Andrew mumbled and waved over his shoulder the vicinity of the bed.

Mattie went as far as to drop his backpack, but left his coat on. He pushed his balled-up hands deep in his pockets as he sat down on the edge of the bed, waiting. Finally, Andrew threw the papers aside with an agitated sigh and strolled on over to the bed. Mattie had to fight to not flinch when the back of Andrew's meaty hand stroked his cheek.

God. He was nothing like Simon. Where Simon was slim and neatly presented, Andrew was overweight and constantly disheveled. Where Simon was quiet and thoughtful, Andrew was crude and inappropriate. Simon would practically fall all over himself apologizing if he were to ever unintentionally cause anyone offense. This guy? This guy was cocky.

"What's up with you? I know you're not usually bowled over to be here, but it's a little difficult to get in the mood when the guy who's supposed to go down on you looks like he's going to burst into tears, you know?"

"It's nothing." Mattie took a deep breath and shrugged off his jacket. "Just get on with it."

"Color me flattered."

"Since when did you need romance?" Mattie snapped.

"True, but I'd settle for willing."

"I'm here, aren't I?"

Andrew sighed, and instead of dropping the towel and getting on with it like usual, he sat beside Mattie on the bed with a huff. "You know what? I don't even have it in me tonight."

"B-but I came all the way over here!" Mattie glared, relieved and pissed at the same time. There had been something about blowing Simon's editor that felt a little extra wrong.

Andrew waved a hand dismissively. "I'll still pay you. Relax. It's just been a hell of a day."

Well. That was… kind of decent of him. Feeling as if he owed the man something, Mattie relaxed a little and attempted to at least act as a listening ear. "You want to talk about it?"

Andrew actually laughed, looking at him. "One of my writers is being a pain in the ass. You know him, actually. You met him at that art show, remember?"

"Simon?" He asked quickly.

A knowing smirk crossed Andrew's lips. "So he *did* pay you a little transactional visit."

Mattie felt his ire rise. "It's not like that."

Andrew raised an eyebrow. "No? Freebie for the writer but not the editor?"

"Fuck you." Screw the money. He'd find it another way, and he'd never set foot back in Andrew's place again. He pulled on his jacket, but Andrew's hand touched his arm. He didn't care for his amused expression.

"Wait a second. Are you telling me you're *dating* him?"

"And what if I am?"

"You're actually serious? You're dating?"

Mattie felt himself deflate a little. "We're... sort of seeing each other. It's a casual thing."

"Huh. He didn't mention it this afternoon."

"Wait... he was *here*?"

Andrew stood up with groan, stretching his arms above his head and then opening a drawer to pull out some clothes and get dressed. "Not *here*, no. We had a late lunch meeting with the publisher at the Grant." He looked at Mattie. "That's a hotel." He pulled on his pants and murmured. "A pretty damn expensive one."

"What was it about?" He was practically leaning off the edge of the bed.

"Kid, I can't tell you that. Hell, he's *your* boyfriend. *You* ask him."

Mattie deflated, wondering if Simon would mention it to him at all, or if Simon was even still speaking to him. Apparently he must have been wearing a kicked puppy expression, because a second later Andrew was sitting next to him on the bed, looking at him almost... kindly?

Andrew heaved an exasperated sigh. "Oh, for the love of—do *not* repeat this. He's scrapping his old book and starting fresh. We just spent a very tense lunch renegotiating his contract for *another* fucking extension." He narrowed his eyes. "You repeat that and I'll screw you over, kid. I'm not even joking."

"I won't." Mattie shook his head, feeling faintly proud of Simon but a little let down too. He'd played a rather integral part in a pretty big decision Simon had made that day, and he couldn't even text him?

Or perhaps it was because of this meeting he hadn't been able to. Maybe his phone had been off.

"Can I ask you something personal?" Andrew asked out of the blue.

Mattie shrugged one shoulder. "I guess." He supposed it was tit for tat.

"How the hell is he okay with you doing what you do if you're seeing each other?"

Mattie contemplated going into the whole spiel of the parameters of their relationship, but didn't have the energy. Instead, he settled for the truth. "I don't know. Perhaps I don't mean as much to him as he does to me."

Andrew stared at him. "That's fucking depressing, kid."

"Tell me about it."

"You're...." He looked at him, squinting. "Ah, *shit*. You're in love with him, aren't you?"

After swallowing hard and looking anywhere but at Andrew, he nodded once. It was supposed to be a happy feeling, wasn't it? Instead he felt like he was heading for a huge letdown. "I don't think he feels the same way. Or if he does, I don't think he'll ever admit it." And with that he suddenly knew that he would never have been able to go through it with Andrew that evening. A line had been drawn, at least where Andrew was concerned.

"Shit." With an angry huff, Andrew walked over to his dresser and searched for his wallet. Finding it, he paced back over to Mattie, standing in front of him. "Here...." He pulled out a large wad of bills. "There's something close to two hundred there. Stop. Hooking."

Mattie looked up at him in shock, and slowly reached for the money in a daze. "You're just giving this to me?"

"I know two hundred won't last long, but figure something out and stop hooking. Stop distracting my writer with this prostitution shit and make him love you back." There was something close to genuine kindness in his expression. "It won't be difficult for him," he said

125

softly. "You're a real nice guy. Just drop the extracurricular activity, you know?"

He didn't know what to say. "I want to. I would for him, but I kind of need him to ask me. I need that reason."

Andrew shook his head. "I don't know what else to say to you, kid."

Mattie stood up, and despite how desperate he was for the cash, he handed it back. "Thanks for this, but uh…." He shook his head. "I can't take it." He knew realistically it was dumb to turn the cash down, seeing as he'd been willing to suck dick for less money a half an hour ago, but when it was being offered to him for free, for some stupid fucking reason his pride wouldn't allow him to accept it. He supposed that what it came down to was the degree of separation being too close between Andrew and Simon. Suddenly even being in the same room with Andrew without Simon seemed like a betrayal.

Andrew took it back, shrugging helplessly. "Take care, yeah?"

Mattie nodded. "Yeah."

SIMON sat at Sarah's dining room table with his legs crossed and his chin resting in his palm. He was tired and wasn't feeling all that great. The meeting had gone better than he'd expected. They were actually on board with him, but now there was just the pressure to deliver, and then there was Mattie. He'd been glancing at his phone every so often for the past two hours, but he couldn't bring himself to respond to him.

A part of him knew he was being immature, and that perhaps his disappearing from the diner without saying good-bye may have worried Mattie, but every time he started to text back, he erased it. Mattie was somewhere with another man, and *he* was the one feeling guilty.

He never lied to you. In fact, you were the one so adamant about being casual. You can't hold it against him while holding him at an arm's length at the same time. Be reasonable.

"Here you go."

He was snapped out of his daydream when Sarah set down a steaming cup of coffee. He smiled halfheartedly and thanked her.

"So if the meeting went so well, why the long face?"

He heaved a heavy sigh, watching Jamie, who was lying on his tummy on the living room floor coloring in another sailboat. (He seemed to really like those.) "Well, the pressure's on now, isn't it? If this doesn't work out then they drop me. That's the deal."

Sarah's look was scrutinizing. "You're going to do great. Are you sure that's all that's bothering you?"

He had to smile at how perceptive she was. "Nothing gets by you, does it?"

"Not really." She gently nudged his forearm with the back of her hand. "Come on, you haven't said word one about who's been keeping you company on the nights I sit for Jamie. Are you at least going to tell me his name?"

"It's complicated, Sarah."

"His name is complicated?" she teased.

"Dippy woman, his name's Mattie."

She smiled. "Okay, so tell me about him."

He glanced at Jamie again and lowered his voice. "We're keeping it very casual. It's nothing serious."

"No? You see him two or three nights every week. That doesn't sound so casual to me. Where did you meet?"

Deciding to gloss over the gallery incident, he told her about how they met at the diner, and the PBJ sandwich Mattie had made special for Jamie. Sarah was smiling, leaning forward on her elbows and blowing on her coffee.

"That sounds rather romantic to me. And you didn't tell me you were seeing him *every* day."

Simon shrugged. "I think of that diner as my place of work too."

"Ah, but now you're mixing business with pleasure."

He laughed at her. "I would never get Mattie into trouble at work. Lord knows how he needs that job."

There was that shrewd look again. "Okay, tell me everything," she said, putting her coffee down.

He took a sip from his mug and shook his head, avoiding her gaze. "There isn't anything to—"

"You're lying. If everything was fine you'd be with him tonight. Otherwise why did you ask me sit for Jamie?"

"Ugh, meddling woman. No wonder I'm gay."

"Stop trying to evade my questions."

"But they're annoying."

"Simon!" She laughed. "Talk. Now."

He smiled sadly at her and unfolded his legs to sit facing her across the table. He cast one more glance at Jamie to ensure he was preoccupied, and spoke in a low voice. "There are certain things about our individual lifestyles that just wouldn't mesh."

She frowned, but nodded. "Okay, I get that you think yours is Jamie, but what about him?"

"What do you mean, I *think* mine is Jamie?"

She rolled her eyes. "I understand, I truly do, about how protective you feel toward your son. You don't want to let anyone into your life that may change their minds and walk away a few years later."

"Right. It upset Jamie the last time that happened. I won't let it happen."

"Simon, he was three years old, and you were still a relatively new father. It disrupted your schedule and therefore his. As he gets older, he'll become—with the proper time and care—more self-reliant. Having Jamie does not mean you can't have a normal romantic relationship. I think what you're not admitting here is that you're as much afraid that this someone will walk away from you, as you are of them walking away from Jamie. Again."

He shook his head. "No, Sarah. It's just too much work. As it is my life is divided between Jamie and my writing. Being with someone means sacrificing some of that time where Jamie needs me."

She frowned heavily. "That's nonsense. The past several weeks have proven that. He's perfectly happy to be here with me for a couple nights a week." She reached over and touched his hand. "Taking time away from him—even just two hours—does not make you a bad father."

He looked at his hands as he rubbed them together. "No?" he asked quietly and knew that this was something else that had been bothering him without his even realizing it. He was so used to being the primary caregiver, that he felt bad for the time spent away from his son. He felt guilty for enjoying not being a father for a few hours, and for spending that time with Mattie.

"My God, you silly man," she laughed affectionately. "No, not at all, Simon. You've been at it full-on for four years without a day's rest, and you've done a wonderful job. Jamie is *happy*."

He looked over at Jamie, and he supposed that, yes, he was happy. They of course had their setbacks, but the two of them got by.

"So why don't you tell me what it is about his life that won't mesh with yours. I know it's not Jamie, because it sounds to me like he adores him."

He smiled reluctantly. "He does, actually. Even though he hasn't seen Jamie since then, he always considers him, asks about him, that sort of thing."

"Then it's him specifically. Is it… just not love?" she said quietly.

He swallowed. "No, I have feelings for him. We're just not very well suited."

"But *why*?"

He sighed heavily. "Well, he's seven years younger than me. He's only recently finished a reading and writing course at the central library for illiterate adults, so he's studying now for his GED so he can go away to school. In New York."

She frowned. "All right, I can see why you might be hesitant to start a relationship with someone who might be leaving soon, but I hope the fact that he doesn't have his GED isn't a factor for you. I mean, you would see how that might be hypocritical of you, right? It would be like someone assuming Jamie was stupid because he's autistic."

He shook his head. "It's not that. I'm actually quite proud of him for trying to get his GED. I'm just trying to give you a full picture, that's all."

She nodded. "All right, so it's the New York thing?"

He hesitated. "Partly, though... he doesn't really talk about that anymore. It's as if he's lost interest in the idea." He looked at her a moment and spoke quietly. "No judging, okay?"

"Simon, I haven't even met him. Why would I—"

"No, I know you won't judge him. You're too good a person to do that. I meant no judging me."

She nodded, looking confused. "All right."

"He's... um," he began in a hushed voice. "He's a prostitute."

Her eyes widened. "Simon, y-you're...?"

"*No!*" he was quick to answer, and checked again that Jamie was still off in his own little world. "No, it's... no money is exchanged between us. It's just a genuine sort of... friendship... thing."

"You don't sound very sure of that."

He sat back in his chair with a sigh and ran his hands through his hair. "I'm not. Sometimes I feel like he wants more, or thinks it's more, and that terrifies me. But then... sometimes it just feels so comfortable and *right*, but that's not what we agreed to in the first place, so...."

She held a hand out palm up. "All right, all right. I see why this is complicated. Why did you think I would judge you?"

He winced. "Because I'm starting to resent him for it." He was quick to carry on when seeing her disapproving frown. "I know it's unfair of me. He explained that it meant nothing to him, he does it out of necessity, and that it's '*water off a duck's back*' for him. What's more, I was the one who wanted to make it clear that it would remain casual between us. I mean, I *really* pressed that, Sarah."

"But now you have feelings for him and... oh boy."

"And now I'm jealous. I'm jealous but I don't want a commitment from him. How messed up is that?"

"I'll admit that seems a little unreasonable. Are you sure you don't want any kind of commitment?"

He shook his head immediately. "I'm not ready for that."

She bit her lip. "Where does he stand on all of this?"

He sighed. "I have no idea what he's thinking. It may be absolutely nothing to him, just a casual and regular hook up with a nice guy, or it could be a lot more."

"Oh, for—*men*, I tell you. Just *talk* to each other."

"And screw up what could be a great friendship with the added bonus of… uh, well."

She snorted. "I know where you're going. Don't worry."

"I think… I think I just need to play it by ear, try and feel him out."

She lifted one shoulder in a shrug. "Perhaps, as long as you don't feel like you're leading him on."

"I guess that's one of the things I need to figure out." He saw her worrying her lip, studying the mug in her hands. "What's wrong?"

"Simon, it's none of my business, but… you are safe, aren't you?"

He frowned for a moment, unsure of what it was she was referring to, then snorted with quiet laughter when figuring it out. "We are always perfectly safe, I assure you. And… well, the one time we talked about what he does sometimes, he told me that he only does… certain things, and is always, *always* safe."

"Do you know why…?"

"Why he does it?" His brows lifted sadly. "He earns minimum wage because he was illiterate. He's also an artist and paints quite a bit. He's just trying to get by. He doesn't really have anyone else to rely on."

"That's terrible, but kind of commendable, with how he's trying to turn it around."

He found himself smiling, feeling proud of Mattie. "Yes, it is, isn't it?"

She nodded, and they both looked to Jamie when he came toward them, picture held out.

"It's a boat."

"Wow." Simon smiled brightly, taking the picture. "This is even better than the last one."

"It's for Miss Protrakis."

Simon snorted and handed it over. "My mistake, Miss Protrakis."

Her eyes danced with mirth, and she gushed and made a show of pinning it up on her corkboard.

"I'll draw one for you too, Dad."

"Thank you, baby." They both held in their amusement as he tottered back into the living room. Simon turned back to Sarah when Jamie was once again engrossed in his drawing. "Well. Charming."

Sarah laughed. "What can I say. The kid adores me."

He lifted one shoulder and took a sip of his coffee. "And he likes it here. One more place we can go without having to plan ahead and visit first."

"Simon, I know I've mentioned this before, but what about your moth—"

"*No.*"

"I know what she did was terrible, Simon, but—"

"I said no, Sarah."

"But Jamie could really benefit from having more people in his life, especially fami—"

"Sarah, the answer is *no*."

She looked sad, but held a hand out, palm forward. "All right, I'm sorry."

He sighed. "You don't have to apologize, but you need to understand that the woman tried to take my son away from me."

She nodded, looking into her mug. "You're right. I'm sorry."

"Like I said, you—" He was interrupted by the vibrating of his cell phone. Out of habit he whipped it out quickly, forgetting that Jamie was actually with him, and then felt alarmed when realizing who it was calling. "It's him."

She waved at the phone quickly. "Well then answer it!"

"And say what?"

She frowned. "What do you mean? You say hello!"

"But what about everything we just talked about?"

"Didn't you say you were going to 'feel it out' with him?"

"True." He looked at the phone to hit "answer," but it went silent. He glanced up to see Sarah glaring at him comically. She pointed to the hallway.

"Go and call him back. I'll be with Jamie."

He smiled his thanks, walked into the hallway, and called him back. Within two rings Mattie answered, and just the sound of his voice felt comforting to him. He made the excuse of having been in a long meeting and then getting Jamie settled at Sarah's as a reason for not texting him back. And although it sounded feeble to even him, Mattie didn't question it or ask him about his sudden departure from the diner earlier that day.

"How was your day?" Simon asked in a soft voice. Mattie had that ability; he could talk him out of the worst of moods.

"It was a little slow, and I was worried about you, but I'm glad the meeting went well."

"Better than I thought it would, anyway."

"It's so great that they let you renegotiate your contract, or whatever."

Simon frowned. "I hadn't mentioned that yet." Had he? No, he was pretty sure he hadn't, and there was an uncomfortable silence coming from the other end of the phone. "Mattie?"

"N-no, you didn't. Um. I was… that is, Andrew might have mentioned something, just in passing—"

"Andrew?" His eyes widened. "Andrew, my *editor,* Andrew? You were... *God.*" He felt sick, and suddenly his talk with Sarah seemed not only ridiculous but laughable. "He was your 'other plans'? You were with *him*?" He couldn't help it; the disgust dripped from his every word.

"Simon, listen, it wasn't what you're thinking—"

"So you didn't go down on him for money?" Even *he* winced at that, and heard the intake of breath from Mattie. "I...." he sighed, "I didn't mean to say that."

There was a shuddering breath across the line and then a quiet "I think you did."

"No, Mattie—" He softened.

"I think I actually fucking disgust you, but you like an easy lay."

"Jesus, Mattie, no."

"For your information, I didn't do anything. He offered me two hundred dollars for nothing, and I still turned it down because even a whore has some pride, you know?"

"Please don't call yourself that. I'm sorry—"

"I didn't do anything with him because of you. I'm fucking broke and can't pay my rent, but I turned down free cash because it felt disrespectful to you." He took another shuddering breath. "Fuck you, Simon."

The line went dead.

Simon let out a quiet curse and resisted the urge to bang his head against the wall. Where exactly did that leave them? And what the hell did this mean? What did they mean to *each other*? He had no clue, but what he knew for damn sure was that Mattie had not deserved to be spoken to like that. He walked back through to the living room, and his face must have been a picture, because Sarah was already standing from where she had been crouched by Jamie, and was giving him that familiar "men are useless" look.

"Tell Jamie you'll be back soon, and then go fix whatever the hell just happened."

HE'D spent about ten minutes with his head in his hands, warning himself to not shed one goddamn tear, and then he'd pulled out his sketchbook. Usually he'd head for the paints, but of course, he was completely out of supplies and didn't have the cash to buy anything new. So now he lay back, propped up with a cushion behind his back, and sketched furiously in a bid to unwind the coil inside that was choking the life out of him. He was so disappointed he could scream.

When he heard his buzzer, he deliberated on just ignoring it. He didn't want to talk to anyone. But then he thought that it might be his elderly neighbor, Mrs. Tiller, who was constantly locking herself out, and his conscience demanded he get up and answer it.

"Hello?"

"It's me."

Mattie blinked in surprise; he'd honestly thought that he'd had his last conversation with Simon. He certainly hadn't expected him to turn up at his apartment, at any rate.

"Mattie?"

"Um. I'm here."

"Can I please come in?"

Mattie bit his lip. His pride wanted him to say no, but the part of him that was crazy for Simon wanted to beg him to come up. He settled for saying nothing and buzzed him in. He left the door open a crack and sat himself on the sofa, waiting.

When Simon came in, he hesitated by the door a moment before closing it behind him. He made his way over to the sofa, not saying a word, and eventually sat himself sideways next to Mattie and touched his knee. "Mattie, I'm so sorry for my actions today. I'm sorry for leaving the diner without a word, I'm sorry for ignoring your text, and I'm sorry for the appalling way I spoke to you on the phone."

"I thought we understood one another, Simon. I thought you understood that I don't like what I do sometimes, but that it doesn't define me either."

"I do, I...." He swallowed a little pride and forced himself to expose some of his true feelings on the matter. "I know that we agreed to slow and easy. I know that, and quite frankly I need that. I can't deal with anything else. But today I just... I got jealous, and it made me cruel."

Mattie felt delighted at the revelation, but was reluctant to allow Simon to see any of these emotions. Instead, he hedged for further information. He licked his lips nervously. "You were jealous?"

"At the idea of you being with someone else, yes. But I do understand, and please don't feel that I think less of you for it."

"So... so what does this mean for us?" Mattie held his breath.

"I suppose... I know that I want to keep seeing you, but I also know I still need to keep it slow and easy between us, f-for now."

Initially, Mattie felt let down. The words "slow and casual" were too broad, too intangible, and would only confuse matters further. He wanted clarification but didn't want to push too far. But "for now?" He could work with that. There was hope there, and he supposed he could be patient.

"What do you think?" Simon asked, looking worried.

"It's okay if you get jealous, but don't make me feel that way again, all right?" he whispered.

"Mattie...." He shook his head. "I've come to more or less think of you as my closest friend, and I promise you I will endeavor to always treat you with the respect you deserve."

Mattie allowed a small smile. "You're always so wordy." He looked him up and down. "And you look really handsome in that suit."

"Does that mean...." Simon smiled, looking a little nervous.

Mattie found it charming. "It means you should kiss me." He spoke quietly.

A look of relief crossed Simon's face, and he immediately leaned close to take Mattie's face gently between his hands to kiss him softly. He murmured one more quiet "I'm sorry" against his lips, and Mattie pulled away, took his hand, and wordlessly pulled him toward the bedroom.

WITH Mattie's flesh under his hands and lips, Simon suddenly felt overwhelmed with gratitude for being forgiven for his actions. He followed Mattie into the bedroom and quickly divested Mattie of all clothing, finding himself in a more dominant mood that evening, and wasted no time in slinking down Mattie's flat, toned stomach to below his waistline.

It had been an unspoken rule between them that oral was something they would not bring into the bedroom for obvious reasons. Simon didn't want Mattie to be reminded of anything unpleasant, and he suspected that Mattie didn't want him to be thinking of those things when being intimate together. But tonight Simon just wanted to please; he wanted to pleasure. It had been too long since he'd done this, since he'd felt that exhilarating power of making someone else feel *that* good, and he wanted Mattie that way. He wanted Mattie desperate for him.

It didn't take long. Within minutes Mattie was panting and begging him to stop. His chest was slick with sweat, rising and falling rapidly. He looked almost lost in a haze of pleasure, those beautiful hazel eyes looking at him for direction. Simon knew exactly what Mattie wanted, and with a quick rummage in the bedside drawer, he wasted no time in giving it to him.

He could tell almost immediately that it had been a long time since Mattie had bottomed for anyone. In fact they'd discussed their respective lack of boyfriends previously, but it was never more evident than when Simon was sliding home through the slick, hot, *tight* glove that had him squeezing his eyes shut in an effort to stave off his approaching orgasm.

Mattie's harsh breath and intense gaze was fodder enough, but when he desperately pulled Simon down to him, hitching his legs higher over his hips, countering every thrust and looking at him with those desperate, helpless hazel eyes, Simon was just about done in.

"Mattie, oh my… *nugh.*" He found himself thrusting madly and without rhythm as that familiar rolling sensation began at the bottom of his spine, spreading through his pelvis. "*Mattie!*"

Just before the peak, he felt a spreading of warmth bloom between them, and it was Mattie's inarticulate cry of pleasure that sent him over. He growled out an expletive that was meant to be Mattie's name, tensing and clenching all over before collapsing over Mattie with an almost pained sigh of relief.

Christ, he had needed that. He had needed to take charge and show Mattie just what it was he did to him, and he had a feeling, as Mattie's hands travelled lazily over his back, that Mattie had needed it too.

He didn't know where this relationship was headed, or if indeed it was a relationship they had, but what he did know for sure was that Mattie had become a part of his life, and he needed him.

Chapter
Six

"HEY, you."

Simon looked up from his laptop, having been for the first time in months thoroughly engrossed in attempting to brainstorm and lay out a skeleton of a manuscript. Mattie was distraction enough, however. Something had shifted between them. It was subtle, but they had—despite all odds—laid down the foundation of a genuine friendship and the beginnings of something perhaps more meaningful. Mattie was happier; that much was obvious. He always seemed to light up when Simon entered the room, which was humbling in itself, but there was also no denying that his day improved tenfold in the younger man's presence.

"Hey, yourself. Are you on lunch?"

"Yup, do you want a few more minutes to finish where you were?"

Appreciating the offer, he nodded and rounded up the notes he was working on, glancing over his laptop as Mattie blew on his cup of soup. He grinned to himself; just about everything this man did lately turned him on. The shift in their relationship—he was admitting to himself that, yes, they had some sort of casual relationship—had come from his playing a more dominant role in the bedroom. For some reason, to begin with he had decided to merely follow Mattie's lead, perhaps still stunned that a guy like Mattie was so attracted to him in the first place. Now that they'd had their small fight, and Simon had finally admitted to himself that he wanted Mattie, he had turned a corner of sorts and returned to what felt more natural to him in bed. And while he never said no when Mattie decided to take charge for an evening—those were some of the more spectacular evenings that came to mind—he felt more himself playing the instigator and the more dominant of the two.

"You're asking for it." He grinned.

Mattie looked up, innocent and oblivious. "Huh?"

"Blowing on your soup like that."

Mattie snorted and shook his head, going back to his soup, but Simon could tell he was pleased. "I mean it. Here I am trying to work, and you come over being all sexy with your tomato and basil soup."

Mattie laughed quietly. "Stop being cute."

He shrugged one shoulder. "Stop being all sexy, and I'll stop being cute."

It was ridiculous, really. They'd been seeing each other for a few months now, and had only just hit that honeymoon period where the flirting was second nature and the texting at night was downright dirty. He felt as if he were back in his twenties. He was beginning to remember his old self before he became a father, but instead of reminiscing on this, he felt as if he were now a pleasant mixture of his past and present. He felt a small part himself, that had been the carefree Simon with the world at his feet, meshed with the stay-at-home dad in him. And thinking about it, that was exactly the person he wanted to be, because even though he missed how his life had been before Jamie, he realized that he didn't want to give up who he was now. That had a lot to do with the person sitting opposite him, throwing him shy glances over his cup of soup.

"Anyhoozles, how's the writing going?" Mattie frowned slightly and reached a hand across the table to where his satchel lay open and pulled out the small plastic wrapper that had caught his eye.

Simon watched, taking a moment to save the document he had open. "It's going really well, actually. I thought it would be absolute hell to begin with, but I've got the hunger back, and the ideas are just flowing. I've missed this feeling."

"That is so great." Mattie held up the packet with the end twisted shut and lifted his brows in question as he took another sip of his soup. "I didn't know you had a sweet tooth."

"I don't. Jamie got it into his head that he wanted gummy bears for breakfast." He shrugged guiltily. "Not exactly healthy, I know, but I was helpless against those big brown eyes, so...."

Mattie laughed quietly. "You big softy."

He shrugged. "I was just kind of thrilled that he wanted something other than Lucky Charms for once."

He took the packet from Mattie. It was still half-full. "I guess he changed his mind." He smiled softly. "Jamie has this habit of putting empty wrappers, juice boxes—anything he doesn't want or is done with—in my briefcase or bag. I'm not sure why."

"Cute kid just keeps getting cuter." Mattie shook his head.

Simon decided he liked hearing how fond Mattie sounded of Jamie, despite their limited introduction quite a while ago. He popped a gummy bear in his mouth and then held the packet open toward Mattie in invitation.

Mattie shook his head no, and then nodded toward Simon's laptop. "I think I'm proud of you."

"You think?"

He nodded and hunched his shoulders as he rested both elbows on the table and took another sip of his soup. He seemed to almost regret his comment.

"I know you don't need me being all proud of you, or whatever, but uh—I am anyway. It takes balls to move away from what's familiar and safe—trying something new."

He didn't quite understand the remark, but it pleased him nonetheless. "Thank you. You know, I was up until three last night. I just pictured this scene in my head and had to get it down before I forgot it. I'm honestly beginning to feel like the writer I used to be."

"I can't wait to read it."

He'd promised Mattie that, once he had a small portion written, he'd be the first to read it. "Are you still plugging away through my other novel?"

Mattie hadn't mentioned he'd been reading his other novel until Simon had spotted it one night on his bedside stand. And it wasn't that he was eager for praise, but Mattie's opinion meant a great deal to him, and he was proud of him for keeping up with the reading and writing exercises. He grinned when Mattie's eyes widened and he rushed to put his mug down.

"I just got to the part where the mechanic is hallucinating about seeing the woman he buried in the—"

Simon interrupted him with a held up finger. "Ah, but *is* he hallucinating?"

"Oh, man, it sucks that I'm not a faster reader, you know?"

"You'll get there."

He took another sip from his mug. "If you weren't so wordy, maybe," Mattie muttered with a small grin.

"Writers are supposed to be 'wordy'," he laughed softly. "Otherwise I wouldn't have a job."

"Kind of like an artist without any paint," Mattie groused.

There was that uncomfortable feeling again. It always reared its ugly head when the subject of money came up. It rarely did, and he thought that perhaps it was only him who felt this way. He'd promised Mattie that he didn't think any less of him for what he occasionally resorted to for extra cash, but that didn't stop him from feeling jealous.

He'd offered *once*, choking out the uncomfortable words, to lend him some money, but Mattie had turned that down flat, and he hadn't dared mention it since. They spent three nights a week together and more or less saw each other all day at the diner, but on the nights they didn't see each other, he couldn't help but wonder what it was Mattie was doing and with whom.

It was pointless getting himself worked up about it, though. He'd still insisted that they take it slow and keep it casual. It felt hypocritical of him to demand Mattie stop what he claimed did not disgust him, when he wasn't ready to offer Mattie a commitment in return, no matter how basic. So he chose to assume that on the nights they didn't see each other, Mattie spent studying with Ty.

There was one small indication that the hooking had stopped, however, in that it appeared Mattie had—for now—ceased painting due to his lack of funds. He didn't necessarily think that was a good thing (he was trying to get into art school, wasn't he?), but the hooking was a way of helping with the rent and paying for his art supplies, or so he'd come to understand. So surely if he wasn't painting, then….

"Man, you can't stop that brain of yours from ticking away even for a minute, can you?" Mattie smiled, bringing him out of his daydreams.

"Hmm? Oh, no. Apparently not."

Mattie reached over and squeezed his hand. "It's okay if you want to keep working. I'll just grab a paper, or something."

That was another reading exercise he praised Mattie for, but he shook his head. "No, it's all right. I just got distracted for a second."

Mattie raised one sneaky looking eyebrow. "Oh yeah, thinking about what?"

He could play this game. "Oh, just a certain telephone call that gave me sweet dreams the other night."

Mattie smirked, playing it cool, but there was a telltale flush creeping up his neck. "Those damn telemarketers again?"

"Yeah. They're becoming a real pain in the ass too. Like this one I had the other night, he wanted to know what I was wearing," he droned, "if I was hard for him, if I was imagining riding him until—" He laughed and handed Mattie a napkin when he spluttered soup.

"Damn, those guys are really getting out of control. No wonder you were distracted."

That's what Simon wanted to see: Mattie's cheeks a nice rosy pink. The phone sex *had* been getting a little heated lately. It wasn't as if they did it every night. Sometimes they'd just talk for a few hours, but the fact that they couldn't spend the night together was wearing a little thin. So... when needs must, and all that.

"Do you have a study date with Ty tonight?"

Mattie nodded. "Yeah, he picked up all these study guides, bless him. There's actually an adult basic education program available and GED preparation classes I could take, but I just can't pay for any other courses, and it's only a few weeks until test day, so I'm cramming like a madman."

"How's it going?"

Mattie shrugged one shoulder, pushing his empty mug to one side and wiping his mouth with a napkin. "Not bad. Once I got used to the idea of actually studying, it stopped feeling so weird. Like... I'm picking up where I left off as a kid." He shook his head. "It's strange, and *tough*, but I don't know... makes me feel a little more human, somehow."

Christ. What does a guy say to that?

"I'm struggling in some parts, but surprising myself in others. I'm not bad at math, actually."

"So... wait, what are the areas you have to cover, again?"

Mattie ticked them off on his fingers. "Language arts, reading and writing, math, social studies, and science. I'm struggling with science and social studies, and I'm *so* glad half of it is multiple choice. It's the essay writing portion that's really gonna kick my ass."

"Do you...." He bit his lip, again hesitant to broach the subject of money. "Do you have the entrance fee covered?"

Mattie nodded and glanced away. "Ty spotted me sixty dollars. I just hope I don't have to pay to retake any parts."

"And it's at one of the high schools here in San Diego?"

"San Diego Union High School, yeah. I think there's a way to do it all online, but I'd probably screw that up. I'm no good with computers." He shook his head. "It's gonna feel so freaking weird walking into a school after so many years." He chewed the inside of his cheek. "Just makes me wonder... if I hadn't quit, where would I be now? Who would I be?"

Simon cleared his throat. Most serious things Mattie said were difficult to take in. He felt foolish when those brief insights threw a light on how much depth lay just beneath that nice guy smile and happy exterior. "You'd still be a great guy, I think." He smiled. "Perhaps working in a gallery somewhere."

Mattie smiled sadly, as if his thoughts were far away. "Maybe," he murmured quietly. He glanced up and leveled a soft look at Simon that practically projected his thoughts.

But then I wouldn't have met you.

Simon glanced away, not quite uncomfortable but nonetheless uncertain as to how to deal with the unspoken but coherent words.

Letting him off the hook, Mattie took a deep breath and let it out with a sigh. He ran his hand through his hair. "Going back to school, man. Lockers, teachers, chalk boards…."

"Well, you're going to have to do that with New York sooner or later," he pointed out, feeling the bitter pill sliding down his throat at the thought of Mattie doing so well, but then moving away.

Mattie became quiet, giving nothing but a noncommittal "umhm."

He carried on in an effort to see that smile again. "So… five tests. Are you doing that in one sitting or…?"

"Ugh, I don't know. It's an option, and part of me wants to just get it all out of the way, but I'm worried I might burn out and bomb the second half. I'll probably do it over two days."

Simon smiled gently. "You've come really far."

A proud grin tugged at Mattie's lips. "Maybe, still a long way to go, though."

"How long do you have to wait for the results?"

"It'll take three or so weeks to get the transcripts. So I'll be an *iddy* bit tense."

"I'll see what I can do to keep you occupied." He winked. *Winking? You never wink.*

"What did you have in mind?" Mattie grinned.

He was just about to suggest a few ideas when he felt his cell vibrate. He reached into his pocket and immediately flipped it open when recognizing the school's number. He had another two hours before he was supposed to pick Jamie up, so something must be wrong. "Hello, Simon Cas—Sarah? What's going on, is everything... *what*?"

In a panic, he began to gather his things: his wallet, his keys. He closed his laptop and was grateful when Mattie—who had quickly gathered that something was wrong—was already holding open his bag for him to slide his laptop inside while he finished up the call to Sarah. "I'll be right there. *No*, no, please just, can you keep him with you? And keep her away from him. I'll be right there." He stood and slung the strap of his bag over his head.

"Is Jamie okay?" Mattie asked, looking worried.

"He will be. He's just a little upset." He walked toward the entrance of the diner, Mattie following him. He gritted his teeth. "My *mother* just tried to take him out of school."

"*Oh*." Mattie's hand touched his shoulder, knowing how Simon felt about his mother and the history there where Jamie was concerned. "Call me later, okay?"

Without even thinking about it, he put his arm around Mattie's waist and kissed him quick on the lips. "I will. I've gotta go."

"Go on," Mattie urged with a gentle push to his arm.

HE RUSHED up to the reception desk, panting from his quick dash to the school. "I'm Simon Castle; there's been an incident with my son, Jamie?"

"Mr. Castle?"

He turned quickly to see a familiar-looking man. He searched his memory bank and remembered him from his last visit. Adam. "Yes, yes that's me. My son? Where is he?"

"Follow me. He's with Sarah. The two of you know each other very well?"

"Yes, Sarah babysits for me on occasion. She's a good friend. Can you tell me what happened?"

"I believe Sarah knows the details. They're just through here."

He was led into a quiet room that was anything but quiet, and the scene that greeted him made his heart sink. Sarah knelt in front of Jamie, giving him his distance but speaking soothingly to him to try and calm him down. But Jamie was past that point. He was past the point of humming or reciting his numbers. He was sitting on a small couch, either thumping himself in his knees with his little balled up fists, or slapping the sides of his head and ears as he sobbed his heart out. Sarah spotted Simon and tried to tell Jamie that his daddy was there, but Jamie was already following his instincts and was trying to lie on the couch in an attempt to roll back and forth.

It was at times like this where he had to make a judgment call. If merely distressed but not at the point of having a full-blown fit, it was usually best to leave Jamie to calm himself down. Trying to touch him at that point would only escalate his anxiety. However, if Jamie were already in a full panic, then he needed pressure against his body. The pressure against his back and front would slow his heart rate and allow him to gradually calm down.

There was no doubt in his mind what to do, and though initially it would frighten Jamie further, he strode forward, and Sarah automatically moved out of the way, knowing what he was going to do and closing the door to give them privacy. He did the only thing he could at that moment, and pulled Jamie off of the couch and into his arms. Jamie's cries instantly grew into a wail that tore his heart right open, but he held the full length of him against his chest, wrapping his arms tight around him and making soft shushing noises.

Eventually Jamie's legs stopped kicking against him, and he rested his cheek underneath Simon's chin and against his chest as his loud screaming became nothing more than an unhappy and downright woeful cry of a little boy who had been frightened terribly.

"Shh, we're all better. That's my good boy. Daddy's here now, hey?" Eventually he was able to turn Jamie sideways and sit with him on his lap. He rubbed his back and rocked him gently. He looked over at Sarah, and even she looked harried from the experience and as if she might want to cry herself. "Are you all right?" he asked her.

She waved him off and sat across from him. "Don't worry about me. I'm fine. It's just, no matter how used to it you get, it's still difficult to watch a child become that upset when you're powerless to help them, you know?"

"Oh, I know, all right." He nodded over to the table beside Sarah with a box of tissue on top. "Can you pass me a couple of those?"

She handed over the box, and he pulled a tissue out and craned his neck back to get a look at Jamie's face. "Let me see, baby."

Jamie looked up, and Simon swallowed hard around the lump in his throat when seeing his small face, red and blotchy from his crying. "That's it, good boy." He wiped at his damp cheeks and then grabbed another tissue to hold over his nose. "Give a big old blow now."

Exhausted from his upset, Jamie did as he was told and blew as hard as he could, which wasn't much. Still, Simon wiped his nose clean and kissed his forehead gently. "We're going to have a little sit here, okay? Then we're going to go home, maybe play with Gizmo, or do some coloring and drawing. Does that sound good?" Simon gave him a gentle bounce and was relieved to see him nod and then rest his head back against his chest.

Once he knew that Jamie was settled and that he himself felt calm enough, he turned to Sarah. "All right, start to finish, what happened?"

She let out a heavy sigh, her shoulders slumping. "I left him on the bench to go check on one of the other kids. He was perfectly fine eating his lunch. Next thing I know, I turn around to check on him and there's a woman sitting beside him that I didn't recognize. I immediately headed back, but before I could ask who she was, she tried to hug him and...." She trailed off with an upturned palm. "It was zero to sixty. She frightened him quite badly, I'm afraid."

"Well, no wonder. *God*," he bit off furiously. "She knows he's autistic. Why the hell would she do something so *stupid*?"

"I don't know, but… Simon, I had no choice but to pick him up. The other kids were getting scared. I had to pick him up and carry him in here. I think that's what really set him off."

"It's all right," he reassured her. "You did the right thing. Did she leave?"

"No. She saw her mistake right away, Simon. She explained who she was, and she's been apologizing ever since. She didn't want to leave. I think she wants to see you—"

"Not a chance." He stood, pulling his bag strap over one shoulder.

"Simon, please, she's your mother. I know she—"

"We've talked about this before, Sarah. And right now I don't want Jamie to see her. It might set him off again."

"I understand that, but can I at least give her a message?"

"Yeah, you can tell that if she pulls a stunt like that again I'm calling the cops."

"Simon, *please*."

"*What?*" he snapped and then closed his eyes in frustration and gently cupped the back of Jamie's head when he began to hum. He needed to calm down; otherwise Jamie would pick up on his mood and the whole upsetting ordeal would start over. "I'm sorry, Sarah," he began again, more calmly this time. "But I don't think you fully understand the relationship I have with my mother."

"You've explained the situation to me. I get that she let you down when you were younger," she said softly. "And I understand that you haven't forgiven her for trying to take you to court, and *today* probably hasn't helped much either, but she's asking to speak to you. Now I know she's gone the wrong way about it, but couldn't this be her backward version of an olive branch?"

"Sounds to me like she was trying to snatch him."

She shook her head. "I really don't think that, Simon. She said she just wanted to see him, that's all. She absolutely did it the wrong way, but honestly? She just looks like a lonely old lady."

Simon sighed. Damn it. "There's a lot of bad blood between us, Sarah. I don't know if it can ever be right between us again."

"What about Jamie?"

"I'm trying to *protect* Jamie."

"I know this isn't my business, and that I'm taking liberties here, but it sounds to me like you're trying to protect yourself."

"That is *not* the case."

"So what if you never see eye to eye with her again? Is your relationship with her to mean Jamie doesn't get to have a grandparent, just like most other kids?"

"That's not fair, Sarah."

"No, it's not. But Jamie's entire family is *you*. He trusts only two people, and they are standing in this room. There is no downfall for him here; he would only gain. He could let another person into his life, and he could have a female influence around that isn't his teacher."

"We do just fine by ourselves, Sarah. He doesn't need a female influence."

"You're right; you are a fantastic father, but what if I suddenly get a job elsewhere? What if I move or get married and can't sit for you anymore? Then it's back to just you in his life. *One person*, Simon. What if, God forbid, something happened to you? What would happen to him then?"

He closed his eyes tight, gently swaying Jamie in his arms. She had a good point. It was just difficult to imagine putting aside the anger he felt toward his mother, especially after today. "Fine," he said in a low voice. "But I don't want to see her now. I don't want Jamie around when I speak to her."

She nodded quickly. "I'll come by around six tonight to pick him up."

"All right, can you get the door please?"

She walked him out and through the gates of the school, away and in the opposite direction from where his mother was apparently sitting in the school's reception waiting area, wondering if she were about to be arrested or see her son for the first time in nearly a year.

"Simon?" Sarah said gently. "You know that you have my support, don't you? You know I'm on your side? I'm just thinking of Jamie here."

He leaned close and kissed her cheek. "I know, and I'd be lost if I didn't have you to push me in the right direction every now and then."

"Good. I'll tell her to come by your place around six thirty."

Simon nodded, and watched as she turned to walk back through the gates. "Sarah?" he called, and she turned back. His brow creased with worry. "You're not really moving away, are you?"

She smiled. "No, you foolish man."

"OKAY...." Ty began. "So in the fourth stanza, what does the dark line cutting through the snow represent?"

"Give me the choices."

"Come on, Mattie," Ty groaned, frustrated. "Get with it. Just try to think it through first."

"It's a multiple choice test!"

"So what? Try and learn it this way. Then when you're taking the test, hopefully you might be thinking of an answer automatically before reading the choices."

"It's taking a hell of a lot longer this way, and I've got a lot of material to go through."

"You've only got so long to *do* the fucking test. I'm trying to get you to think for yourself, to give you a better chance!"

"I'd have a better chance if we could get through the rest of these textbooks!" He closed the cover of the literature textbook and shoved it forward, across the table.

"No, you'd have a better chance if you'd stop daydreaming about your fucking boyfriend and listen to me!"

"Why are we yelling at each other?"

"I don't fucking know!"

Mattie fought to not smile. "Do you want some coffee?"

"Please!" Ty threw the study guide onto the kitchen table and leaned back in his chair with a groan, running his hands through his hair. "On a serious note, Mattie, you need to get your head out of the clouds. You've been distracted all afternoon."

Mattie glanced back over his shoulder as he poured the coffee and quickly looked away again. "I'm just worried about him."

"He called you to tell you the kid was fine."

"I know, but the thing with his mom…."

"Oh Christ, he's a grown man, Mattie. You've got more important shit to be thinking about."

Mattie stopped himself from cussing out his best friend, but Ty's attitude toward Simon was beginning to piss him off. "You don't understand. You don't know how his mother is."

"Oh please, and you do?"

He paused before setting the mug down in front of Ty, surprised at the very transparent dislike he could hear in his buddy's voice. "Yeah, I do."

"Oh, so he's introduced you to her?"

He rolled his eyes. "Yeah, Ty. He's introduced his boyfriend to his homophobic mother. In fact, I had her over for tea and cookies just the other day."

"What about his friends, this Sarah person. Does she know you exist?"

"Oh, fuck off, Ty." He sat heavily in his chair.

Ty raised his eyebrow sarcastically and reached for his mug to take a sip. "I'll take that as a no. What about his kid?"

"Why are you being such an ass?" *Please don't burst my bubble.*

"Have you even been over to his house, or do you just hang out here?" *Where no one can see you together.* The words were unspoken, but hung in the air between them nonetheless.

He didn't want to have this conversation. He and Simon were at a good place. He didn't want that spoiled by anyone. "We hang out at the diner." It was a feeble comeback, and he knew it.

Ty just sighed and looked down into his mug. "I'm not trying to be a dick here, honest, but I am not going to let some guy who you're all hot and bothered over fuck up your—"

"Will you give me some credit? *Jesus*."

Ty blinked in surprise. "What?"

"It's a lot more serious than that, all right?"

Ty frowned and then looked down into his mug. "That's what's getting to me here, Mattie."

"What are you *talking* about?"

"You're on cloud fucking nine, and he's—" He glanced away a moment, looking guilty. "—and he's not, all right? I'm sorry to say that, but—"

Stunned for a second, Mattie all but burst out of his chair. "That is *not* true, and do you get what a horrible fucking thing that is to say?"

Ty's voice became soft, which just made it worse. "I'm sorry, Mattie, but I don't think he's worth the effort. You should be treated better. You should want *more*."

"He treats me just fine, thank you."

Ty held his hands palms up. "Okay, okay. I mean… I guess I don't know what you're like in private together, so…."

"We're boyfriends in private. If he's reserved at the diner, it's because he's working and so am I."

Ty hunched his shoulders, his hands up again in defense. "*Okay*, God. I'm sorry, all right? It's just… I want so much for you to do well, and you're just distracted and fucking it up. You are so fucking close, Mattie. You can do this. You're smart. You can get your GED. You could even make it to New York… but only if you make every effort. And just recently… well, it's like you don't even care anymore."

Mattie swallowed, turning sideways in his chair to look away from Ty and rest his elbow on the table, his hand running over the back of his head. He bit his lip. "Maybe my goals have changed a bit."

Ty rolled his eyes and stood, shoving the kitchen chair with its torn seat cover roughly under the small table. "I fucking knew it." He stalked into the living room and all but threw himself onto the couch, his head back as he rubbed his hands over his face.

Mattie stood hesitantly, hovering in between the two connected rooms. He rubbed at his left elbow absently. "I still want my GED, Ty, but… I don't want to go now. I've got something better waiting for me here."

"No." Ty shook his head.

"Ty—"

"*No*, Mattie. Do you hear me? I said no!"

Mattie sighed and sat next to Ty, who was unwilling to meet his gaze. "My mind's already made up. I'm still going to get my GED, okay? But I want to be a part of his life more than I want New York."

"That's unacceptable, Mattie."

"Look, I appreciate that you—"

"You've had a shit life, Mattie," Ty interrupted, meeting his gaze straight on. "You are such a good guy, one of the best, all right? And I hate the thought of you not getting—not even *trying* for everything you deserve, because that's only going to happen in New York. It was a big goal for a reason…. It's a big goal because you're meant for big things."

Touched, Mattie could only stare at his friend. Ty rolled his eyes again and shoved at Mattie's shoulder playfully.

"Come on," he groused. "Don't look at me like that. Anybody'd think you didn't know how much I care about you. And yes, I'm aware of how gay that sounded."

Mattie let out a breath of a laugh and then swallowed. Ty was the first person who had really cared about him on such a genuine, personal level. No mother, a dead father who hadn't noticed him during life, and a high school dropout with nothing going for him but a pretty face…

he'd been alone. But he had one good friend who wanted to see him do well and who wanted good things for him.

"Look…," Ty began softly. "I know you had this huge crush on him and that the past few months have been good for you, but…." He trailed off, looking away.

"What?"

Ty shook his head sadly.

"No. Say it. I'm giving you permission right now to say anything, no matter how blunt, as long as it's honest."

Ty looked at him. Took a breath. "Are you sure he's not ashamed of you?"

Goddamn, the coil was back and wanted to kill him. "Ty…," he choked out, and Ty screwed his eyes shut for a second.

"I know, and I'm sorry. I only ask because, if I'm supposed to let you give up on what has been a lifeline for you—this dream of art school and New York—then I gotta know that he'd be worth it. It doesn't seem like it, but I'm trying to be a good friend here."

"I know," he said softly. "What… what is it you see when you look at the two of us together? What is it you see that makes you think he's ashamed of me?"

Ty winced. "I do genuinely see someone who is crazy about you. It's not like I think he treats you like crap or anything, but…."

"Then what?"

"It's just… *shit*," he sighed. "You look like you're in love. And he does look like he cares about you. I'm not saying he doesn't…."

Mattie nodded, encouraging him. "But…?"

"But I don't think you're at the top of his list of priorities."

Mattie felt a wash of relief. He even smiled. "Well, of course not. Ty, Jamie will always be—"

"No." Ty winced again, shaking his head. "No, it's more than his kid. I do get what you were saying about him having to integrate people into the kid's life slowly and all, but… I don't know."

"Well, figure it out!"

"You've never even been to his house or met any of his friends—
"

"He doesn't have any!"

"He's never going to introduce you to his kid," he continued.

Mattie blanched. "You've got no idea what you're talking about, Ty. Jamie's situation is so much more delicate than—"

"When's the last time he brought the kid to the diner, huh? Isn't it a coincidence that you guys start dating and then suddenly he doesn't bring Jamie there anymore?"

Mattie looked away. "He has a sitter so he can write and spend time with me alone." He swallowed hard when feeling Ty's hand on his shoulder.

"I am so, *so* sorry to say this nasty shit to you. I know how you feel about him, and it's not like I even think he's a bad guy, but you have got to ask for more if you're really considering giving up New York for him. I mean, does he even know that you want to stay? Does he have the first clue?"

Mattie sighed. "No, but it's… it's this time scale thing. We have to go slow. It has to be easy and gentle for now. But that's okay." He nodded earnestly at Ty. "It's okay because we're headed in the right direction." He glanced away. "And if I have to miss that time slot—that window to get to New York—on the off chance that we could be a family a year down the line… then I think it's worth it."

"Crap," Ty whispered.

"There are art schools here in San Diego."

Ty shook his head. "I know there are other schools. Shit, you think I want my best buddy to leave town? Hell no. It's the meaning it has behind it. All those times you'd tell me about 'when you got to New York'. And then that one New Year's in that basement, the one you keep going back to, all alone, watching the ball drop? You said New York seemed like a new beginning, and you know what? You were totally right. Why else would I be here going over these fucking textbooks with you?"

Mattie smiled sadly. "Simon could be that new beginning, Ty. I haven't let go of the dream. It's just changed shape, that's all." He waited for Ty to say something. Anything. And when he didn't he nudged him in the arm. "I promise you that I am going to get that GED."

"Make me a different promise. Promise me that after you get your GED—and you will—you'll still apply to this school anyway." Seeing Mattie about to interrupt him, he spoke over him. "*That* way, at least in a couple months down the line and, worst case scenario, it hasn't worked out between you two, you can still have New York to fall back on."

Mattie bit his lip. "And if Simon and I are still going strong?"

"Then I will shut the fuck up and genuinely be happy for you. Boy Scouts honor."

Mattie snorted. "You were never in the Boy Scouts."

"No, but for credibility's sake…."

"You're a good buddy. That's all the credibility you need."

"You know that I have no personal vendetta against him or anything, right?"

Mattie slapped his knee. "And here I thought you were secretly in love with me."

"Oh, fuck off." Ty blanched, and then laughed anyway.

Mattie laughed quietly, feeling unsettled by their conversation but oddly satisfied with the compromise they had agreed upon.

"Can, um… can I ask something?"

"What?" he asked cautiously, put off by the hesitant note in Ty's voice.

"He… he knows, right?"

Mattie knew immediately what Ty meant, and felt the familiar uncomfortable, shame fuelled heat rush up his neck. He nodded, looking away. "He knows."

"And he's all right with it?"

Mattie lifted one shoulder. "He's… accepting. He gets a little jealous sometimes, but it's not like I'm… I haven't even, um…."

Ty lifted an eyebrow in surprise. "You've stopped?"

"No. Well, yes. I mean not officially, or even intentionally. I just haven't since Simon and me… not since we started to get a little more serious." He trailed off with an embarrassed laugh.

Ty snorted. "You're getting shy? Wow."

"Yeah, well… that's how it is." He felt something twist in his stomach, knowing that he had actually planned on regretfully breaking his dry spell later that evening when Ty left. No paints were one thing; no groceries were another.

Ty looked around the sparse living room. "I did notice that you don't have any paints lying around." He frowned. "I don't know if that's a good or bad thing."

"Bit of both, I guess."

"What about thumper over there?" He nodded over to the open rabbit cage in the corner. "He pulling his weight?"

Mattie laughed. "No. Little asshole."

Ty grinned for a moment, and then a note of seriousness crept back into his voice. "You're doing okay, yeah?"

"I'm getting by. Who needs to eat every day, anyway?"

"*Mattie*," he groaned, reaching into his back pocket for his wallet. "You know you can ask—"

"No," he snapped, frowning. "No. I already owe you sixty for the exam entrance fees. I told you, I'm getting by."

"Ten bucks is hardly—"

"Ty, come on. You're not exactly made of money yourself, are you?"

"*Ahh*, but I have the winning ticket right here." He pulled a card out of his wallet and held it up, smug as anything.

"Oh, for fuck sake," he snorted. "You shouldn't be lending me money, let alone wasting it on scratch cards."

"You'll change your tune when I'm a gazillionaire."

"That's not even a word."

He put the card back in his wallet and pulled out a bill. "Whatever. Just take this."

"I can't keep borrowing money off you, Ty." He closed his eyes a second, hating to admit his next words. "It's embarrassing, not to mention unfair. We're practically on the same wage, for fuck sake."

"Perhaps, but I also have parents who'll send a check to their underachieving son if I can't make my rent."

"That may be, and I appreciate the offer, but I cannot keep coming back to you for cash. Believe it or not, but I actually have a bit of pride left." Something that would probably disappear that very evening. He was already worried about how he'd act around Simon the day after.

Ty nodded, unwilling to press him any further. "Well…." He pushed up with his hands on his knees to stand. "Shall we hit the books?"

"Yes," he sighed. "You were saying something about snow…."

HE'D called Mattie to reassure him that everything was okay and would have given anything to be within hugging distance of the man right now. But Mattie was studying, and Sarah had just taken Jamie— who was back to his normal, smiling self—and he was now waiting for six thirty.

Simon felt like he was in some sort of western, waiting to draw guns at high noon, or in this case, evening. He sat on the sofa, elbows resting on his knees, fingers steepled and pressed against his lips. He felt troubled that he couldn't remember the last time his mother had been… his *mother* to him. It certainly had to be before he came out to her.

If anything, that would be the starting point to all contention between them. She hadn't liked it and had reacted badly. And stupidly, he'd actually hoped that maybe his announcement would be a small thing to them, just kind of like a heads up.

You'd have thought he'd told her he had the plague.

Goddamn, why couldn't she have been a better mother instead of the conservative, disapproving, *disappointed* woman she turned out to be? And he hated that word. Conservative. It was just another word for disapproving, wasn't it? Another word for cautious. As if a person has to pick between being a patriotic do-gooder, or a free thinking, loving human being who would never consider choosing between their children and keeping up appearances. And just why the hell did it have to be choice, anyway? Why wasn't there a middle ground by now? A word for someone who was all about the family values but smart enough to recognize the need to change the way we think.

He knew his mother had come from a very conservative background. His grandparents had been as right-leaning as could be: American flag out in the yard, addicted to FOX News, an intolerance for foreigners, and a dislike of anything that hinted at being even the slightest bit unpatriotic. He'd always suspected they'd been unhappy with his mother over... well, *him*. He knew next to nothing about the relationship between his mother and father. For all he knew his father could be dead, but what he did know was that they'd never been married.

And there was no greater shame to a conservative family than having—other than a gay grandson—a daughter knocked up out of wedlock. It'd always been a strained atmosphere when they'd visit, because not only had their daughter gotten knocked up at a young age without a wedding band, but she'd gone and done it again a few years later with Carol-Ann.

Carol-Ann's dad, well... he'd visited her at least, but barely spoke to his mother and had absolutely zip to do with him. He'd always felt bad for his mom when he'd visit, because she'd get this young, desperate look in her eyes that'd always made him feel uncomfortable—like she was waiting to be rescued.

He'd always suspected that his mother's feelings toward him must have something to do with her parents' stern disapproval of her. Perhaps showing a hate of his "lifestyle" was a belated way of proving to her folks that she wasn't a total lost cause. Or maybe love just *was* conditional.

He was working himself up. With a frustrated, sharp exhale he stood and swung his arm out to swipe at a houseplant leaf. Was it a generation thing? He could never consider loving Jamie less over something he just *was*. Surely he'd proven that. But could he have said the same thing thirty—hell, fifteen—years ago? Perhaps he wasn't being fair. His mother hadn't had the easiest of times raising Carol-Ann and himself alone, and he had to admit, they had, once upon a time, been a happy threesome. They'd gotten along, cared for each other, and been interested in each other's lives. Now? Now it felt as if they'd all gone their own separate ways. The Castle family that had at least once a week turned off the TV to play charades, the family that had held family meetings over what color the kitchen should be painted—this *normal*, content family had evaporated.

How could something so good and natural disappear? Carol-Ann was gone. She was dead, and he would never *ever* see his friendly, loving sister again. His mother, who had played the role of both parents, who had taught him all the usual stuff like tying his shoelaces and riding a bike… the woman who had bought him his first suit and taken him to the San Diego Museum of Art when all of his friends had gone on a father-son camping trip, that wonderful woman had turned on him.

He'd tried to announce it so casually. The three of them were in the living room. Carol-Ann was fifteen and curled up next to their mother, her head resting against her shoulder while watching a rerun of *M*A*S*H*. He'd been eighteen and about to leave for college, sitting on the love seat and terrified of leaving his small family without them really knowing him. Stupidly, he'd thought he *owed* them, and that they'd be pissed he hadn't mentioned it to them earlier.

And so, during a commercial for 7Up, he'd just blurted it out. Carol-Ann'd lifted her head up from their mom's shoulder, a knowing smile slowly creeping over her face, and he'd begun to smile back, but their mother's low voice had put a halt to that.

She had not smiled. In fact, she'd yelled as if it was the final straw that broke the camel's back. She made threats and screamed things about being shameful and backward. Carol-Ann, as surprised by the venom in their mother's voice as he was, had cried quietly and slinked away to her bedroom. He'd left for college early.

That was the last time he'd thought of her as his mother.

There was a knock at the door.

MATTIE took the crumpled piece of paper out of his pocket, checking the address and then looking up at the apartment building. Okay, first? He did not want to be there. He hadn't been with a john since getting serious with Simon, and the thought of slipping back into old routines now wasn't sitting well. He wasn't sure how he was going to look him in the eye after this, but he needed the money and couldn't bring himself to ask Simon or Ty, so he'd have to figure it out.

Second? He'd never met the guy. Usually, he'd pick 'em up in a bar or at a gig, establish a few regulars, and just stick to those few when money got tight. That way he could get a feel for the guy before going ahead. After all, it wasn't exactly the safest way to make money. This particular guy was a friend of one of those regulars, who had recommended him.

Recommended. Fuck. How had he ever let any of this happen?

He shook his head quick and then hit the buzzer. Time to dig deep. Usually, he could scrape by on the rent, and he always made sure to have an emergency stock supply of rabbit food, but damn, his kitchen cupboards were embarrassingly empty. A guy can survive on graham crackers for only so long. He shuffled his feet, waiting for a response, his shoulders hunched and his hands deep in his pockets to stave off the cold wind.

No answer. He looked up at the apartment block. Something didn't feel quite right, and he couldn't decide if it was the complications with Simon, the fact that he was going into this completely blind, or a genuine gut feeling that was telling him to walk away.

"Yeah?" A grainy voice came back at him through the intercom.

"Uh, yeah. It's Justin."

There was no answer but the sound of the buzzer, letting him in. He opened the door and stood there, stalling and holding the door open. In or out? He didn't want to be doing this. He did not want to be there, and there was something throwing him off.

With an angry shake of his head, he let go of the door and made his way up to the third floor. Of course it wasn't sitting right with him. It never had, but now that he had Simon it felt like he was flat-out cheating.

"Mattie. You have. No. Fucking. Food," he muttered as he jogged up the stairs, the elevator apparently out of order.

He counted along the doorways, 3A, 3B, 3C. Wait. Had he checked with the regular—who he couldn't help thinking of as a fucking pimp now—that only oral was on the table? He couldn't remember what he'd said over the phone. Something about twenty minutes, in and out. He glanced up at the doors and stopped still. Shit. He'd passed it. He backtracked until he was standing in front of 3G.

"Quit being a pussy."

He knocked on the door.

HE'D never seen his mother look so nervous, and so *small*. She was standing there, looking up at him—seriously, she'd shrunk—offering a small smile that seemed all at once nervous, hopeful, and worried. He should probably say something, or at least let her in. He stood back, opening the door wider.

"Mother." *Quite the greeting, Simon.*

"Simon, thank you for seeing me." She walked past him, searching the room.

His heart sank a little. "He isn't here. He's with his sitter." Of course, that's why she was smiling.

She looked back at him and gently shook her head no. "I didn't expect Jamie to be here, not after today. I was just—I was looking. It's been a while since I've been here."

Feeling remotely pacified, Simon closed the door and strode past her. The two of them stood awkwardly in the hallway. "Still take your tea the same way?"

"Coffee, if that's all right?"

Simon raised an eyebrow. Sure it was all right, just unexpected. Of course it was only a hot drink, but his mother usually stuck to what she knew. "Okay."

"Actually, um… I went into one of those coffeehouses a while ago." She gave him a friendly smile that just fucking *grated* on him. "Had one of those lattes? It was very nice. I like trying new things every now and then."

"Is *this* a new thing? Talking to me with some degree of familiarity and warmth?" Damn. He honestly hadn't meant to snap so quickly. There was just so much built up resentment and feelings of betrayal. This was the first time he'd faced the source of that pain in years.

She visibly blanched. "No. *No*, Simon. I was just…." She trailed off and looked down to fiddle with the clasp on her purse. "I can't believe I've forgotten how to talk to you."

He was not going to tear up. He could be civil. He shoved his hands into his pockets. He would not feel sorry for her. "Kitchen's this way." He indicated with a nod of his head. "I can make you a latte, if you like."

He didn't look to see if she'd followed, and instead busied himself over his coffee machine. He heard a chair being pulled back at the kitchen table and looked over his shoulder to see her sitting there, hands still grasping her purse like a lifeline as she looked around the kitchen. She looked out of place sitting there. Out of place and intimidated. Good.

"You have a lovely home."

Yes, I do. And you'd know that if you visited more often. "Thank you." He opened a small tin to spoon in the latte powder. He liked his fancy coffee/latte/cappuccino machine that had cost him $350. He hoped she noticed how expensive it looked.

"*Oh!*"

Simon looked over his shoulder at the breathless exclamation and watched as she rose and walked over to the fridge. Feeling confused, he turned, about to ask if she was hungry at all, before realizing that it was the drawing of a sailboat that was causing her to react so emotionally. Clenching his jaw, he turned away to pour the two steaming lattes.

"He drew that for me last night."

"It's so *good* for a four-year-old! Look, all colors are inside the lines. It's so neat."

"He's a smart boy. He can read and write at the level of an eight-year-old, you know." Yeah, he was smug. What of it?

"Well, that's incredible! You must be so proud."

That made him glance up and look her in the eye as he was sitting at the kitchen table. It was the first time that she had—in a roundabout way—spoken to him as if she recognized he was a parent. "More then you could ever know."

Her cheeks flushed with what he assumed to be shame as she took her seat again, and then a godawful silence fell over them. Simon cleared his throat and tapped the side of his mug. Just what was he supposed to say? They were here to talk about her disastrous visit to the school earlier that day, but there didn't seem an awkward-free way to segue to it. He watched as she began to shoulder off her coat and managed to stop himself from sputtering out an apology for his poor manners.

"Let me take your coat." He rose from his chair.

"Oh no, no. I'm fine, see?" She draped her coat over the back of the chair and then faced him with a smile he supposed was meant to appear approachable and easy, but only made him feel sad. How had they got to this?

He sighed and pushed his mug away. "You feel like a stranger," he admitted quietly. Goddamn, he wanted to be angry. It would be so much easier if he could recall the hate he'd felt for her this afternoon.

She shook her head. "I don't want it to be that way."

"It's your doing." *Is that entirely true?*

The sadness that washed over her features was almost enough to make him apologize. Almost. "I know, Simon. I—I have a lot to apologize for."

"You think a simple apology is going to make what you did three years ago okay? Not to mention this afternoon." There it was: the anger he needed.

"Simon...." Her hand reached across the table but stopped short of touching his. "I am so, so sorry for trying to take Jamie from you, I—I was...." She let out a sharp exhale of frustration as he pulled away from her attempt to hold his hand. "It's a pitiful excuse, but... I was grieving, Simon. It was so terrible."

"You don't think *I* was gr—"

"No." She cut him off firmly. "Not in the same way, Simon." She glanced back at the picture held up on the refrigerator door by magnets. "Can you begin to imagine the pain of losing Jamie, of your child *dying*? Your *child*, Simon. That's a special kind of hell. There is nothing else in the world so painful."

He had to glance away. He remembered the funeral. She had been beside herself, frantic with the pain of losing Carol-Ann. He'd wanted to comfort her, but he'd been afraid to.

"So...." He began in a voice that was not completely steady. "Grief is why you tried to take Jamie from me? From the *faggot* who might hurt him?" he spat out.

"Oh, Simon." She shook her head, looking away and anywhere but at him as she tugged uselessly at the strap of her handbag. "I never used that word."

"You may as well have."

"It wasn't because you're gay."

A noise of disbelief left his throat as he stood and turned to lean against the counter. "*Please.* You accused me of being unfit to take care of him, which is hysterically ironic, if you ask me."

"You'd had no experience with children! And... and I admit that I—I wanted him. I just wanted my children back, but they were gone. Carol-Ann was gone; you despised me. My...." Her chin trembled and her voice cracked. "My arms ached, Simon. They *ached*. I don't know how else to describe it."

He was unaffected. "Tell me something. If you thought you stood a chance in the courts, would you try and take him now?"

"No," she answered immediately. "Absolutely not."

"*Then what was today?*" he exploded, making her jump and surprising even himself. "You were at his *school*!"

"Oh!" she choked out, tears flowing freely as she turned away from his hard stare. She dug in her handbag and pulled out a tissue. "I—I didn't want us to yell," she cried. "I wanted this to go well. I wanted to talk!"

He realized he was leaning across the table, practically bearing down on her. This wasn't how he wanted things to go either. He pulled back, rubbing his hands over his face before pulling out his chair and sitting back down, level with her. He clenched his jaw tight and took a deep breath. "I'm sorry for shouting. Just... tell me why you were there. You have to be honest with me now: were you trying to take him away?"

"No!" she gasped. "I would never try and snatch him!"

"Then why—"

"Because I miss you! I miss you, Simon!"

That gave him pause. "Me?" He blinked in surprise.

"I wanted to see my grandson. Of *course* I did. But I knew you would be there to pick him up...."

"That doesn't make any sense. It was during lunch."

"Simon," she sighed, her shoulders slumped. "My days are empty. I don't work because of my back. I have nothing to do but sit and think of every single mistake I've ever made. There's...." She glanced up, as if afraid to admit what she was about to say. "There's a park across from the school. Sometimes I go there, waiting for the children to have their recess, hoping to see him...."

He knew that this should alarm him. Instead, he found himself wondering what was wrong with her back.

"I mean, really, they're too far away to see, but I can hear them playing, and I wonder which one is my grandson."

He pressed his lips tight together. "And today you thought you'd talk to him?"

She shook her head. "I promise you I had no intention of stepping through those gates. Like I said, I was hoping to wait around long enough to see you both together. Just see you. I wasn't going to try and talk to you because I knew you wouldn't have wanted that. You never return my calls."

Something dawned on him. "You've done this before."

She nodded guiltily. "I'm sorry."

He closed his eyes for a moment, trying to understand what all it meant. "Why did you try to talk to him?"

She didn't answer right away, but folded and unfolded the tissue in her hands. When she spoke, she was quiet. "He looks so much like Carol-Ann. It's almost shocking up close." Finally she wiped under her eyes with the tissue before folding it and stuffing it up the sleeve of her cardigan.

"I saw him sitting there alone, eating his grapes, his little feet swinging happily." She smiled tremulously. "And I just wanted to be in his life so badly, Simon. I just wanted to tell him who I was. I wanted to ask him if he ever got any of the birthday cards I sent. I started walking toward him without thinking."

"You scared him."

"I am so very, very sorry, Simon."

"I could have had you arrested, you know." Oddly enough, there was no fire in his words.

"Why didn't you?"

"Sarah—his teacher, Miss Protrakis," he clarified. "The person sitting for me now. She convinced me not to. She convinced me that it would be best for Jamie to talk to you, to…." He bit his lip. "To try and work things out with you."

A smile bloomed across her face. "Oh, Simon, nothing would make me happier!"

"Hold it right there." He held up his hand. "Just because I'm willing to talk does not mean all is forgiven."

She leaned back in her chair and nodded, seeming hopeful. "I understand that what I did today was appalling."

His brows rose together sadly, and the teenager who had been thrown out by his mother wanted to shake her and make her see him. "I meant for what you did to me." He spoke quietly.

"I—I know I should never have sought legal advice against you—"

"No!" he cried out unhappily. "No, Mom. For—" He looked away, biting off his words in fear that they would make him appear too vulnerable. "Christ. Do you even know how scared I was to be cut off by my mother, to know that you didn't want me in your house anymore?"

A look of horror crossed her face, the lines around her mouth and eyes accentuated. Her hands crept across the table as she shook her head softly. "Simon, *no*, it wasn't like that."

"Don't you tell me what it was like!"

"You were already going to college. Y-you were moving out into one of those dorms—"

"You made me get on that bus a week early. You were supposed to drive me down there, but you put me on a bus and you barely said a word. You didn't even stay to watch the bus *leave*!" It was all coming out, and there wasn't a thing he could do to stop it.

"I'm sorry," she gasped, her head shaking from side to side. "I'm so sorry. I—I thought you'd change in college, that you'd grow out of it and then come home…."

169

"You took my home away from me!"

"No, never, Simon!"

"I'd call home and you'd pass the phone over to Carol-Ann without a word." Damn it, he could feel his eyes stinging.

She closed her eyes tightly a moment, pulling her hands back when it was obvious Simon would not allow her touch. "I was just trying to show you how unhappy I was with your decision. I admit I was trying to punish you, but—"

"What *fucking* decision?"

"Simon, please! Don't—"

"Let's get one thing straight right now. Being gay is no more a choice than being straight is. Sexuality is not black and white. I did nothing wrong, and it was *you* that disappointed *me*."

Her voice was almost breathless when she spoke. "Simon, believe me when I say I *know* that. I promise you I hold no illusions as to who failed who."

"Then how could you let this carry on for so long?"

"No." She shook her head firmly. "No, I've tried constantly to get in touch with you over the past few years."

"To take my son away!"

She sighed, her shoulders drooping as she shook her head. "This is such a mess. I've made such a mess of things."

A brief silence passed between them. They'd spoken more in the past five minutes than they had in the past three years, and it was a lot to take in. Simon swallowed. "Let me ask you this. Do—do I still disgust you?"

She was quiet for a good ten seconds, as if taking time to choose her words, and for a horrifying moment, Simon was sure she would say yes.

"All right." She nodded, straightening her posture. "All right, now I want to get this right, I want you to understand what I'm trying to say. I did not like that you were gay, and…." She looked him in the eye apprehensively, "and I still don't, Simon. I don't like it."

He felt something inside shrivel up. God, he'd actually thought there was a chance of making things right. But not now, not with her still feeling he was doing something utterly immoral and disgust—

"Simon," she said sharply, interrupting his chain of thought. He swallowed hard and couldn't bring himself to move when she pulled her chair around the table. "Don't do that. You did that as a boy—you went off somewhere in your head when you were unhappy. You can't do that right now. I need you to listen to me."

"Go on," he whispered, feeling resigned.

She took a steady breath and let it out slowly. "Back when you were just a boy? When you told me? All I could think about were all the things that would be taken away from you. No marriage, no children. All I could see was how hard you would have to fight. All I could see was the way people were going to look at you, speak to you—"

"Like how *you* looked at me?"

She closed her eyes. "Yes." She grasped his hand and wouldn't let go when he tried to pull away. "I know how hypocritical that sounds now."

"Don't pretend that you were just worried about me. You were genuinely disgusted by the idea of homosexuality." He wanted the truth if they were really going this far.

"I—I didn't like it. I couldn't picture you with a man. Two men together just...." She shook her head. "It was just odd. It was embarrassing."

"*God,*" Simon hissed, yanking his hand away.

"No, Simon, Simon!" She gripped his arm and tugged until he reluctantly sat back down. "I was being shortsighted. If—if I'd have known what my reaction would entail, please believe me when I say I would have done things differently."

"You can't just change your mind."

"No, I can't."

He could feel a bitter twist to his mouth forming. "And you never even tried to become a part of my life again until Jamie. I stopped existing for you."

"Now that is *not* true," she said firmly, and for a moment she sounded like his mother again, scolding him for talking back at her. "You cut me off just as much as I did you."

He yanked himself out of her grip and stood, needing the distance. "Oh, *please*."

"You hear people go on about tolerance, understanding, and patience. Where was your understanding and patience, Simon?"

He was afraid his mouth was gaping. "You have to be joking. You're my *mother*. You're supposed—"

"Yes, I know that! I know I failed, Simon. I was a bad mother, and I pushed you into college and away from me. But what about afterward? I tried, Simon, I tried to talk to you, but you'd become so cold to me."

"Can you blame me?" he scoffed.

"Not one damn bit! But you say 'how could I'? Well, I'm your mother. Why was it so easy for you to cut *me* out? Because I'll tell you this, the way I treated you?" She slashed her hand through the air. "The biggest regret of my life. But I'm willing to back down, to grovel if need be, because I would give anything to be back in your life. But you? You wouldn't hear it back then, before I so *stupidly*...." She screwed her eyes closed tight for a moment. "Before I so stupidly tried to take that boy away from you. You had cut *me* off. And maybe I deserved that, but the difference between us is that I couldn't keep up with it. I can't live without my son in my life!"

She was shaking now, both with fury and fear. "Where was *your* understanding, Simon? No matter how underserved. I tried to apologize, but back then? You didn't even give me a chance to understand you being gay."

"Y-you hurt me too deep."

"And I am so, so sorry. My God, I am. But am I wrong in thinking that as much as you deserved my patience and understanding, that *I* deserved the same in return? Please, can you grasp that?"

Simon raked his hands through his hair. He couldn't deny that she had a point.

"I just needed time, time to understand and wrap my head around the whole thing," she said.

"To 'understand'? You just said you still don't like that I'm gay!"

"Simon," she spoke tiredly. "I'm an old woman set in her ways—"

"Don't give me that. I *hate* that. As if anyone over the age of fifty gets a free pass when it comes to being a bigot."

"I am trying to be completely honest with you. Seeing two men— or two women together, for that matter—it makes me uncomfortable. It looks strange to me."

"So why are we even talking, if nothing's changed?"

She stood and strode over to where he leaned against the counter. "Because now I can see that my feelings on the matter will make no difference. I know that's it simply something you are, and that just because I don't like it, does *not* make it wrong."

He felt like an open target; he felt exposed. "But you still don't like me, Mom." He swallowed at how feeble and vulnerable he sounded, and closed his eyes when he felt her small hand touch his cheek.

"You're dead wrong about that. I love you. Open your eyes. Look at me."

He did as he was told.

"I love you up to the sky and back. And however I might feel about your homosexuality? That's my problem to get over. There is nothing wrong with you, and I have been a terrible mother to you."

"Mom," he whispered, fighting the urge to lean into the hand against his cheek.

"We had such a great little family, you, Carol-Ann, and me. And I ruined it, didn't I?"

He tried to turn his head away, but she pulled him back to face her. "Answer me. Tell me everything you've ever wanted to say to me."

"Yes," he whispered. "You split us all up. I felt like an orphan."

She closed her eyes, but she didn't move away, she didn't take her hand away from his cheek. "I'm so sorry," she choked out. "I am so, so sorry, Simon."

He bit his lip. "Can I say something else?"

"Go on."

"I'm afraid you'll hurt Jamie." He hurried to explain when she lowered her hand, a deep frown marring her brow. "What you saw today was nothing. I'm worried that once you see him on a really bad day when he's been unsettled by something—when he's screaming and rolling on the floor and trying to slap himself—I'm worried you'll be disgusted with him for being different, like you were with me."

"Oh no," she whispered, her breath hitching. She shook her head sadly. "I can't believe I did this to you."

"You abandoned me." Alarmed by the hot streak against his cheek, he quickly wiped at it with the heel of his hand.

"You only thought I had. I promise you I was always thinking about you. Always."

"What if you're just saying all this to get to Jamie?" He didn't care if he sounded exposed or childish; they were way past keeping up appearances now.

"Simon, if I have to keep away from Jamie to prove to you that I am sorry and that I want you back more than I can possibly say, then I will. I will never try to be a part of his life again, if it means I can be a part of yours."

"Don't play with me. If this is some trick, then—"

She pulled him into her arms, holding him tight and rocking him in a way that, although he hadn't felt it in years, was immediately

174

familiar to him. "Oh, Simon," she cried. "Oh, honey, I'm sorry! I'm so sorry!"

Unable to do anything but, he completed the hug. He felt no shame as warm tears trickled down his cheeks when she brushed his hair away from his face, as if to get a good look at him after being denied the sight of him for so long.

"I, well…." He cleared his throat. "Okay."

"Okay?" she asked quietly.

"Okay. We can talk about Jamie now."

THEY wasted no time at all. This guy who hadn't even gone so far as to offer a name had merely sat himself on the sofa, beer in hand, and sneered at him while unzipping his pants. Now Mattie was on his knees, his eyes closed, and his mouth full as a complete stranger used him.

He honest to God felt like crying. The grip in his hair was too tight, the slap against his chin with every thrust, along with the loud grunt above him, drowned out any sound from the TV. He didn't want to do this anymore. In fact, at that exact moment, he didn't want to *live* anymore.

"*Fuck*," the deep voice above him growled before moving to perch on the edge of the sofa to gain more leverage as his thrusts passed unkind and became brutal.

The tight grip on his hair was bringing tears to his eyes, and he could feel himself beginning to gag. He gripped at the guy's thighs hard to try and silently convey this and received nothing but a hard yank at his hair in response.

"Don't you dare fucking stop—*ah*! Shit, yeah!"

Please just come. Just finish and get off of me. He couldn't take much more. A particularly hard piston into his mouth made him cry out—as much as he could—around the solid flesh down his throat. And just like that, he was past the point of trying to get on with it. There was no keeping up a natural façade now. He was struggling and pounding against the guy's thighs with his fists.

"You. Fucking. *Bitch*!" The john ground out between thrusts, and then finally, he was coming. He grunted and lost his rhythm as his hips stuttered and flexed unevenly against Mattie's jaw.

He tried to pull away from where his face was pressed against the guy's hip and could feel the grip in his hair relaxing, when he gasped in shock as a liquid—beer, judging by the smell—trickled down over his head. There couldn't have been much left in the bottle, but it was in his eyes, blinding him when he already felt suffocated. The john laughed.

"Fucking slut. That's what you are, hey?" he panted, tucking himself back in. "Little whore. You like being a come-dumpster, you little bitch? Like sucking dick for cash? You subhuman piece of shit."

Before he could even respond with a well-deserved "fuck you," the air whooshed straight out of his lungs when a booted foot wedged itself into his stomach with shocking force. He'd never felt anything like it, the deep, cramp-like pain that stole his breath and vibrated through his entire body.

"You're not getting a fucking dime out of me. Not for that piss-poor blowjob. You're disgusting, hear me? Fucking disgusting."

Mattie's head was being yanked up again by the hair, but he couldn't even cry out or begin to stand. He gasped for breath and closed his eyes in shock when the guy's face loomed close to his. The john spat in his face.

"Get the fuck out of here."

He tried to stand to ease the searing sting in his scalp as he was more or less dragged to the front door. When the door slammed behind him, it took him a moment to realize that the grip in his hair was gone and he was out in the hallway of the apartment block. Still gasping for breath and wiping at his face, he scrambled to his feet, stumbling as he tried to rush.

Making it to the first flight of stairs, his clumsy feet tripped over themselves. He reached desperately for the railing as he flailed and stumbled down the first few steps. It wasn't until he'd reached the bottom of the second set of steps that his knees gave out and he crumpled, sliding down against the wall, his arm wrapped around his stomach as he gasped for breath between hiccups of fear.

After taking a minute to collect himself, he carried on down the last flight of stairs and walked unsteadily toward the front entrance. He wiped at his face to make sure it was dry, and reached into his pocket for his phone.

He didn't care about having to explain to Simon where he was and what he was doing there. He just needed to speak to him, have him come get him and take him away. His hands noticeably shook as he scrolled down his contacts for Simon's number. Hitting the green button and putting the phone to his ear, he pushed the entrance door open and walked slowly down the sidewalk.

"Please pick up, Simon, please...."

HIS phone vibrated on the counter, but after checking it wasn't Sarah and seeing that it was Mattie, he decided to let it go to voice mail. It wasn't every day that his mother was sitting in his kitchen, offering to mend fences and build bridges. He couldn't help but smile a little as he poured two more lattes—the first untouched and now stone cold. Mattie was probably checking that he was okay. It felt good to have someone checking up on him. He'd make sure to call him back as soon as his mother left.

"Aren't you going to answer that?"

"No, I'll call him back later." He almost winced when he realized what he'd said. He glanced cautiously over at his mother, bracing for whatever her reaction may be.

"So... is—is that the young man you were in a relationship with a few years ago?"

There was some mild discomfort but no look of outright disgust. "Tim? No, we parted ways a while back." He set a mug in front of his mother and sat opposite her, blowing over the rim of his own.

"Oh?" she asked hesitantly.

Simon couldn't help but snort. "You're seriously asking me about my love life?"

His mother actually smiled, and it was a good, familiar smile he recognized from years ago before everything went so wrong. "No, I suppose it's a bit soon for that."

He studied her a moment and then shrugged with a small sigh. "Tim didn't want to be a father, and to be fair, it was sort of thrust upon him."

His mother nodded slowly. "So, you wanted different things?"

He nodded in response. "Pretty much. I was set on being a family man. I swear." He smiled. "Not even a month old and Jamie *owned* me, heart and soul. There just wasn't room or time for the kind of life Tim and I shared beforehand."

"So you chose Jamie over your, um...."

He nodded, almost enjoying her discomfort. "Boyfriend. And no, choice had nothing to do with it. If he didn't want to be a part of Jamie's life, then there's no being a part of mine. They go hand in hand. He's my *son*."

He was surprised to see his mother actually tear up, and when he asked what was wrong, she waved him away and covered her mouth. She reached for her mug again and let out a short breath, smiling still. "I love hearing you talk like that. You sound so proud of him."

"I *am* proud of him, Mother."

"Please go back to calling me Mom. I miss that."

He swallowed hard.

"Am I allowed to ask if there's someone new in your life, or is that...?" She trailed off with a nervous hand gesture.

"Well, that depends on whether you really want to know, and how you're going to react. I'm telling you now; I'm not going to stand for—"

"Simon," she interrupted with a rueful smile. "You can answer yes or no. In all honestly, I'm not ready for details." Her eyes widened slightly. "That's not to say that you can't talk about—about any, um, significant other you might have, if you want to. I told you I'm determined to be the mother you deserve. I'm going to get over any—"

"Oh good God, stop waffling." He laughed, and felt a flush of genuine warmth when she waved him away with a laugh and reached for her mug again. It almost felt like everything could be right with them once more, and he knew that if his sister were able to see them now, she'd be smiling from ear to ear. Still, a small part of him held back. It felt good to be talking to his mother—to have that feeling of a mother looking at you with some sort of ownership in their eyes. He hadn't realized until now just how much he'd missed her, and wasn't quite ready to have Mattie enter the delicate mixture. Whether he was protecting his relationship with Mattie, or himself, he didn't want to examine too closely. Time for a change of subject.

"So... Jamie." He'd brought the large scrapbook of photos and drawings by Jamie he kept in his office, and they'd spent a good half hour warming up to the subject of them meeting while they played catch-up with Jamie's every mannerism and achievement. "You want to be a part of his life," he stated flatly. He watched her put down her mug and swallow hard.

"If you're willing, but I want you to understand that I recognize that you are his father, and I will abide by any rules you want to put in place concerning him."

Something in his chest slowly loosened its grip, and he was able to breathe a little easier. As much of a breakthrough that evening had been so far, he couldn't trust her completely, not yet and not by a long shot. But he knew now that he at least wanted to.

"I think, perhaps to begin with at least... a telephone call?" He felt guilty when her face fell in clear disappointment, but she was quick to agree, nodding away.

"Absolutely. Get him used to my voice first, right?"

"Uh, yeah, actually." He frowned.

"I understand, Simon. I know I frightened him terribly when I tried to hug him. To be honest, I can't believe I showed such a lapse in judgment. For all the research in infant autism I read, you'd think—"

"Wait a second. You—you read about that sort of thing?"

She suddenly looked nervous. "Well, there was a time when I was adamant on—on taking him from you, wasn't there?"

The look on her face could be described as nothing other than shame. She wasn't to know, however, that he appreciated hearing the truth. It went a long way to building a little trust between them.

"And then, of course, I just hoped to be a part of his life, so... yes, I read quite a bit about the subject. Though I can't imagine it compares much to actually raising a child with autism. So... we go at your speed here. Whatever you think is right."

A snide part of him wanted to point out that she'd probably say anything to get him to trust her again, but he could only read sincerity in her expression, and there had been a time when he'd trusted her implicitly. He dared hope to feel that way again.

He nodded. "Maybe a phone call a few times a week. He likes using the phone. It makes him feel grown up."

She was beaming. "I can't wait, I really can't. Thank you."

"And uh... well." He cleared his throat. "Depending on how that goes, his birthday is coming up real soon, as you know, and I was thinking of throwing him a small birthday party." He almost smiled at the hope he could see building in her face. "Perhaps you could drop by early and help us blow up some of the balloons?"

"Oh, Simon!" She laughed, standing and rounding the table to hug him. He couldn't help but laugh himself. Christ, it felt good to finally, or at least *begin* to, forgive. "I could bake the cake! What's his favorite flavor? Lemon? Chocolate? I bet it's fudge, isn't it? You always loved fudge."

He hugged her for a moment and then gently held her back. He didn't want them getting ahead of themselves. "Remember, it all depends on Jamie. If I don't think he's ready for someone new...." He shook his head apologetically, but she was already nodding along.

"Then I will be perfectly content to sing him happy birthday over the telephone."

He sighed quietly in relief. "All right. All right, good." He nodded. "So…." He smiled. He'd quite enjoyed playing catch up with regards to Jamie and carrying on like a proud father, despite his clock-watching. He'd have to pick up Jamie soon, and he wanted to return Mattie's call. He wanted to tell him all about it. "What else do you want to know?"

She bit her lip, something he wasn't accustomed to seeing her do. "Everything, absolutely everything. But…."

"But?" He raised an eyebrow in surprise. Where the hell had that "but" come from?

"I'd like… tell me about you?"

"Me?" he asked softly.

"I want to hear everything. Have you travelled much? Is spaghetti Bolognese still your favorite food?" She smiled, shrugging slightly. "What are reading lately? What are you *writing* lately?"

He felt blindsided, and not just a little bit emotional. "You want to talk about my writing?" Why the last surprised him the most, he didn't know.

"Well, of course, silly. I've read all of your books. When's the next one out? Oh! You can autograph the ones I have at home!"

He smiled sadly. He never expected to have this back, and it was throwing him a little. He glanced back at her when her small hand covered his own, larger one. Her eyes were glassy.

"This is something I should have told you years ago. I am, and always have been, blindingly proud of you, Simon. You are incredibly talented."

He swallowed hard. "Thanks, Mom."

She patted his hand and then sat back and picked up her mug. "Come on. I want to hear absolutely everything."

He smiled, feeling oddly nervous. "Well, I've just started a new manuscript…."

THE rain had gone a small ways to washing the scent of beer from Mattie's hair, but he still felt fucking filthy. What had happened in that guy's apartment could have been so much worse. All sorts of fucked-up scenarios were now going through his head.

He sniffed and shivered as a droplet of rain dripped from his hair and trailed down his neck and the back of his shirt. What was he doing with his life? What the *fuck*? He thought he'd hit rock bottom before— he'd been wrong. *This* was rock bottom.

For some reason, he didn't want to go home. He needed company. He pulled his phone out of his pocket again to check for any messages from Simon. Nothing. He wasn't mad. He knew it was an important evening for Simon. Still. He felt so fucking raw, so alone, and Simon was the only person who could probably make him feel better right now. Though, thinking on it, perhaps it was best Simon hadn't answered his phone. He was calmer now and didn't like the idea of telling Simon where he'd been.

One positive thing had come out of this. He was done with hooking. Fucking draw a line through him, stick a fork in him, *done*. He'd told himself such things before, but there was no way in hell he was ever putting himself in that situation again. He was just going to have to tighten his belt and hang on until he got his GED and could apply for a better-paying job.

And he wasn't sure why, but he didn't want to let on to Simon that he was calling it a day with hooking. It wasn't that he wanted to make him jealous; it was something more important than that. He needed Simon to ask him to stop. He needed to know he was important enough to become a fixture in this man's life. And nothing would smack more of commitment and feeling needed than Simon wanting him all to himself. Perhaps Simon'd catch on when he noticed how much weight he was losing from lack of *food*. Nah, he was being stupid. It would never get that far. Ty would never let it get that far, and he was pretty sure that Simon would eventually broach that uncomfortable subject of money if he noticed how bad things were getting for him.

And if he had to swallow his pride and ask for a handout? Then so be it. Simon knew he wasn't with him for the money, and Ty would be relieved as fuck. Ty. That's where he was headed right now, Ty's place. He needed some food in his stomach, a friend to talk to, and—he wasn't too proud to admit it—he needed a fucking hug. The worst night of his life, and his lover wasn't answering the phone. He needed a friend. Now if he could only stop sniveling....

Raising a hand, he knocked at Ty's front door. He quickly wiped at his cheeks, hoping any residual dampness could be blamed on the rain. But when Ty opened the door, and his usual friendly smile of greeting slowly slipped away to be replaced by a look of concern, a sound frighteningly close to that of a hiccup escaped his throat.

"Fuck, Mattie, what the *hell*...?" Ty stepped forward, out of the doorway and into the rain. Following Ty's gaze, he hadn't even realized he was still guarding his stomach with his arm. His voice was unsteady and sounded thick with impending tears when he spoke.

"Can I get that ten bucks?"

Chapter
Seven

HEAVEN.

That's what this was. For the first time in a long time, his life, in all aspects, was coming together. The words were flowing freely with his new manuscript. He no longer procrastinated and dreaded the blinking curser of an open Word document. Now? He whipped out his notes, got himself settled with a coffee, and poured his every experience, fear, and triumph into his manuscript. If ever he began to worry about his new venture and felt tempted to return to what felt safe, he kept one thing in mind, one fantasy: he pictured Jamie reading his book ten years down the line. And with that one image, that one goal, Simon threw himself into writing what he hoped was a manuscript that would justify the struggles any parent raising an autistic child faced on a daily basis. He tried valiantly to put into words how much he treasured and adored his son, hoping that one day Jamie would read it and know just how much his father loved him.

Speaking of, Jamie was doing just fine. And his relationship with his mother? Still tenuous, but... better. It was good between them, and it truly touched him to see Jamie chattering away to his newly discovered grandmother on the phone. They were becoming fast friends, and he only hoped that the same easy relationship would develop in person. Despite the resentment he'd felt, and the residual caution he still felt with regards to his mother, he had to admit that when it came to Jamie, Sarah had been right. His mother was good for him. His fears of any awkwardness between the two of them due to Jamie's condition were unfounded. His mother was kind to him and more patient than he thought her capable of. The idea that there may be another person in the near future that Jamie would feel comfortable enough to look in the eye filled him with hope. And he had to admit, he felt happier, *lighter*, having begun to forgive his mother and integrate her back into his life.

Then there was Mattie.

Heaven.

Coming down from their intense lovemaking, he lay on his side with Mattie—the only word for it was snuggled—into his side. His lazy kisses along Mattie's shoulder brought a content, lazy hum from the beautiful young man beside him.

He didn't deserve to be this happy, surely? Mattie brought out a side of him he had long forgotten about. The side of him that liked to laze about in bed and laugh about stupid, unimportant shit. The part of him that had always loved sex. Mattie was turning out to be not only his dearest friend and the most energetic lover he'd ever had, he was fast becoming one of the most important people in his life. He felt safe with Mattie.

"You're just about the sweetest thing I know," he said gruffly.

Mattie lifted his head slightly to look him in the eye and gave him one of those perfect, loving smiles that seemed to be reserved just for him. "Ditto, handsome," Mattie said quietly.

He was feeling bold. He wanted to declare something. He wanted to give Mattie something, but he didn't know what. More than once he'd contemplated asking Mattie if he wanted to come over to his place. He liked the idea of having Mattie in his bed, of cooking for him and seeing Mattie in his home, among everything that was familiar and important to him. But there were so many complications that came with moving things from Mattie's place to his.

He wasn't sure how he felt about letting Mattie close to Jamie, and even thinking that made him hate himself, but the parameters of their relationship were still hazy and barely defined. They hadn't talked their way past that casual status, even if their relationship felt anything but. And as head over heels as he may feel, he knew it might be a whole other kettle of fish for Mattie. Sure, he knew Mattie liked him a great deal, but as far as he knew, Mattie was still planning on leaving for New York at the first opportunity, and he was still... he was still earning extra money on the side through methods Simon couldn't bear to think about.

He didn't know if it was foolish to carry on like this if he were setting himself up for some sort of fall, but what he did know was that, if or when things ended between them, it was going to hurt like nothing else. And the thought of Jamie feeling a fraction of that kind of pain or loss was flat-out unacceptable. He couldn't let Jamie near any of the harsh realities Mattie's life involved.

Yet he hoped, didn't he? He hoped that, despite the fact that they'd never spoken of it, and despite the fact that he knew Mattie wanted to leave San Diego, he hoped that something permanent could solidify between them.

God. He didn't want to lose him, but he couldn't let him in either. There had to be a middle ground. Somewhere to test the waters. He needed *more*.

"Hey," he murmured quietly, his throat feeling thick.

Mattie's answer was the slide of his hand along Simon's side, up along his back to hook over his shoulder. A leg slinking over his own thigh to draw him closer as Mattie pressed his face against his neck. Nothing had ever felt so intimate. "Yeah?" the younger man murmured sleepily.

"How, um, how'd you feel about occasionally moving this over to my place?" He felt Mattie's body still and wondered if he'd been foolish to say the words out loud. Mattie's head pulled back, looking at him questioningly.

"Yeah?" Mattie smiled wide.

Oh man, that smile was gorgeous. He couldn't help but offer a matching grin, but he needed to make something clear. "Yeah, I could swing by the diner after I drop Jamie off at Sarah's, bring you home, we could hang out for a few hours, and then I can take you home on my way back to Sarah's. It'll save you some bus fare at least...." *Please don't pick up on my keeping you and Jamie separate....*

Mattie sat up slightly, leaning on one elbow. "That sounds great, but... can I ask why the sudden change?"

"Well...." He ran his fingers through Mattie's bangs, pushing them aside. "I figured it was time I played host."

Mattie watched him. "Nothing else?"

Simon bit the inside of his cheek until Mattie's thumb gently brushed his lower lip. "I want something more, something... something different for us. I thought a change of scenery would be like a... a baby step."

Mattie's smile lit up the bedroom. He nodded. "Yeah, yeah okay."

"Yes?" he asked hopefully. "It's okay that we're still, you know, keeping it slow and all, but changing it up a little?"

"Hey," Mattie said softly, leaning into Simon's space until he was flat on his back with Mattie lying over him. "We're still good. I just like the direction this is going."

A happy grin spread across his lips. That was exactly what he'd wanted to hear. "I'm so glad," he breathed.

A downright devilish smirk touched Mattie's mouth, and he pressed their lips together for a kiss. Simon groaned helplessly as Mattie rubbed their groins together in a slow circle. "Speaking of switching it up a little," Simon said unsteadily, his hands encouraging Mattie's gyrations. "How about you take advantage, now you've got me lying beneath you?" Christ, he wanted Mattie to have him.

The loud groan against his neck and the hand hitching his thigh up was all the answer he needed. His hands slid over the expanse of toned muscle that was Mattie's back. "Did I mention?" he asked breathlessly. "That I have a flat screen?"

Mattie's groans turned into muffled laughter. "You got more than Ramen noodles in your cupboards too?"

"Oh yeah." His breath hitched as Mattie pushed up on his hands to look down at him and grind their hips together.

"Then we have a match made in heaven, beautiful."

A helpless sound escaped Simon's throat as Mattie leaned down for a deep, heart-stopping kiss. Like he was saying…

Heaven.

"SO, HAVE you started to draft your entrance essay?" said Ty.

"Hmm," Mattie replied, half-listening as he doodled in the corner of his textbook. He glanced at his watch.

"And you feel prepared for next week? Feeling confident?"

"Yeah, I'm fine." Five o'clock had never felt so far away.

"Okay, so we'll finish this chapter, and then we'll grab some buckets and spades and take care of that eel problem."

"'Kay."

"You know, in my hovercraft? My hovercraft that's full of eels?"

"Yeah, su—wait. What?"

"Dude, you're totally ignoring me. I just threw some *Python* at you and you didn't even bat an eyelid. What gives?"

"Sorry, just distracted."

"About what?" Ty stood and strolled over to the fridge to help himself to some juice. "Did you, uh, have another run in with that guy, or something?" The look he gave Mattie was nothing short of brotherly concern.

Mattie sat up slightly, reaching for his textbook. "No, Ty. I told you, I'm done with all that. Utterly and completely *done*." It'd been more than a little humiliating explaining to Ty what had happened after only a few hours earlier declaring to the same person he no longer hooked.

Ty nodded with what seemed like relief. "Hey, man, I wasn't judging or doubting you or anything. I've just been a little worried, you know? My offer still stands, if you ever want to go back to this guy's apartment and teach him a lesson, let me know. I'd quite happily introduce him to my baseball bat."

"That's… sweet."

Ty nodded. "As honey." He stared into the fridge, subconsciously curling his lip at the lack of contents inside. He pulled out the OJ. "So, what's got you so distracted?"

"My date, later."

Ty glanced over with a frown. "You're always hanging out with Simon. Why are you nervous all of a sudden?"

"He's cooking for me at his place. As in, you know, a *date,* date."

Ty housed the juice back in the fridge and sat back at the small kitchen table with his glass. The fucker was smirking. "*Oh.*"

"Yeah, '*oh*'."

"Well…." He shrugged. "I don't see what you have to be nervous about. I mean, you'll probably do the same shit, just at a nicer place."

"Thanks, man."

Ty looked around the kitchen, grinning. "I've got nothing against this shithole, but he's a published author, right? He's probably got all expensive furniture and stuff."

"He has a flat screen, and one of those new Mercedes in his garage."

Ty put his glass down with a thunk. "Hell, can I be his boyfriend?"

"Nope. Position of hot young boyfriend has been filled, thank you very much." Hell yes, he was smug.

Ty leaned closer. "He have a pool table? Because, seriously man, if he does, you're gonna have some competition."

Mattie laughed. "Actually, he used to, but then he threw it out and converted the space into a playroom for Jamie."

"Lucky kid."

"Yeah."

"Is, uh, is Jamie going to be there?"

Mattie shook his head. "No." He glanced at Ty and couldn't help but feel warmed by the protectiveness he sensed in him. "Ty, we're taking baby steps. Just, sorta finding our way into something serious and more permanent-like. It's a delicate situation."

Ty nodded, looking uncomfortable. "I get it, just, um...."

"What?"

"Just don't forget what's important for you, okay?"

"How'd you mean?"

"Well, the taking it slow thing, which makes sense, I get that. But in the meantime, well, you've got applications to fill out, tests to take, and a portfolio to think about."

Mattie sighed. "I know that."

Ty's hands went up in a defensive gesture. "I'm not trying to piss you off or start something, I promise."

"No." He nodded. "I know what it is you're talking about."

"There's only so much time to apply, Mattie. Then the chance is gone for another year."

Mattie worried his lip. "Would that be such a bad thing?"

"Mattie, if you don't do it now while you have a chance then you're never going to do it, and you know it."

He wanted to put up an argument, but he couldn't deny that what Ty was saying was true. He couldn't imagine leaving Simon in a year's time any more than he could in a few months' time. Who was he kidding? A year to get closer to Simon, close to Jamie? Maybe living with each other, only to leave and disrupt whatever it was they might have built together? Ty was right; he wouldn't be able to go.

Problem was, they were getting serious. They were going in exactly the right direction, just not fast enough. It wasn't something that could be pushed, but with the pace they were going at, the time was going to come when he was gonna have to consider giving up what could be a concrete dream ready and waiting for him, for another dream which might just be exactly that: a dream and nothing more.

"How about, just for now, you concentrate on this?" Ty tapped the textbook. "Don't make any decisions yet. Concentrate on what you know you definitely want regardless of the future—your GED."

Mattie nodded. "You're right."

"Always am."

Mattie pulled the textbook closer and sat up. "Can't believe it's not even a week away."

Ty nodded. "Just a few days. You're gonna do great."

"God, I'm terrified of the essay portion."

"Just think of it as practice for your entrance essay to art school."

"What if I get in there and go blank? Or pass out? What if I *throw up*?"

"You're not going to do any of those things, idiot. You'll get in there and breeze through it. You'll be a rock star."

"You could be one of those life coaches."

"Nah, whining makes my dick soft."

Mattie snorted. "How you've managed to remain friends with me is a miracle."

"It's not a question of remaining friends; it's a question of remaining flaccid."

Mattie laughed and shook his head at him. Ty gave him a shit-eating grin. "This got weird." said Mattie.

"Yes, it did," Ty agreed. "How about we call this a day for now? Seeing as you're distracted over fretting about what to wear for your big date and all."

Mattie's eyes suddenly went wide. "Shit, I don't have anything nice to wear!"

"Oh my God. I was kidding, you girl."

"Well, I'm not." He stood up. "Up. Come on. Help me pick out something smart—oh! What time is it?" He glanced at his watch. "Even better, we've got enough time to head on over to your place so I can borrow something nice to wear. All I have are jeans and T-shirts, man."

"I swear you just grew a vagina before my very eyes."

Mattie was already looking for his keys. "Shut up and get your jacket on."

"You're just going to end up naked anyway," Ty argued. "Just wear what you usually wear."

"This is a big deal. I want to look good."

"*Annnnd*… there's the tits."

Mattie threw Ty's jacket at him, which Ty deftly caught. "Get the fuck up."

"You *will* go to the ball, Cinderella!"

SIMON glanced over at Mattie when slowing down at a stop light. He looked nice. "You look nice."

Mattie smiled, touching the collar of his shirt for the hundredth time. "Thanks, you too."

Simon didn't think he looked any different than usual, but he was starting to wish he'd made more of an effort. It was touching that Mattie was treating this as something special, and he supposed that it was, in a way. It was a new step in their relationship. A small one, but a step nonetheless. "Is that a new shirt?"

"Uh, no, not really. I um, I borrowed it from Ty, so…." He trailed off with a small self-conscious shrug, smiling and looking back out the window.

Simon had to fight to keep a silly smile from his face. In that moment, he was so happy to be taking Mattie home with him. His Mattie. "Well, you look great."

Mattie actually flushed, looking pleased with himself. "I gotta be careful not to get any wine on it or anything." His eyes widened slightly. "T-that's if we're having wine. I don't know what you have planned."

Yes. *His* Mattie. "I have wine," he laughed softly.

"Okay." Mattie nodded, smiling across at him. "So," he asked brightly. "How's Jamie doing?"

Simon felt his happy glow dim slightly. Any time Mattie mentioned Jamie, he felt pressure to introduce the two of them again. He knew Mattie was merely interested and wasn't trying to force any kind of meeting between him and his son, but Jamie was his boy, their relationship was still new, and it had gone so very wrong with Tim.

"He's just fine. He's with Sarah for a few hours."

"How're things going between him and your mom?"

"Um, yeah, yeah they're getting on." Simon swallowed and tapped the side of the steering wheel with his thumb. The thought of Mattie and Jamie together made him anxious, sure, but the thought of Mattie and his mother in the same room—the same *sentence*—was enough to give him palpitations. His mother would scare Mattie off. Mattie could scare his mother off. *Change the subject, Simon.*

"I made risotto with lemon chicken; just have to heat it up when we get home—*back,* when we get back," he amended quickly, swallowing thickly as he glanced between the road and Mattie. Mattie seemed oblivious to his discomfort. He was also as gorgeous as ever.

"That sounds great. I can't wait to try it."

"I hope you're hungry. If not, we can always heat it up later and I could give you a tour around the house in the meantime?"

"I'M starving, actually." No truer words had ever been spoken. Mattie's cupboards were becoming alarmingly bare at home, with no means to fill them again until he was paid in a week's time. "But I'd like that tour afterward."

"Great." Simon slowed down and pulled into a more residential area. "Here we are," he said unnecessarily as he pulled into the drive.

Mattie blinked up at the house. It was nice. It was fancy looking.

It was a whole other world.

He'd known Simon owned his own home and that said home was *comfortable*; he was a fairly successful writer, after all. He drove an expensive car, had an expensive-looking laptop, his clothes were always smart-looking, so of course it would make sense that the house would follow suit. But for some reason, he hadn't expected the well-kept front yard, complete with a painted royal blue gate to match the royal blue door. There were shutters on the windows. Rose bushes. A mailbox with a red flag. Mattie swallowed.

"It's looks nice."

"Thanks." Simon smiled, unbuckling his seat belt and opening the car door.

Mattie looked down at himself. The shirt was okay, but it was still him underneath. He was wearing sneakers, his smartest pair of jeans, and a smile that was starting to feel strained. For the first time during their relationship, he wondered what it was they looked like together.

"Hey." Simon rested one hand on the open door and the other on the car roof. He dipped his head slightly to catch Mattie's gaze. He looked nervous. "Need help with your seatbelt?"

"Oh." Mattie forced a small laugh, looking down as he unbuckled. He stepped out of the car, closed the passenger door, and stood there nervously with his hands stuffed in his back pockets as he waited for Simon to round the front of the car and lead the way.

Instead of heading to his front door, however, Simon strode over to Mattie, looking a little uncertain himself. Mattie felt a moment of panic, sure that Simon had changed his mind.

He stopped just in front of Mattie, and for a moment, the younger man was arrested by the sincerity he could read so clearly in Simon's now familiar, steady gaze. He watched, feeling strangely exposed by the frank expression as Simon reached for his hand, holding it loosely between his own. Simon's smile was utter kindness, as if he could read Mattie's every thought.

Mattie swallowed again, looking down at where Simon's thumb stroked over his wrist. "I knew this was a nice neighborhood, but…."

"Don't back away now," Simon pleaded quietly. He looked worried, slightly fearful even. As if Mattie might make a run for it.

Mattie chewed the inside of his cheek. He couldn't look away from their hands. "Should we be doing this?"

"Didn't you... I—I thought—"

"I want to be here." He dared look Simon in the eye. "Was just asking if I *should* be, that's all."

Simon looked inexplicably saddened, and the words of apology were on the tip of Mattie's tongue, but he found himself unable to speak when his hand was raised to Simon's lips and a kiss was brushed against his knuckles. It was a sweet gesture. Simon's eyes looked up at him over the rims of his glasses. Mattie took a quick breath.

"I'm hungry because I have next to nothing to eat at home," he blurted, feeling as if this was something he should come clean about—something he should say to test the waters.

Simon looked both surprised and troubled by this, and there was that sad look in his eyes again, but then a small smile touched his lips. "Then let me feed you my risotto and lemon chicken," he said with a slight hitch in his voice.

When Mattie didn't move, Simon gave his hand a gentle tug, and finally, Mattie felt the coil loosen its grip inside, and followed. He felt himself returning that tentative smile.

Not five minutes later, his worries had been, for the moment at least, placed on the back burner as he enjoyed a delicious home-cooked meal. He felt himself relax as Simon casually talked about his manuscript, and allowed himself to sit back with a glass of wine and just watch the man he was beginning to adore beyond words.

"So, how long do you think until it'll be finished?"

"I'd say about ten or eleven months, not including editing, of course."

"Really?"

Simon sat his own glass down. "Oh yeah, it's a long process, getting a book out. Writing can take a year, editing can take two or three months, and then there's actually getting it produced and out on the shelves. Not to mention that I actually rewrite everything at least three times anyway. From start to finish, it can take two to three years, depending on the publisher."

"No kidding."

"A year to write a book is actually a little embarrassing."

"I don't follow."

"Well, I've always been able to churn out the pages rather quickly when an idea takes form, but for most writers—at least for the writers I know—it usually takes up to two or three years." He shrugged. "I've always wondered if it was a reflection on the quality of my writing, but, uh…." He waved a hand dismissively. "Oh, ignore me." He bailed with a self-conscious smile.

"Well…." Mattie frowned, setting down his fork and laying his forearm across the table to slowly turn the stem of his wine glass. "We all develop and work at our own pace, don't we? I mean." He snorted. "I'm going to back high school in a few days to take my GED."

Simon let out a surprised laugh, and then, raising his brows and nodding, he dipped his head slightly and lifted his glass. "You're actually quite the savant, aren't you?"

"Uh… yes?"

Simon shook his head, still grinning, and stood to take his plate over to the spotless kitchen counter. "Would you like some more?"

"I'm good, actually, and so was the food. I didn't know you could cook."

"Well, I didn't want to raise Jamie on microwave meals and takeout, so I had to learn."

Mattie snickered. "I can just see you glaring at a cookbook, mixing spoon in hand."

Simon narrowed his eyes playfully as he held his hand out for Mattie's plate. "I went to a cooking class, actually."

"Yeah? Was it fun?"

"Uh, no, not really. I was the only guy there."

Mattie rolled his eyes. "Let me guess: single, cute dad learning to cook for the first time… they were on you like white on rice."

Simon shuddered. "You have no idea how frustrating it is to be so appealing to women but a lost cause to men."

"You're far from a lost cause, but it hardly matters what other guys think when you're already spoken for."

Simon turned around, leaning back on his hands against the counter. "I'm spoken for, am I?"

Mattie couldn't help but smirk with satisfaction at seeing the faint flush spread along Simon's cheeks. He pushed his chair back and slowly strode—no—*sauntered* over to where Simon stood. Mattie took Simon's hips in his hands, pulling him close. He brushed his nose against Simon's cheek as one of his hands wandered south and splayed over the other man's ass.

"Yes, you are."

"I—I'm agreeable to that."

"That's just as well, really." Mattie pressed a soft kiss against his throat.

"I think I rather like it when you get like this."

Mattie shook his head and stole a chaste kiss, keeping his hands on Simon's trim waist. "You really have no idea how much you tie me up in knots, do you?"

Simon let out a reticent huff but couldn't quite hide his pleasure. "Think I'm beginning to see, actually."

"It's about time." He brought his hand up to cup the side of Simon's face and kissed him like he'd been jonesing to do all day.

They pulled apart a fraction, and Mattie watched from under his eyelashes, pleased at how ruffled Simon appeared. Simon's eyes remained closed. He wet his lip and then swallowed hard. Having this sort of effect on the writer did a lot for Mattie's ego, not to mention his libido.

"Do—" Simon cleared his throat and opened his eyes. "Do you want to take our drinks into the other room?"

Mattie grinned, feeling for once confident and brave, and gave Simon room to breathe. "Lead the way."

Mattie trailed after him with his wine glass in hand, and took in his surroundings as he followed Simon into the living room. It really was a nice place, spacious and homely all at the same time. He bit his lip against a smile as Simon set his glass down and fidgeted, brushing his hands down his khakis and straightening his glasses. Fucking. Cute.

"Um, music?"

"Sure." Mattie didn't take a seat right away and instead wandered over to a large glass cabinet that held a series of photographs. Mostly all were of Jamie. He tilted his head to the side slightly as he studied the pictures, practically seeing the boy grow in years. He smiled broadly when noticing that, in all recent photographs, Jamie was wearing his cape.

"I know people are supposed to say this when they see pictures of other people's children, but you really do have the cutest kid, like… ever."

Simon smiled over his shoulder as he looked up from where he flicked through what appeared to be a large CD collection in a hefty folder. "Yeah, I do."

"Little guy's going to be a heartbreaker when he's older."

Simon groaned. "Don't. I can't believe he's nearly five years old. It feels like just yesterday that he fit in the crook of my arm."

"Five, huh? That's sort of the first milestone."

"Yes, I suppose it might be."

"Doing anything special for the big day?"

"Well, Sarah suggested a small birthday party with a few of the other kids from his class. Just some party games, some crafts, that sort of thing."

"That sounds great."

"It sounds scary." Simon laughed, still flipping through his collection of CDs.

"Why?" Mattie frowned, picking up another photo frame and smiling broadly at the picture of Simon and Jamie both dressed up as... hobbits? He wondered who took the picture.

"I guess all I can think about is what might go wrong." He shrugged. "Pointless, really. Sarah will be there, a few of the other kids' parents will be there... my mother will be there."

Mattie's brows rose. "Holy crap, that's huge. *Great*, but huge."

"I don't know; it might be." He shrugged. "All the same, I'm not looking forward to Saturday. The party'll kick off around five. She'll be over at around three to help set up and... I don't know, meet Jamie officially, I guess."

"I'm sure it'll go just fine." Mattie bit his lip. "Do, uh... do you need some moral support?" He asked, attempting to pass it off lightly.

Simon snorted. "I'm going to need all the help I can get come Saturday. Ah ha! Here we go." He slotted a CD into the machine and then turned and strolled up to Mattie almost awkwardly.

Unsure if that had been an answer or not, Mattie let it go for the moment. He frowned, tilting his head toward the stereo like a hound catching a scent. The strands of a very old-fashioned, 1940s-era song drifted through the living room.

"You don't like it." Simon paused, looking unsure of himself. "It's corny, isn't it? I'll change it—"

Mattie shushed him, waving his hand in a hushing gesture. "I know this, but I have no idea who it is, if that makes sense?"

"Yeah, it's one of those classics everyone knows. It's 'You Go to My Head', by Louis Armstrong."

"It's romantic."

"That's... kind of what I was going for." Simon laughed nervously.

"Come here." Mattie didn't wait, however, and pulled Simon close. With one hand at Simon's waist, his other held Simon's hand, curling it so that the back of Simon's hand rested against his chest. It was something he'd seen in an old Jerry Lewis film once, and he'd always wanted to do it. He nuzzled close, his nose brushing Simon's as he led them in a gentle sway. There was no real dancing involved—he didn't know how—but this was enough.

"Mattie," Simon whispered his name, and they stayed that way for a few minutes, until the next oldie began to play. Simon pulled away almost reluctantly. His voice was a low murmur. "Did you, uh, did you want that tour?"

"Does it start upstairs?"

A smile split across Simon's face. "As a matter of fact...."

Mattie turned Simon in his arms, his hands at his waist. "Let's go."

There had been a tour of some sort, but Mattie knew he wouldn't know where the bathroom was if asked. He'd more or less pushed Simon down onto an ohmygod comfortable bed and stripped him without preamble. It reminded him of their first time together, actually. And at that thought, he mentally cooled his heels a little, attempted to rein in the excited horny puppy and summon any seductive prowess he possessed.

Simon's reassurance earlier that night and his oddly endearing nervousness during their meal had led him to one thought: *fuck* feeling intimidated. He may not have the cash or the security, but he could sure as hell be Simon's man. There were ways to take care of people other than financially. He couldn't bring home bacon, but he could make Simon scream in the bedroom, he could be that shoulder to lean on, and he could be the best friend Simon ever had.

As worked up as he felt, he kept the pace slow. He leaned up on one hand, just above Simon's shoulder. His other held Simon's flushed cheek with his thumb gently soothing over warm skin as he moved, his back arching and his head hanging low with his bangs in his eyes. His hand moved down to gently clasp Simon's throat, and Simon's eyes fluttered open.

That's right. I'm your man. He didn't tighten his grip on Simon's throat, but his movements became less languid and more forceful. Simon's breath hitched and became ragged, and Mattie had to grit his teeth against the coil of pleasure forming in his groin as Simon moaned and gripped desperately at his shoulders and back.

He went down on his elbows, their chests rubbing together, so he could press his face into Simon's throat. The sudden vice-like grip on his shoulders and the feel of Simon's hips bucking against his own was the signal he was waiting for. With Simon on the cusp of losing it, he let go and fucked him good and hard through his orgasm. His own followed a millisecond later.

A sweaty, panting mess, Mattie collapsed beside Simon and raked his hands through his hair as he attempted to catch his breath. He tingled all over and felt fucking incredible. He glanced over with no small amount of pride when Simon near enough mirrored his thoughts out loud.

"THAT was…." Simon broke off and laughed. "That was incredible. Just… wow."

Mattie bit his lip against an obnoxiously proud grin. "You uh, you were really into that."

"You caught that, did you?" Simon laughed breathlessly.

Mattie shrugged. "Most guys tend to lean either one way or the other. I thought I had you pegged. I'm not so sure now."

Simon turned his head on the pillow, watching Mattie as he caught his breath. "You did have me pegged."

"Then you put on one hell of a show."

Simon looked up at his ceiling, letting out a deep breath and smiling lazily. "I guess you unpegged me. I'm more of a fifty-fifty man now."

"I kind of feel like thumping my chest."

"I kind of feel like giving you a standing ovation."

"Aw, what the hell." He thumped his chest, and Simon laughed. "This is one hell of comfy mattress."

Simon winked. "Memory foam."

"Ooh. Nice, man."

"Yup."

Mattie watched as Simon squinted and leaned up on one elbow to search for his glasses on the nightstand closest to him. "Here," Mattie supplied. He'd gently pulled them off and set them aside before rocking Simon's world.

Simon reached for them with a quiet "thanks" but looked at Mattie quizzically when they weren't immediately handed over. He had to smile and close his eyes as Mattie placed them gently on his face for him, then climbed out of the bed, presumably to clean up.

"Uh… bathroom?" Mattie hesitated, still naked, sweaty, and a little roguish by the bedroom door.

Simon raised an eyebrow, teasing. "I already showed you where the bathroom was, if I recall correctly."

"Nah, I was looking at your ass the entire time."

Simon barked a laugh and shook his head. He pointed over to the door that joined his bedroom to his own bathroom. "It's that way, one track."

"Two bathrooms?" Mattie strolled over to the bathroom and left the door open behind him. "Well I do *declare,* Mister Castle!" he cried in his best Southern belle voice.

Simon snorted and collapsed back on the mattress. "Dork," he muttered affectionately. He heard the faucet turn on and off, and gladly took the damp washrag handed to him to swipe over his stomach. He felt the mattress dip next to him and looked over at the sight of Mattie with his arms resting behind his head, eyes closed, looking sated, relaxed, and utterly gorgeous.

Mattie opened his eyes blearily, looking suspiciously like the cat that got the cream. "You all right?" he asked softly, a frown appearing on his brow. "Did I hurt you?"

Simon shook his head. "No, I'm fine. I, uh…." He swallowed and moved closer across the mattress. He cast Mattie a quick, cautious look before easing his arm around Mattie's middle and finally giving in. He laid his head across Mattie's chest, his shoulders drooping and relaxing instantly.

He let out a deep, weary but contented sigh as Mattie's fingers stroked through his hair and across his back. It felt so goddamn good to be held. The feel of Mattie's skin under his cheek, the regular thump of his heart, and the steady rise and fall of his chest was the safest feeling in the world.

"This is nice," Mattie crooned.

Simon hummed in response; it was more than nice. "It's been so long. I'm always the one to plan ahead. I'm always worrying," he said in a voice that was not completely steady. He cleared his throat before continuing. "It's difficult, being the one in charge, the one to comfort… this *is* nice," he repeated Mattie's words.

He felt Mattie curl beneath him slightly, and a kiss was pressed against his temple. He closed his eyes tight for a second, worried that he might actually ruin what had been a very pleasant evening by inexplicably tearing up.

"Am I that person now?" Mattie said softly, his fingers still combing soothingly through Simon's hair.

"That person?"

"The person you tell your secrets to," Mattie murmured quietly.

Now his eyes really were stinging. He nodded against Mattie's chest and laughed softly at himself for getting emotional. "You just might be."

"Good. I wanna be that guy for you."

In no time at all, the few hours alone together had ticked by, and it was, unfortunately, time to call it a night. More than ever Simon didn't want the evening to end, but he needed to pick up Jamie. Now they sat in his car, the engine idling outside of Mattie's apartment block.

"So, this is where I say I had a great time," Mattie provided.

"Usually, yes."

"I had a fucking awesome time."

Simon laughed. "Me too. We'll do it again soon?"

"Absolutely, come here." Mattie unbuckled and leaned close. He gently gripped the back of Simon's neck and kissed him. "See you soon." He winked and climbed out of the car, missing Simon's troubled expression.

MATTIE was at the apartment entrance when Simon climbed out of the car. At the sound of the car door closing, Mattie looked back over his shoulder to see Simon following him.

"Hey, miss me already?" he teased.

"No—I mean, I—I want to, um…."

"You know, you're either very wordy, or you can't speak at all," Mattie laughed softly.

"Please just… don't get offended, okay?"

Mattie frowned. "What's going on?"

Simon looked ridiculously uncomfortable for a few seconds before reaching into his back pocket and pulling out his wallet. He pulled out a twenty and three tens, hesitated a moment, and then held it forward, urging Mattie to take it.

"I don't want you reading into anything, I don't want you misinterpreting this, and I don't want you to be offended or proud right now. You said you had no food in your cupboards, and as a, um, boyfriend of sorts, I can't let that happen. So, here." He extended his hand forward again, urging Mattie to take the money. "Please, just take it."

"You're giving me money?" Abruptly, there were several feelings at war within him. His pride *was* rearing its ugly head. There was a hint of relief, a good measure of embarrassment, but mostly, he was attempting to wrap his head around the word "boyfriend" having finally popped out of Simon's mouth.

"Giving, loaning, whatever makes you more comfortable, but yes, you are taking this money whether you like it or not."

Mattie's lips lifted at one corner in a sad smile. He took the money and watched Simon's shoulders sag in relief. "Thank you," he said quietly.

Simon finally smiled and pulled Mattie into hug. "You know you can always ask, right?" he said quietly. "I know it's awkward, but please don't be afraid to ask if you need to." He hummed happily when Mattie completed the hug by wrapping his arms around his neck. He rubbed his hands in soothing circles along Mattie's back before pulling away a little, gently touching the back of Mattie's elbows and looking him in the eye. "All right?"

Mattie nodded, looking down at his hand that held the cash. "I just don't want you to think I'm using you or—"

"Hey," he interrupted. "If you're the guy I tell my secrets to, then I'm the guy you lean on when you need help, understand?" He snorted. "Hell, how long have we been seeing each other? Four, five months? And tonight's the first time *I* cooked for *you*. I've been over at your place three nights a week, eating you out of house and home. If anything, I owe you."

Mattie swallowed but pulled the twenty separate and held it out for Simon to take back. "Thirty's enough for groceries, Simon. I get paid soon."

Simon took his hand and pushed it back. "Then buy some art supplies; I haven't seen you drawing or working on any new paintings in a while, and I have to say that bothers me."

"Why?" Mattie asked quietly.

"Because you're talented and because it's something you love to do."

Mattie looked back down at his hands, afraid to speak in case his voice cracked. He nodded and folded the bills, putting them in the back pocket of his jeans. He reached forward, tugged Simon close by his open jacket, and nuzzled his nose against Simon's cheek affectionately. He whispered one more thank you, offered him another kiss goodnight, and then watched Simon climb back in his car and drive away.

Later that night in bed, for the first time in a long time, he didn't lie awake worrying about money or Simon's feelings for him. His head hit the pillow free of worries for once, and the familiar anxiety that usually hindered his dreams, taking the form of a frayed, coiled rope, was absent.

To say his nerves were on edge would be an understatement. The hardest part was over, he supposed. His mother had arrived a few hours ago, and since then she and Jamie had been in his playroom, getting to know one another in person. He'd stayed with them for the first half an hour, worried his mom might accidently forget herself and try to hug him, which was an entirely reasonable thing for any grandmother to do under normal circumstances, but not when Jamie was so clearly wary of this new person.

Simon had to give her some credit. She hadn't overstepped once, and he thought that perhaps her biggest worry might be that Jamie would associate her with the scary woman who had sat next to him at recess those few weeks ago. Whether Jamie recalled that event or not, he seemed quite content to at least show her Gizmo, his beloved hamster. The few times he had taken a break from filling party bags and laying out markers and crayons, he'd joined them to check that all was running smoothly, and it was.

He stood now outside the playroom and smiled at the sight of them together. His mother had crouched down to sit on the floor, and was stroking Gizmo's head with one finger as Jamie held him in both hands proudly, expounding on what a good hamster he was. Just about every time he caught his mother's eye, she looked about two seconds away from tears. He was hesitant to walk away. He didn't like the thought of his mother struggling to stand without help, and Jamie needed to get changed, but a knock at his front door pulled him away from the picturesque scene.

He opened the door to greet Sarah and reached to help her with her carrier bags, ushering her in.

"I'm sorry I'm late. My car wouldn't start."

"When are you going to scrap that thing?"

"When I can afford to buy a new one. Is there a lot left to do?"

"Not really, just the food."

"Is your mom here?" she asked carefully.

Simon nodded. "In the playroom with Jamie."

"How's it going?"

One corner of his mouth turned up in a sad smile. "Really well, actually."

"Hey…." She touched his forearm. "If it's going so well then why the face?"

He lifted one shoulder, emptying one of the carrier bags onto the kitchen counter. "It's just nice seeing Jamie with his grandmother, and it's something he could have had years ago if I'd pulled my head out of my ass sooner."

"You had your reasons, Simon."

"I know," he said softly, nodding. He turned to lean against the counter and look her in the eye. "I just really want today to go well. It's a big day."

"Everything'll be fine. You'll see."

"There's so much that could go wrong."

She rolled her eyes and lightly slapped his upper arm to get him out of the way of the counter. "It's a party, Simon."

"With five autistic children."

"And your son's teacher, your mother, and two other parents. It's not like we're outnumbered."

"I know, I know. I just feel like this is the first birthday Jamie's really going to remember. I want it to go well. I want it to be normal."

"And why wouldn't it be?" She pulled out several slices of bread onto the chopping board and opened the drawer that held the knives, forks, and spoons. She knew her way around the kitchen as if she lived there herself.

"I…." He sighed and threw the dishtowel he'd snagged up and been twisting between his hands down on the counter. "I'm being stupid."

"Yes. Sorry, but yes."

"I don't know why I'm being like this."

"Well...." Sarah turned and offered him a sympathetic smile. "Your family is a group of three again. You're, I don't know." She shrugged. "You're rebuilding a relationship and introducing someone else into Jamie's home life. I can understand why you might feel uneasy."

"Yeah," he scoffed. "'Uneasy' is one way of putting it."

"Just... remember that these kids pick up on other people's moods all too easily. If you're tense, chances are Jamie's going to feel tense too."

His shoulders slumped. "You're right."

"Okay, look at me. Take a deep breath in...." She took a deep breath and then let it out with a laugh when Simon glared at her. "Jamie's going to have a great time, and so are you. So relax!"

"All right!" He laughed. "I'm relaxing."

"Good. Now why don't you carry on with these while I go introduce myself to your mom and say hi to Jamie?"

"They can wait a few minutes; I'll introduce you. Then I have to go get Jamie into his party clothes."

"Party clothes?"

Simon smiled. "I got him these little khaki pants and a sweater vest with a picture of a train on it. He'll love it."

"If you say so," she laughed.

"Okay, so I'll at least *force* him to love it long enough for me to take a picture. Then he'll probably be back in his favorite PJ's."

"That does sound more likely."

"Smartass," he sighed. "All right, come meet my mom."

HE HAD no idea what he was looking for. Just what did five-year-old kids like these days, anyway? In a bid to distract himself from thoughts about tests, art school, and money, he'd taken himself off to the mall to search for a great birthday gift for Jamie. Now, Mattie found himself not only stressed about his transcripts and finishing up a portfolio and entrance essay he wasn't even sure he was going to submit, but about what kind of an impression a teddy bear or train set would make to a five-year-old.

He mentally shook himself. It was done now, and there was no point in getting worked up about it. He'd taken the tests, done his absolute best. Now all he could do was sit back and wait a minimum of four weeks for his results.

He mulled over what a long journey it'd been for him: nearly two years of adult reading and writing classes, three or four months of hard-core studying, and five long-winded tests that could make all the difference to his future.

And here he was, close to having the qualifications that, at the very least, could enable him to get a better-paying job, if not start him off on the path to his original goal: art school. Not to mention the shopping for a birthday gift for his boyfriend's son.

At the thought of meeting Jamie again in a capacity as more than the guy from the diner, but as someone important in his dad's life, he had to stave off the nerves that wanted to overwhelm him. He thought that he was fairly likeable, and it wasn't as if he hadn't met the kid before, but he was also so desperate for Jamie to like him. If Jamie didn't, then his relationship with Simon didn't stand much of a chance.

He stopped in place when he caught sight of what might just be the perfect gift; not too much but something Jamie might genuinely like. It was a set of special edition *Lord of the Rings* top trump cards. Surprised that toy stores would even still stock *Lord of The Rings* merchandise, he picked them up—not even bothering to look at the price because they were absolutely the perfect gift—and made his way over to one of the cash registers.

Now it was only a question of having the balls to wrap them up, slap a bow on there, and deliver them. There was the true dilemma: give them to Simon tomorrow, or nip over there during the party—just for a few minutes, mind you—to give them to Jamie himself.

At first he'd attempted to kid himself into thinking he'd been invited, that his offering to be there for moral support had been taken seriously. But honestly? He couldn't say for sure if it had. Simon had laughed it off, too wrapped up in his worry about how the party would go to consider his suggestion for what it was.

What he couldn't decide on, and what was making him hesitate about just showing up like any other boyfriend would, was whether— invite or no—his appearance would be a happy surprise for Simon. It could play out one of two ways: Simon would become awkward and overly polite but ultimately be unhappy at his presence, or Simon would be relieved.

Heading home with the small bag looped over his wrist, hands tucked in his pockets and head down against the wind, he couldn't help but smile a little wistfully at what it might be like to evoke that look of pleased relief. To feel welcomed into the home of someone you were very significant to.

There was the issue of Simon's mother being there, his friend Sarah and the parents of the other kids, not to mention Jamie, but Simon had made some serious progress with his mother, or so he'd told him. He'd felt proud of Simon for being willing to begin to forgive his mother while maintaining his stance of a proud gay man. If he were in Simon's shoes, he didn't know if he could be so brave. The sometimes disapproving looks from anyone who might overhear conversation that included any homosexual activity—hand holding included—was enough to make him want to shrivel up.

Not Simon. He wouldn't hide who he was after already coming so far. It was merely a matter of judging whether it was too soon to include himself into that mix. Mattie thought perhaps with his mother meeting Jamie—officially—for the first time, that it may be too soon to introduce the boyfriend on the same day. A shame, really, because things were so good between them at the moment. *Really* good. Every instant Simon wasn't with Jamie or writing, they were together. Like a real, devoted couple.

Surely five minutes wouldn't hurt? He could nip in, drop off the gift, and let Simon know he was thinking of him. He wouldn't ask to meet his friends, his mother, or Jamie. He'd just let Simon know that he was in his thoughts and that he loved him. Just without the actual words.

Five minutes.

"WOULD you calm down already?"

Simon leaned against the kitchen counter, craning his neck to see through to the living room where the kids all crowded around the coffee table, scribbling away on the several coloring books he'd bought that morning.

"It's going fine, Simon," Sarah said in a hushed voice so his guests seated in the next room wouldn't hear. "They're actually having fun."

He watched as his mother carefully crouched down on the floor beside Jamie to ask him about his drawing. Jamie wouldn't look at her, but he saw his lips move in answer. It was good to see. It was heartwarming to see Jamie having such a nice time, and to see his mother so happy to boot. He had to admit, it *was* going fine, and he felt foolish for worrying so much.

"Can you give me a hand?" Sarah asked.

"Sure. Here...." He took the coffeepot from her hand. "Let me do that."

"Great. You do the adults, and I'll see to the kids. Did you get ice cream?"

He nodded. "Chocolate and vanilla. Oh, and some sprinkles in the cupboard." He stopped short. "I don't know which flavors they all like."

"I teach those kids, remember? Three vanillas and two chocolate."

"Thank God you're here."

"You, Simon Castle, are a drama queen."

He paused in pouring his coffee. "Did you seriously just call me a queen?"

Sarah grinned and opened her mouth to answer, but a happy squeal followed by the giggling of young children caused them both to glance to the living room and laugh quietly.

"Queen or not, your son is having a great time."

"He is," he agreed. "And he looks abso-friggin-lutely adorable."

"Oh my God, Simon." She swooned, licking the ice cream from her thumb. "I just want to eat him up in his little sweater vest. I can't believe he's actually kept it on."

"He even stood still and let me take pictures."

"He's a good little man."

"I only wish he'd have left the cape in his room."

"Baby steps."

He glanced at her fondly. "You sound like a mother. You know that?"

She placed the ice cream bowls on a tray and smiled sadly. "I'd kind of like to be, one day."

"You will be, and you'll be the best mom ever."

"Thanks, Simon." She sighed and put her hands on her hips as she glanced around the kitchen. "Where did you say those sprinkles were?"

Simon pulled the milk out of the fridge and tried to remember who had wanted their coffee black, and who wanted white. "In the cupboard, next to the tomato soup."

"Ah, I know where."

Simon watched her as she moved around his kitchen with ease, as if she knew it as well as her own. "Anyone who didn't know the dynamics of our relationship would think you were my wife. I swear it."

She snorted in quite an unladylike fashion and set the sprinkles on the tray. "Well, they'd be sorely disappointed."

He hummed in agreement. "Like my mom."

"What? Your mom's been great."

He smiled sadly and shook his head. It saddened him to see the glimmer of hope in his mother's eyes when watching him with Sarah. Not to mention that the hastily dodged questions about Jamie's mother from his guests had set his teeth on edge. "You didn't see the way she watched you in this kitchen."

"She's probably just not used to seeing you so familiar with a woman."

"No, she's definitely not, and she's not alone. Did you see how Tommy's mother was—?"

"Simon," she interrupted. "You're not happy if you're not worrying about something, are you?"

He sputtered, offended. "I admit I'm tightly wound at the moment, but I think that's a little unfair."

"Then for the tenth time, *relax*. Everything's going great. Jamie's having fun, the other kids are having fun, your other guests are *not* watching your every homosexual move despite what you think, and your mom knows you're gay. Gay as a goose."

He sighed. "I think I need a Valium."

"You don't take Valium."

"I think I need to start taking Valium."

She slapped his forearm and then picked up the tray of ice cream. "I'm taking this in before it melts. Hurry up with that coffee."

"I'll be right in." There was a knock at the front door. "As soon as I've answered that."

"All right."

He watched her leave the kitchen and smiled at the delighted response from the kids when asked who wanted ice cream. He walked through to the hallway, opened the door, and was more than a little surprised to see Mattie standing there.

Mattie offered him a delighted smile. A smile Simon couldn't seem to offer in return.

"Hey." Mattie spoke quietly, stepping through the door and giving him a quick hug. "I hope I didn't interrupt the party?"

He barely returned the hug as panic began to prickle along his spine. "Mattie. W-what are you doing here?"

Mattie reached into his pocket and pulled out a small wrapped gift. "I got this for Jamie. I was just going to drop it off—"

"You can't!" Simon hissed.

Mattie's smile faded. "What? I wasn't—" He wet his lips quickly. "I wasn't going to stay or nothing. I just wanted to give you Jamie's gift so he could have it on his birthday."

Simon shot a quick look over his shoulder and then more or less snatched the gift from Mattie's hand. "That's very sweet of you, Mattie, but you have to get going."

Mattie still held his hand out from where Simon had hastily taken the gift, and slowly lowered it as he looked at Simon with confusion. "Um, okay. Is everything all right?"

Simon sighed and took hold of Mattie's upper arm to gently encourage him toward the door. "I'm fine, everything's fine. You just... you can't be here right now. I'm sorry."

Mattie pulled his arm out of Simon's grip, feeling hurt. "Why are you being like this? All I was trying to do—"

"Oh, for the love of—" Simon cut himself off, pinching the bridge of his nose. "It's inappropriate that you're here."

"*Why?*" Mattie hissed, feeling pissed but alarmingly close to upset at the same time.

"Because this is my son's birthday party!" Simon hissed back. "My mother is here. I have guests. You can't just invite yourself—"

"Simon? You're guests are getting thirst—oh."

Simon's mother paused in the hallway behind them, and he could gauge her expression perfectly. Surprise turned quickly to schooled discomfort. How close they stood together, along with the undeniable tension between them, were fairly obvious indicators as to what the nature of their relationship might be. Simon swallowed hard, upset at the thought that everything he and his mother had worked at was about to go up in smoke, and that Jamie was about to lose his new grandmother. He wanted to mesh these two worlds together—his past and present—but not yet. It had to be done delicately. He could see the question forming on her lips, and panicked.

"Who—"

"He's nobody," he blurted, regretting the words instantly. He shook his head, shocked at himself. "I—I mean to say, um...."

His mother frowned, stepped forward. "Simon—" An unhappy wail from the living room made them both jump, and with a last worried glance at Simon, she turned and left the hallway.

Simon looked back at Mattie and felt his heart sink. The only word to describe that look was "betrayed." "I—I'm sorry. It just came out. I didn't mean to say that."

"No, of course you didn't." Mattie bit his bottom lip and then shook his head. He put his hands in his pockets, stepped backward. "I'm so stupid." He swallowed, then nodded to himself. "Okay, I—I think I'm done," he whispered.

"Oh, come on, Mattie...."

"No," he ground out between clenched teeth, turning his body away sideways when Simon tried to reach for his hand. "I'm done, you hear me? I can't wait for you anymore, not when it's one step forward and then ten steps back. I thought—" His voice faltered slightly, and he swallowed hard. "I thought this was going somewhere, but I'm just kidding myself, aren't I?" He clenched his jaw. "You can be so wonderful sometimes, just—just the best guy in the world, you know? But when push comes to shove, you let me down. You turn nasty." He shook his head. "And I don't need that shit."

Simon's mouth worked uselessly, unable to say anything for a second. "That's not fair, Mattie." His voice sounded weak and pleading even to him. "I—you don't know what it's like, you don't *know*—"

"Oh, fuck you, Simon," he said breathlessly. "You think you're the only one who struggles? Stop using your kid as an excuse to keep me at a distance, because it's *bullshit*. I'd be great with Jamie, and you know it. It's you. *You're* the problem. Either you're too chickenshit to take a chance with me, or you just don't care enough to."

"I do want you," he whispered. "I—I just don't…." He trailed off, lost for words.

Mattie nodded and then turned away, taking a deep breath. When he looked at Simon again, his eyes shone with unshed tears, and he smiled without humor. "Screw you for leading me on," he whispered. "And screw you for not having the balls to love me back. *Screw you,* Simon."

"Simon?" Sarah appeared in the hallway, and much like his mother had, halted when noticing Mattie. "Oh, I'm sorry to interrupt, but it's Jamie. One of the boys pulled on his cape. You should probably come."

Simon groaned and ran a hand through his hair. He didn't move.

Sarah leaned around him, offering Mattie a shy smile. "Hi there, are you Mattie by any chance?"

Mattie looked back at Simon and shook his head once. "I'm nobody." He turned and ignored Simon's call as he slammed the front door closed behind him.

"*Fuck,*" Simon hissed.

"Simon, what did you—?"

Simon ignored her question, pushing past her and toward his son, who was calling for him.

Chapter
Eight

SIMON stared at the blinking cursor. He'd been sitting at his kitchen table, staring at the open document for what felt like hours. The house was quiet. It had never bothered him before, but just recently it was all he could do to not turn on the stereo, TV, and radio just to not feel so alone. He supposed he could always go to the library, or find an Internet cafe to write in, but he knew he wouldn't be able to concentrate there either. He sure as hell couldn't go back to the diner, not after last time.

His voicemails went unanswered and his texts ignored. He'd taken one step into the diner three weeks ago, and Ty had more or less thrown him out—banning him, apparently—before he'd even made it to the sandwich counter. He hadn't been there to work. His laptop had stayed home. He'd gone there in a desperate attempt to talk to Mattie, to apologize and beg him to just hear him out. Not that he even knew what to say.

He hated himself, pure and simple. He'd fucked up too many times with Mattie, and as the days had ticked by, he'd found he could no longer kid himself into thinking Mattie had overreacted. He'd strung him along and insulted him by keeping him away from his son. Neither had been deliberate, but that hardly mattered.

What made matters worse was that Jamie was picking up on his morose mood, but he could not shift the heavy feeling in his chest. He felt like he'd lost his best friend as well as his lover. He missed Mattie.

He missed him so much that he just didn't care about anything else. His usually pristine house was a mess. He hadn't written more than a paragraph in the past four and a half weeks. He had his editor and Sarah breathing down his neck to get back into the swing of things—to get writing, to get Mattie back—to get on with his life either way. But he felt oddly stuck in place, unwilling to move on.

It'd been different with Tim. When Tim took off, he'd felt terrified, panicked even, at the thought of being alone. But being alone wasn't the problem. It was no longer being a part of Mattie's life that was killing him. He hated that Mattie doubted what it was he felt for him. He hated himself for not having had the balls to make it clear how much he adored the man. Now? Well, now Mattie was under the impression that, what? He'd been his plaything? Someone to pass the time with?

He leaned both elbows on the table and pressed the heels of his hands into his eyes. He'd fucked up so bad, and as a result he'd never felt so low in his life. He needed Mattie. He hated not speaking to him. He hated not knowing if he was okay or what was happening in his life. And he had no idea how to fix it.

"*Think*," he ground out, his voice thick, his eyes blurry, and the heels of his hands damp as he leaned back in his chair with a sniff.

The timer on the oven went off, reminding him it was time to leave and pick up Jamie. He'd taken to setting the alarm after the one (and first) time he'd been late picking Jamie up from school a few days ago. He'd been sitting at the kitchen table, much as he was now, not working but lost in thought, only to glance at the clock and realize he should have been at the school ten minutes previously. Needless to say he'd had a very unhappy five-year-old to answer to.

He closed his laptop and reached for his keys. It was frustrating, really, because he kept going back to one thing in particular Mattie had said.

"*I'd be great with Jamie, and you know it. It's you. You're the problem. Either you're too chickenshit to take a chance with me, or you just don't care enough to.*"

It struck him as frustrating because Mattie was right, but he'd also never been more wrong. He'd genuinely worried about allowing Mattie to get close to his son, for a number of reasons. But he *had* been using Jamie as an excuse to keep the pace of their relationship as slow as he had. He *was* a chickenshit. He was afraid of Mattie. He was afraid that this gorgeous, talented, younger man would one day just take off. He was afraid of not being enough. He was afraid of Jamie being *too* much. And, if he were honest, he was afraid of resenting his own son for potentially being the reason for losing someone else he loved.

But Jamie hadn't pushed Mattie away. He had.

"Enough," he growled, pulling on his jacket and tucking his phone and wallet into his pockets. "Enough of this bullshit."

IT HAD been a lonely, miserable four or so weeks. By rights he should be feeling high as a kite. A little over a year ago, he'd been almost completely illiterate. Now he had American high-school level academic skills and a general equivalency diploma to prove it. His boss, Don, had even allowed him to pick up some extra shifts waiting on tables for the first time. And as a result, he'd been able to pay Ty back, and even had enough cash for groceries and rent that month.

Then there was the biggie. He'd finished his entrance essay (which had ended up being far more personal than he'd originally planned) and portfolio, and in a fit of *"fuck this town and everyone in it"* he'd sent it off to the Art Institute of New York along with his transcripts.

He'd come so far. He'd worked his fucking *ass* off. And here he was, miserable. He missed Simon so much it literally hurt him, right in the chest like indigestion, and it made him feel pathetic. He missed his quiet nature and unsure smile. He missed how it felt to lie in bed with him. He missed making Simon blush. He missed that feeling of equality, of normalness that Simon and only Simon had given him.

He'd forced himself to ignore every voicemail and every text. He wanted more than anything to call Simon back and pretend that everything was normal. He wanted his happy bubble back. But he couldn't do it to himself. He'd worked too hard on changing who he was and pulling that coil loose. To go back to Simon now, knowing that it wasn't the lifesaving relationship he'd thought it was, would be the biggest step backward.

Instead, he was focusing on the normal stuff. He went to work; he still made the sandwiches but waited tables now too. He came home; he sketched and he painted until the lighting was too poor to continue. But most of the time, he'd catch himself thinking of Simon, wondering what he was up to, how his book was going, how Jamie was doing. No matter how much he wished it, he couldn't turn off the feelings that had developed during their strange relationship.

Mattie was painting now, making use of his recently restocked supplies, and imagining what it would be like to actually go to New York and achieve everything that had seemed too much of a challenge a year ago. Just the thought of him, former illiterate prostitute, going to *college*. It was almost enough to make him smile. Almost.

There was a knock at his door, but he decided to ignore it. If it was a visitor they would have called him or buzzed. It could only be his landlord or a neighbor, and he didn't feel like speaking to either. With no music or TV on in the background, it was easy to play possum.

There was a silence, lasting approximately ten seconds, before there was another knock at the door. He thought idly of one of the passages he'd liked by some dead guy that he'd studied for his English Lit test. Something about a bird, knock knocking at his chamber door.

"Mattie? Are you in?"

He dropped his paintbrush and felt his stomach drop. He wanted to run to the door, while feeling contradictorily annoyed that Simon had dared turn up at his apartment after several very obvious brush-offs.

"Mattie, please open the door? *Please*? I know you're in. I just spoke to your neighbor."

Mattie ran his hands over his face. Simon sounded terrible. He sounded unsure and a touch desperate. Instead of it being a turn off, it almost softened something inside of him.

Almost.

He strode over to the door, intent on firmly asking Simon to leave. He opened the door, and any words of dismissal escaped him. Simon stood there, a small Ninja Turtle backpack hanging over one arm and a small child wearing a cape in the other.

IT WAS easier to get into the building than he'd thought it would be. He knew Mattie wouldn't buzz him in if he were home, so he'd intended to either wait outside the building and ambush him, or plead with a neighbor to let him in. Fortunately, having a cute kid on his hip was apparently the easiest and fastest way to charm his way through the front doors.

Having made his way in, and with Mattie standing opposite him now, looking utterly shocked, all the carefully planned and rehearsed words left him. Simon couldn't think of a thing to say, except…

"Hi." *God, I've missed you.*

"Hi." *You bastard.*

Simon cleared his throat. "Can I—can we come in? Please?" he asked quietly.

Mattie leveled him with a displeased look that made him swallow nervously. Perhaps this wasn't going to work. Perhaps it really was over. But then Mattie sighed softly, glancing at Jamie and tilting his head as if to catch his gaze. Something that at that moment was not possible as Jamie clung to him, nervous in these new surroundings.

"Hi, Jamie. I don't suppose you remember me?"

He felt Jamie's head move under his chin, but he knew Jamie wouldn't look Mattie in the eye. He could feel one small hand twisting the collar of his jacket nervously.

"You cut the crusts off my sandwich," Jamie replied quietly.

Mattie's smile changed from polite to genuinely quite enamored in a second flat, and Simon felt something inside of him unwind. He bounced Jamie gently on his hip, proud of his son for responding.

"That's right, little guy." Mattie glanced back at Simon, some of the warmth leaving his eyes to be replaced by wariness. He looked back at Jamie. "You know what, Jamie? I hear you don't like to talk too much, and I also know that new places are a little scary for you, but that's okay. How about you come on in with your dad, and I can show you around. Then I'll make you one of those PBJ sandwiches? Would you like that?"

He could feel Jamie squirm a little restlessly against his hip, and he knew his child was conflicted. Jamie's instincts were telling him to not reply and to say his numbers until his dad took him home to where his building blocks were. But all of the practicing they did about manners and the fact that his dad hadn't taken him away was confusing him. Not to mention that, despite being autistic, Jamie was still a child and, at times, as curious as any other.

"No crusts?" he asked after some time, and Mattie's smile in response could have lit up any room.

"I remember just how you like it." He glanced at Simon and moved aside. "I'll even give you a tour."

"Thank you," Simon said quietly and passed Mattie into the familiar surroundings. The entranceway led to the kitchen and living room, which was essentially one large divided room with a doorway leading to the bedroom.

"Well," Mattie drawled, then spread his arms comically. "This is it!"

"Your house is small," Jamie said against his dad's shoulder. Simon let out a breathless little laugh and bounced Jamie against his hip as he gave Mattie an apologetic smile.

"Sorry," he offered.

"That's okay." Mattie smiled, not even bothering to look up at Simon. "It's only me here, so it doesn't need to be big. *Well*...." He put his hands in his pockets and tilted his head to one side. "That is, it's just me and my bunny rabbit."

Jamie's head came up off of his shoulder, though Simon knew his son's gaze rose no higher than Mattie's chest. "You have a bunny?"

"Yeah, I do. Do you want to meet him?"

Jamie was already wriggling against him, attempting to shimmy out of his dad's arms. Simon snorted and set him down, though he took his son's hand when Jamie reached for his.

"He's over here in his pen, and you know what? He really likes cool, smart little boys."

As far as he could tell, Jamie wasn't even listening to Mattie. He was too busy dragging Simon by the hand over toward the pen. Jamie eventually let go of his hand and knelt down next to the open pen, peering in at the rabbit that sat there with its nose twitching.

"Is it okay if I just crouch down next to you a second?" Mattie asked.

Jamie nodded, and Simon found himself oddly choked up. He didn't know why, but he hadn't expected Mattie to be so at *ease* around Jamie. He hadn't expected such patience.

"Come on, fluff ball," Mattie kidded, encouraging the small rabbit to take a hop forward. And one hop was all it took. This was a lazy animal that was content to be so as long as it was fed regularly and got to hop around the living room occasionally. "Do you want to touch him? He's friendly. I promise he won't bite."

Jamie nodded and shuffled forward on his knees. He reached out slowly and stroked the top of the rabbit's head with one finger.

"Soft!" Jamie exclaimed in delight. He looked back at Simon. "Daddy, it's soft!"

"Like Gizmo?" he asked, pleased at his son's reaction.

"Softer then Gizmo. Gizmo's always *wiggling*."

Both Simon and Mattie laughed at the apparent annoyance in the child's voice and then glanced at each other. Mattie's smile faded ever so slightly, and Simon felt his heart sink.

"I'm going to make you that sandwich—no crusts."

"Jamie?" Simon crouched beside him when Mattie stood and moved into the kitchen. "I'm going to be just over there—look at me,

Jamie." He waited until he had Jamie's attention. "I'm going to be just over there, okay?"

Jamie nodded, already going back to the endlessly patient rabbit. "Your backpack is just here at the table. I'll set your coloring book and crayons out, okay?" He pointed to the small coffee table, though he doubted Jamie would move an inch. "Can you answer me, baby?"

Jamie looked up at him, offered him that sweet little smile. "Okay."

"You just call me if you need anything." He strode over to where Mattie stood at the kitchen counter, cutting the crusts off a peanut butter and jelly sandwich.

Mattie glanced up at him, licking his thumb, and then looked away to reach for a small plate. He put the sandwich on it, and Simon watched as he took it over to where Jamie sat, still crouched next to the rabbit. He smiled when Jamie leaned down and gently rubbed his cheek against the top of the rabbit's head. Soft textures had always fascinated his son, and he had no doubt that he would have to purchase Jamie his own bunny in the near future.

"I'm gonna set this down on the table right here, okay?" Mattie asked.

When Jamie nodded, Simon cleared his throat. "What do we say, Jamie?"

"Please and thank you," Jamie answered, sounding rehearsed.

Simon shook his head, smiling faintly. "Close enough," he said quietly and pulled out a chair at the kitchen table to take a seat. He hesitated, however, and glanced at Mattie. That displeased look was back, and there was a definite pause before Mattie nodded. He sat.

Mattie sat opposite him. "Well, talk about inviting yourself over," he said quietly.

Simon winced, remembering the similar words he'd spoken not so long ago. "Thank you for letting me in."

"As if I'd close the door on your kid. You just happened to be with him."

"*Okay*," he drawled nervously, offering a tremulous smile as his hand folded and unfolded in his lap.

"And by the way?" Mattie glanced over at Jamie, then folded his arms and leaned forward. "Using your son to talk to me? Low."

Again, he winced. "I know. Believe me, I don't feel good about it."

"I mean even for *you* that's low."

Simon stared at him for a moment, at the unwavering glare offered to him. He felt something twist in his stomach. He pressed his lips together in a tight line and suddenly felt humiliatingly on the verge of tears. Mattie hated him. This kind, loving man who had for some reason adored him and offered him refuge from even himself could now barely stand the sight of him. He'd ruined everything. "I made a mistake," he spoke quietly.

"A bit of an understatement, don't you think?"

"No I, I mean… it's too late, isn't it?"

Mattie didn't reply, but his brow creased in a frown, as if that was the last thing he'd expected Simon to say.

"I royally messed this up. You meant it. We're done, aren't we?"

Mattie looked away quickly, lifted his shoulder in a shrug. "Perhaps we could be friends, still."

Simon clenched his jaw and splayed his hands out on the table. He kept his gaze on his hands, swallowing hard as they began to blur. "I don't think that'd work. Not after what we—what we used to be."

"Oh, come on, Simon. What were we exactly? There's no reason—"

"Don't. Don't act like it was nothing, because it meant something to me."

He looked at Mattie when there wasn't an immediate response, and saw the anger back in those hazel eyes.

"Then why?" Mattie ground out. "Why would you *fu*—" Mattie shot a quick glance at Jamie, catching himself, and then lowered his voice. "Why would you just… *sabotage* us like that?" He sat back in

225

his chair, his expression sad. He threw his hands out to the sides in a helpless gesture. "Was it all in my head? Did I have some sort of twisted *Pretty Woman* fantasy going on?"

"No, not at all—"

"Then why?" Mattie interrupted. "Why pretend we were dating?"

"We *were*," Simon snapped.

"I only just recently saw the inside of your house, after how many months of so-called 'dating'?"

"You *know* my reasons," Simon practically pleaded, aware that he was sounding needier by the second.

"No. You're not doing that. You're not using him as an excuse. I respected every boundary, save for turning up *once* unannounced."

"I wasn't expecting it."

"You weren't *expec*—? I don't care!" Mattie hissed, before letting out a frustrated breath and standing, taking two steps to lean against the kitchen counter. "The way you looked at me?" He glanced at Jamie, still preoccupied across the room. "I felt like trash. You looked at me like I was a stranger." He clenched his jaw. "It was like going back in time, to that party when Andrew let slip that I hooked. Standing in that hallway at your son's party, it was… it was like everything we knew about each other, everything we felt for each other didn't matter. You just…." He shook his head and lowered his gaze, swallowing hard when his voice wavered.

Simon stood and approached Mattie, who leaned against the counter with his arms crossed, eyes to the floor, and so vulnerable that it hurt to look at him. "Mattie," he murmured, saddened when Mattie shook his head "no" and wouldn't look him in the eye.

Simon wiped a hand over his mouth, sighed softly, and nodded, as if reaching an agreement with himself. "Okay," he said softly. "Here it is. When Tim left—"

Mattie immediately shook his head in a "here we go" gesture and pushed away from the counter. "If you're not using your son as an excuse then it's your ex. Christ."

"Hear me out." Simon crowded him back against the counter, dipping his head and tipping Mattie's chin up to look him in the eye. "Please."

Mattie regarded him closely, and then his shoulders slumped. He leaned back against the counter. "I hate this hold you have over me," he whispered.

Feeling a slither of hope, Simon took a deep breath. "Just let me explain."

"Everyone's been burned by an ex before, Simon," he spoke sadly.

"Yes, true. But when Tim left? He was close to the same age you are now, and he loved me too. We had a future."

"I get that Jamie was a problem for him and that's why he took off," Mattie said in low murmurs, not wanting there to be any chance that Jamie would hear. "But I believe the problem here is that I want to be a *part* of yours and Jamie's life. You're the one who—"

Simon pressed the tips of two fingers to Mattie's lips, almost amused. "Mattie, please. Let me talk."

Mattie rolled his eyes and moved Simon's hand away, then raised his eyebrows in a bid for Simon to continue.

"Yes, I do have a hang-up about our slight age difference, about how annoyingly gorgeous you are, and the fact that you're so talented you could go anywhere and do anything you wanted at any time." He quickly pressed on when he could see Mattie about to argue. "But that's not what it came down to."

"What, then?" Mattie asked.

Simon pressed his lips together and lowered his voice to whisper, the timbre of his voice sounding all the deeper. "I—I resented Jamie, when Tim left." He met Mattie's gaze, feeling nervous and guilty, whereas Mattie showed only surprise. "He was three years old, completely helpless, and thought the absolute world of me, and I *resented* him. I resented him because he was the reason the man I loved walked out."

Something in Mattie's eyes softened. "Oh, Simon," he sighed, a sound of disappointment.

Simon cringed. "I know, fucking terrible, right? I hate myself for having felt that way, but—"

"No." Mattie interrupted with a shake of his head, his voice soft. "I can't even imagine how you must have felt."

"It was bad. Really bad, for a time. Tim left, I was heartbroken, and Jamie was missing his presence and was twice the work. My mother wanted custody, I couldn't write, and I didn't know how to do *any* of it."

Mattie begrudgingly touched his arm, offering sympathy despite still not actually wanting to. "But you love Jamie."

"Oh, absolutely. That little boy has my whole heart, he *owns* me, but I loved him back then, and still...." He shook his head. "I don't want you to think I was nasty to him or mistreated him, but—"

"Oh, of course not," Mattie scoffed. "You'd sooner cut off your own arm than say a single unkind word to Jamie. I know that."

"But the feelings were still there, you know?"

"Well." Mattie frowned. "You were mourning, weren't you?"

Simon frowned. "How so?"

"The life you thought you'd have, the lover you'd lost. It's a big blow."

He ran both hands through his hair. That was it *exactly*. "I can't understand how you always know what to say, how you're always so understanding."

Mattie sighed and ran his hand along Simon's arm again. He shrugged helplessly. "I know you, Simon Castle. I *know* you."

And that's what it came down to, really. Having someone else know you, good and bad, inside and out. That was the once in a lifetime connection that people sang about, wrote about. Simon nodded, unable to speak for a moment.

"But, Simon...." Mattie tilted his head, clearly indicating that he hadn't heard enough for amends to be made. "I understand what you're saying, but...."

"No, you don't. Not quite, anyway."

Mattie took a deep breath, clearly losing patience. "Then what?"

"I was devastated when Tim left, and my emotions got all tangled up. It took me nearly two years to recover, for *both* Jamie and I to recover. And then I met you."

"And then you met me," Mattie echoed.

"I'm being frank when I say it frightened me that you're younger and so beautiful, but what worried me most is what might happen when you leave. Because what I felt for Tim?" He took a short breath, his eyes stinging. "What I felt for Tim is not a *fraction* of what I feel for you."

Mattie's brows rose in clear surprise, but he was pleased too.

"I kept you at an arm's length because, at first, I didn't want the option of actually falling for you to be possible. Then when I fell for you anyway? I tried to keep you at a safe distance because I wanted to be sure, *absolutely* sure that you were in this all the way, and that—that I could trust you, *rely* on you to stay. Because if you left, Mattie, that would ruin me. It would ruin me."

"How could you not know that I'm completely in love with you?" Mattie choked out.

Simon swallowed. "Because Tim was in love with me too."

"I'm not Tim."

"No, you certainly are not. But...." He closed his eyes tight, willing himself to be completely honest, no matter what. "But I had to keep you away for other reasons, *one* other reason." He willed Mattie to please, *please* understand.

A certain light in Mattie's eyes dimmed, and that look of shame that Simon *hated* briefly flashed over his face. But Mattie nodded.

"Please understand," Simon begged.

Mattie nodded again, looked to the small patch of tile between their feet, then back up. "It's not nice, what I had to do. It's serious stuff. Not the kind of thing you want around a child. I get that."

"I'm not trying to hurt you. I don't *want* to hurt you."

"No, I understand. Jamie is the priority here." He nodded. "I've never once felt bitter or angry because of that. I hope that much was clear."

Simon nodded. "Yes. From the start, actually."

Mattie frowned, looking annoyed. "You know what? You always see these movies or those dumb TV shows where the guy and girl don't talk, and then there's always some predictable misunderstanding and someone gets hurt. Do you know what I'm talking about?"

"Yeah?" Simon replied hesitantly.

"Well, we talked. We talked all the time and we *still* fucked things up."

Simon let out a small, watery laugh, and couldn't help but pull Mattie into a hug. "You're not wrong." He was pleased when Mattie returned the hug, rubbing his hands along Simon's back, but was disappointed when Mattie pulled away, putting that small, safe little square of space back between them.

Simon shrugged sadly. "That's it, Mattie. I know it doesn't undo how I've acted toward you, how I've hurt you, but I don't know what else to say. I was scared of losing you—whether it be by you leaving for New York or getting tired of me—so I kept you away. I was afraid of my mother being unable to cope with seeing her gay son actually *be* gay and walking away out of Jamie's life. I was afraid of *you* walking out of Jamie's life."

"And out of yours."

"Yes. Yes, that's it."

"And…." Mattie bit the side of his thumb. "And you didn't like that I was a—a prostitute," he almost whispered.

Simon looked him in the eye and said softly, "No. No, I didn't like that."

"Because it's dirty?" Mattie asked, sounding younger than his years but bravely looking him square in the eye.

"Because I was *jealous*," Simon said firmly, hating how vulnerable Mattie looked, as if one blow from Simon, and only Simon, would kill him.

Mattie looked away, nodding once, and Simon felt the beginnings of panic. Mattie's shoulders were slumped in resignation, and even though the air had been cleared, nothing felt resolved.

That was it then.

He swallowed hard, knowing it was time to leave and not come back.

"Mattie?" There was something inside of him, twisting so hard that he didn't even care about the crack in his voice. "I know we're done. I know I messed up and it's over now, and this isn't me trying to get you back. I just really, really need you to know that I love you. I loved you from the start, and I'm so sorry that we're not going to be a family."

He turned away, intending to collect Jamie and get out of there before he lost it and broke down completely, but Mattie's hand on his arm stilled him. He watched, as if a butterfly had landed there and he was afraid of scaring it away, as Mattie's hand slid down his arm to his wrist and then to his hand, cradling it.

"That's it?" Mattie murmured, clutching his hand tightly. "That's all the fight you've got left?"

"I don't know what else to say...."

"You love me, right?" Mattie asked, his voice hitching.

"Yes. Very much," Simon whispered.

"Then do better."

"I—I don't know what you—"

"Do something. *Say* something else. Beg me, or get angry with me. Make demands, do *something*." Mattie quickly wiped at the corner of his eye with the heel of his hand. "Don't let me just slip away."

"Are…." Simon quickly wet his lips. "Are you saying that there's a chance here?"

"For fuck's sake, Simon, I loved you even before I knew what your name was. Yes, there's a chance."

Simon let out a startled breath, and a beaming smile threatened to split across his face, but he stopped himself in time. Mattie did not look happy. He looked alone, he looked scared, and Simon knew that Mattie needed some sort of guarantee, just as he had. He quickly brought a hand around the nape of Mattie's neck, and suddenly knew exactly what he needed to say, and what he should have said a long time ago.

"I'm not letting you go, Mattie. You're not going to slip through the cracks with me. I want you in my life and Jamie's, to be a family, the three of us. And above all, I do *not* want you to ever let another man touch you intimately." His thumb slid under Mattie's chin, lifting it. "That all stops *now*. I'm not saying that as a jealous boyfriend, I'm saying that as your partner. If there are money issues, then we hash it out together, because that's what partners do." He pressed his brow gently to Mattie's, closing his eyes. "You're mine, and I'm yours. That's it. That's *it*."

Mattie let out a soft, choked up laugh, his hands moving from Simon's waist up his back to grip both shoulders, pulling him close. "See, was that so fucking hard to say?"

Simon smiled and wiped the dampness from the corner of Mattie's eye with the pad of his thumb. "I missed you." His gaze fell to Mattie's lips as Mattie whispered his response. He tilted his head to the side to brush—

"Daddy?"

They both pulled apart with startled intakes of breath, having forgotten that they were not alone. Jamie stood by the kitchen table, one hand twisted up nervously in his cape, the other holding up a childlike—but nonetheless very good—drawing of a rabbit.

Simon and Mattie took a step apart, shooting each other sheepish glances. Mattie turned away to cover his smile as Simon knelt in front of Jamie.

"Oh, hey, that's a rabbit," Simon said with the appropriate amount of awe in his voice.

"It's a bunny."

"It's a very good one. Well, I tell you what, when we get home, that's going on the fridge."

Jamie shook his head, looking at his dad's shirt, where he reached out to toy with a button. "Not for you." As if to clarify who the picture was for, he held it out in Mattie's direction, but turned his body in toward Simon, suddenly shy.

Simon snorted and looked up to see Mattie—who was already a little emotional—crouch and take the picture, handling it as if it were the most precious gift that had ever been bestowed upon him. One look at the expression on Mattie's face, and Simon had to press his lips together to keep from looking too smug. He already knew it was a done deal; with one drawing of a bunny, Jamie had snared the man for life.

"Guess you have something to put on your fridge now," Simon murmured.

"This is wonderful, Jamie." Mattie smiled. "Thank you so much, little man. This is going front and center, for all to see!"

"Can I play with the bunny some more?" Jamie whispered into his dad's chest, still too unsure of Mattie to speak directly to him.

"Of course you can," Mattie answered for Simon. "Any time you want."

Simon stood as Jamie went back through to the living room, and couldn't help but smirk a little as Mattie turned to him, speechless. He laughed and pulled Mattie back into his arms, and it wasn't until that moment that he realized how empty his arms had felt over the last few weeks. "I missed this," he whispered, clutching Mattie close. "I'm never going to risk losing you again."

"You'd better not," Mattie warned, bending to press a kiss to Simon's neck and then detaching himself, much to Simon's annoyance.

"Hey," Simon protested.

"One sec." Mattie pulled open a drawer to rifle through for something, then strode over to the fridge to tack up the picture. "That's one hell of a bunny picture," Mattie said with pride.

"Whether you realize it or not, that's pretty much a stamp of approval from Jamie."

"Yeah?"

Simon walked up behind him and wrapped his arms around Mattie's waist, pulling him in tight against him. He took in the scent of Mattie's hair. "Yes. He only draws pictures for the people he likes. Of course, having a *real* bunny probably scored you major points there."

Mattie turned in his arms. "I think you were about to do something before we were so adorably interrupted."

Simon didn't waste a second longer and captured Mattie's lips in a quick, searing kiss, pouring every ounce of regret, passion, turmoil, *everything* he had felt over the past few weeks into it. Eventually Mattie pulled away for a quick intake of breath. He cleared his throat.

"You *have* missed me."

"Don't even joke. You've no idea." He gently pushed the bangs off of Mattie's brow, raising his chin to plant a soft kiss there. "I can't believe I haven't been able to do this for more than four weeks."

Mattie closed his eyes and ran his hands up along Simon's arms. "Four weeks is a long time," he agreed, then bit his lip. "A person could do a lot in four weeks."

Simon pulled back to look at him. "Like what?"

Mattie considered toying with Simon, but eventually just came out with it. "I got my GED."

Simon's eyes went wide, and he held Mattie at an arm's length before quickly pulling Mattie back into his arms, hugging him tight. "That's fantastic! I knew you'd do it, Mattie. I'm so proud of you."

Mattie laughed, pleased that he'd finally been able to tell the one person he'd most wanted to share his news with. "I'm on a higher wage now too."

"That's great, Mattie, it really is. Come here." Simon took Mattie's face in his hands, kissing him again, and then on the cheeks, his brow, over his closed eyelids.

Mattie felt his smile grow shaky as a lump formed in his throat. "I got my transcripts, and you were the one person I wanted to tell."

"You've told me now. Come here." He pulled him into a tight hug and whispered, "Never, never letting you slip away again."

MATTIE slowly came to wakefulness, feeling warm and comfortable. He stretched and rolled onto his side, reaching for the space where Simon had recently been. His hand splayed over the still-warm spot before reaching to hug Simon's pillow close in the man's absence.

He sighed contently into the pillow, hearing Simon and Jamie's chatter not far away, and finally rolled onto his back, opening his eyes to look up at the ceiling. It still amazed him at how quickly they had managed to fall into routine.

He was not a morning person, and so, more often than not, Simon and Jamie would be up and dressed long before him (something the pair enjoyed teasing him about). But then he didn't take much time at all to get dressed and ready for the day, so he figured it evened out.

Not only that, he also liked to give Simon and Jamie a little alone time first thing in the mornings. It'd become some sort of unspoken understanding over the past month between the two of them that Simon would get Jamie up and ready for the day ahead on the occasions that Mattie stayed the night, and then Mattie would join them for breakfast. There was strictly no slap and tickle in the mornings when five-year-olds might be awake and listening, which he couldn't agree more with.

He still lived in his shitty apartment, more or less. What had begun as one or two nights a week where Mattie would spend the night had become more like four or five. He had a toothbrush and razor in Simon's bathroom. There was a spare drawer where he now kept a few essentials. The house, along with Simon and Jamie, *felt* like home to him. But he instinctually knew that this relationship would not progress along at the same speed as other couples might. He and Jamie had become fast friends, but there were still boundaries to be respected.

He at least knew it was more than some trial period to see if Jamie would accept this new person into his home. He and Simon had discussed as much, and both knew where the relationship was heading, and that was toward something permanent. But he also knew it would be all too easy to overwhelm Jamie, or to unintentionally cause him distress by taking up too much of his dad's time. It was a careful balance, but they were steadily finding their way.

He heard the door creak open and lifted his head, expecting to see Simon with a cup of coffee in hand, but instead looked down to see Jamie hovering in the doorway, clearly uncertain of his next move.

Mattie pulled the quilt up under his armpits and sat up a little. "Hey, little man. Have you come to say good morning?"

Jamie's finger traced the edge of the door, but he remained silent. Mattie noticed that Jamie was still in his PJ's, and the cowlick that was ohmygodadorable had yet to be tamed by Simon. He rolled onto his side, along the edge of the bed, and beckoned Jamie over with a crooked finger and a playful "*psstt.*"

He saw a ghost of a smile on Jamie's lips (which always felt like the biggest victory in the world) and smiled as Jamie came over toward the edge of the bed.

"You're still in your PJ's."

Jamie nodded, his eyes on the coverlet as he traced the swirling pattern.

"I'm in my PJ's too," he whispered conspiratorially. He *was* wearing boxer briefs, so technically he wasn't lying.

Jamie giggled, and then to Mattie's utter surprise, he climbed up onto the bed beside him. Mattie cautiously made room for Jamie, not wanting him to fall off the edge of the bed and also not wanting to crowd him. He'd seen first-hand what happened when Jamie felt crowded.

It had been something so small that had set him off, but Jamie's reaction had stunned him nonetheless. Jamie had been playing with his building blocks, stacking them into tall (and rather impressive) towers as he, Simon, and Sarah chatted over coffee in the living room. He stood to take Sarah's mug, and unaware of how close by Jamie was playing, he'd accidentally stood on his cape just as Jamie was moving away. As a result the cape had tugged at his neck, and the usually quiet, happy kid had burst into tears. Those lovely brown eyes had screwed tightly shut, his small fists pounding into his knees as his anxiety increased.

He'd stood by helplessly as Simon tried to comfort him, eventually cutting Mattie an apologetic glance and taking Jamie into another room while Sarah tried valiantly to assure him that he hadn't hurt Jamie in any way.

After that he'd discovered a newfound respect for Simon. Not because it felt uncomfortable or awkward to be around Jamie when he was in such a state, but because it was painful to see the little boy so deeply upset and frightened. Simon dealt with that every day. He took it in stride and was one of the few things that could calm Jamie down. Oddly enough, he now saw Simon in an all-new light, suddenly even more attractive than before with an almost alpha-like quality. What had cut him deep, however, was the downright worried look Simon had cast him when rejoining him and Sarah afterward. It hurt him that Simon had reason to feel that fear, and he'd been more than eager to prove to Simon that same night that he had not been scared off.

So he was hesitant now, with Jamie kneeling close to him, to move even a fraction. He was left speechless, however, as Jamie reached forward with one hand to touch the beaded necklace around his throat.

"You like my necklace, little man?" he asked as softly as possible, feeling somewhat privileged to be the subject of Jamie's close attention.

Jamie nodded and then pulled his hand away. "You sleep over sometimes." He spoke quietly, still so shy around Mattie.

"Yeah," Mattie answered quietly. "Is that okay?"

"My dad makes my lunch."

"I know. You like your grapes, don't you?"

Jamie nodded. "He lets me pick my grapes, and he tucks me in, and he writes stories in his books."

"Your dad's real special."

Jamie nodded. "He's my dad."

"Yep." Mattie hesitated a second. "No one's ever going to take your dad away from you, okay, Jamie?" When there was no answer, he bit his lip, and then dipped his head to catch a glimpse of those chocolate brown eyes. "I'm your dad's special friend, Jamie, which means I might be here quite a lot. But if you ever want it to be just you and your dad for a little bit, you just let me know. Okay, little man?"

Again Jamie reached to touch his beaded necklace, and he held still. The door behind creaked open further, and he felt downright proud to see the at first stunned, then delighted smile spread across Simon's lips at the sight before him.

"Will you bring your bunny with you next time?" Jamie asked, and both Simon and Mattie laughed.

"How about we go have supper at Mattie's home one night next week, hey?"

Jamie turned to look at his dad and then climbed off the bed. Simon rubbed his hand over the top of Jamie's head when Jamie made to squeeze by. "I want you to go start getting dressed, okay? Then we'll drag Mattie out of bed for breakfast."

"Okay."

Mattie pushed the bedsheets away and stood to stretch. Simon's arms circled around his middle, and he hugged him back for a second, then pulled away with a playful slap to Simon's ass. As nice as good morning hugs were, he had to piss.

He headed into the bathroom to take care of business, and when he came back into the bedroom, Simon was perched casually on the side of the bed, waiting for him. He offered Simon a cheeky wink as he strode past to retrieve his jeans off the floor, but Simon's hand caught his and tugged. He landed in Simon's lap with an "oof."

"Hey now." Mattie chuckled, quite happy to be manhandled. "You have some sort of objection to me wearing clothes today?"

Simon pressed a kiss to his neck, smirking. "Not so much an objection as a preference."

"Well, as nice as lazing around in my shorts sounds, I think modesty might be called for here. You know, with a certain little someone running around in cowboy pajamas and all." He stood, snagging up his jeans.

"Want me to iron them for you?"

"Nah, they're fine." Mattie cut a glance to Simon, who was still perched on the edge of the bed, leaning back on his hands. "What's up?"

"Hmm?"

"You've got something to say, but you haven't found the right words yet. I can see it in your devilishly handsome face, Mr. Castle."

Simon snorted. "You've pretty much got my number."

Mattie sat on the bed beside him, pulling on socks. "I had your number from day one." He yanked on his T-shirt and then looked at Simon. When Simon said nothing, he nudged him with his shoulder. "Come on, we talk about everything now, remember? Spill."

Simon smiled and nudged his glasses up along the bridge of his nose. "Jamie was talking to you."

"*Yes*," he drawled.

Simon raised his eyebrows, as if the point he was making was obvious. "Unprompted, Mattie."

"Well, I'm pretty interesting, you know. Little guy probably couldn't help himself."

"I'm serious, Mattie. That's a big thing for him. He doesn't even do that with my mom yet."

Something puffed up in Mattie's chest. "He sees more of me then he does your mom, that's all." And it was true. If it wasn't three or four evenings and mornings a week, then there was the diner. "He's getting used to me."

"It's a big deal, Mattie."

"Even Sarah said that he's coming out of his shell more. He's opening up, being more social, and that's thanks to you, by the way. No one else."

Simon stared at him for a moment, and when Mattie was about to speak again, a slow smile slid across Simon's lips, and he shook his head. He leaned over and pressed a kiss to Mattie's cheek.

"Love you," he said simply, and stood, leaving a mystified but nonetheless pleased Mattie sitting on the bed.

"Come on, it's time to be out of bed, lazybones," he called from the hall, and then: "What do we call Mattie?"

"Lazybones!" Jamie shouted, and then giggled.

Mattie laughed and stood to go join them for breakfast.

THE ten minutes where he would walk with Simon and Jamie in the morning was arguably one of the best parts of his day, with him heading off to work and Simon taking Jamie to school. When they reached the park, their paths split. Mattie would carry on to the diner, and twenty or thirty minutes later, Simon would arrive with his laptop, ready to work. But the ten minutes spent walking toward the park together? It was wonderful. It was family time.

"Can we feed the ducks?" Jamie asked.

"Maybe after school, before we go to the diner, okay?"

"Okay," was the disappointed reply, and Mattie couldn't help but shoot Simon an amused look.

"Do you want to have mac 'n cheese later?" Simon counteroffered.

"I want a sandwich."

"All right then." Simon chuckled fondly.

"Mattie cuts the crusts off."

Mattie felt a pang in his chest and glanced at Simon to see if he'd noticed too. One look and, yes, Simon was grinning.

"Yes, Mattie does."

It was the first time Jamie had actually used his name.

"Well, this is me." Mattie tilted his head toward the sidewalk that would lead him to the diner.

"See you soon, don't forget to ask about shifts for… you know." Simon grinned and pecked a quick kiss on his lips.

"Oh, yeah, yeah of course. Have a good day at school, little man." Mattie stood a moment and watched as father and son walked away through the park.

HE ENTERED the diner in a damn fine mood. Until he spotted Ty, of course.

"Hey," Ty greeted.

"Hey." Mattie set his backpack on the counter and looked at Ty, feeling dumb and guilty. "How's it going?"

"All right, I guess."

"Cool."

"Cool."

Silence ensued. They stood there in the empty diner, staring at each other awkwardly.

"This is fucking stupid!" Ty practically yelled and then took a step closer to shove him. "Be my friend again. Now."

Mattie actually laughed, slightly incredulous. "*You* stopped talking to *me*, remember?"

"I was being a good friend by being pissed at you."

"Ty, you *said*—"

"I *know*, I know," Ty grumbled.

Mattie sighed. "I've got something really good going on for me right now, Ty. I don't want to give that up. You said you'd support that."

Ty sat himself on a stool. "I know, but that was before I saw that fucking letter. That was before you *got into art school*."

The letter. The letter offering him a place at the Art Institute of New York. With financial aid, even. The letter daring him to reach for everything he'd always wanted for himself. The letter he could not bring himself to throw away and that travelled with him everywhere in his backpack.

"Just tell me that you're sure. Tell me you're 100 percent certain that you're doing the right thing."

"My feelings for Simon and Jamie are the one thing I am certain of, Ty. I'm not leaving them."

Ty's shoulders slumped. "Fine, I guess. I suppose he's really happy with your decision, then?"

Mattie looked away, shrugging. "He doesn't need to know." He cut a glance back at Ty and sighed at the totally disapproving glare his friend was leveling him with.

"You're not even going to mention it to him?"

"Nope, my mind's made up. There's no point."

"You know, here I am, blaming this guy for everything, and he has no idea. What, are you afraid that he'd be mad, or…?"

No. Simon wouldn't be mad; that wasn't what he was afraid of. He was afraid of the exact opposite. "He'd never be mad. There's just no point in discussing it. I have what I want, Ty. So please, just… drop it, okay? Let it fucking be already."

Ty sighed. "Okay, this is me, dropping it once and for all." He waited a heartbeat. "Even if it is the wrong decision."

Mattie reached into the glass counter and threw a croissant at him. Ty ducked out of the way with a laugh, holding up his hands in surrender.

"Okay, okay, enough."

Mattie shook his head and unzipped his backpack. "Hey, do you think you could swap a shift with me next week?"

"Uh, um, um...." Ty squinted, obviously shifting his schedule around in his head. "Yeah, should be able to, why, where you off to?"

"We're taking Jamie to the zoo." He grinned, excited.

Ty even managed to offer a reluctant smile in return. "Yeah? That's kinda cool, I guess."

"Aw, you want to come too?" He laughed.

"Fuck off."

"You don't want to see the lions and tigers and bears?"

"Don't say it."

"Oh my!"

"Ugh. You're pathetic." He swiped a cloth over the counter. "And everyone knows that the penguins are the best."

"Loser," Mattie snickered and reached into his backpack to pull out the crumpled piece of paper that was his work schedule.

"Says the dude with...." Ty leaned over the counter, peering into Mattie's backpack. "Says the guy with *trash* in his backpack." He plucked a gummy bears wrapper and a squashed juice carton out of the bag.

Mattie snatched them back, putting them back in his bag. He shrugged. "Jamie has this thing where he likes to put his trash in Simon's suitcase or satchel. Or in this case, my backpack. It's cute."

"It's weird."

Mattie pointed a warning finger at Ty. "It's. Cute."

Ty laughed. "Okay, man. Cute, whatever." He slapped Mattie's arm with his dish towel. "Hey, you want to go see this band play at the Noisy Cricket next week? They're supposed to be a cross between Nine Inch Nails and the Smashing Pumpkins, what do you say?"

Mattie mulled it over. The Noisy Cricket would usually conjure not so great memories of his first foray into prostitution. And though he doubted he'd ever feel completely comfortable there, he didn't feel afraid of the place. He shrugged. "Sure, why not."

"Yeah? Great! It's been ages since we've hung out, got wasted, and listened to some truly dire amateur bands. High five!"

"Put your hand down. Now."

"Fine. Mr. Sensible."

Mattie waved his work schedule in front of Ty. "Come on. What day do you want to swap?"

THE bell dinged above the door as Simon strode in. Out of habit he glanced at the sandwich bar where the unfriendly guy with the thick, indefinable accent stood in Mattie's usual spot. A quick search around the room and Simon spotted Mattie, taking a patron's order. He walked over to his usual booth and pulled out his laptop.

"Good morning, sir. What can I get you?" a familiar voice asked.

"So many inappropriate answers...." He glanced up and grinned, feeling roguish.

Mattie laughed. "Okay, coffee coming up. Let me know if you get hungry, all right? I've got a break in twenty minutes."

"May I suggest you spend your break in my booth?" He winced. "I—I wasn't trying to be dirty or metaphorical there...."

Mattie barked out a laugh and covered his eyes with one hand. He was still chuckling when he squeezed Simon's shoulder. "I know, honey."

"Mattie?" Daphne, the waitress, called from behind the diner cash register. "Hon, could you go sign for the delivery out back? I got my hands full here."

"Sure thing, Daph." Mattie turned to Simon, winked. "Back in a bit."

Simon watched Mattie walk through the "Employees Only" door and then turned back to his laptop. He looked up, however, when someone sat opposite him in the booth. He had a sudden sense of déjà vu, seeing Ty sitting there. "Um. Hello."

"Hey."

Simon waited for him to say something else, but he didn't. It didn't take long for things to become awkward. "Um, was there anything else?"

"Yes, but…." Ty rolled his shoulders. "I'm just debating on how much to say."

"Uh. Okay. Do you mind if I…." He nodded at his laptop. "Just while you gather your thoughts?"

"I guess."

With that permission, Simon attempted to go on writing. For approximately ten seconds. "Actually, no." He closed his laptop. "What you're doing…." He gestured between them. "It's a little intimidating."

"I'm trying to think of how to phrase this without biting your head off."

"That isn't comforting."

"You need to let Mattie go."

Amused up until that point, his smile disappeared and he sat up straighter. "Excuse me?"

Ty sighed and leaned forward across the table, shooting a quick look at the door Mattie had used a few moments ago. "Don't… don't you think you're holding him back?"

He was speechless. He felt as if the rug was being pulled out from beneath his feet. "Mattie and I care about each other very much," he replied seriously.

"I don't doubt that, I mean, I know he's crazy about you and all…."

"And I'm crazy about *him*."

"Yeah, but… he could be doing so much more with his life right now, you know? Rather than playing happy families."

"I'm not keeping him against his will," he bit out.

"No, you're not. But it's not like you've got his best interests at heart either, is it?"

"Of course I do!"

"Then why haven't you even asked him about his plan for school, huh?"

"I…. He gave me the impression that he didn't really want—"

"Don't. Don't even." Ty shook his head. "Look, I know you're not a bad guy. All I'm asking is for you to pop your head out of your happy bubble for a sec, and look at the bigger picture."

"I know what the bigger picture is," Simon hissed. "The bigger picture is Mattie someday moving in, Mattie and I getting married, Mattie becoming a second father to Jamie!"

"What, so you've just got his life planned out for him now?"

"No!"

"Because everything you just said there, as happy as I'm sure it'd make Mattie, does not include any of his goals, just yours."

Simon took a steadying breath, not wanting to draw attention to them or the conversation they were having. "If Mattie didn't want to be with me, then he wouldn't be."

"It's not a matter of whether he wants to be with you. I told you, he's head over heels for you, has been since you started coming here, in fact. It's a matter of what he's giving up to be with you."

"He could still go to school here, in San Diego."

"No," Ty said sadly, shaking his head. "You don't get it, and I don't even think it's your fault because he obviously hasn't said a word about it, but he's not just giving up the chance at—at—" He gestured, frustrated. "—at just furthering his education or some shit. It's more than that. New York is what kept him going. You don't know, you don't even *know* the hell-like shit he's been through just to feed himself. He's degraded himself, he's put himself in dangerous situations where he's been *attacked*. He had zero, *zero* self-worth at one point."

"Mattie and I don't have any secrets, not anymore. I know all about his past," Simon offered weakly, feeling ill.

"You don't know how much encouragement it took to get him to take those reading and writing classes. How much it took for him to begin to believe that he could get a GED and actually accomplish what it was he wanted. New York? That was his... his fucking redemption, or something. Just the idea of actually taking his art to this fancy college was something to keep him going when everything else was

just shit. It was like he believed if he could get to New York, then—"
He shrugged helplessly. "—then he'd done it. He'd changed who he
was. Who he *hated*."

"He hated himself?" Simon asked weakly.

Ty nodded. "Yeah, he did. And you know what? Despite all that
nasty, ugly shit he put himself through, he did it. He got his GED, he
got… he could do the art school thing, but he's settled." Ty leaned back
in his seat, looking as unhappy as Simon felt.

"You think Mattie is settling for me and Jamie?"

Ty pressed his lips together in a thin line. "Yes. And I know that's
an asshole thing to say. I'm sorry."

"You—you don't know anything. This could be the making of
Mattie. For all you know we were meant to be together."

Ty groaned. "Look, I haven't handled this well. What I'm
basically trying to say is that he is still in his twenties, and before you
came along, he had these aspirations of being an artist. Now? Now he's
settling for being a fucking waiter so that he can be with you."

That hit home. It really did, but he and Mattie… they'd been
through so much together. He may not be New York and all the
meaning this college apparently had behind it, but he could try and be
something more for Mattie, something that could give him that feeling
of self-worth that New York would have.

"I… I appreciate what it is you're trying to tell me. You
obviously care a lot about Mattie too. You must be a very good friend."

"Or a really bad one. I'm not sure." Ty spoke glumly.

"*But*—"

"But?" Ty raised an eyebrow in question.

"But I can give Mattie that self-worth by—"

Ty groaned and pressed the heels of his hands into his eyes. "You
don't get it."

"By loving him like he deserves to be," Simon continued sharply.
"Anything he needs, I will provide him with until he's in a position
where he can do it himself. If he wants to go to college close by, then

I'll pay for it. I will. But mostly, mostly I am going to love him. I am going to love him so hard until he *knows* what an amazing person he is."

"Or you could let him do it for himself...."

"I promised him that I would never let him slip through the cracks again, and I'm going to keep that promise. Now you can disapprove all you want, but that's the way it is. We're together. We're *staying* together."

Ty stared at him, sighed, and then nodded once. "Fine. All right, I tried."

"I understand that you did this out of kindness for Mattie, and out of respect for that, I'm even going to do you a favor and not mention this conversation to him, because we both know how mad he'd be with you right now."

"You've got that right."

"But you have to leave this be, all right? Please just trust that I am not going to let him down."

Ty watched him, clenching his jaw. "Fine, just make sure that you don't."

Chapter
Nine

MATTIE had come to the conclusion that there was nothing more awesome than seeing a five-year-old lose his shit at the zoo out of excitement. They'd been there a good two hours, and the kid showed no signs of tiring. He couldn't help but laugh as Jamie tugged Simon by the hand, making the man stoop clumsily over toward the chimpanzee enclosure. He trailed behind with Simon's fancy digital camera in hand, taking shots of the adorable two.

Taking Jamie to the zoo had been a great idea of Simon's. The kid was seriously enjoying himself, even if he did shy away from some of the animals, and even people at times. But they knew, even though Jamie would be excited, that this new place would be a challenge of sorts for him. Every new place was. They'd told him a few days before to try and get him used to the idea, and chose a weekday when most people would be at work and most kids at school so there wouldn't be a crowd to contend with. So far it had panned out just fine. Jamie was loving it. Hell, *he* was loving it, and he'd never seen Simon so happy and relaxed.

"Hey, let me get a photo of you two."

Mattie blinked in surprise. "Really?"

Simon nodded. "Yeah, go stand under that tree. Come on, champ." Simon took Jamie's hand and stood him under the tree. He stood back a few feet and fiddled with his camera.

Mattie crouched beside Jamie but wasn't foolish enough to try and touch him at all, no matter how much he'd love to put his arm around him. He especially took care to not accidentally stand on his cape.

"Look." Jamie pointed to the ground, and then they were both leaning with their heads close together, inspecting a line of ants.

Mattie sneaked a look at Jamie, a now familiar feeling of protectiveness swelling in his chest. He knew without a doubt that he could so easily love this kid like he was his very own flesh and blood. The idea thrilled him. A flash pulled him out of his thoughts, and he looked up to see Simon prodding at the camera, a frown on his face.

"The flash went off, should be fine," Mattie offered, knowing that, despite the fact Simon owned a laptop, a fancy phone, and an even fancier camera, the man just was not technically inclined.

"I screwed up the lighting somehow. It's a nice picture, but you're all... silhouetted."

"Take it again," Mattie offered.

"Daddy, look!" Jamie chirped and pointed to a couple that strode past, hand in hand. The woman was carrying a large stuffed panda bear. "It's a panda!"

"It's a big one," Mattie offered enthusiastically, and Jamie nodded.

"Do you like pandas, Jamie?" Simon asked, as always, trying to engage his son in this sudden new interest. Jamie nodded, and Simon reached into his back pocket for his wallet.

"Let me get it for him," Mattie offered quietly, hoping Simon wouldn't mind.

Simon practically beamed. "Sure, thanks. I think the gift shop is this way." He nodded and then reached for Jamie's hand. "Mattie's buying you a panda! What do we say to Mattie?"

"Thank you, Mattie," Jamie chimed, clinging to his dad's hand.

"No problem, kiddo."

They had the gift shop in their sights when crude squawking caught their attention. An excited squeal of "Penguins!" from Jamie had them veering off course toward the penguin enclosure, and Mattie had to admit, Ty had been right. Penguins *were* the best.

"Having fun?" Simon asked him with a mixture of teasing and amusement.

"Hell yeah!" Mattie laughed.

"You know they don't sing and dance like *Happy Feet*, right?"

Mattie elbowed him in the side, and Simon laughed, hugging him close before speaking quietly in his ear. "It's getting a little late. I think that gift shop might be closing soon. Do you want to stay here to watch the penguins with Jamie while I go get that panda?"

Mattie looked over his shoulder. "You're okay with that?" Aside from sitting on the couch, watching *Lord of the Rings* and being schooled on Tolkien by Jamie while Simon was in his office writing, he'd never really been left to look after Jamie by himself before.

"I trust you. More to the point, so does Jamie."

Mattie stole a quick kiss and then reached into his back pocket for his wallet. "I still want it to be from me," he whispered and put a twenty in Simon's hand.

"Be right back," he murmured, then louder for Jamie to hear over the noisy birds. "Jamie? I'm going to be right over there, okay? I want you to stay with Mattie."

Jamie nodded, and Mattie crouched down beside him. "Can I hold your hand?" he asked softly. Jamie hesitated, and then with a nod, placed his own much smaller hand in Mattie's.

Mattie glanced back at Simon. "We're good."

"I won't be long."

Standing there, alone with Jamie and trying to make him giggle by giving voice-overs to the penguins, he felt like a whole new person compared to who he had been a year ago. This gorgeous little kid who barely spoke to anyone was letting him hold his hand. The man he loved and adored was thirty feet away buying a giant panda. Life was good.

Noise drew his attention to the small crowd walking toward them. He felt Jamie squeeze his hand as a group of schoolchildren, all in uniform and obviously enjoying a day trip to the zoo, approached the penguins with excited chatter.

"Shall we go find your dad?"

Jamie didn't answer. Instead, he was humming to himself and mumbling a list of numbers as the noise around them grew and the kids jostled for the best position to see the penguins.

"Off we go," Mattie spoke cheerily, gently pulling Jamie's hand closer to him in an attempt to keep any of the children from bumping into him.

No such luck. He didn't know which child had knocked Jamie into his side, and it didn't matter, because the tears were as quick as they were noisy. Jamie was clearly torn between wanting to yank his hand away from Mattie and wanting to move closer to him to escape the crowd. Mattie glanced around them quickly and gritted his teeth, realizing that to leave the penguin enclosure would mean having to walk back through the gated entranceway that was now crowded with excited schoolkids.

Instinctively, he edged them both to the back of the crowd, away from the noise, and again glanced toward the busy exit, praying to see Simon with giant panda in hand. "It's all right, Jamie. We're just fine, little man." He tried to soothe, rubbing his thumb over Jamie's knuckles.

He glanced behind them and felt a rush of relief that was short lived. The enclosure, and the standing area around it, was surrounded by a low fence. He could easily step over this fence that didn't quite reach up to his waist, but Jamie could not. He crouched in front of Jamie, who was squeezing his eyes shut.

"Jamie, we can go back to where your dad took that picture of us under the tree, remember that? There won't be anyone else there, but I'm gonna have to pick you up for a second. Is that all right?"

There was no answer, only Jamie's unhappy humming as small hands gripped at the edges of his blue cape, pulling it close around him.

Mattie crouched, and instead of scooping him up, he loosely put one arm around him and more or less encouraged Jamie into his arms. As soon as he stood with Jamie in his arms, the frightened tears returned and Jamie began to squirm. He was over the fence and had Jamie back on his feet in two seconds flat. Any attempt to shush Jamie or take his hand to lead him toward a quieter area was pointless. He bit his lip, unsure, and then reached for his cell and called Simon.

"Hey, can you come back? We're near where you took that picture. No… no, Jamie got frightened by some kids and needs you." The phone immediately went dead, and Mattie slid his cell back into his pocket. Jamie was still tugging at his cape.

He seemed to remember Simon mentioning this to him a few months ago. Something about the pressure to Jamie's nervous system calming him. Looking at Jamie now, it didn't seem to be working. He slid off his jacket.

"Here, kiddo. You want my jacket?"

The jacket dwarfed him, but Mattie draped it over his small shoulders, not daring to pull it around him tight. Jamie seemed to calm a little, at least, and now only stood with his eyes closed, breathing heavily.

"Let's get this buttoned up, hey?" He reached for the top button under Jamie's chin, and was startled by the insistent "No!" Jamie yelled.

"Mattie?"

Mattie looked behind him to see Simon jogging toward him with a giant panda under his arm. He sighed in relief and moved out of the way for Simon to crouch in front of Jamie.

"Hey, now," Simon crooned softly, smoothing a hand over Jamie's head while trying to catch his gaze. "What's all this?"

"A group of schoolkids—that came out of nowhere, by the way—crowded us and kind of… jostled him. I'm sorry."

"Come here, baby," Simon murmured, and Mattie watched, impressed at how Jamie just sank into his dad's arms, letting himself be held. "Don't be sorry," Simon spoke quietly to Mattie while rubbing slow circles into Jamie's back. "You did great, Mattie. You did just the right thing."

Mattie rubbed the back of his neck, feeling guilty regardless. "You sure? He was pretty upset."

"Trust me, give it a little time and he'll be all smiles again."

Mattie nodded. "Okay. I hope this didn't spoil the zoo for him. He was having such a great time…."

"Just you wait." Simon smiled. "He'll be begging to come back here in a few days. He loves animals."

Mattie heaved a sigh of relief. "Good. Are we heading off now?"

"Yes, I think so. They close in forty-five minutes anyway."

"Okay, let me grab this." Mattie hefted the panda under his arm.

Simon frowned, only seeming to just realize what it was Jamie was wearing. "Is this your jacket?"

"Uh, yeah. I remembered you saying something about pressure calming him down." He shrugged, feeling a little embarrassed. "Probably didn't work, but at least he's toasty."

"Come here." Simon pulled him close by the front of his T-shirt and craned his head away from Jamie to kiss him softly. "You just continue to surprise me."

"I hope that's a good thing."

"It is. You're not cold, are you?"

"Nah, I'm fine."

"All the same, let's get going—*Oh*, I got you something too."

"I only see one panda, mister."

"In my back pocket, and no goosing me in public, you."

Mattie snorted and reached a hand into Simon's back pocket, taking a moment to go ahead and goose the man anyway. He pulled out a small plastic wrapper. "A key ring?" He pulled it out of the clear wrapper and laughed. "A penguin key ring, nice."

"Well, you need one. You can't go around keeping your keys on a piece of string. You're just asking to lose them."

Mattie laughed, remembering the horrified look on Simon's face when he picked up the keys that, yes, were in fact hooked onto a shoestring. "Ty's gonna have a fit. He'd love this." He was already pulling his keys out of his pocket to transfer them over.

"Look a little closer."

"What am I looking at?" He turned it over in his hand and noticed that there was something on the plastic penguin's stomach. The middle of the penguin was almost hollowed out, and there was a small bubble of liquid with a moving arrow inside.

"It's a compass."

"You are such a boy scout," Mattie laughed. "Come here." He kissed Simon on the cheek. "Thank you for my compass."

"You're welcome. No getting lost on me, okay?"

He looked at the small plastic compass in his hand, smiling softly to himself and not quite able to meet Simon's eyes. He settled for gently nudging him in the side. "Love you."

"You too. Now guide us home."

"DONATELLO was my favorite."

"You're making me feel old."

"You're not old."

"Just older than you."

"You're distinguished."

"Writing books and owning a house doesn't make a person distinguished."

"Then what does?" Mattie drew lazy circles on Simon's chest. His head nestled comfortably on his shoulder. "What makes a person better than other people? What makes a person respected?"

"Aren't we getting a little deep?"

"I want to know what you think, that's all. Come on, in your opinion…." He lifted his head from Simon's shoulder and leaned up on one elbow to look down at him. "In your opinion, what makes a person better than any other?"

Simon squinted at Mattie, smiling slightly as he pretended to give it some thought. "Let's see... I'm guessing you're expecting me to say something along the lines of... kindness? Compassion or intelligence?"

Mattie hummed and reached to run his fingers through Simon's hair. "Something like that. Though I was expecting you to put it more eloquently. Being as wordy as you are and all."

"Well, you'd be wrong." Simon reached for the duvet, pulling it up higher over the both of them.

"This should be good."

"I think that remembering your favorite Ninja Turtle at the age of twenty-six is pretty special."

"The word 'special' can be taken in *so* many ways."

Simon laughed. "Special as in beautiful. Beautiful and individual and untainted by the grind that is life, sometimes."

"Now who's getting deep?"

"I'm just saying I wish I'd known you years ago. I'm saying that you're special in the beautiful way." Simon tugged him by the arm, encouraging Mattie to lie back down, and then draped an arm around his shoulders to hold him close. "I'm saying that I find it cute that you had a favorite Ninja Turtle."

"I didn't think the show would still be airing. It's from the nineties, right?"

Simon shrugged, his fingers ghosting up and down Mattie's bicep. "Not sure. I don't think Jamie's actually ever seen it." He frowned. "He's not really a fan of cartoons."

"Then why'd he choose that backpack?" Mattie asked, referring to Jamie's Ninja Turtle school bag.

"He might have liked the colors. And he does love animals. *Oh*...." Simon poked him in the shoulder. "Thank you, by the way. Because of you, I'm probably going to have to buy him a bunny."

"Ha ha."

"A hamster, a rabbit… he's going to have his very own zoo by the time he's ten."

"You're exaggerating. You love seeing him get excited over animals."

"Hence why he'll probably have his own zoo."

At the mention of the zoo, Mattie thought about the trip earlier that day. Something was niggling at him. "Jamie's cape…."

"The security blanket that will outlive us all, yes?"

Mattie huffed a quiet laugh. "That's what it is?"

"Actually, no. I mean, perhaps it is on some subconscious level, but I did ask him why he needed his cape once."

"Yeah? What'd he say?"

Simon began to speak, stopped to chuckle softly, then wet his lips and continued. "He said it wasn't a cape at all. It's a cloak, as in what a Hobbit wears."

"You're kidding."

"Nope."

"That's adorable," Mattie laughed.

"Yep," Simon agreed, grinning. "In his own words, it's 'his magic cloak that makes him invisible'."

"You sure he isn't thinking of *Harry Potter*?"

"Where are you up to on the books and movies?" Simon asked.

"I've seen *The Fellowship* and *The Two Towers*. Me and the J-man are gonna watch the last one tomorrow. I'm still on the first book."

"I think it mentions it in the first book, but you see it in the last film. Them elvish cloaks be wicked cool."

"You just said wicked cool."

"I know. Sorry about that."

Mattie laughed and pressed a kiss to Simon's neck. "So… if he thinks his cape—sorry, *cloak* makes him invisible, then it *is* a safety thing."

Simon shrugged. "It's a bit of both. Tolkien is his favorite storyteller—"

"That's awesome, by the way," Mattie interrupted. "Having a favorite author at his age."

"Not so much a favorite author as a favorite story, but yeah, I know what you mean."

"So, both? Security and plain old little boy hero worship?"

"Yes."

"He, um… he did this thing, at the zoo," Mattie began slowly.

"What thing?"

"When I put my jacket on him. I was going to button it up, but he froze up and wouldn't let me touch him. I didn't know if it was because he thought I was going to untie the cape, or…?"

"Ah. No." Simon shook his head. "That's his neck thing, remember? He doesn't like the area around his neck to be touched; it's like a trigger for him."

"With other things…," Mattie began, "I mean, there are a fair few things that upset him, right?"

Simon nodded. "Right."

"But those are usually gradual things. Like when he's in a noisy atmosphere, or somewhere unknown? He'll hum, and he'll do the number thing before he gets *really* upset…."

"Kind of like stages, yes."

"But you touch him near his neck or accidentally step on his cape—which I guess tugged at his neck, now that I think about it—you do that and it's like… he cuts out those stages."

Simon nodded. "It's pretty much zero to sixty," he sighed. "I don't really know what it is, and believe me I've read every book there is, spoken to all kinds of doctors… it's just a part of him. For some kids—kids like Jamie—it could be touching their ears, hair, holding their hand… it's just something that terrifies him."

"Like he's being choked." Mattie spoke softly.

"I guess so."

Mattie nestled closer. "I know that feeling."

Simon's hand stilled in Mattie's hair a moment. "What do you mean? Someone choked you?" he asked with a sense of dread.

"No—well, yes. But I didn't mean it literally."

"You were *choked*?" Simon asked thickly.

"Simon," Mattie sighed in a tone of voice that did not invite further discussion. "I told you… it was a dangerous profession, if it can be called a profession."

Simon closed his eyes, nodded. "Sorry. So, if not literally…?" he encouraged, forcing the image of Mattie being hurt out of his mind's eye.

Mattie hesitated. He watched his thumb gently graze through the light stubble on Simon's chin. "It's not something I've ever really talked about before," he offered quietly.

"Then you should probably get it out." Simon slid an arm across his waist, his touch possessive. "You can tell me."

Mattie cleared his throat quietly and shrugged one shoulder. "No big thing, really. It's just… it's this picture I keep in my head. Like…." He took a breath, then sighed in frustration. "You know when you're feeling anxious, or… I don't know, like you can't cope?"

"Yeah, sure. I've been there."

"Well, I'd sometimes picture this… this rope. A coil of rope, wound tight inside of me."

"Inside you," Simon echoed quietly.

"Yeah. Like when things got really bad… say like when I really, really hated who I was…."

"Why would you ever hate who you are? You're amazing." Simon spoke sadly.

Mattie shook his head. "Personality doesn't come in to it, believe me. When you can't afford to buy yourself socks that don't have holes in them, or you can't pay back a friend without resorting to getting on your knees in front of a stranger…." Mattie twisted his fist closed around the edge of the pillow. "You'd be surprised at how quickly a guy can learn to hate himself."

"Mattie," Simon said weakly. "All of those things… they're circumstances, not who you are or were."

Mattie let out a deep breath. "The worst of it, though, the worst of it was feeling *helpless*. Prostitution is degrading. But not knowing how to even begin to make a better life for yourself? That's the kind of stuff that can make you feel hopeless."

Simon gently rolled Mattie onto his back so that he could lean on one arm beside him. He cupped Mattie's jaw, his thumb stroking over his cheek. "You *did* do better for yourself, Mattie."

Mattie smiled a little tremulously. "I know. I met you."

Simon felt something heavy settle uncomfortably in his stomach. "No, Mattie. You got your GED. You're waiting tables now." Even before he'd finished speaking, a sense of shame settled deep within him. Was this what Ty had meant? Had he seriously just told the man he loved that he was a different person now because he was allowed to take a customer's order?

"No, Simon. I don't think you get it." Mattie rolled on his side to face him, and worried his lip as he struggled with his words. "Every day I was treading water, Simon. I was working so hard to just not *give in*, you know?"

Simon opened his mouth to say something, but couldn't. He shook his head unhappily. "I—I don't—"

"Twenty-six, and I couldn't do shit. I—I didn't know how to look after myself, how to function normally like other people. I'd watch the customers that came into the diner. I'd look at you, with your laptop, with your son, and I'd wonder what the hell was wrong with me. I'd wonder how all these other people managed to lead normal lives so easily. I'd look at them. I'd feel so fucking alone, Simon, you've no idea."

Mattie quickly wiped at the corner of his eye with the heel of his hand. He kept his eyes downcast, wanting to flush all the built-up bile out of his body, out of his *heart*, but to do that he couldn't look up.

"I'd see you writing away, and then I'd go to these adult reading and writing classes and struggle to understand such basic shit. Every day I'd try, I'd try harder to feel like I belonged with other people, but I'd fail." He shrugged helplessly. "I'd fail and I'd fail and I'd fucking fail."

"Jesus, Mattie," Simon whispered.

"So I'd picture this coil, right?" He dared look up into eyes that were glassy and sad. "I'd picture this rope just winding itself tight around—around the *me* that's inside, you know?"

"I—I…."

"And it's like the tighter it wound, the safer I was. If the rope pulled hard, then it'd stop me from just completely floating away. But at the same time—" He frowned and shook his head. "—it would choke me. The more I gritted my teeth, the more I'd try and then fail. Try and then fail… it *suffocated* me. But I needed it." He let out a deep breath. "God, does that make any sense?"

"I had no idea," Simon replied, his voice barely there.

"One of the few things that kept me going was trying to get my GED, wanting to go to *school*—"

"New York?" Simon asked quietly, swallowing hard.

"Yeah. Man," Mattie laughed quietly. "I wanted it so bad. Did I ever tell you why?" He frowned. "I don't think I did, seems so unimportant now… anyway, I spent my teens crashing on the couches of various friends, and then there was this one New Year's that I ended up in this basement…."

SIMON listened with a sinking heart as Mattie explained why he had so set his hopes on New York. He felt overwhelmed with guilt. This young man who'd had a less than supportive start out in life, who had lost all sense of self-worth along the way, and who had somehow managed to plow through and find a way of changing a rather bleak future… this man was now setting all these hopes in him.

"And I really do feel like I've made it out to the other side, Simon." Mattie smiled and kissed him softly. "Because of you. You and Jamie."

"But what about New York?" he asked thickly.

Mattie shrugged, and Simon could feel the sense of loss that Mattie was burying. It made him want to throw up.

"Hey, I have you now. You're all I want." Mattie said it reassuringly, but for Simon, it felt anything but. "I'm not going anywhere."

"So you're going to keep working at the diner?"

Mattie relaxed back into Simon's side, and Simon rubbed the arm that lay across his middle, though his throat felt tight and his head dizzy.

"For now. Maybe when I'm feeling a little more confident with the reading and writing I'll try and get a better paid job. Perhaps an office somewhere." He shrugged. "I'll be normal, just like everyone else."

Simon ran a hand over his face. An office. This brilliant young man was going to wait tables and then learn how to type letters for a living, just so he could be a part of his and Jamie's life.

Mattie sighed. "I couldn't be happier."

Yes, you could.

HE'D tried his best to put it out of his mind. He wanted to be selfish. He wanted to keep Mattie away from the rest of the world and all to himself. He wanted to ignore his conscience, but he couldn't. It'd been bad enough knowing the upsetting truth about Mattie's past. Just knowing that Mattie had tortured himself so much killed him, but *knowing* what it was Mattie was giving up and actually having it in front of him in black and white was the deal-breaker.

Mattie was in the shower, and Simon had been brushing his teeth when he'd suggested the two of them go out to dinner one night.

Somewhere nice, on him. The sweet guy that he was, Mattie was excited, but needed to check his work pattern for the next week. He'd offered to check it for Mattie, and after going through his backpack kept by the front door, he'd found the letter. The fucking letter.

Mattie was oblivious. He had no idea he'd found the letter, and had no idea that Simon had agonized over it ever since. A place at the Art Institute of New York for three years. Financial aid. Everything Mattie had worked for was here, in this letter, offered to him on a silver goddamn platter.

He'd come so close, *so* close to ignoring what he knew was the right thing, and keeping Mattie to himself. He'd come so close to letting what was rightfully Mattie's just slip away, so that they could be a family. But the simple truth was that he loved Mattie too much to let him settle. He couldn't do it.

Now he sat at his kitchen table, the letter in front of him, as he waited for Mattie to come home. He rubbed at his already wet, stinging eyes and clenched his jaw when he heard Mattie let himself in.

"Si?" He strode into the kitchen. "Hey, you. Sorry I'm late. I picked up a few things before coming over."

Simon watched, saying nothing as Mattie put the brown paper bag on the kitchen counter and began to unpack. "I got some popcorn for me and gummy bears for J. Are you watching the movie with us, or are in your office tonight?"

"Mattie, come sit down."

"Where's Jamie?" he asked, his back still to Simon.

"He's with Sarah tonight. Please, just come sit down."

"I thought we were watching a movie?" Mattie glanced over his shoulder and did a quick double take. "Hey, you feeling okay?"

"Mattie, we—we have to talk."

Mattie smiled nervously. "That doesn't sound too good." His smile slowly slipped away. "Why do you look like that?"

"Mattie—"

"Why are you looking at me like that?"

Mattie strode over to Simon, but stopped dead in his tracks when he saw what was on the table. He shot Simon a quick, nervous look, pressed a palm to his forehead, and then took a steadying breath. He knelt in front of Simon, his hands resting on Simon's leg.

"Okay. I understand why you might be freaking out, but I promise you, I *promise* you I am not leaving. I was just... it's only—"

"You're leaving, Mattie."

"No, that's what I'm trying to tell you, silly, I'm not. Simon, I'm your guy, remember? I am *not* Tim, I'm not taking off."

"You're going, Mattie!" Simon raised his voice, shoving Mattie's hands away from him as he turned away, elbow on table and his face covered by one hand. "I *want* you to leave," he forced out.

Mattie stood slowly, frowning. "I don't get it. I—I just told you I wasn't going to take off. Simon... what the *hell*?"

"You are going to New York, Mattie. We can argue about it until we're both blue in the face, but you're going."

"I don't...." Mattie shrugged helplessly, struggling to say anything. "I'm telling you that I don't want to leave. I'm not leaving! What... is this you pushing me away before I can leave you? A 'hurting me before I can hurt you' kind of thing?"

Simon shook his head, feeling drained. "No. This is me letting you go because you deserve—"

Mattie's hands flew up into the air before landing on his hips. "So it's some sort of 'if you love it set it free' kind of bullshit!"

"No, this is called doing the right thing."

"Simon!" he snapped. "I don't *want* to go!"

"Then why are you carrying the letter of acceptance around in your fucking *backpack*?"

Having no response, Mattie finally looked away, walking back over to where he'd set down the groceries and leaning both hands on the kitchen counter. "I've just... I've never accomplished anything like that before. I didn't want to throw it away." He turned around, wet his lips. "But, Simon... getting in is enough. I don't need to go."

Simon shook his head, pushed away from the table, and stood to pace. He finally stopped in place, his shoulders slumped in resignation. "I called the Dean of Student Affairs, made up some bullshit excuse about there being a death in your family. You still have your place, but you've got—" He looked at his watch. "—until tonight, about four hours, to call and confirm your place yourself."

"Simon, come on, *please*," he choked out.

"I…." He took a deep breath. "I booked you a flight. It's in nine days. It'll have to be enough for you to give notice at the diner and say good-bye to your friends. Any later and you miss the beginning of the semester. You're going to be in a pinch as it is finding an apartment at such short notice."

"Will you just *shut up* for a minute?" Mattie bit out, his hands raking through his hair.

"It's best to just end things now, I think." Simon spoke quietly, nodding to himself and then turning away to swipe the back his hand across his eyes.

"You don't get to make all the decisions here, okay? You don't!"

"This has come out all wrong, but… *fuck*," he hissed. "There is no right way to do this."

"We're *not* doing this!"

"I wrote you a check." He pulled the folded check out of his pocket, placing it next to the letter on the table. "Five grand to help you with rent until you find a part-time job out there, okay?"

"Simon, just—"

"And it is not a loan. Any money you make you have to put toward school, not paying me back." He looked at Mattie sadly, who said nothing. "Mattie, are you—"

Mattie was rubbing his hands over his face, his shoulders hunched and tight. He turned suddenly, picked up the grocery bag, and lifted it in the air before slamming it down on the tiled floor with a loud cry.

Simon took a step back, but was quick to pull Mattie into his arms when the younger man's shoulders began to shake, his breath catching in a desperate attempt to not break down in tears. "I know," Simon choked out. "I know it's... I'm dying here too, Mattie. I don't want to lose you, but if you didn't leave, I would fucking hate myself."

Mattie turned in his arms, burying his face in Simon's neck. "I don't want to go. I want you and Jamie. I want to be a family with you."

"I want that too, honey, I do."

"Then why are you doing this? Why are you sending me away?"

Simon looked up the ceiling, his jaw clenched for a second, before gently pulling Mattie toward the kitchen table. "Sit." He pulled a chair up close next to him, Mattie's knees between his as he gently wiped away the dampness under those gorgeous hazel eyes. "This isn't like before, when we hadn't found our rhythm together yet. There aren't any misunderstandings here, and we both know we love each other. This is about you going out there and getting what is *yours*."

"I already have that."

"Mattie, you haven't done anything with your life yet. You haven't had the opportunity to find what it is that sets your soul on fucking *fire*. I did. I loved writing, and now I do it for a living. Now you need to go do that with your art. You need to go to that college and soak up absolutely *everything*."

"I could go to school here," he offered weakly.

"No, you can't. You've missed the enrolment period; you'd have to wait another year."

"Then I'll do that!"

"*No*. If you wait another year, you won't go, you know you won't. You'd get settled here with me and Jamie. You'd find some shitty office job and never leave. Time will pass, and you'll have missed this window. You worked for New York, the one thing that kept you going when you had *nothing*." He cupped Mattie's face. "You achieved that, Mattie. And I am so fucking proud of you." He swallowed hard. "I told you I wouldn't let you slip through the cracks, and that's what I'm doing."

"Don't I get a say in this?" Mattie pulled one of Simon's hands away from his face and cradled it in his own.

The corner of Simon's mouth lifted up in a sad smile. "No. Sorry."

"What would this mean for us? I mean…." He sniffed, looking at their hands. "Are you talking about a long distance thing here, or…?" He trailed off, unwilling to say the words.

"I gave it some thought, and… and I guess the best thing to do would be to—to just—"

"Don't," Mattie whispered, closing his eyes and shaking his head no.

"Mattie, three years is a long time. It's just going to make it more painful to drag this out. You'll be meeting new people and—"

"Oh, you asshole." Mattie laughed sadly. "We both know how deeply I'm invested here. Don't even pretend that I could—"

"Okay, okay," Simon interrupted him, even if he did think he had a valid point.

"I, um." Mattie pressed his lips together in a tight line, swallowing hard. "I suppose you're thinking that it'd be better for Jamie if we didn't try and keep this going… that it might confuse him."

"That *is* something I have to consider," Simon murmured sadly.

Mattie nodded yes, then let out a harsh breath and shook his head no. "Simon, what we've got here? Comes around once in a lifetime. I can't just…." He choked up. "I can't just not have you in my life. I *can't*!"

"Okay, okay. It's all right, hey now…," he comforted, scooting closer in his seat and pulling Mattie into his arms. He pulled back quickly to avoid knocking heads when Mattie sat up.

"Come to New York!"

"*Mattie,*" he groaned.

"You can write anywhere!"

"I can't do that to Jamie."

Mattie's shoulders sagged in disappointment, and in that moment Simon truly hated himself. He shook his head. "I'm sorry. I can't do it to him, I can't pull him out of school and away from the few people he's comfortable with. Not when he's only five...."

Mattie nodded. "I wasn't thinking. *Shit*." Mattie covered his eyes with one hand, his head bowed. "Ah, shit," he repeated, his words garbled this time with tears.

Simon leaned close, stroking a hand over Mattie's hair and pressing a kiss to the top of his head. He closed his eyes tight. This was horrible, this was absolutely fucking *terrible*. He let out a deep sigh, whispering to himself. "Fuck, fuck, fuck, fuck."

Simon sat up straight, his hand thumping down on kitchen table. "Fuck. Fuck it!" He stood and walked over to the kitchen cabinets and drawers, rummaging through them. "Where are they?" he muttered to himself.

"What are you doing?"

"Where are—ah!" He strode back over to the kitchen table, sat back down, and held out a stack of postcards he'd purchased absolutely months ago when looking for inspiration.

Mattie took them, frowning. "Postcards?"

"So this is what it comes down to, right? You're going to New York. I can't go with you. To keep up a long distance relationship isn't feasible with what it would cost you to travel here and me being unable to leave Jamie, not to mention how torturous Skyping would be—"

"Simon!"

Simon shook his head, turned Mattie's hand palm upward, and placed the stack of postcards in his hand. "This isn't a normal breakup, where something has gone irrevocably wrong. Nobody fell *out* of love here. And you know what? You're right. This is a once-in-a-lifetime relationship we have here, so... so maybe...."

"Christ. Like I always say, you're either too wordy or you can't speak at all," Mattie managed in a watery laugh.

Simon placed his hand on top of the stack of postcards held together by a red rubber band. "Why don't we think of this as your time to go find yourself, before you make your way back to me?"

Mattie's brows rose together sadly. "Why the postcards?"

"I don't want you to call me. I don't want you to e-mail me. I want you to focus 100 percent on you and your art for the next three years, all with the knowledge that I'm still here in San Diego, missing you, still loving you, and waiting patiently for you."

"I don't understand."

"I know you think that your feelings aren't going to change." He spoke softly, squeezing Mattie's hand when he knew the younger man would protest. "But you don't know... you've no idea what might be ahead of you, and I am not going to stand in the way of that. So, you are going to take these with you, and when you find somewhere to live, you're going to send me one with a return address, and that's it."

"I don't understand. Why would I send you one without a message?"

"Because I'm going to send you one back, and we're going to keep doing this every few weeks. This way, I know that you're still coming back to me, or that perhaps when Jamie is older, I could be coming to you. No talking, no pain, just an 'I'm still here.'"

"To say 'I'm still in this.'" Mattie spoke quietly, looking at the postcards.

Simon nodded and cupped the nape of Mattie's neck, bringing their brows together. "And if they stop coming." He spoke softly. "Then I'll know you've moved on."

"Ah, hell." Mattie pulled away but kept hold of the cards.

"You get everything this way, Mattie. You get to go to that school, and when you're done? I'll be here, waiting for you."

"What if you meet someone?" Mattie whispered miserably.

Simon actually laughed. "Mattie, this is it for me. I'm done. I have my career, I have my son, and I have the man that I am going to love for the rest of my life. I swear to you, there will be no one else while you're gone."

Mattie sighed, shaking his head. "I hate this." He pulled Simon into a kiss. Too upset to deepen it with any real show of finesse, he pressed their lips together, took a gasping breath, and then did it again. "What now?" he asked.

Simon swallowed. "Now? We go to bed to say good-bye in private. Then I'm going to take you home. And that's it. I won't be at the diner. No airport farewells. You get everything tied off here, and then you head out to New York."

"Promise me you'll stock up on postcards, because you're gonna need a lot. A *fucking* lot," Mattie choked out, and not waiting for an answer, he dragged Simon to the kitchen floor.

HE'D stuck to his word and stayed away from the diner until now. Two weeks had passed, and Simon had his first postcard. Only now could he return to where it was he used to write. Ten minutes after sitting in his booth, however, and he hadn't written a word.

He missed Mattie so much he ached.

Jamie was fine. There had been questions, sure. He'd certainly noted that Mattie wasn't around anymore, but thankfully Mattie hadn't been a part of Jamie's life long enough to cause any major disruption.

He closed his laptop. He couldn't come here anymore. He looped his satchel over his head and went up to the counter to pay for his half-eaten salad. He met Ty's unreadable gaze, and only just stopped himself from rolling his eyes. He just did not give a *shit*.

"Hey, man," Ty offered lamely. "How're you doing?"

"Just peachy." He pulled out five dollars. "For lunch."

"Hey!" Ty called out, following him to the entrance. "Wait up a sec."

He held up his hand. "Just don't, okay? I don't want to talk about him."

"You don't want to know how he's doing?"

That gave him pause. He had a blank postcard with a return address. He'd even gone as far as to look it up on Google Maps so he could at least see where Mattie was. But that was it. He sighed. "How's he doing?" he relented.

Ty offered a sympathetic smile. "He's fine, even managed to get a roach-infested apartment with another student." Ty tilted his head. "I hear you helped out on the money front. That's pretty decent of you. To be honest, I thought he'd left it too long to get in."

Simon shrugged. "Yeah, well."

"Simon?" Ty asked, waiting for eye contact, then continued. "I know it sucks, but you totally put him first. My hat's off to you."

Simon nodded. "You're keeping in touch with him?"

"Well, duh. He's only my best friend."

Simon smiled. "Keep an eye on him, okay? Let me know if he needs help or anything."

"Will do." Ty slapped Simon's forearm with his dishcloth. "Hey, he starts at that fancy college tomorrow. He's shitting it, man." He laughed, and so did Simon.

"He's going to do great."

"That's what I keep telling him. You know...." Ty paused, uncharacteristically tentative. "You can talk to me whenever you want. I know you two have some kind of weird pen pal thing going on now, but if you ever want to cheat and know how he's doing, just ask."

Simon huffed a quiet laugh and nodded. "Thanks. I just might do that." He adjusted the strap on his shoulder. "Anyway, I have to get going."

"Can you wait just one more second? I have something for you."

"Uh, sure." Frowning, he watched Ty dip into the "Employees Only" door, and then let out a genuine laugh when he returned, holding an animal carry case with a familiar-looking bunny inside. "You're kidding me?" He laughed, crouching to check that it was in fact Mattie's rabbit blinking sleepily back at him.

"I've been bringing him in with me every day, hoping you'd stop by."

Simon shook his head. "Looks like I'm well on my way to building that zoo."

"Say what now?"

"Never mind." He carefully took the carrier from Ty. "Well, I apparently have a bunny."

"Actually, no, you don't."

"I thought—?"

"I'm under strict instructions to make sure this gets to Jamie." Ty glanced away for a second. "Up until the last moment, I think he was waiting for you to turn up and beg him not to leave. You did him a kindness, you hear?"

Something inside of Simon throbbed, but he managed a small, sad smile. "I'll make sure Jamie gets his new bunny. Don't worry."

"All right then. Well, take care, man."

"Yeah, you too. Thanks."

Three years ahead of him.

Three years.

Epilogue

HE'D tried his best to sneak a quick peek. He'd craned his neck slightly, keeping his body obscured behind the line of people in front of him, looking for just a glimpse of Simon. Just a glimpse of those thin-rimmed glasses that he'd always found classy and sophisticated-looking. A quick look at his short, light-brown hair, graying slightly at the temples. That unsure smile that had, for him, always been flat out gorgeous

There was no line to hide behind now. For two hours he'd queued and debated over what he would say. For two hours he had tortured himself with questions he could not answer unless he actually grew a pair and forced himself to voice them to the one person who could answer him. But what was he doing? He was hiding. He was hiding in the young adult section, clutching the latest hardback by Simon Castle to his chest like a lifeline.

Did that intense spark between them still exist? What if it wasn't the same? The easy conversation, the comfortable silences, the simple reassurance of Simon's cologne, and the very basic luxury of his presence. What if *he* didn't love Simon the same? He sighed, instantly dismissing the thought. His mind would stray to Simon and their brief time together at least once every day. At least once a day he'd allow himself to feel utterly heartsick. He'd let himself remember and regret leaving, even if it had been the right thing to do. He knew that the only way he'd no longer love Simon was if he'd changed: if he was no longer the sweet, loving, and adorably boring Simon he'd known years ago.

Perhaps the more important question was whether *he* was too different for *Simon*? The past few years had been the making of him, really. He'd never wanted to leave, but after nearly three years of living independently in New York, of having had the chance to change and to develop his work in different mediums, he knew now what he couldn't understand then. Simon had given him the permission he hadn't been able to give himself to pursue something life-altering. And though it had broken both of their hearts to do so, he had never felt so at home in his own skin as a result.

The coil of rope that he had manifested and pictured inside of himself for so long was completely absent. He still had moments where he doubted himself, but he knew who he was. More importantly, he liked who he was now. But would the person he was now be able to engage with whoever it was Simon had become? Not to mention Jamie. Would Jamie remember him at all? He'd been five years old when he'd left without so much as a good-bye. He'd be eight now and held memories of him that only his five-year-old self would have. He supposed another big question that threatened to drive him into a full panic was whether Jamie was old enough to leave the only home he'd ever known, and what would that mean for the three of them?

He knew the only way to answer any of these questions would be to walk up to the man in question and ask them. He edged out from the hidey-hole he'd sequestered himself in, and chanced a casual glance toward a large table at the back of the store.

The hours of queuing and inner monologue had not prepared him. With a harsh intake of breath, Mattie spotted him, seated at a long table stacked high with copies of the book he held in his hands now, facing away from him. He'd recognize the back of that head anywhere.

The place had emptied out, and Simon was speaking with a woman who he assumed (judging by the name tag) worked in the store. One hand rested on the table, fingers drumming. He couldn't help but notice a slightly defeated slump in Simon's shoulders, and wondered if his thus far absence could be the cause of it.

Telling himself to stop being a chickenshit, he slowly approached the table. He had every intention of saying something suave, of appearing cool and collected, like a whole and newly self-possessed and well-balanced individual. But the second Simon glanced his way, doing an abrupt double take, he was back at the diner, watching the hot single dad typing away at a laptop.

Simon stood, ignoring how the woman he had been speaking to seconds before patted his arm before walking away. Everything they had been through and all the changes he had made in his life accumulated to that moment of them standing opposite one another, nothing but a table between them.

"Hey," Mattie croaked, hating himself for sounding so scared and not like some sexy bastard who had arrived to reclaim his lover.

"Mattie," Simon breathed, a smile so relieved and happy splitting across his face.

Mattie felt an identical smile begin to spread across his lips. He reached to slide the copy of Simon's book across the table in the hopes of sounding witty by asking Simon to sign it. "Would you do me the pleasure of—"

Only to knock over a stack of books.

"Shit! I—I'm sorry, let me just…." He quickly crouched, feeling himself flush red hot as he gathered books and attempted to clean up the mess he'd caused, his hands shaking.

"Mattie." Simon spoke softly, a look of amusement, relief and devotion on his face as he reached for Mattie's hand, stilling him. "It's fine, honey."

He looked up sharply at the endearment, and saw Simon's throat bob nervously. They stood, and both shuffled awkwardly before speaking at the same time.

"That's not the impress—"

"I'm so glad you're—"

They both laughed nervously, and Mattie rubbed at the back of his neck. "You look really good," he offered, and it was true. Simon's hair was longer and styled back with streaks of silver on either side of his temples. His glasses were the same, which for some reason Mattie found reassuring, and he was also sporting a light scruff that made him flat-out devastatingly handsome.

"You too." Simon nodded, putting his hands in his pockets and then taking them out again a second later, as if he didn't know what to do with them. "I—I was worried you weren't coming. I was going to go over to your apartment if you didn't show."

Mattie smiled and pulled a scuffed and broken compass in the shape of a penguin out of his jacket pocket. "I guess this thing still works."

Simon let out a quiet, breathless laugh, nodding. "Guess it does."

"Is, um… is Jamie with you?"

"No, not this trip. Next time, maybe."

"How is he?"

Simon smiled. "He's doing wonderfully. He's with his grandmother right now."

"Oh yeah?" Mattie smiled. The last he'd known, Simon's relationship with his mother had been a tenuous thing. If she'd been left in charge of Jamie in Simon's absence, it boded well. "Just your mom, or your mom and Sarah?"

"Oh, Sarah's got enough on her plate." He grinned. "Seeing as she's newly married and eight months pregnant."

"Shit!" He laughed.

"Yep."

He bit his lip. "That's great about Jamie and your mom, Simon."

Simon nodded. "We're all doing pretty well." His eyes widened with curiosity, and he moved a fraction closer. "How's art school going? Shouldn't you be nearly… you know, finished?"

Mattie, of all things, felt himself begin to flush again. "Yeah, nearly. It's been…." He shook his head, at a loss for words. "It's been *incredible*. I have this part-time job working in a gallery; the guy who owns it even sells a few of my pieces every now and then."

"Wh—that's *great*, Mattie!"

276

Mattie smiled, enjoying how pleased and impressed Simon appeared. "Yeah, I love it here."

"Is it, uh, a job that could lead to something more permanent, do you think?" Simon asked carefully.

"I think so, yeah. My three years at school are nearly up, so...." He honest to God had not meant to utter such a loaded sentence.

Simon looked at him, his mouth opening and then closing before he glanced away. Mattie laughed quietly.

"You're either all wordy, or you can't speak at all." He spoke softly.

Simon let out a breath and nodded, smiling wryly.

Mattie could see a million questions circling in Simon's annoyingly big brain, all fighting to make their way out. It reassured him. It showed him that the man he knew he was without a doubt still in love with was as terrified and nervous as he was. Simon had been the one to take them this far, to make him leave and go find himself in a city of skyscrapers. Mattie could do the rest. But first....

"Simon?" he began softly, forcing the other man to look him in the eye. "I need to thank you."

Simon shook his head, almost sadly. "Mattie, you did all this yourself."

He too shook his head no. "That isn't true. You knew I was too afraid to do any of this alone. You knew I couldn't leave you and Jamie. So thank you." He swallowed hard. "Thank you for making me go. Thank you for *letting* me go, just for a little while."

Simon looked him in the eye, as if trying to read him. "F-for a little while?" he echoed with an unmistakable lilt of hope.

Mattie took a deep breath and let it out slowly. "Simon, these past three years have been *painful*, without you. But they have also been the making of me. I... I *like* who I am now." He gave a tremulous smile, shrugging helplessly. "I feel good about who I am, I like the work I do... but it's not complete." He shook his head. "It's not right because you and Jamie aren't here."

"Are—" Simon wet his lips. "Are you saying... what are you saying?" He laughed nervously.

"I'm saying that if you're still in this, like I am, then after I've finished up at school, I'll be coming home to you. If I'm welcome, that is."

"You'd give up your job?"

"I've had my time, Simon, and I can paint anywhere." He swallowed. "I miss my family."

Simon clenched his jaw, his eyes taking on a sheen. He sniffed and then shook his head with a quiet laugh. "Mattie, I won't lie and say that New York was the only place I could have had a book signing. I came here for one main reason, and that's you. I couldn't wait any longer, and I needed to see if we could still be... *us*, I suppose."

Mattie nodded, his heart in his throat but unwilling to interrupt.

"But, following that, and I suppose dependent on whether we were still an 'us', I came here for one other reason. I came to shop."

Mattie stared at him. Blinked. "Shop," he repeated. "Um. Okay."

Simon laughed. "Mattie, shop for *schools*, and by extension, an apartment too."

Mattie felt a smile shakily begin to spread over his mouth. "A-an apartment?" he stuttered, his voice thick and his breaths coming in halted little gasps.

Simon swallowed and finally reached out to gently cup the side of Mattie's neck, his thumb brushing along his jawline. "There's a school here for autistic children. The New York Center for Autism Charter School. It's one of the leading and most progressive schools for high-functioning kids with autism in the *country*."

"But I thought... J-Jamie's used to San Diego."

"Yes, he is. But he's not five anymore, Mattie. He's doing well, and I think he's ready for something new. He's been seeing a behavioral therapist for two years, and he is just...." Simon shook his head, overcome with pride. "He still has his challenges, believe me, but he is the bravest kid you'll ever meet. He's ready, Mattie. We both are."

"You would… you would actually move here, the two of you, to be with *me*?" He'd had himself ready to up and change his entire world; now Simon was throwing him through a loop.

Simon pressed his lips in a tight line to smother a smile. "You know how we cut all ties, with the exception of those damn postcards?"

"Yeah?"

"No contact, just space for you to explore college and all that?"

"Yes?"

"Yeah, I totally cheated."

Mattie barked out a strangled laugh. "What?"

"Ty's pretty much become my link to you over the past few years. Or rather, I've become the bane of his existence." He shrugged, grinning and unconcerned. "Every time I ask, you're doing great, apparently. Now I come here and see that, yeah, you are. So I came up with this alternative, because I'm not taking you away from this if you're happy, and I'm sure as hell not staying away any longer."

"You…? H-he never said a word!"

Simon nodded. "Because I told him not to."

Mattie laughed, wiping his hands over his face. "Okay." He held out his hands and then rested them on Simon's chest. "Okay, let me just get this clear. We can do this? You came here… not to end it, but to… to…."

"Make a beginning?" Simon frowned, clearly amused, and then chuckled quietly. "Mattie, how long have you been in this store trying to ante up and come over here?"

Mattie cringed. "A few hours, why?"

Simon let out a breathless laugh, closing his eyes for a second. "And you've been clutching a copy of this, right?" he asked, holding up a copy of his book.

"Uh, yeah?"

"Okay, assuming the cover of the book isn't evidence enough that I love you beyond all measure, did you at all during this time crack open the cover?"

279

Mattie frowned and snatched the book out of a laughing Simon's hands. He went straight for the dedication....

My undying love to Carol-Ann. Thank you for Jamie.
To Jamie, you are the source of my continuous pride and joy.
And to Mattie, the man I will love for the rest of my days.

"Aw, fuck," Mattie whispered, something inside of him slotting into place as a tear dared to escape. "Simon," he whispered, closing the cover and then closing his eyes as Simon gently wiped the pad of his thumb at the dampness clinging to his eyelashes.

"So this is you telling me that—that you're in? We're doing this? For keeps this time, no holding back?" Mattie asked, breath hitching.

Simon's hand at the nape of his neck gently pulled him close until their brows touched softly. A kiss ghosted over his lips before Simon replied.

"This is me, telling you that you are *still* the guy I tell my secrets to." Simon swallowed. "You always will be."

Mattie let out a harsh breath before gripping the front of Simon's shirt, and pulled him into a kiss that was as urgent as it was shattering.

Like the first time round, he didn't know how long it would take them to find their groove around each other, but what he did know was that it was going to work. Simon had let him go so that Mattie could change and become the person he was meant to be, and then he'd come back for him. If there was a greater evidence of devotion, he didn't know what it was. People who loved you, people who chose you, who made you their family and made you *belong*, they're the ones you have to hold onto with everything you have.

Mattie was holding on, and he'd keep holding on.

With everything he had.

L.A. GILBERT currently lives in a small British town where not much of anything ever really occurs. Jumping from job to job, she has no real qualifications in anything and is blithely proud of it. Between spectacularly failing driving test after test, she generally spends her free time reading about beautiful gay men, if not attempting to write about them. She is perhaps not the most outgoing of people, but is certainly one of the most cheerful.

Her aspirations are to eventually leave England and see a real, live whale (London's zoo is poorly lacking in that respect) and to perhaps one day hold in her hands a published copy of her own work.

One down.

Twitter: @L_A_Gilbert

E-mail: L.A.Gilbertmail@gmail.com

Livejournal: http://l-a-gilbert.livejournal.com/profile

Website: http://lagilbert.WebStarts.com

Also from L.A. GILBERT

http://www.dreamspinnerpress.com

Also from L.A. GILBERT

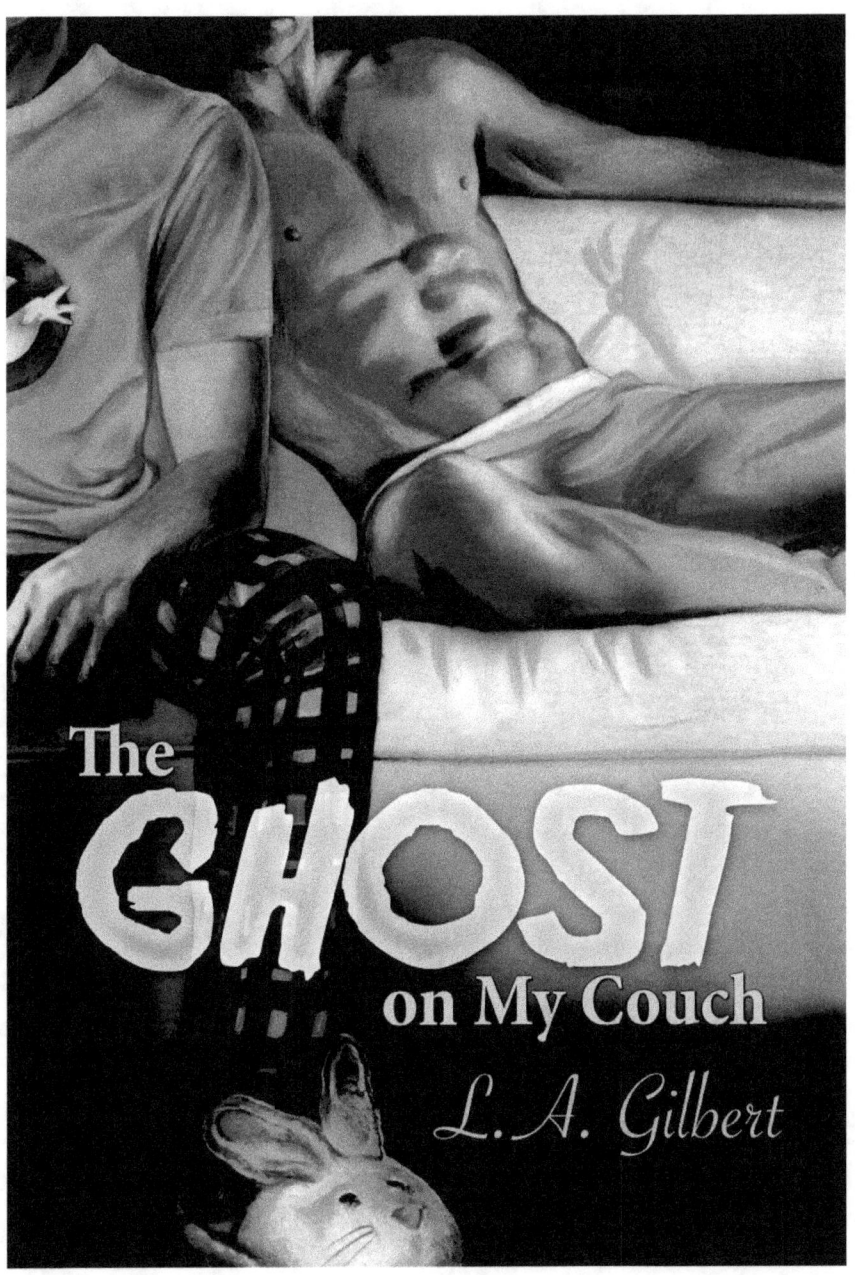

The GHOST on My Couch

L.A. Gilbert

www.ingramcontent.com/pod-product-compliance
Lightning Source LLC
Chambersburg PA
CBHW051533260626
47170CB00003B/922